The Diary of a Gunfighter

Also by Eddie L. Barnes:
    The Legacy of the Desperado (self published)
    Western Tales and Such (self published)
    The Bar-B-Que Circuit

The Diary of a Gunfighter

Eddie L. Barnes

iUniverse, Inc.
Bloomington

The Diary of a Gunfighter

iUniverse books may be ordered through booksellers or by contacting:

iUniverse
1663 Liberty Drive
Bloomington, IN 47403
www.iuniverse.com
1-800-Authors (1-800-288-4677)

ISBN: 978-1-4502-9476-8 (sc)
ISBN: 978-1-4502-9477-5 (e)
ISBN: 978-1-4502-9478-2 (dj)

Library of Congress Control Number: 2011907221

Printed in the United States of America

iUniverse rev. date: 10/27/2011

Preface

I wrote a self published work, a collection of interconnected poems; it is called The Legacy of the Desperado. The work was inspired by a song from an album by the band, the Eagles. The Legacy is about a young man. His name is Judas Bones. He is a bandit and a notorious killer. In those poems, I thought about having Judas Bones kill a character named Rhyming Simon. I liked the name and it rhymed. However, that character was never included in The Legacy of the Desperado.

One morning I was sitting on the side of my bed getting dressed for work. An advertisement came on television for the movie <u>Diary of a Mad Housewife</u>. I thought about it for a while and could not remember ever hearing or seeing anything about the diary of any gunfighter. So the idea was born that morning, and the main character evolved into Simon James Sublette whose gun fighting moniker became The Rhymer or Rhyming Simon to some.

I originally wrote his diary in long hand using quill pen and pencil and some paper that looked old. After it was finished, I had my good friend Sandy Vandevender of Muleshoe, Texas, read it and critique it for me. He suggested I turn the diary into a novel since it was difficult to read in long hand—especially my scribbled version. It took many years of part time labor for me to finally finish the book.

Chapter One

Northern New Mexico Territory

The wind blew fiercely across the open plains. The sky was angry, unforgiving. Ice pellets were hurled to the ground like bullets. A horse and its rider struggled against the wind, the ice pellets and the deepening snow. The pellets stung both the horse and the rider—but neither could feel the pain. For four days the horse and rider had wandered aimlessly through the driving, blinding snow, not knowing where they were going. In every direction the rider looked all he could see was the whiteness of the blinding snow. They had not given up on finding a place for shelter. They had to try and continue forward—to stop was certain death. The only way from them to survive was to, somehow, stumble upon a shelter.

Underneath the large brimmed hat, behind the frozen bandana he was using as a mask for protection, Simon Sublette's world was gray; slowly turning to black with each passing minute. He and his horse would not last much longer in the freezing cold. It seemed both were doomed to die from exposure.

Four days ago he had been riding across the north, central plains of the New Mexico Territory. It was a brisk, sunny spring day in April. Suddenly a freak winter storm developed. The wind went from a gentle breeze to a gale force in a matter of seconds, and a raging blizzard caught him and his horse in the middle of the open plains. The storm came so quickly he had no chance to find shelter. He could see, dimly, in the distance, some hills or mountains, and he headed in that direction. He rode fast but the snowfall was so heavy he was unable to see more than a few yards. He had to ride on blind, hoping that he would soon find those hills he had seen. His only hope was that his horse would continue going in the right direction. He rode on, but he never found any place to use as a haven from the relentless raging storm. The cold, ice, snow and wind were taking their toll.

On the fifth day, the blizzard subsided but the bitter cold remained. Simon thought it was odd the sun was shining bright but there was no warmth—he himself was like that sometimes, warm but cold with no feeling. He almost smiled at the thought, but it was too damned cold to smile. To make matters worse, the sunshine, reflecting off the snow, sent blinding white daggers to stab at his eyes. He could not open his eyes for very long even though the driving snow had ended—the brightness hurt his eyes—he feared he was becoming snow blind.

Relentlessly, he rode on. He rode for hours, and days, for what seemed like a life time considering the situation, and then suddenly, a voice from inside told him to look up. *Look up Simon....open your eyes....endure the pain....let the daggers pierce the brain.* Slowly, reluctantly, Simon raised his head. He put his hands over his eyes in an attempt to shield them from the harsh, snow–reflected, sun light. He thought he saw something, a dark outline, in the distance. Did he really see something or was his mind playing tricks on him? He wasn't sure. He continued to look, to stare, with great concentration. Then he decided something was there, something indeed. The dark figure was a settlement perhaps, or maybe a town. A ray of hope for survival sprang to his mind. He tried to spur his horse, to urge it on, but his legs wouldn't move. They were frozen and wouldn't respond.

"Come on horse, last a little longer, shelter is just a step or two away."

Simon knew spurring his horse would not have done any good. The horse couldn't go any faster. It was mostly dead, too. Simon also knew that if, and when, his horse finally fell, he would cut its stomach open, pull out the innards, and then crawl inside for the warmth until his own demise came.

A soldier, from his lookout position at Fort Defiance, saw a rider, in the distance. He called out to some of the other soldiers, and they helped to get the frozen hulk of a man to safety. They brought him and his horse into the confines of the fort, out of the weather, into the shelter of a warm stable. The soldiers tried to get him off his horse—but his legs were literally frozen to the saddle. They hurriedly got some fire logs to melt the bond between the saddle and Simon's legs. They got the fire logs so close to his legs his pants would start smoking. Simon didn't care. The heat felt good. He didn't care if they set him on fire, at least he would die warm. Dying of cold was a long slow process. He thought everyone had it backwards. Hell should be cold; it would be a lot more miserable than if it were hot. One of the soldiers used his saber to cut the saddle from the horse and lifted Simon, still frozen to the saddle, to the ground next to the fire. Eventually, after repeatedly warming his legs, they peeled him away from the frozen leather of the saddle. They had to use a saber to help loosen his right leg from the saddle. They not only cut part of the saddle, but also his trouser and right leg—Simon fell unconscious from the pain.

Quickly, they rushed Simon to the fort infirmary and to the fort's nurse, Abigail Sweeney. If anyone could bring a dead man back to life, it was Abigail Sweeney. Lord knows how many of the soldiers she had saved time after time. She had saved them from bullet wounds, Indian arrows, snakebites and various other injuries that occurred from living on the open frontier. She might not be able to save this one, but at least he was in good hands.

The army doctor, Doctor James A. Fadden, came to look at his newest patient, a half frozen corpse. He examined him closely and then he shook his head and shrugged his shoulders. He let out a long whistling sigh. He did not have much hope for the man. The exposure and the frostbite had taken its toll, and the tear in the right leg was not good. It would take all he and Abigail knew of medicine to keep the leg wound from becoming infected and to save this man's life.

"Well, Abigail, his right leg doesn't look good. It's real bad, real bad indeed. And his right foot isn't any better. If he survives the rest of his problems, we may have to amputate that leg or foot. Right now, I don't give him much of a chance. Do what you can and I'll look in, in the morning."

Doctor Fadden applied what medicine he had; it was up to a higher power than him to save this one. Maybe the Almighty would be kind to this man.

They put him in a room with a fireplace. They decided it would be better, given his condition, instead of putting him in the general hospital bay.

Simon was lucky. He had his own private room.

Abigail put on three blankets and kept the lamps lit so she could create as much heat as possible. She wrapped his leg and foot in several layers of cloth and hoped for the best. Abigail dressed his wounds every four hours—and prayed.

A soldier brought Simon's personal effects, his saddle, saddlebags and bedroll, to Abigail that same evening. She had the soldier take the saddle to the livery stable for storage.

As Abigail attempted to store his bedroll and saddlebags on the top shelf of the closet, the saddlebags opened and a small book, tied across both ends with a red ribbon, fell on the floor. Abigail picked up the book. It was a tattered loose set of pages, on the front page was written the word *Diary*. The first thing that came to her was—why would a man have a diary? Usually diaries were women things. She put the diary on the shelf with the rest of the man's belongings. The diary made her curious about this man laying in the bed fighting for his life. Sure, they were going to try everything they knew to bring him back to life, but he had to do the most work, he and the good Lord. He had to want to live. But why would a man carry a diary? Was it his or did it belong to someone else?

Abigail tended to Simon for the next four days. He seemed to be getting better, maybe a little stronger, even though he had never awakened. The color was returning to his right leg, but there was still a problem with the right foot. Only time would tell how much damage had been done.

Abigail's curiosity about a man carrying a diary piqued her interest. Finally, she decided that if this man were to die, then at least she should know as much about him as was possible, so she could say the proper words and put the correct markings on his grave. She went to the closet, got the diary, untied the red ribbon, and sat down to read.

Abigail turned the top page that read *Diary*; her heart was beating fast like she was doing something wrong. Like when her father had caught her kissing her first boy.

At the bottom of the inside of the first page was inscribed *Simon James Sublette*. A poorly taken photograph fell to the floor. She could not tell for sure, but it resembled the man lying in the bed. Well at least, she thought, now I know his name. As Abigail read, the half frozen, half dead man remained in his dream like state.

The Beginning

I'm starting this diary, hopefully to get things out of my head.
One said, it's not a diary, call it a Journal instead.
He said diaries are for girls, Journals are what men write.
I don't care either way, but for the ego, perhaps he is right.
I wonder what he would think, me writing this in verse.
Would he think me sissified ~ or maybe something worse?
I'm not sissified by any means. My fighting has proven the contrary.
I am just the opposite, and at times, I can be quite scary.
So far I have survived this mess, but there is more fighting I dread.
This War Between the States has left all of my kin folks dead.
I enlisted when only sixteen, and it has wreaked a terrible toll,
but now I'm headed home, a scarred man with a cold soul.
The politics of this conflict, I don't understand.
I came to help brother, father, to return home again.
I failed in my endeavor, to protect them at all cost.
At the battle Lynchburg, they were both lost.
General Jubal Early is a good leader, but can't protect us all.
Murdock is the problem, under him, too many men fall.
One day Murdock will get his, and I hope it is by my hand,
and then Heaven's light will shine again, on this great land.

Just before my eighteenth birthday, I got a present I didn't want to receive.
I buried my father and brother, and didn't have time to grieve.
I covered them, gently draped in flags, the prayer was about to begin,
but the Union Army didn't care, they attacked us again.
Merciless bastards.
I was enraged with more hate than I ever felt before,
and I vented my rage on the attackers ~ I tried to settle the score.
I killed many men that day, and some probably didn't deserve to die,
but if they want to know the reason, they'll have to ask the Devil why.
I don't ask for much, just a moment in peace to be content,
And then we can fight for days, till we're bloody and spent.
In the paper it said, the rivers ran red, with the blood we shed,
flowing from the battle field covered with all those who had died.
I fought possessed, crazed, and I was never fazed
by the dismembered, mangled bodies strewn across the countryside.

The thought of it haunts me, and has changed me for the worse.
How can I not feel badly about the deed, is it some evil curse?
What if the South were to win, how would it affect me?
But the North IS going to win ~ and from that, what change will we see?
How will my life be better? I can rightly say I don't know.
I do not understand the benefits. Perhaps some Yank can come and tell me so.

I got home today, July 1866, but was it still home?
I found out from the church, my mother had passed, she's gone.
It tore my heart out, I got sick to my stomach, and I cried a tear.
She was all I had left, and I am now all alone I fear.
The woman whose breast I suckled, who nursed me time and again.
I am now deprived forever, of feeling the warmth of her soft skin.
Who is going to hold me, warm me against the cold?
Who is going to help me, restore my scarred, darkened soul?
The war left me with a demon, he needs to be controlled,
but I don't think I'm strong enough, I am in the Devil's hold.
The demon comes when danger is nigh ~ but I can't explain why.
Today is my birthday, July 6, 1866, twenty years to the day.
I came to town to celebrate, when things turned the other way.
I'm fresh back from the war. I survived, and I'm still a young man.
I came out of a side street today ~ all of a sudden this shooting began.
There are two families still feuding, and now it was a full–scale war.
I got shot across the face, and I don't even know what for.
It really bothered me, all that blood dripping from my head.
I raised my rifle, steadied myself, and shot a man dead.
I guess I went a little crazy. I shot three more before they finally ran,
and I suspect I've made blood enemies of the survivors of that clan.
I went over to the barbers to get patched and what I saw made me reel.
My cheek was blown open ~ this kind of wound would take time to heal.
I had lasted through the war and now right here in my own home place
a bullet has passed through my cheek and has forever ruined my face.
My life splattered ~ just like blood when it drops to the floor.
This clan was going to hunt me ~ I am now part of their public war.
It wasn't my fight to begin with ~ I was just acting in self–defense today.
I won't wait for them to come ~ I'll seek them out, and then each one, I will slay.
My last few birthdays have all been dangerous ~ people firing shots my way,

with brother and father in sixty–four, Atlanta in sixty–five, now today.
Sixty–four it was war ~ Atlanta and today, someone else's fray.

Simon was in the alley, between the stables and the saloon. As he turned the corner, he felt the stinging, burning pain and knew it came from a bullet. His reaction was immediate, just like in the war. He grabbed his guns and defended himself. The people whose stray bullet accidentally shot Simon were not ready for someone like him. Simon was a vicious fighter and killer. The Confederate Army saw to that. The army refined his innate talents made him an expert marksman. On occasion, when the Confederacy needed an assassination, they called on Simon. Simon killed many men in the war, some from a long range and some up close—close enough to smell their body odor. His commanders found out quickly that he was well suited to killing and demonstrated no conscience about the results. So when this hostility was directed towards him, he reacted in the only way he knew, the way he was trained. When the shooting was finished four of the Henrys lay dead. The rest fled with what was left of their family.

It happened so fast the sheriff couldn't get involved. Simon went to the barber to see how bad the wound was. The sheriff came to check on Simon, to see how badly he was hurt. The sheriff, J.T. Johnson, was Simon's cousin.

"Simon, you okay son?" asked J.T.

Simon turned and showed his face but didn't speak. The bullet has entered his face near his left lip and came out just before his left ear, leaving a huge gash.

"Simon, I'm sorry you got involved in all this. The Henrys are a mean lot, and they'll be back to kill you. Maybe you should leave until I can get all this settled down."

Simon looked up from the bowl filled with water, water stained red with his blood. The side of his face where he had been shot started to twitch uncontrollably. He talked in a voice never heard before by his cousin. It was a low, harsh voice and in a controlled, paused, rhyme.

"J.T.....I fought in the Great War....and I didn't even know what the hell we were fighting for. They killed my daddy and they killed my brother.... then when I get home....I find that I've also lost my mother. I've stood in person, face to face, against thousands....and I never ran....and I'll be damned....if I'm going to start with this clan."

"Well, I was just trying to warn you. I'm only one man and I can't chase them all down."

"You should warn them, they'll need it. I'm only one man and I'm going to seek them out. I'll give them each a chance to flee....but if they don't....if they die....then don't come looking for me."

Johnson looked into Simon's eyes. He saw Simon's ice blue eyes. They were cold, glazed over like he was looking past Johnson. Simon's eyes, and his face, unnerved Johnson for a moment, made him queasy. It was Simon's manner of talk, the paused, controlled rhyme, as much as it was the way he looked, that made Johnson nervous.

Simon left Johnson's office, went out the door and turned right in the direction of the saloon. As he came out of the door he brushed past a man. Simon, hesitated, politely said excuse me, and continued his walk.

I happened to bump into a man today. I didn't have time to reminisce.
He was a general in the Confederacy, but something was amiss.
There were two like him, General Murdock was the other.
I served under Murdock along with my daddy and my older brother.
There was a battle, many black soldiers lay wounded, in need of aid.
The command was given, the reprehensible decision was made.
Over one hundred men were found dead, their fate was sealed.
Killed while they lay helpless, wounded on the battle field.
Another was hanged for the crime, but who gave the command?
Felix Robertson was the general, was by his hand?
It comes to me at night, invades my dreams,
the massacre, men being killed, their only defense, their screams.
Perhaps another was involved ~ I'll never know.
I served in special units with him ~ his name, Ian Calcough.
Some thought I was involved, but I was far away, in another fight.
I should have killed Robertson on the spot, but the timing wasn't right.
Have decided I will kill Ian Calcough. If I ever see him again,
for being despicable, reprehensible, and for all his other sins.
War is hellish ~ when it comes, you must stand and fight,
destroy the enemy with all means ~ with all thou might.
When the smoke clears ~ through the gore, and the bloody mess,
If you have kept your honor ~ you have no crimes to confess.
I have NONE, not ONE!

General Felix Huston Robertson walked into Johnson's office. He immediately saw Johnson standing behind his desk. "Do you know that young man?"

"Yes, he's my cousin. He's fresh back from the war and ran into some trouble today."

"Is his name Simon, Simon Sublette?"

"That's him, how do you know him?"

"Did he tell you anything about the war? Did he tell you what he did?"

"No, no, I can't say he ever mentioned the war. With his troubles, we didn't have any time to catch up."

"He was a fearless fighter. He fought in many battles, killed lots of men, but he saved a lot of lives, too, such an honorable trait, saving men's lives."

"He never mentioned any of it. I did hear of it some though, as news got back to us."

"Well, I can tell you. He was a hero. He received many commendations and several medals."

"How can that be?"

"What do you mean?"

"Mister, he's only nineteen!"

"I don't care if he's eleven, or new born, you don't want to be on the other side in a fight with him. Where's he off to?"

"Unfortunate for him, he got caught in the middle of a fight between two families. They shot him in the face. He told me he was going to set things right."

"Sheriff, it is probably unfortunate for the others. I hate to be the one to tell you."

Johnson stared at the man but didn't reply.

"These others, whoever they are, they all are going to die. The men, the women and the children, he will rid them of this land. That's what he was taught, retaliation and elimination, and I believe that's what he will do."

"He said he wouldn't. He said he would give them a chance to apologize."

"Good luck with that, I think I know him better than you. He served under a man named Murdock. Murdock served under my father, Jerome Robertson, then later with Jubal Early. My father and Jubal cared about their men and how they were treated. Murdock did not. Simon was in a special group of men who did extraordinary things, if you know what I mean. The things they did, well, there were only two survivors, that's how dangerous their missions were. If you run across a man named Calcough, Ian Calcough, keep an arm's length. They are skillful in what they do. He's not as dangerous as Simon, but he's close." Roberts pronounced the name Calcough as Cal–co.

"I didn't catch your name."

"I'm Felix Robertson. I was a general in the Confederate Army. I know well about this Simon James Sublette. He's a different person now than he was before, be careful, be very, very careful." Former General Robertson tipped his hat and exited the office.

Johnson sat heavily in his chair and pushed his hat backwards. He was uneasy before, but now this. Johnson, thinking he knew Simon really well, believed that Simon had only spoken in anger. He believed when Simon did cross the Henrys' path, he would give them a fair chance. He hoped Mr. Robertson was wrong. He had no way of knowing what was underneath Simon's gentle exterior, but the general might have given him a clue.

Johnson had read the articles, read the accounts in newspapers, about General Felix Huston Roberson. His command, as a general, was surrounded by controversy. It happened during a battle at Saltville, Virginia. The Union Army, at Saltville, was mostly black soldiers. The south was victorious and when the smoke of the battle cleared, hundreds of soldiers were strewn about the battle field, wounded and in the need of help. That very night, Confederate guerrillas, commanded by a man named Champ Ferguson, murdered them all instead of rendering them aid. Ferguson was later convicted of the war crime and hanged to death. There were those that tried to implicate Ian Calcough in the incident, but they were not successful. Simon's name was never mentioned in any of the documents. Somehow, miraculously, General Robertson escaped prosecution, but his reputation was forever damaged.

Simon had grown up with Johnson's son, Wesley. J.T. Johnson remembered when Simon had left for the war. He was just a skinny kid of sixteen and not yet a grown man. Now he had come back and had grown to about six feet tall and was a muscular young man. Simon was strikingly handsome, with his tan skin, his blond hair, blue eyes and war–hardened physique. The shot to the face today changed his appearance forever. Johnson wondered when and where and how Simon picked up this trait of speaking in rhymes—and that voice of his. It was scary, eerie. Johnson wondered just what in the hell had happened to him in the war?

Abigail continued her reading.

I'm killing the Henrys one by one. I can't see much value in making a fair fight.
I killed some during the day, and I killed some in the shadows of night.
One I killed in the deep black of a sweltering, miserable night.
He had no chance with only a knife ~ to me it was a gunfight.

Abigail looked at this symbol; it marked the end of brief chapters, or sections, in the diary. On close inspection, she realized that the small symbolic gun was comprised of two S's that made up the gun handle. Clever she thought. The two S's for Simon Sublette. She wondered how a man could get away with killing someone who was only armed with a knife, especially when the other man had a gun.

I caught the one Bunk Henry and his wife, casually riding along.
For whatever reason they left their ranch, they both knew it was wrong.
Instantly Bunk Henry knew me and reared his horse.
My shotgun roared ~ he was blown backwards into his wife by the force.
She was knocked to the ground ~ I was on her in a spark.
I wanted her to see my face up close ~ where her bullet left its mark.
I pinned her down and yanked her head back by her hair.
I told her it was over and she best be saying a prayer.
I said, "Look at this mess, look at what you have done."
I rubbed the length of my wound with the barrel of my gun.
I said, "I'll carry this forever no thanks to you."
She said, "It's too damn bad my aim wasn't true."
Then she spit in my face ~ I gave a little grin.
I took out my knife, and I shoved it in.
"Sorry pretty lady that you have to die,
look upon my face and you'll know why."
The knife was killing her slow like the knife usually does.
"At least you're not a whimpering coward like your blue bellied daddy was."
She tried to struggle but I finished it and put her to sleep.
I grabbed the handle of the knife and shoved it in deep.
Something smelled sweet, was it her blood or her perfume?
Or maybe it was the field of wildflowers in bloom.

I wondered about killing a woman, but she bled and died the same as the others,
her coward daddy, her husband, cousins and all her shit—heel little brothers.

Simon had this special sense to smell blood, much the same as some horses can smell blood. Simon was not especially fond of this unique talent. He didn't know where or when this nasty trait was acquired. He guessed it happened in the war sitting in the bloody gore of the aftermath of a battle.

I caught up with one a cowering in a corner, crying, blowing a snot bubble,
he was the last one and with this clan would end my trouble.
He begged me "Mister, I don't want to die"
I came close to feeling sorrowful watching him cry.
But his kind are dangerous once the cowardice turns to hate.
Back—shooting and sneak killing becomes their trait.
When I cocked the hammer, he screamed and turned his head,
I grabbed his hair, so he could see my face when I shot him dead.

Abigail wondered what Simon had done to give this poor soul an even chance. Did anyone see Simon commit this seemingly cold—hearted killing? How did he explain this to anyone?

I don't believe in a fair fight. I wouldn't last long here in the west.
I'm not interested in standing face to face just to see who is best.
If I get cross ways with a man, or he does something that he hadn't of ought,
then I'll kill him any way I can and I don't care of how I'm thought.
I carry a rifle and a pistol and I'm not interested in standing in the street.
I never intend to give an even chance to those who have death to meet.
I've seen quite a few come along who've had the blinding speed,
but graveyard nerves and deadly accuracy are also a need.
If a man is just fast and has no nerve then he'll likely end up stone dead,
for the steady hand and eye is better and so is keeping a cool head.
Dueling is for civilized folks ~ and here and now, well, civilized we ain't.
The people and the lands are rugged, and wild, and free from constraint.

I killed one woman and all six men of that clan,
and I wiped, forever, their seed from the land.

I went to J.T. Johnson, my cousin, the sheriff, and told him my tale,
of all the Henrys, and about each one, and how I sent them to hell.
Each time, each one, I told him, I gave the chance to leave, to flee,
but each time, each one, was hell bent on killing me.
J.T. couldn't disprove my story, and in a cold voice said so.
And he told me I couldn't stay, sell the farm, collect my things and go.
Everything I ever loved is now gone, except for a few friends,
I sold the farm, the cows, the horses, and now, a new venture will begin.

After all of the Henrys were dead, Simon went to J.T. and told him what J.T. wanted to hear. He told him the facts about each one he killed, about how, each time, the Henry's started the trouble first and never gave Simon the time to ask them to leave the territory. Simon embellished the story of the one blowing snot out of his nose, Simon thought it was funny. Sooner or later Simon would be forced to kill him anyway, maybe in a street, with innocent bystanders in the way. This way Simon thought, hell, he probably saved some other person from getting shot in the face. Besides, any grown man who would cower in a corner, cry and blow snot bubbles deserved to die.

Simon sold off the family farm. It distressed him to have to do so. He loved the area around Marshall, Texas. His father, brother and mother were all gone, and now with this trouble, he no longer had any reason to stay in Texas.

"Do you have any idea where you might go?" asked Johnson.

"Not sure, maybe north, Indian territory," replied Simon.

"Man might want to change his mind on that. It's damn tough in there. Plenty of rogues and bandits they say, just damn right mean they are."

"Maybe that's a good choice....for me anyway....don't know about Wes and Boyce."

"Are they going with you, Boyce and Wes?"

"Don't know, maybe they will, maybe they won't....but I'm going on even if they don't."

I asked my lifelong friends Boyce and Wes to come along.

They declined, said they'd just rather stay at home.
Boyce was in the Great War, too. He has the Shooters eye.
At two hundred yards I believe he could pick off a fly.
I called him "Rooster" 'cause when he's drunk he would act like a chicken.
He'd strut, flap his arms, move his neck back and forth like he was peckin'.
We'd had some good times both as kids and as young men.
I wondered if I'd see the Rooster or Wes ever again.
But I can't stay. I have to go, and it needs to be soon,
~Promises to keep, adventures to seek.
I have to find a place called Nellie Jacks' Saloon.
Lots of blood I shed here, but it's perfectly clear,
I'm guilty of no crime.
I'm not wanted by the law ~ at this time.

Abigail interpreted from the Diary that Johnson and Simon not only were related but must have been friends also. To her way of thinking, Johnson had given Simon too much leeway in the destruction of the Henry family. But then, she was only reading what was written and was filling in her own assumptions.

Who was this man lying in the bed, sick from the cold, this man who writes in verse? This man who seems to enjoy killing? What would he do if he awoke and caught her invading his most private thoughts? Would he kill her too, would he smell her blood mingled with the fresh flowers she had placed on the fireplace mantle to decorate his room? Maybe she should just let him die!

Abigail had no way of knowing that Johnson was Wes Brown's father. But her assumptions were accurate; Johnson was Simon's friend.

Nellie Jacks

Henrietta, Texas

I sold all I owned today ~ I headed to a place called Nellie Jacks.
I fought in the war with her man ~ I'm bringing his belongings back.
His name was Denzel Jacques ~ they changed the way it's spelled.
I came to fulfill a promise and tell his woman how he was felled.
Denzel broke during a bloody battle ~ he went to desert during the night.
But a bullet from my rifle ended his wrongful flight.

At Nellie Jacks ~ I told a different story, a hero's story to a grieving wife.
Of how he stood tall and of how the Bluecoats took his life.
She asked? "Did you kill my man's killer? Did you avenge my man?"
I lied, "Yes ma'am, I did, I killed him with my own bare hand."
"I took my saber and viciously slashed his face.
His own mama wouldn't have known him when they laid him in place."
The truth wouldn't have served any good as far as I could see.
Nellie Jacks said, "If you ever, ever need anything you come calling on me."
You know ~ it's better for a man to be remembered this way.
He's a hero ~ and the truth I'll never say.

What Abigail just read was contradictory to how she felt about this man, Simon Sublette. What she read showed some compassion for a fellow human. Maybe there was hope for this person after all. Perhaps he was worth nursing back to health. Maybe she wouldn't let him die.

For a moment, Abigail thought she saw Simon's eyes blink. Was he waking? She checked and found he was still in a coma–like state.

Abigail heard footsteps in the hallway. Quickly, she returned the diary to the top shelf.

The footsteps belonged to Doc Fadden. He came to check on Simon. After his examination, he called Abigail to Simon's bedside. He told her to prepare the instruments. Simon's leg was healing well—but two of his toes must be amputated. The surgery was done quickly and expertly. Although he jerked and moved because of the pain, this man named Sublette did not wake up. That alone worried Doc Fadden.

It scared Abigail. How could any one person endure that kind of pain without crying out?

Abigail came in the next morning, dressed Simon's wounds and noticed that he had a very restless night. The bed covers were scattered and mussed. The heavy quilt was lying on the floor. The pillow case was soaked in sweat. Abigail fixed Simon's bed the best she could, having to work around him still lying there unconscious. After she got him settled again, she retrieved the diary and began to read. She thought it was lucky for her the infirmary was virtually empty, so she could spend many hours with Simon—and with his diary.

The Mason Gang

Like everyone else I need money for whisky, room and board.
So I track down those with a price, bring them in and collect a reward.
Some are just misbegotten souls, others are as mean as a snake,
but with either kind you have to be careful, not give them an even break.
Dead or Alive ~ they don't care how you bring them in, they'll pay.
Dead cold stiff, strapped across a horse and saddle is my preferred way.
In the Oklahoma territory, I made a mistake trying to bring one in alive.
His gang cold jumped me ~ shot me ~ luckily I managed to survive.
A girl, Audra, found me, her and her father have nursed me back to health.
I'd consider staying here, except in farming; there isn't any wealth.
Besides, I got a score to settle, as soon as I am fully on the mend.
I'm going back after Mason, bring him and his gang to an end.
I'm getting fond of this young lady, we've had a little romance.
Her father is against my kind, he wants me to leave, he's firm in his stance.
I told her after I got Mason, that I'd come back and for her not to fret,
that we'd convince her father about us and that he'd see our side yet.

Abigail was learning something new about this man with each page she read. He is a bounty hunter and from what she just read, not a very good one either. Abigail quickly read more.

I rode into Guthrie today and learned the whereabouts of Mason's gang.
I told the so–called sheriff I was going to bring them to justice, see them hang.
He said they weren't wanted in this territory and that he wouldn't assist.

I think he's afraid of them, doesn't want to get into a fight if they resist.
Mason was easy, he wasn't very tough without his gang at his side.
I found him in a lady's bed ~ I guess contented, was how he died.
I had more trouble with the gang, we ended up having a hell of a battle.
I tracked them to the river where they were over branding some rustled cattle.
I managed to kill two with my rifle, the third I only wounded in the leg.
I went straight at him, he fired 'til his bullets ran out, then he started to beg.
I said "Mister, when you shoot someone, better make sure the job is done well,
if he doesn't die, he'll come back to find you and send you to hell."
I asked him why did he think today was the day he chose to die?
Then I sent him to hell so he could ask the Devil why.

Abigail wondered what his voice sounded like. Was it soft, or hard, like some of his other characteristics?

I killed the poor bastards, none of them had an even chance.
As soon as I collect the reward, I'm going back to continue my romance.
The sorry excuse of a sheriff has wired Dodge, I'll get the reward in due time.
Since they were wanted in Kansas, it's agreed, I committed no crime.

Simon left the hotel in Guthrie. He was headed out of town and back to the farm where Audra was waiting. Four men approached Simon as he packed his saddlebags. The one who seemed to be the leader said he wanted to talk.

"Are you, Sublette?"

"I am Simon Sublette, if that's who you're looking for." Simon replied.

"My name is Will Cadence. I'm up from Texas and we've been chasing this bunch of thieves and killers. The sheriff said you killed 'em. Up here I understand he was known as Mason, but he was known as Danfield Cutter in Texas. I need for you to sign this paper saying you killed 'em, so I can take it back to the judge."

Simon took the paper. He read the names, Mackie Dolittle, Blade Cathron and Two Crows Cawson. He now suddenly realized he didn't know the names of those he had killed. They had just been reward money to him. He signed the paper and handed it to Will Cadence.

"I wanted to kill this bunch real bad," Cadence continued. "They robbed our town and killed the marshal and all the family I had. This way

I get no satisfaction, no peace. You know mister. I was bent on getting my revenge."

Simon carefully considered what he was about to say. He was weighing how the man would react. Simon's answer sent a cold chill up Cadence's spine.

"If you got the notion that bad....and need revenge for them killing your kin....hell, I'll help you dig them up....and you can kill them again!"

Cadence looked at this man named Simon Sublette. He had a huge nasty scar on his left cheek, and it twitched when he spoke. Cadence knew this man was dangerous, was a cold ruthless killer and would kill him if he crowded him too close. Cadence did not give The Rhymer the chance. He turned and walked away.

Abigail read what Simon had written in the diary about the incident, it continued.

I felt Cadence wanted to take it out on me.
He was the problem, there was no hate in the other three.
He looked at me long and hard, then finally turned and went.
He'd need to find a different way for his hate to vent.
If you've never festered inside with hate ~ it's hard to understand.
The satisfaction isn't the same less the dying comes from your own hand.

Abigail did not understand. She had hated someone before, but not enough to want to take that person's life. All she wanted to do was to pick up a shovel and beat the hell out of him. She thought back to that time and wondered if the world would have been better if she had killed her no good drunken slob of a husband.

I got back to Audra today ~ her father is against me so we ran away.
He followed us to our camp and a whole lot of me died today.
His bitterness, my temper led to a fight ~ he pulled a gun right at the start.
My demon came forth, unfortunately, and I shot him through his heart.
When I killed him, I also killed her love for me.
Her love for her father is greater ~ now for us, it will never be.
Why am I like I am, I don't know ~ why is it I have to make men die?
Maybe when I get to heaven or hell someone can tell me why.

I'm running from the Oklahoma territory and I'm running long and fast.
With Judge Parker in Ft. Smith, guys like me just don't last.
They may come for me, try me for the fathers slaying,
and that is exactly why I am not staying.

Kansas

Simon was sitting in one of the local saloons. He had left Guthrie in the Indian Territory and moved on to Abilene, Kansas. His only intent was to drink some whiskey, maybe find a card game of some kind and then later enjoy one of the local girls. He had not found a girl that drew his interest, but the night was still young. Simon did not care much for the regular saloon girls; most of them were just receptacles for any old drunk that had the money. Simon thought it sad that these women had lost pride down to that point. He liked the girls who were a little more expensive, who could and would make some kind of intelligent conversation. He also liked those that would drink with him and could hold their liquor.

Simon was not looking for trouble—but it found him anyway, as it usually did. Trouble didn't have to look long to find Simon. Trouble was like a light that followed Simon wherever he went. All it took was for someone to turn on the switch.

A young cowboy, just off the trail, had had too much to drink and got mad when Simon spoke to this particular girl. She was the only one who had caught his eye. Simon guessed the cowboy thought the girl was his private companion. If the cowboy had known what had happened just an hour before he would know she was there for public usage. Simon didn't care what happened an hour ago. This working girl seemed like she was intelligent and Simon liked that.

The cowboy finally reached his boiling point and Simon saw the cowboy reach for his gun. Instinctively Simon did the same, but the cowboy's trigger finger was too fast and his gun fired before he got it out of its holster. The drunken cowboy fired down his leg and into his boot.

A look of shock came across the cowboy's face. Then he started hopping around in pain, and it caused Simon to start laughing, and he laughed hard. The cowboy quickly sat down in a chair and pulled off his boot to inspect his foot. When he pulled off his boot a bloody toe fell out on the floor. Then the whole saloon joined Simon in laughing at the boy.

Simon decided to leave before the cowboy had time to recover. He knew the young man was humiliated by all the laughter. He wrote about it in his diary.

I was hoping I'd never see that young man until his humility was forgot,
'cause if he ever came looking for revenge, more than his toe would get shot.

It's hard to believe, I'm a deputy here in Dodge, probably won't last too long.
You're supposed to arrest them first before you kill these men gone wrong.
I'm just like them, hell, I don't know who is protecting who from who.
I'm just here healing some wounds, doing what I'm told to do.
I was told to protect the citizens from the bad ~ to keep a sharp eye.
It made me chuckle a bit, 'cause hell, I am the bad guy.
I'm just not tolerant, or patient, in getting a man to lay down his gun.
And I'm also not the type who'll leave it be and cut and run.
I'm working here with a man named Wyatt Earp and Jim Bob Purcell.
Jim Bob claims to be a lawyer but I think he's a huckster, only time will tell.
The only law I've seen him practice is law to suit himself, or laws of the saloon.
For the right money, he's like those performing minstrels, he will sing any old tune.
His two cousins are with him, they are worthless as lawmen go.
Ollie Gerald and Rudy Tom are a source of amusement though.
They think being deputies give them an inside slant on making easy money
Wyatt thinks the same thing. If they cross him the results won't be funny.

Well, that didn't take long, today Earp asked me to leave town.
I got into it with a drunken cowboy, and I gunned him down.
He said I should have knocked him out ~ there wasn't any need for gunplay.
I told Mr. Earp I wasn't in to fist fighting ~ a man could get hurt that way.
The cowboy did pull his gun ~ and I probably could have avoided the killing,
but in the heat of the moment the cowboy wanted to die, and I was willing!

Abigail had seen the many wounds on Simon's body. When she first saw his scars, she thought he got them in the war. Now she knew he had gotten some of them in the war, but he also got a lot of them in one incident after another.

Abigail continued to violate Simon's private thoughts as she read more of the diary.

I was having some drinks tonight with another gunfighter.
He knows I'm not someone to be trifled with.
He was there for a woman, some drinks.
He was traveling under the name of Mr. Smith.

We talked about what it might be if we lead a different sort of life,
like working on a ranch, raising kids and having a pretty wife.
I told him my tale, how it didn't work out ~ he said he'd done the same too.
He said, "Fate always calls, then a man does what a man must do."
I guess we're both sort of alike ~ in some ways ~ when our temper goes bad.
We both will do anything we can to kill the son of a bich who's made us mad.
The saloon girls tonight were pretty. The one I chose was a little plump.
When she was naked, I saw this big o rose tattooed on her rump.
Now we were about to get cozy, me 'n' Rosey, when shots rang out everywhere.
Out the window, I saw Mr. Smith jump on his horse in nothing but his underwear.
On the side street there was a man taking aim on the back of Smith's shoulder.
So I got my rifle and shot the cur, Smith would now live to be a least a day older.
No one, not even the lowest scoundrel of the earth deserves to be back shot.
Some of these lawmen are worse than the outlaws ~ believe it or not.
No need to be worried about getting caught, they'll blame Mr. Smith for the crime.
But they might wonder how he shot from the front, and back at the same time.
Oh, back to Rosey, the softness of her and she smelled oh so sweet.
I slowly embraced her body and there for a moment our souls did meet.

When Abigail read this passage it made her blush bright red. But slowly, slowly, she was coming to understand this Simon Sublette. She did start to wonder though, why his diary was written purely in verse. Who was this man? She was beginning to think he was someone special.

Bitter Creek

I went into the general store today, the one over in Bitter Creek.
I saw this big burly man slap this little girl ~ hard ~ across her right cheek.
It chafed me a bit ~ but then it wasn't any of my affair,
but when he slapped her hard again ~ it bristled my hair.
The Demon interrupted, he grinned as he came out to play.
The man should have been in a different place on different day.
I interrupted, "Mister, a man shouldn't treat a little girl like that."
He replied, "Drifter, this ain't no concern of yours." Then on my boot he spat.
I was going to let it go, but when he spit on me,
he made the Demon mad, and he didn't leave it be.
With the Demon loose, I slapped the big son a bich.
He went for his gun ~ but he never got to scratch that itch.
My derringer flashed to my hand and I shot him right in the eye.
Then I took the little girl outside so she wouldn't have to watch the bastard die.
Naturally with all the violence, the little girl had started to cry.
I held her and took my kerchief and wiped a tear from her eye.
I gathered the little girl and took her home to her ma.
The woman said he'd been mean to the girl ~ but he was only her step–pa.
She said he beat both of them so she guessed he finally got his just due,
and if I was willing there was something more I could do.
She gave me my supper and told me there were more beaters across the land,
And that I should go forth and kill every last sorry woman beating man.
I ate in silence and took my leave, it wasn't my crusade,
but I guess for supper with pie, killing a man like him is a pretty good trade.

Beaters, Beaters everywhere
Decent women got to fear
Strike at will
Seek out the Beaters
Kill! Kill! Kill!

Only a small whimper ~ no others cried, the day the beater died.
Laid six foot deep, in a cold damp grave ~ no soul to save.
No mourners, no service ~ I left town, citizenry no longer nervous.

Abigail could tell from his mention of Bitter Creek that this took place in Colorado. Anyway that's where the Bitter Creek she knew about was located. Abigail came to the conclusion that Simon went from place to place doing what he damned well pleased. That's the way the diary read to her. The thought crossed her mind that the only work Simon ever mentioned in his writing was either being a deputy or a bounty hunter. Either way, they both led to the same thing—the death of another human being.

Abigail did not condone senseless violence. But for some reason, she felt good when she read that Simon had killed this wife and child beater. Simon should have been around when she took all the abuse from her ex–husband. Simon would have shot him in the eye, too. She knew he would.

Abigail tied the pages of the diary back in place, put it up for safe keeping, and then went to her room to go to bed.

The next morning, Abigail took care of her normal duties. She tended to Simon's wounds, and bathed him. Abigail then took the diary from its resting place, settled in her comfortable chair and read more.

Murdock McKenzie

I picked up a piece of information last night as I was leaving the bar.
Someone I've hated a long time is up north, where he's at is not far.
He's a man from the Great War ~ a nightmare from the past,
and if he ever sees my face ~well ~ my face will be his last.
I made a promise to myself as I held my dying daddy to my chest,
that if I ever ran across this man ~ I'd kill him ~ or die trying my best.
On to Denver ~ track him down ~ be relentless ~ like a good bloodhound.

I've never gave much notion that I write in verse like I do,
and I know at times, especially when irritated, I tend to talk that way too.
I don't know how it happens ~ writing and talking in verse.
It comes to me natural ~ I don't have to think about it or rehearse.
Last evening in a Denver saloon some cowboy wanted to make a fight.
I wasn't of the notion, so I talked to him, trying to give him a fright.
I told him "You ask around cowboy and your life you'll save.
If you don't leave me be then I'll send you to your grave.
I hold thunder in my left hand and lightning in my right,
so back on out of here and you won't have to die tonight."
One man started laughing, then the whole saloon. The cowboy eased his stance.
I got a new nick name ~ and on life ~ the cowboy got a second chance.
I bought him a drink, convinced him to leave violence to those of us so inclined.
It takes more guts to remain sane, more than to become a depraved mind.
I told him it takes a brave man to back off like he just had.
He knew I gave him his life ~ he'd think about it the next time he got mad.
That's when he said it ~ as I eased off my stand.
"Hell boys, look here, we have done and got us a Rhymer man!"
His name was Don Alejandro, said he was white, looked Mexican to me,
but out here in the west a man can be anything he wants to be.

Abigail almost dropped the diary when she read the words *"Rhymer man."* She had heard vague stories, rumors mostly; about a ruthless gunfighter people called The Rhymer. Surely, this couldn't be him—or maybe it was! If he actually was the Rhymer then may God bless their souls to have such a man in their midst. Maybe she was right about this man being someone special, if one could call a gunfighter special. Quickly, she retied the diary, put it on the shelf and ran out to find Doc Fadden. He was tending to the only other patient in the infirmary.

"Doctor, I think I know who our mysterious, frozen man is!" Abigail said with excitement leaping from her voice. "Have you ever heard of a man called the Rhymer?"

Doc Fadden looked curiously at Abigail.

"It's him Doctor, the Rhymer. Our frozen man is the gunman who talks in rhymes."

Doc Fadden raised an eyebrow and looked Abigail in the eyes. "Now, Abigail, let's don't jump to conclusions. How did you come to decide on this anyhow?"

"Well, you know that I have to dress his wounds. I also have to bathe him, and he has all these scars on this body. They look like gunshot wounds, just like a gunfighter would have. And ..."

"Abigail," Doc Fadden interrupted, "he probably got those in the war or some other way. Just because a man has scars doesn't mean he's a gunfighter. A lot of men in this fort have a lot of scars, but they aren't gunfighters, especially a notorious one named the Rhymer, for God's sake."

Abigail had to confess about the diary. She had to, at the risk of making Doc Fadden angry. Abigail explained, "Well, at first, I thought he was going to die. I was putting his belongings up in the closet when this book fell out from his saddlebags. If he were to die, I didn't think it would be right for us not to know who he was, for us not to put a name on the gravestone if we had the chance, so I opened the book. It turned out to be just loose pages of a diary. I'm sorry Doctor, but I felt compelled to read part of that diary."

Doc Fadden gave a disapprovingly scowl at Abigail. "So, you read a man's private writings, his thoughts, without permission?"

Abigail was now embarrassed. She didn't answer. She lowered her head to avoid Doc Fadden's eyes and nodded yes.

"You really think this is the diary of a gunfighter. The one called the Rhymer?"

"Yes, that's what is written in the pages," she said with her head still lowered.

Doc Fadden looked soberly at Abigail. "Well, if he is a gunfighter maybe he killed this fellow called the Rhymer and took his diary."

Abigail raised her head. She looked Doc Fadden in the eye. "Not likely Doctor. In the diary there was a photograph, and it sure looks like the same man to me."

"Abigail, where is this diary with the picture? Show me so I can see for myself."

Abigail took Doc Fadden to Simon's room, and after making sure Simon was still sleeping, showed him the photograph and the passage about Simon being named the Rhymer man.

Doc Fadden took the diary, retied the red ribbon and returned the diary to the saddlebags where it belonged, not to the shelf where Abigail kept it.

"It could be him I guess. Looks vaguely like him. You really think it is him don't you, Abigail?"

Abigail nodded her head and nervously said, "Yes, oh yes, it is him."

Doc Fadden walked to the door then turned back to Abigail. "Leave the diary alone. If he wanted us to read it, he would say so, and since he's in a deep sleep he can't say so. Besides, if he really is the Rhymer, why, men like him, if he found out, well, you know what I mean?" Doc Fadden left the infirmary shaking his head.

Abigail knew what he meant. But Doc Fadden did not know the Rhymer like she did, and each day she came to know him more. Hours later, deep into the night, she was reading the diary again.

"My hand is twitching, my fingers are itching,
I can feel it coming down deep in my bones.
When it finally gets here, there'll be great fear,
People won't even be safe in their own homes."

"It is pure wickedness and evil, a freakish upheaval,
Straight from the bowels of hell.
No one has ever seen, something this pure obscene,
And never will again I hope to tell."

Simon moaned real loud, almost eerily. Abigail wondered what Simon was writing about in that last passage. Hurriedly she read more.

I met a girl in that Denver saloon ~ her hair was as red as the flame.
The whole time I was there ~ I never did learn her proper name.
Everyone liked her ~ and, oh my, the things she could do for a man.

The only thing I ever heard her called was, "Tits Monahan."
I asked Tits if she'd seen or heard of this McKenzie, she asked why?
I said he's one of a mad dog breed and he deserves to die.
I told her he'd killed thousands during the Great War.
She said maybe she was mistaken but isn't that was what war was for.

"I saw it once before, during the Great War,
And it consumed all in its path.
Maiming and death, fire from its breath,
Only charred remains in the aftermath."

"I stood aside in the past, shocked and aghast,
And let it destroy mankind.
I've lived with it since, unable to rinse,
The malevolent memory from my mind."

There was that different verse again, right out of the blue. It did not seem to fit with the other sequences of this part of the diary. She looked, but the pages were not out of order. It sounded like Simon was writing about some sort of monster.

I told her this McKenzie killed scores of people, mindlessly, to glorify his own name,
and even destroyed his own troops to gain favor and personal fame.
Tits Monahan said "What makes you better? You're hell bent on killing!"
I said, "Yeah I am, but in this case both parties are willing."
"What if he ain't willing?" she asked.
"Willing? He likes killing like a child likes a sweet.
He likes spilling someone's guts more than he likes to eat.
Besides, unlike what he did for us ~ I'll give him an even chance."
Tits knew I was lying ~ I could tell by her glance.

"It's not natures storm, it's not anything norm,
It's born of the killing frenzy.
It comes in a nightmarish dream, it's what makes you scream,
Its name is Murdock F. McKenzie.

"This time I won't stand aside, my courage hasn't died,
On sight, I'm shooting him in the head.

Then I'm going to lob it off, bury it in a separate trough,
To make damn sure he stays dead."

Murdock F. McKenzie, the jackal of the south!
A chill shivered up my spine, and numbed my mind,
As I spit his name ~ nastily ~ from my mouth.

Simon sat straight up in bed and screamed. Abigail jumped out of her chair in a fright spilling the diary on the floor. Simon screamed again. Abigail rushed to his side and calmed him. He was screaming in his sleep. In her arms, he instantly fell asleep again. She laid him back in his bed, straightened his bed covers and then returned to her chair. She gathered the diary and knew she must finish quickly. She knew he was coming out of his coma–like sleep, and she felt it would be soon.

Simon's screams were caused by a nightmare. In his nightmare, he was riding along a steep escarpment when his horse lost its footing and fell over the edge. Simon hated dreams about falling. Simon and his horse landed in a bed of old tree limbs. Simon looked around and the tree limbs turned into snakes. There were many snakes. Each snake's head looked exactly like a person Simon had killed. He screamed and fought, but they kept biting him. Waking up was his only escape!

Abigail now knew what Simon was writing about. She knew it was, in fact, General Murdock F. McKenzie. She wondered why Simon was so afraid of a southern general, a true war hero. Why did Simon think of him as a monster?

Simon's second nightmare came from a different source. It came from the Federal Prison in Yuma, Arizona. Simon had the dream often.

Colorado has great mountains and trees, scenic ~ a little too cold for my taste
I'm here, tracking down McKenzie to lay the son of a bich to waste.
You know, there's not a lot to write about when you hunt and camp all day.
Seems the words don't come unless I'm drinking or in some kind of fray.
Murdock has managed ~ always ~ to stay just a day or two ahead,
but the morning wind turned sour today as I got out of my bed.
I've tracked him across several states for nigh well over a year.
The wind turning hot and sour gives me reason to think he is near.

I came up from behind his camp ~ he didn't seem to know I was near.
I called to him, when his gun hand moved ~ I shot him in front of his ear.

"I could tell from the walk, and his accent of talk,
He was upon us this most evil person.
In the black I moved silent, it would be violent,
I didn't want the situation to worsen."

"Up from behind, I blew away his mind,
But he still had the gall to turn around.
He grinned with green teeth, then crumpled beneath,
Still grinning when he hit the ground."

Simon left his horse tied to a tree some five hundred yards downwind. He carefully navigated the woods on foot, through the fallen tree limbs and the dead leaves, and came upon McKenzie's camp. He approached in Indian fashion not making any noise. McKenzie's horse did not notice Simon coming, giving no warning of the impending danger. Simon saw McKenzie sitting in a small clearing. From his position, Simon had an unobstructed view and a clear firing path. Simon called to McKenzie using his last name. He did not call him General, that was a name of respect, and McKenzie would not get any respect from Simon; all he would get was dead.

"McKenzie, it's time to meet the devil!" General Murdock McKenzie went for his gun and slowly turned his head toward Simon. Simon fired hitting McKenzie in front of his right ear. The noise of the shot echoed over the trees and the rocks. McKenzie, though dying, turned his body in the direction of the shot, facing Simon, gave a grin, and then slumped over dead.

Simon walked, slowly and carefully, to McKenzie's body. Cautiously, with his foot, Simon turned McKenzie's body over to make sure he was dead. Simon shot him again for insurance. Simon was glad he was finally dead. A thought flashed through his mind.

The noise of the shot danced on tree and rock,
The Jackal slain by one of his own flock.
By the one he trained to kill the other.

Revenge taken for Father and Brother.

Simon heard a movement coming from the trees. Instinctively he knelt behind the stump that McKenzie had been sitting on and aimed his pistol at the intruder.

"Don't shoot Mister, I just want to talk. I'm comin' in unarmed."

A man walked out from the trees with his hands raised over his head.

"Is that Murdock McKenzie?" The man asked, pointing to the still warm corpse.

"It was McKenzie, now it's just bug bait."

"I come in peace. See, I been tracking McKenzie, too. I have been hunting him for years hoping for the chance to kill him like you just did."

Simon looked at the young man. He still had his gun pointed at the man's head. "Same difference I guess. What's McKenzie to you?"

The man walked over to have a look at McKenzie lying dead on the forest floor. He didn't seem to be nervous even though Simon was holding a gun on him. He never gave Simon a second thought as he pulled his revolver and blew the top of McKenzie's skull into hundreds of pieces. He replaced his revolver before he turned to Simon.

"I served under him in the war. He sent a lot of men to die for no reason. To me, he was the most hellish person ever that walked on two feet. He was a devil of a man. Hell, I bet he could've stood in hell fire itself and not even of felt the heat."

"Well, he'll damn sure get the chance now....maybe he'll find out if that's true....I'm not going to bury the son of a bitch....how 'bout you?" said Simon still pointing his gun at the man.

"Let the bugs eat 'im," said the man. "Maybe they'll eat his soul, too. He's got so many enemies that even in the hereafter he ain't gonna find no peace. Least ways now we won't have to worry 'bout him no more on this earth."

The man extended his hand to Simon. "My name's Miller Jackson, from Virginia. I have been tracking McKenzie ever since the war. It's been a hell of a long time. Tell me Mister, I'd like to know the name of the man who killed Murdock McKenzie?"

"Name's Sublette, Simon Sublette. I served under his command too.... served him true. So did my daddy and my brother....swore to my daddy that I'd kill him for what he did to all the others. I swore it to him as he died in my arms. Least I kept one promise....McKenzie won't do any more harm."

The man took off his hat, slowly scratched his head as he paced back and forth, like he was trying to remember something, trying to call something up from deep in his memory. Then he put his hat back on, turned to Simon and grinned.

"I'll be damn. I heard of you back in Lynchburg. They call you the Rhymer now, don't they?"

Simon weighed the question for a moment and then decided to tell him the truth. "Yeah, I'm called that by some, but I like to be called Simon by my friends."

The man stood there not saying anything, merely shaking his head.

Simon knew the young man had wanted revenge, just like Will Cadence had wanted his revenge. Simon tried to comfort him.

"I know the revenge is sweeter....if it comes from your own hand....but when I saw him....I had to take the life of that most evil man. It makes no difference who killed him....at least the bastard's dead. Tell me Miller.... how long do you think it'll be....before the memories are gone from our head?"

Miller Jackson shrugged his shoulders. The gesture saying he did not know.

"Probably never....is what I suspect, Miller....but at least we've rid the world....of one mindless, senseless killer."

Miller finally spoke. "When I get back home, there'll be lots of folks that'll be glad he's dead and I'm gonna tell 'em that Murdock F. McKenzie was killed by Simon Sublette, the Rhymer Man."

"Don't tell it too loud....and don't be overly proud. It might cause some to come looking for me....then I'd have to dispute what you say. Some southern zealot's might not take too kindly....to me killing their hero today."

"The people I'm telling damn sure don't think he's a hero, and we're all from the south. Anyway, I suspect if someone did take offense we'd get 'em before they came looking for you."

"That's good to know, thanks."

Miller Jackson walked back into the trees, fetched his horse, mounted and rode toward the east, headed back to Virginia to tell the story of General Murdock McKenzie and the Rhymer Man.

Simon thought it curious, as he watched Miller ride away, back toward home, how the nickname "The Rhymer" had already begun to spread.

Another man approached, he was also tracking this killer.
He was from Virginia, went by the name of Miller.
Like Cadence before, he wanted the dying to be by his hand.
He wanted to kill McKenzie, to rid him from the land.
Though dead, he shot him anyway and scattered his brains forever.
Making sure McKenzie wouldn't hurt anyone again ~ EVER.
He was surprised, I think, when he learned my name.
When he left he said he was going home to spread my fame.
We didn't bury McKenzie ~ we left him to rot, the evil beast.
Forest animals don't care if he's human ~ for them he's another feast.

Murdock F. McKenzie
R.I.P.
"The nightmare -- has finally ended!
Hopefully ~ not just suspended!"

    The Rhymer

Well, Abigail thought, maybe folks do know who killed General McKenzie. They certainly do if this man Miller had done what he said and told everyone when he got home that the Rhymer had done the killing.

Abigail decided to leave it alone. She decided not to tell the Colonel or Doc Fadden. She didn't know why. She simply chose not to tell them. Abigail read the signature and was now absolutely positive that this man in the bed was next to her was the Rhymer. She looked up and Simon was awake!

He was sitting upright and was staring at her, with a glazed look in his blue eyes. Abigail was startled. Her jaw dropped—so did the diary. The diary scattered across the floor in disarray. She couldn't say a word.

Simon blinked, and then lay down, turned over and went back to sleep.

Hurriedly, Abigail gathered the pages of the diary and quickly put the pages in proper order. She retied the pages and placed them near the saddlebags.

Abigail went to Doc Fadden and told him that Simon had briefly awakened. Doc Fadden returned with Abigail to Simon's room to give him an examination. When Doc Fadden and Abigail walked into Simon's room they received a surprise. Simon was awake and sitting upright in bed.

"Well, hello there mister, it's good to see you're finally awake! My name is Doctor James Fadden." Doc Fadden nodded his head toward Abigail. "This is your nurse, Abigail Sweeney."

Simon now tried to talk, but his speech was harsh and not understandable.

Doc Fadden raised his right hand. It was a motion telling Simon not to speak. "Don't try to talk right now. You're in an army hospital at Fort Defiance. You've had a tough go of it. You've been asleep for about ten days. We almost lost you a couple of times." Again Doc nodded his head toward Abigail. "Abigail is mainly responsible for saving you. Now I want you to lie still and we'll get you something to eat. Let's get your strength back and then we will see about getting you up on your feet. As soon as you're ready, and able to talk plainly, I'll come back, and we'll visit a spell. For now, eat and rest."

Simon nodded his head in agreement.

Doc Fadden patted Simon on his shoulder and left the room.

Simon's right foot hurt like hell. He wondered what was wrong with it. He hoped the doctor would do something to ease the pain. God, what he would do for a good drink of whiskey right now.

Abigail left and quickly returned with some hot chicken and dumpling soup. Abigail had no way of knowing it was Simon's favorite soup.

With the first swallow of the soup, memories of his mother flooded Simon and made him feel warm and safe.

Abigail spoon–fed him the soup and then gave him some pain medicine.

Simon still wanted the whiskey; he wished he could talk plainly so he could tell her. Soon Simon was fast asleep.

Abigail got the diary, wrapped it in her apron and went to her room. If need be, she would stay awake all night. She was going to finish reading the diary, and she knew this would be her last chance.

Ernestine Coffee
Colorado Springs, Colorado

I'm putting McKenzie out of my mind ~ I've stopped here in Colorado Springs.
I need to relax after tracking him so long ~ and to replenish a few things.
Naturally I migrated to a saloon, where else was I to go?
There's no other place for a man to relax except at a good watering hole.
I guess I looked worse for wear or maybe looked off my feed.
A voice behind me said, "Some hot black coffee is what you need!"
I spoke as I turned, I replied, "I came for whiskey to drink and to have a rest."
When I turned around, I was looking straight into a woman's chest.
My eyes moved up to her face and I saw that she was black.
She said her name was Ernestine Coffee and that I should take my words back.
I thought about it for a moment ~ then it finally got through to my head,
and exactly what she meant with those words she had said.
Now I'm not saying that being with a black woman will drive a man mad,
but it was the hottest, sweetest, blackest coffee that I'd ever had.

"Hot Black Coffee can heal a man's soul.
Add in some whiskey, it'll make you whole.
Good Whiskey and sweet tasting women,
isn't anything better if you got to be sinnin'."
"Hot Black Coffee, come and get your fill.
It'll cure what ails you if only you will.
Hot Black Coffee, get your fill indeed,
it may not be what you want ~ but it's what you need!!"

The Rhymer

Abigail was taken aback by what she had read, a southern gentleman admitting to sharing a bed with a black woman. Oh, she had heard that plenty of them did it in the south, but they would never admit to it. It seemed to Abigail that the only people Simon didn't care for were men. She surmised he wasn't a bigot, at least not to black women; maybe he was to the men of color. Abigail was beginning to like this Simon Sublette, though she did not understand why. She wished he did not like these saloon girls so much. Was she jealous? She reasoned that it was difficult for gunfighters to settle down with a decent woman. Did they fear for the life of the woman or did they fear the prospect of staying in one place too long? Maybe she would get the courage to ask him. She mused, could she, Abigail Sweeney, be with a man like Simon Sublette?

Petey Joe Tyree
Deaf Smith County, Texas

"What's that book you got there, is that a bible? Are you a preacher man?"
I guess the voice talking to me was referring to the journal I had in my hand.
I said "No, I'm not a man of the cloth ~ I walk too close to the other side.
But I have been known to say a few words ~ over other men as they died."
I stepped up and ordered a whiskey, laid my money down on top of the bar.
I took a sip of the whiskey and felt the twitch come to my scar.
I said, "This is just a pile of papers ~ I write down things to clear my head,
and then I can think better on how to make a nosey son of a bich dead."
He said, "That wouldn't work for me, I can't read and I can't write,
but I am pretty good at drinking beer and at making a good fight."
I sized him up, scruffy blond hair, still in his teens, and he appeared to be fast.
If it came to fighting with fist and such, I'm sure I would never last.
Good thing for me I carry my guns.
He said, "I don't like nosey people either, sticking their nose where it don't belong.
I don't know why they can't be off by themselves and leave everybody alone."
I said, "Tell me son, how is it that you get your fighting done?
Do you use your fist or do you use some kind of gun?"
He said "Oh no, guns make me nervous. I just beat 'em up with my hands,
or I bite 'em or gouge 'em or kick 'em whenever I can."
He said "Mister, looking at your face, looks like you been in a scrape or two."
I said, "Yeah, you're right, this is the result of what a crazed woman will do."
He said, "Mister, I didn't catch your name, or from where you came."
I said "Now you're being nosey just a bit, sticking your nose where it doesn't fit?"
He said, "That ain't being nosey." And he gave me a little grin.
"It's just things you ought to know when you call a man friend."
I told him I was born in the Territories, but claim Texas soil, the name is Sublette.
And then I said, "I don't believe I've got your name yet."
He replied, "My name's Petey Joe Tyree, the town makes fun of me!"
When they do I whomp 'em with my fist real good
I beat's 'em to hell, the sheriff puts me in jail.
Then tells me I need to control my temper, if I could."

It occurred to Abigail that when Simon wrote in the diary about what others said, he wrote their conversations in verse. It was Simon's way of writing and it was Simon making their speech rhyme.

Early on I knew Petey Joe was dim–witted and probably suffered ridicule.
It's strange about people like him and how folks can be so cruel.
Petey Joe and I took a table and I raised a glass to Petey Joe for a toast.
It should be noted that Petey Joe Tyree drank the most.
He was drinking beer and I didn't see no harm,
and all of a sudden two men approached, one grabbed Tyree's arm.
He said, "I told you Petey Joe, next time I saw you, you better have a gun.
So get it strapped on and let's get our fighting done."
Petey Joe said "Wendell, I don't have a gun, shoot you know me,
I don't know how to use one, so go away and leave me be."
These two seemed extra nervous ~ Petey Joe and I were both calm.
Wendell said, "I want to fight right now, give him your gun Tom."
I butted in, "Why don't you two just give them guns an unbuckle,
be fair about it, fight oh Petey Joe here bare knuckle."
Tom said "Hell no, we ain't doing that, last time he beat us black and blue.
Just what the hell do you have to do with this ~ who the hell are you?"
My scar twitched ~ the killing mood heightened.
If they had of known the Demon was near ~ they would have been frightened.
I said, "I am just a friend. I am his and he is mine.
And I am not going to say this, but just one single time."
I took a sip of drink, pausing for time to think.
I said, "Tyree here did get him a gun and that gun is me.
He knew you were coming so I'm his protection you see.
Now you get along and you stay away from Petey Joe for good,
or do you want to be laid to rest in a box of piney wood?"
I took a sip of my drink, giving them time to think.
"Now I have no more to say ~ either get ~ or make your play."
Derringer to my fist, sawed–off up to privates' level.
If need be, I'd send these two to see the Devil.
My scar was twitching, they didn't know what to do.
My sawed–off would kill them as soon as my finger wanted it to.
But I just waited ~ letting them make the selection,
and then I'll play the hand as it goes ~ follow their direction.
The law came in, broke it up, and got in between.
"Stranger, you better leave if you know what I mean."
I stood, paid my bill and left, keeping my back to the wall.

Whatever happens to Petey Joe in the future, is now the sheriff's call.
Someone will come along someday and kill Petey Joe, for good reason or not.
I guess by being there this time a few more days of his life was bought.
Cruelty like that chafes me a bit, next time I won't hesitate.
I'm going to make my own selection ~ stand them at hell's gate.
I hate people who find fault with another person's affliction.
Sometimes it's only their speech or accent or their diction.
They just better not do it in range of my ear.
I'll tell you outright ~ there'll damn sure be a fight,
and my southern diction is the last they'll ever hear.

Abigail thought to herself, he likes women and children and he is not bigoted about the color of skin. He stands for those with afflictions. He's good in those ways, maybe a hero to those he helps. However, he does not seem all too fond of men, at least not the men in this dairy, those men who are cruel to the disadvantaged and the meek. He seems to believe men like that need to be killed. Abigail didn't know what to really think, but she had this feeling she agreed with him. Abigail was ashamed of herself for thinking like that. She would never have thought like that before reading the diary.

The Slobber Dog
Tucumcari, New Mexico

Slobber Dog Deacon, if there was a nastier looking man, I haven't seen one.
He came into the PowWow saloon, skunk drunk and firing his gun.
It wasn't a place for me to be ~ I finished my drink, and then headed to the door.
I had only taken a couple of steps when a bullet hit at my feet, splintering the floor.
Slobber Dog said "I'm the one here who says who can leave and who cain't.
So stop right there stranger, 'cause leaving you ain't."
I said "Mister, you can shoot this place all to hell, with me it's fine,
but I'll pick another time and place to make a stray bullet mine."
He said "Oh no! There's no way I'm going to let you go.
I think you ought to dance for us ~ put on a little show."
He started shooting at my feet ~ one bullet nicked the heel of by boot.
I didn't move ~ dancing never was my strong suit.
The next thing the Slobber Dog knew my derringer had parted his hair.
With his bullets now spent, defenseless, he just stood there.
I said, "Deacon, see little Sweet Pea here, pointed at your head,
one twitch of a nervous finger, and you'll be dead."
He started to drool ~ the old fool ~ taking him down was simple.
I grabbed his gun and slapped him alongside his temple.
Two others and I took the fat belly swill to the livery, to sleep it off in the hay.
When he sobers ~ I'll deal with Slobber Dog Deacon another day.

I was readying myself to leave when I ran into Deacon by chance.
It'd been two days past since he wanted me to dance.
He said, "Mister, where you shot me in the hair sure does hurt."
I said, "Well, it beats being face down dead sucking up dirt."
"Deacon, when you shake a man's tree, you ought to know what's inside.
If I wasn't the benevolent sort, you know you would have died."
"You can't corner a man like you would corner a rat,
he'll come out vicious, and mean, when you treat him like that."
He said, "It's the demon whiskey that makes me act that way."
I said, "If that's so then you better learn to keep the whiskey at bay."
Whiskey can be the Devil's brew, especially when it gets a hold of you."
He said "Yeah, guess I'll quit." If he did, I knew it would only be for a bit.
Except for Deacon, everything here has been tame.

Anyway, how the hell could a person get Slobber Dog for a name?
I gathered by belongings and horse, and I readied to go.
I'm riding over to the western part of New Mexico.

Slobber Dog Deacon sounded reminiscent of Abigail's first and only husband. She had married young, too young, at the age of fifteen. She gathered the courage to leave him, and move away from east Texas, a couple of years ago. She then came west with the army. When she was married, her husband came home many times soaked full of the demon rum, stinking drunk. In his drunken mood, he would talk abusively to Abigail. He never beat her though, and she counted herself lucky in that respect. If Simon had been around in those days and had met Briceton Sweeney, and heard the way he talked to her, Simon might have killed him. She would have not tried to stop him.

Getting Well

Abigail went to Simon's room early in the morning, before the first rays of sun and returned the diary. Simon was asleep, but Abigail could tell he had had another restless night.

Simon had dreamed about the Yuma prison again.

Abigail sat in the chair beside Simon's bed until he awoke.

Then she went to the kitchen and made his breakfast. After she had fed him, slowly and hoarsely, Simon spoke his first words to Abigail Sweeney.

"Thanks, ma'am, your name is, Abigail, right?"

Abigail nodded her head in agreement.

"Well, Abigail, my foot hurts something fierce. I don't know what's wrong with it. Could you get me some whiskey? It's there in my saddlebags. And please, get me the Doc, so he can take a look."

Abigail was shocked and disappointed in Simon's first words to her. She wanted him to speak in a rhyme, but he didn't. Abigail went for Doc Fadden; thinking it was time to tell Simon about his foot.

Abigail met Doc Fadden coming down the hallway.

"Doctor, Mr. Sublette is awake. He's asking for whiskey, and he's complaining about his foot hurting. I guess you better see him and tell him we cut off two of his toes and that's why his foot hurts."

Doc Fadden stopped what he was doing and went to see Simon. He entered the room and pulled a chair next to Simon's bed and sat down. Simon's face showed the strain of the hurt he was feeling.

"Young man, before we start, I need to know your name."

"Where am I?"

"I told you before, remember? You're in an army hospital in Fort Defiance. Now could you tell me your name or do I just call you mister from now on?"

"My name is Simon. Simon Sublette." Simon grimaced from the pain in his leg and foot. "My leg and my foot are causing me pain. Can you get me some whiskey or do you have something better? The whiskey is in my saddlebags."

Doc Fadden ignored Simon's request. "When we found you, you were almost frozen to death. We had to use fire logs to heat your legs just to get you off your horse. We don't know how long you had been riding in that blizzard, but I suspect it was a long time. You developed some infection in your right leg and two of your toes had severe frostbite. I had to remove the toes before gangrene set in. That's why your foot hurts. Whiskey won't help. Healing properly will."

Simon sat straight up in bed. "You cut off my toes, son of a …!" He stopped short of saying the word when he looked at Abigail. A grimaced grin came across Simon's face. His scar turned red and twitched. He threw back his bed covers. He looked at his foot and saw the bandages. He saw the gap where the toes were missing. He fell back against his pillow. "Good God All Mighty, couldn't you have saved them? It's one fierce pain, Doc. How long before it goes away?"

"Well, Mr. Sublette, I had no choice, I had to remove them. I had to take them before the gangrene set in, or you would probably have died. When the pain will go away, I don't rightly know, maybe never, some people heal differently than others."

"Good God All Mighty," Simon repeated. And then he sat up and looked at his foot again. He stared at it for several minutes before he spoke.

"Will I be able to walk, Doc? Or am I going to be crippled?"

"Oh, I don't think you'll be a cripple, might need a cane at first, but you'll be able to walk all right. You'll probably have a little limp. As soon as you're able, we'll get you up and teach you how to walk again without those two toes, shouldn't be too difficult."

Simon looked at Doc Fadden. He was mad because of the loss of the toes, especially since he had no say so in the matter. His scar turned red and it twitched. The Demon came, and he could not help himself. He smiled at Doc Fadden with a cruel smile, his killing smile. It was a good thing his gun was in the closet. Sometimes, most times, he could not control the Demon.

"Two toes frost bit and cut....guess I'll walk with a limp from now on.... it beats the alternative I reckon....to be all dead and gone."

Doc Fadden looked at Simon. Goddamn, he thought, maybe he really is the Rhymer.

Abigail shot a quick look at Doc Fadden, and then she turned her face away and smiled.

Doc Fadden thought for a moment, rubbed his chin with his left hand, then finally said, "Tell me, Mr. Sublette, you by chance go by the name The Rhymer?"

Simon looked at the doctor for a long time without saying anything, still smiling. He wondered how the doctor knew of his other name. Maybe it was because he had just spoken in a rhyme? It didn't make any difference

Simon guessed. He needed these people to help him heal and get well. Finally, Simon spoke. "Yeah, some call me that name....The Rhymer.... Simon....Mr. Sublette....they're all the same."

"I thought that might be so, should have named you the cat. As many wounds as you have, you've probably used up nine lives or more already."

"Yeah....I guess I've abused this body of mine....if all those bullets were sticking out of me....I'd probably look like a porcupine." Simon grinned, and then grimaced with the pain.

"I'm curious, Mr. Sublette. How did the rhyming come to you anyway?"

Simon didn't need all of this small talk. He needed the whiskey. Maybe if he indulged the man, he could finally get a drink.

"I don't really know, Doc....one day it just popped into my head....they came out as a rhyme....the things I said."

Doc Fadden looked at Simon and started laughing.

Simon laughed, too.

So did Abigail.

Doc Fadden started for the door, and then he turned and gave Simon some advice.

"Let's keep who you are between the three of us. If the word were to get out that you were sick and in bed, some might come to finish off what nature started. Abigail and I don't want or need the trouble."

"I won't tell anyone. And I'd welcome a peaceful rest for a change. But I sure could rest easier with some whiskey."

Doc Fadden sent Abigail to get some whiskey from his private stock.

Simon told Doc Fadden that the sunlight bothered his eyes some.

Doc Fadden said he suspected Simon was partially snow blind from being exposed for such a long time. He said his eyes were overly sensitive to the bright light. Later that day, Doc Fadden brought Simon some small, round, dark glasses to wear.

Simon did not particularly care for the glasses, but his eyes did not hurt when he wore them in the bright light. And now he could see without squinting.

He looked at Abigail closely for the first time. She was a pretty woman with long flowing hair. Its color was blonde, like a flaxen blonde. She was about five feet two or three inches, he guessed. Her skin was fair and had not seen much sun light. He also guessed she didn't weigh more than a hundred pounds or so. Simon liked her.

Over the course of the next couple of weeks, Abigail nursed Simon back to full health. In the warm afternoons, she helped him learn how to walk without the use of a cane. He was always gentle with Abigail and a perfect gentleman to all others he encountered. Abigail took full notice of Simon the first time he stood to walk. He was about six feet tall, muscular build of one hundred eighty pounds and had long, blond hair that he combed straight back before he put on his black, large–brimmed hat. His hair had a natural curl and was not stringy like some men who wore their hair in this manner. His hair fell to the top of his shirt collar. What she noticed most was Simon's hands. They were strong hands with longish sleek fingers. They could have been musician's hands, she mused.

When Abigail touched me, her strength, her warmth, I could feel it.
Whatever is wrong with me, I knew, in my heart, she could heal it.
Perhaps keep the Demon at bay, or fully exorcise him some day.

During the time Simon spent with Abigail, he learned she wasn't married and was born in Texas. Her father was an army man, a doctor, and that was how she came to be a nurse. Her father and mother had both passed a few years ago. Simon also learned she was twenty years old. Simon was quite taken with Miss Abigail Sweeney. He wished he wasn't who he was.

Abigail did not accompany Simon when he went outside the fort to fire his weapons. He only went once. The near cold death had not hurt his hands, and he could see quite well with his new glasses. He had a limp when he walked, from his bad foot. But then he thought, you don't kill people with your feet. You do it with your hands—and steely nerves.

Glad my hands weren't cut off ~ they're what I need.
I went to see if I still have the necessary speed.
Derringer to my hand ~ it found its mark.
Forty–five roared to life ~ it was good to hear it bark.
Cans, bottles, and rocks spewed into the air.
Men will be too, if they dare.

That one time was all Simon needed. He knew he had not lost anything while he was laid up half frozen. He was still fast and deadly accurate. The Rhymer was alive and well. He had spoken in a rhyme only once since he awakened from his deep sleep, that one time to Doc Fadden. He could feel his blood stirring; he could feel the Demon coming. He was healthy. He was restless and it was time to move on.

He was told his horse had not lived through the ordeal. They tried to warm it and feed it some oats, but the animal never recovered. The army didn't have any spare horses he could purchase. He was told a stagecoach, bound for Santa Fe, New Mexico, was coming soon. For now it was his only mode of transportation. He decided he would be on that stage. He would go to Santa Fe or anywhere the stage went. He did not care. He needed to be on the move. He sat and wrote in his diary.

I'm just now getting to where I can write again, it's been a pretty bad spell.
I damn near froze to death, but now am I starting to get well.
An angel came, with flaxen hair and fair skin aglow,
spread her warmth and saved me from a coffin of snow.
I got caught in a freak blizzard, in the north of New Mexico.
The storm came on early and fast and trapped me in a blinding snow.
I tied my scarf over my eyes to keep the snow from ruining my sight.
I rode mostly blind during the day, but I could see fairly well at night.
To keep up the circulation, I used my rope to beat my legs and feet.
When the Fort came into view, I had never seen anything so sweet.
When they tried to get me down, my legs had frozen to the saddle leather.
I had ridden for four days straight in snow and below freezing weather.
They had to get fire logs to get my legs to thaw,
but my legs were so stiff that I couldn't walk at all.
The Doc came in, said it looked like I was going to be all right.
But I lost my right big and middle toe due to the frostbite.
I've got a little limp and for a while there'll be some pain,
but I can get around pretty good and I won't need a cane.
They had to put my horse down so I'm taking the stage to Santa Fe.
I'd prefer to ride a horse, rather than that dusty, bumpy contraption all day.

Simon was gathering his saddlebags, bedroll and saddle. The saddle had the knife marks on the right side where Simon's leg had been cut away. The mark was jagged, like the scar on Simon's face. It, too, would serve as a reminder of things past.

Abigail approached and gently touched him on the arm.

Simon turned and looked into Abigail's pretty brown eyes and spoke.

"I need to ask you....bluntly....would you consider coming away with me?"

Abigail had thought about this at great length. She had agonized over this exact question—but she never dreamed Simon would actually ask her.

"Mr. Sublette, my heart tells me yes, but my gut feeling tells me I can't. I want a man who is ready to settle down, have children. I don't think you are that man. You jump from place to place looking for something, but I don't know what. I can't do that, go from place to place without any plan for a future."

Simon started to speak, but Abigail spoke first.

"Mr. Sublette, I've nursed you back to health," Abigail said. "And, to me, you are a gentle soul. I know who you are and what you've done. I've heard all the talk all over the fort, but I just can't envision you being the coldhearted killer they call the Rhymer."

All the talk, really, her saying that brought a smile to Simon's face. It wasn't the talk going around the fort. He knew better. He knew she had read his diary, all except the pages he'd just written. He knew because of the red ribbon used to tie the diary. He saw it was tied wrong when he removed it from his saddlebags. It didn't matter to Simon. It was of no consequence. Abigail had saved his life. She could have the diary, if she wanted. He was lucky he was still able to write in the diary, lucky indeed, and he owed all of it to her. Abigail was a woman who certainly stirred Simon's blood. He slowly spoke softly and gently.

"I would prefer if you called me Simon. You are a lovely, sweet woman and you no doubt saved my life....and I thank you ma'am....but it's true what they say....that I am what I am." Simon hesitated for a moment then continued. "It wasn't my mother's intention....for her baby son....to become what he is....and be known for using a gun. She wanted me to be a farmer and work the land....but things happened along the way....to change mother's plan. I was made this way by fate....wounds, both physical and mental, all leave a scar....so your life gets changed....and we become what we are."

Abigail started to say something, but Simon put his finger to her lips and continued.

"There are men who are vile and evil....and when they come....they must be eliminated....with the use of the gun. I have a Demon in me,

Abigail....he comes when danger is near....he comes uncalled....and he has no fear. The Demon hates the ridicule of women and kids....cruelty for the color of a man's skin....it's something I can't control....my blood quickens.... and I kill again. I just want good folks and me to be left alone....then, Abigail, I'm as gentle as a lamb." Simon smiled at Abigail. "But when the Demon is provoked....well then, that's when I am what I am."

"Isn't it written vengeance is mine says the Lord!" said Abigail.

Simon reached over, put his finger gently underneath Abigail's chin and lifted it up, so he was looking directly in her eyes.

"Isn't it in the Bible that all evil doers will have their light extinguished? All I want for me is to be left alone in peace....no conflict, no war. That's all I'm searching for. As for the Demon, I don't know."

Abigail didn't answer. She knew he was right. She stood and stared. She hadn't ever met a man like this and doubted she ever would again.

As Simon limped toward the stage to Santa Fe, he turned and said, "Abigail, thanks again....I'll try not to go to the devil....and maybe somehow, someday....I can come back and make things level."

"God's speed, Simon," Abigail said, and then hesitated for a moment before adding, "Simon, please write and tell of your whereabouts. I do care about you."

Simon got on the stage. He knew he would never come back.

Abigail hoped she would see him again. She was sad he was leaving. She wondered if the other passengers knew of him and of the potential violence that would be their traveling companion for the next few days. He would only be a danger to them if they in turn were a threat of some sort. None of them knew what the future held, but if trouble reared its ugly head, they would be damned glad to have this kind of man in their midst on their way to Santa Fe.

Simon thought about all those who had fallen: Murdock McKenzie, the man at Bitter Creek and the Henrys that had started all this. He did not think the Almighty would judge him too harshly—all of the men had the dying coming. He was uncomfortable though about how the Almighty might think of him for killing the woman. Surely somewhere in the Bible, a woman was killed for a good reason. The story of Lot came to mind.

As the stage pulled away, Abigail finally realized that when Simon had spoken, he had spoken to her in rhyme.

Abigail went back inside to clean Simon's room. She found a sheet of paper on his pillow. It read:

There's a fighter born in every human soul,
won't give up his life ~ won't let go.
Embedded in spirit, ingrained deep,
the date with death the soul won't keep.
The struggle is built in the human will,
take the morphine, pain to kill.
Cut off the flesh to remove the disease,
wound will scar ~ pain will ease.
Grim Reaper defeated by inner fight,
infection rescinded by blinding light.
The soul won't give up in defiant stand,
guided in battle by unseen hand.
Fight through hard ~ fight through hurting pain,
let the body mend so it can hurt again.

Simon, the Rhymer, Sublette

Chapter Two

Santa Fe

Not much leg space on this stage, and I can't write a thought.
When I get to Santa Fe a good horse will be bought.

Simon tried to write in his diary during the stagecoach ride to Santa Fe, but it was cramped and bumpy, and he was unable to write legibly. He was traveling with a woman, her husband and two other men. He suspected the man and wife were easterners. Simon determined this by their manner of talk. The other two gentlemen were in fancy dress. Fancy anyway to Simon's way of thinking. They wore matching coats and trousers, ruffled shirts and ties. Their shoes were unlike any Simon had ever seen.

Occasionally, Simon would take out his flask of whiskey and have a small drink. Each time the woman would turn her head and roll her eyes as though the sight of him drinking whiskey disgusted her. Simon did not need that kind of self–righteousness. He was not hurting the woman, not one damned bit. He decided he would ride on top of the stage with the driver when they stopped to rest the horses.

He spent a lot of time staring out of the window at the lay of the land. The last time he passed this way, all he saw was snow. It was a pretty ride, even if it was bumpy. He could have enjoyed it more if he wasn't sitting next to this prudish woman. The country side was rolling, grass covered, hills with the occasional stand of trees. Simon wondered if any of those stands could have offered him any shelter, if only he could have seen them.

Simon could feel the stagecoach begin to slow. They approached the first of several way stations. Here they would change the horses and give the passengers a brief rest from the bump, grind and dirt of the coarse road. When they stopped, Simon noticed two horses tied to the post in front of the way station, for some reason, his senses went on alert—the Demon in him awoke. *Be careful, those horses are wet. Trouble coming, I'm not going away just yet. You go on and pee, I'll stay alert. No need for anyone to get hurt.* He needed to relieve himself badly so he hurriedly went out back as the others unloaded and went inside the way station. Simon finished his business and the Demon told him to enter the way station by the back door. When he walked in, even with his dark glasses on, he could see a man silhouetted against one of the front windows, and, the man was holding a gun. His scar twitched violently. The hair on his neck prickled. The Demon took control. Slowly, silently, Simon removed his glasses with his left hand and his forty–five from its holster with his right hand. He let the gun hang low just inside his coat. He could now see the other man standing close to the front door. The one closest to Simon spoke first.

"Mister, get your hands to where I can see 'em. Franklin, get what money he's got."

The Demon took over. In a low guttural voice Simon spoke, "You should reconsider....'cause you're not going to steal from me....if you're smart you'll back out now....and leave us be."

Simon's reply surprised the men. "What in the hell …"

Simon interrupted. He flipped away his coat and raised his gun to eye level. "Let me explain if you will....you see it's a widely known fact....dead men can't steal!"

The two hold–up men didn't know what to think of Simon. There were two of them and only one of him. Did he have a death wish? They weighed their chances.

Simon gave them one more opportunity to go. "Let me ask you....why are you picking today to die?" Simon looked at the men, and they gave no indication they were going to leave. He knew they were thinking there were two of them and at least one of them could kill him first. He gave them another moment, and then he spoke the last words they would ever hear. "I can send you to hell....and you can ask the devil why!"

The first man's gun hand twitched. It was his last twitch. As he turned toward Simon, Simon fired and killed him. Then in an instant he shot and killed the one called Franklin. Franklin got off a shot, but it went harmlessly into the ceiling as he fell dead to the floor.

Simon checked each man to make sure they were dead. Then he walked to the bar and poured himself a glass of whiskey. He walked to the woman, stood in front her, and drank the entire glass, never taking his eyes from hers. This time she did not look away.

"You shouldn't judge a man....just for the whiskey on his breath.... without me here today....you would have met your death."

The woman stared at Simon without speaking. She knew he spoke the truth.

One of the men in fancy dress spoke up. "I don't think they were going to kill us. They only wanted our money."

Simon turned to the man to stare him in the face. He pointed to the two dead men on the floor with his gun. "Tell that to them....they could have left, but they chose to die....if they weren't going to kill us....then tell me why?"

Simon holstered his gun and moved over to the bar and refilled his flask.

The station manager was grateful he had been there. He knew the two would have killed them to keep from being identified. "Thanks for the help," he said nervously. "The whiskey is on house."

Simon did not speak. He politely nodded his appreciation and touched the brim of his hat with his hand. He went to the stagecoach and settled on the top seat with the driver. He rode there the rest of the way to Santa Fe.

A bead of sweat ran down the side of their faces.
Two of my forty-five bullets found their places.
Now maybe I can get on to Santa Fe and buy me a mount.
I wonder how many I've killed ~ I've never stopped to count.

After they had driven for a few miles, the stagecoach driver spoke to Simon. "That was purty good shootin' back there mister. Seems to me that those two didn't have much of a chance, you dropped both of 'em without 'em gettin' as much as a squeeze."

"They were probably only farmers. Damn sure weren't professional highwaymen. Any good holdup man would've been watching that stage. When I went around back....he would've jumped me cold....he would've made me piss my pants....while he was taking my gold."

The driver looked warily at Simon. It suddenly occurred to him that the man sitting next to him was the killer called the Rhymer. At first he was a little afraid. "Seems to me you were already in a foul mood when you walked in back there, that woman givin' you a hard time?"

"No. It's that I've been suffering for a spell....I'm just getting over a cold day in hell."

The driver shot a curious look at Simon. "I thought hell was hot?"

"One man's hell is hot....another man's hell is not....but hell is all the same. There's the hopelessness and agony....grief and misery....and lots of searing white pain."

"Guess I never thought of it that way."

"Take it from someone who's been to both places....the devil wears many faces....and manages both places."

"I'll take your word for it. Either way it's good to have you on top."

Later, after they had driven for quite a few miles, the driver had had time to think about Simon's words. "So tell me Rhymin' Man, you really think pain comes in colors?"

Simon stared off into the distance. He never looked at the driver as he answered. "Oh yeah, if you had ever had any real pain you'd understand.... the black and blue kind aren't so bad....but the white kind....it's the kind that kills a man."

The stagecoach driver looked at Simon. He was certainly everything he had heard about. He seemed about half crazy, and his looks didn't help any. With that big ugly scar running from his lip to his ear, and wearing those sinister looking dark glasses, he could give a man a fright all right. It made the driver shudder, but he sure was glad to have him riding shotgun. No other conversation was exchanged the rest of the trip. Simon just rolled with the sway of the coach and sipped from his flask of whiskey.

Before they got to Santa Fe, Simon removed his boot and rubbed his foot. It still hurt like hell, and the whiskey was not dulling the pain very well. Simon knew one thing for sure. After the incident at the way station, his instincts and his gun hand were at full speed. Maybe this was what the Demon needed.

I arrived in Santa Fe, and I've decided to stay for a few.
The games are generous and the ladies are too.
I've been here a while now but the peace has been smashed.
One of the painted ladies turned up ~ her throat was slashed.
Whoever did it has killed three more of the painted ladies.
The killer leaves a note on them "I've sent another whore to Hades!"
I tell you one thing I'm really glad about this time ~
that the killer didn't make that death note rhyme.
The ladies have gone on strike until this killer is caught.
Sex has dried up around here ~ none can be bought.

Simon was the one who had found the first girl. He had taken his usual route from the Cerritos Saloon to the La Fonda hotel through the alley. There she lay. Simon could see her slumped against the wall—her throat slashed. Her clothes were rumbled and in disarray, Simon wondered if she had been raped. He went immediately for the sheriff.

After the death of the fourth lady of the evening, the town council decided they should intervene and called a meeting. They wanted to see if they could formulate a plan to catch the killer.

Simon thought the decent women of the town feared that the killer might run out of whores and start on them next.

They called a town meeting about the killer, and I thought I should attend.
The audience was full of over dressed women and farcified men.
I looked at the council, and I thought it curious this was the town's elite.
For me personally I wouldn't vote for any of them to sit on my council's seat.
They talked for a while, and they never did really make any sense.
It occurred to me that this council was probably the killers' best defense.
They each were concerned only about themselves and not the city as a whole,
and with that kind of thinking, they could never come to a common goal.
The thought occurred to me ~ I'd seen people with more integrity sitting in a cell.
If our society is coming to this then I fear it's going to hell.

Simon was not too impressed with what he witnessed at the town meeting. The council never did come to a resolution about an action to catch the killer. At the town meeting, Simon sat next to the man who tended bar at the saloon where Simon drank and played cards each evening. The bartender's name was Cordell Pitifore. They talked as they walked back to the saloon after the meeting. This senseless, random killing was bad for business. Simon and the bartender formed a partnership. They would catch the killer, to hell with the city leaders. They knew they would need one of the ladies of the evening to help them with their plan.

The best girl, and the toughest in Simon's way of thinking, was Aurora Bates. She sure did not mind taking a fist to a man's head, if needed, or give a kick to a groin when called for.

When Simon and Cordell approached Aurora and told her of their plan, she reacted as they thought she would.

"Why, you two sum–bitches are crazy. You'd probably go to sleep or sumthin' and I'll be left standin' there eatin' a goddamn knife for supper," Aurora said.

Cordell replied. "Aurora, there'll be two of us, one on each side of the street. We'll both be carrying rifles, so we'll have a good range of fire. We can set it up so you are standing real close, and I'll be right near hiding in the shadows. The Rhymer here, he'll be across the street with that Sharps of his ready and waiting. Besides, hell, you know the stories. The man who talks in rhymes doesn't miss what he's shooting at."

Aurora looked at Simon. "If you are the Rhymin' Man, how come I ain't knowed it 'fore now, I ain't heard you say shit, except deal, more whiskey and whose gonna get lucky tonight."

"Well, Aurora....I haven't wanted anybody to know I'm the Rhymer....I'm not interested in having to defend my name....against some gun fighting social climber. I just want to catch this killer of women....so we can get back to gambling and drinking and sinnin'." Simon gave Aurora a smile.

"Well I'll be damned. The Rhymin' Man has spoken. But this plan of yours it's crazy. I'm the one takin' the risk. You ain't riskin' nuthin'. What's my take in all of this?"

"You making' any money lately, Aurora?" asked Simon.

"Not a damn red cent. But why me, there're other girls here who ain't makin' no money either."

"We figure you're the only one who would stand there and not scream like hell and piss your pants when the killer comes along and pulls a knife. We just need one good shot. And we're risking a lot too. If this goes down wrong, we might get charged for murder."

Aurora was silent for a moment, and then she spoke, "I'll do it for fifty dollars, not a penny less, cash up front."

"Fifty dollars! Damn, Aurora, that's more than you would make in a whole month of Sundays whoring!" said Cordell.

"I don't know who you been laying with, but I can make that in a week, easy. Take it or leave it!" Aurora said defiantly.

"I'm in," said Simon, "We'll make it back soon enough, Cordell."

"Okay, okay, but it's still too much money."

"One of you two better shoot good, real good. If that sum–bitch cuts my throat I ain't gonna take it none too good. I'll come back from hell and haunt the both of you to your graves."

Aurora Bates was one tough woman.

Simon and Cordell put their plan together. Each night Simon and Cordell took up their positions and watched Aurora walk the streets. It didn't take as long as they had calculated. Two nights later, finally, he came, and they were ready.

We devised a plan ~ to have one girl to serve as the bait.

Me and Cordell Pitifore stood guard ~ it wasn't a very long wait.
I saw him coming. As he approached I saw him pull his knife.
Aurora jumped aside, the Demon took his life.
When I saw his face, I was shocked. I thought how terribly sad.
What in the world could have happened to make a preacher man go bad?
He hadn't tried to disguise himself, he still wore the collar of the priest.
Whatever caused the sickness in his mind is now gone at least.
Time to move on ~ his congregation wouldn't believe he was the one.
The sheriff and I know ~ but he told me in Santa Fe, my business was done.

Neither Simon nor Cordell got to stay long enough to recoup their fifty–dollar payment to Aurora Bates.

Simon and Cordell both left Santa Fe at the same time but went in different directions. Cordell took what he had saved during his time in Santa Fe and headed for Texas. He had heard there was a saloon and bawdyhouse for sale in Sweetwater, Texas. A saloon called the Palomino Palace.

Simon wondered what could happen to a man's mind, any man's mind, let alone a man of the cloth, to make him feel the need to do what he did. Why would a priest, a servant of the Lord, slash a woman's throat, and then rape her while she lay there and bled to death?

Simon did not travel far. He went to Las Vegas, New Mexico.

Las Vegas, New Mexico

I was having a drink in this decent saloon. I don't consider myself lame.
I was just having some good whiskey for my aches when the trouble came.
Damn it, just because I'm not perfect doesn't mean I'm any less of a man.
I'm doing pretty good considering what I've been dealt for a hand.
Ask the inconsiderate slob, who is dead and slumped over the table,
with his mouth wide open, and sucking on the bottle label.
He laughed, made fun and said that he didn't consider me whole.
So I killed the idiot ~ and to hell ~ I sent his soul.

Simon had been in Las Vegas only two days when the trouble came. He asked the cowboy to leave him alone several times. He did not want or need any attention so soon after the incident in Santa Fe. The cowboy kept at him, bothering Simon, making insults about his scar and his limp. Simon knew where this would lead, but he was not in the mood to kill anyone. The Demon would have killed him instantly, but he held the Demon at bay. Simon turned to leave. As Simon turned, he heard the hammer of a gun click. Instinctively, Simon turned and his derringer sprang to his left hand. He dropped to one knee just as a bullet flew past his head and crashed into the wall. Simon shot the cowboy in the head. The dead man fell against the wall, then onto the table, his mouth landing wide open against an overturned whiskey bottle. When Simon went to one knee, he lost his balance and fell to the floor. His right foot, racked with pain, couldn't support the weight of his body.

The sheriff came. The other men in the bar related the story. It went good for Simon. They told the truth.

"Santa Fe warned me 'bout you," said the sheriff shaking his head, staring at the dead cowboy.

"Well....they should have warned you about him....who ever the hell he might be....he started the trouble....damn sure wasn't me."

"Innocent or not, just go. Your kind only brings more trouble."

"Might be more trouble....if there's more in town like that bottle baby.... just bring them on over, we'll talk, and get acquainted maybe." Simon gave the sheriff an evil smile. "We can some drink some whiskey, and trade an insult or two....then I'll rid the town of the shit heels for you."

"Rhymer, go, get the hell out of here, or I'll bring enough men to make you go."

Simon left Las Vegas, New Mexico and rode toward Henrietta, Texas and Nellie Jacks' Longhorn Saloon. Texas might be friendlier to a native son.

On the run again! The way my whole life's been.
Can't find a decent town! How am I to settle down?
Nothing good about me to tell ~ will never hold a woman like Abigail.

Big Legged Kate

Simon got to Nellie Jacks at ten o'clock in the evening and entered the back way. On his way in he saw a big burly man and a woman in the hall, and to Simon, it appeared they were having a scuffle. Simon was not keen on men mistreating women, even if the women were soiled doves. Simon took the sawed–off by the barrel and struck the man across the head with the butt end, knocking him unconscious. The woman turned on Simon.

"What the hell you doing, he's a customer of mine."

"Man shouldn't treat a woman like that ma'am."

"Ma'am, ma'am, I ain't your goddamned ma'am. I got your goddamned ma'am right here."

The woman reared backwards and threw a right cross aimed at Simon's head. He ducked and partially blocked the punch. The force of her swing, and her missing her punch, spun her off balance. She landed with a thud on the floor and with her skirt up around her waist.

Nellie Jacks heard the ruckus and quickly ran to the hall.

"What's all the commotion back here?" She looked and saw the man laying on the floor bleeding and the woman sitting on her butt.

"This mangy assed drifter here just cost me my pay for the night," said the woman.

"I'm sorry ma'am....I thought you were having a fight....come sit and drink with me....and I'll make it right."

"You go piss yourself."

Simon wasn't fazed by her insult.

"You're much too pretty a lady....to take that kind of abuse....there are better ways than getting slapped....to put your body to use."

He offered his hand to her to help me up. The woman gave the finger to Simon.

Simon, not fazed by her reaction said, "I like my women tough too.... but in a different way....you shouldn't have to fight like that....just to earn a night's pay."

The woman sat there—staring at Simon. Then slowly she started to get up on her own. Nellie Jacks spoke just as the woman realized who the intruder might be. "Kate DeLauro, meet the now infamous Simon Sublette, the man they call the Rhymer. I guess you're pretty lucky. They say when he talks in verse; hitch up the hearse, 'cause he usually kills someone."

"The Rhymer, huh?" Kate said as she sat back down on the floor. "Here with us, alive and in goddamn person. I'll be damned. I thought you'd be smaller and a whole lot prettier. Anybody who talks in a rhyme kinda ought to look like a poet instead of the devil, don't you think, Nellie?"

"That's what I thought, but once we get the trail off him and get him shaved and bathed, he'll pretty up enough for most around here, maybe even you, Kate."

Kate stared at Simon for a moment, not saying anything.

Simon reached out and grabbed her hand and helped her to her feet.

She looked at Simon for a minute, then turned and left.

Simon noticed that for such a petite woman, Kate had larger thighs and calves than normal. He guessed she was, or had sometime been, some sort of a dancer. Simon walked into the main room of the saloon and joined Kate at a table. It was a table near the back. He liked where the table was located. It afforded him the best view of the entire room.

"Kate, I'm sorry for all the trouble." Simon offered his hand. Reluctantly, Kate shook his hand.

"You owe me twenty dollars, you quick–hitting bastard—and a bottle of whiskey."

Simon smiled and called to Nellie. "Nellie, bring me and my friend here a bottle of your finest."

"I ain't your friend."

"You know, Kate, twenty dollars is a lot I'd say....just for a fifteen minute roll in the hay."

"Sounds like you screw as fast as you hit."

"That's still a pretty high price Kate, given the service rendered. Do you charge all of your pokes that much or am I special?"

"You're special. It's twenty dollars 'cause he probably won't be back for a while, especially if you're around."

Simon laughed. Kate finally grinned.

Nellie Jacks brought the bottle. Simon, Kate DeLauro and Nellie Jacks sat and drank and talked. Simon and Kate became acquainted—slowly they would become friends.

Later that evening Simon bathed, had his clothes washed and shaved his scruffy beard. The scar was now fully visible. When he was drinking, the scar turned more red than normal.

I entered Nellie Jacks through the back hall. A man was treating a lady rough.
I came to her aid and hit him in the head. Now let's see if he is tough.
She didn't want my help. I was ruining her night's pay she said.
I was surprised. I treat my women gently when I want to take them to bed.

So I got off to a bad start with everyone, made them all mad you see.
Guess I missed the chance for the welcome wagon to open its doors for me.

When Kate saw Simon the next afternoon she noticed how his features did not look as harsh when he was cleanly shaven. His hair was yellow blond, and he was not a bad looking man, except for that damn scar. That terribly jagged scar that ran from his lip up to his ear.

Simon started drinking early that afternoon. He would be in a rare form later in the evening. The one thing about Simon though, no matter how much he drank, he always maintained a level of sobriety, that made him a very dangerous man. There was another thing. No matter the amount of alcohol he consumed, he never recited poetry or verse for money. He did not volunteer and no one dared to ask.

Simon was sitting with Kate, drinking and having a conversation about things in general. As far as he was concerned, Kate was his for the evening. He would pay for her if necessary—even if it was to only have a conversation.

Kate was beginning to find Simon interesting.

A gentleman approached their table to ask Kate for her favors. Kate said thanks, but no thanks, very politely and returned to her conversation with Simon. The gentleman persisted.

"Henry, dad–gum–it, I'm taking the night off. Go on get, come back tomorrow."

"Can't, Kate, tonight is Wednesday, my card playin' night. It's my only night away from the missus. Can't come tomorrow, she won't let me come to town tomorrow. Come on, Kate, please, or I'll have to wait a whole week and I might explode 'fore then." The man was fidgety, shifting his weight from one foot to the other.

"Henry, maybe if you'd stay home, and off the bottle, the missus just might service you herself, pick another girl, can't you see I'm busy?"

"Aw, Kate, I don't like none of the others. It wouldn't be the same without those big–o–wonderful legs of yours wrapped 'round me!"

"Go on, Henry, I'm not in the mood for that, or for none of this arguing either."

Henry started to say something more, but he was interrupted.

"Henry, my man....look in my left hand....Big Legged Kate said no. You're dead I figure....if I pull the trigger....so why don't you just go."

Henry saw the derringer in Simon's left hand. It was pointed at his head. Henry fainted on the spot. As he fell, he tried to grab the table for support, and he sent a glass flying. When it landed on the floor, it broke, and made a sound like a gun being fired. One of the other girls screamed.

Nellie Jacks saw Henry lying on the floor and instantly thought Simon had shot him.

The whole saloon got quiet and still, turning their attention to the commotion.

Nellie rushed over to Henry's aid. "Oh my god Simon, what did you shoot Henry for?"

Simon was laughing. "He isn't dead Nell....he just fainted and fell." Simon could hardly talk for his laughing. "He wouldn't leave Big Legged Kate alone. So I showed him my gun, thinking he'd run....because Kate wasn't getting anywhere on her own."

"Henry wasn't evil, Simon. He just wanted to lay with Kate!" Nellie said angrily.

"I know all he wanted was a slat rattle....with the Big Legged Kate.... and it wasn't my intention....to send him to heaven's gate. I only meant to scare him, Nell. For some that's all it takes....why the hell are you harping on this....for Christ's sakes?"

"Damn it, Simon, we can handle our business without pulling guns. You need to learn better ways of dealing with people."

Simon gave Nellie Jacks a hard stare. His scar twitched, and then he turned away and poured himself another drink. "Sorry, Nell....just trying to help a friend....I'll try to make sure....it doesn't happen again."

Simon didn't know, but Big Legged Kate didn't mind at all.

"Big Legged Kate, now what in the world kind of name is that for a lady? You and Henry trying to insult me for some reason?" said Kate as she slapped Simon on the arm.

"Henry's right you know, Kate....you do have big legs....for a lady built in such a small way....but they are fine looking legs....and shaped nice I must say. I mean hell....I gave it as my way of a complement....you're Big Legged Kate to me....no insult, no harm meant.

Kate turned her glass to her lips and took a drink of whiskey. "I guess there are a lot of people who go by some sort of moniker. People call you the Rhymer 'cause you talk in verse. I can think of One Pony, Short Leg Charlie, Jimmie Two Beers and Punk. I mean Nellie Jacks isn't even Nellie's real name. I guess having a moniker isn't so bad. But I don't know 'bout having Big Legged Kate for mine. A name like that's not too likely to have the gents clamoring at my feet wanting to spend their money for my wares."

Simon put his arm around Kate's neck and leaned toward her. He got so close they could smell each other.

"Big Legged Kate will be heard of far and wide....rich, powerful gentlemen will come to lie at your side. Quickly, the word will be spread.... there isn't anything finer....than Big Legged Kate's bed. Your story will be told....men will come and give you their gold. You'll be infamous....a legend in your own time....made famous by the one....the one who talks in rhyme."

Simon was starting to smile now, with a twinkle of mischief in his eye. "I'll tell of a beautiful dove....who for the right price....will sell the tainted love. A dove with legs so pure and creamy....and inside, so hot, so soft, so steamy." Simon took a drink of whiskey to wet his lips. "Why men will die just to touch a thigh....it is more than most men can take....and for a chance to partake....all riches they'll forsake." Simon was now starting to laugh.

"Rhymer, you're one crazy sum–bitch aren't you? Besides, you don't know, you haven't been between these big o' wonderful legs of mine."

"No need....I just know what I know....and I'm spreading the word.... from here to Mexico....the story of your legs will be heard."

Kate and Simon both laughed. Kate had now seen what she thought were both sides of this man called Simon, The Rhymer, Sublette. What she didn't know was that she had not really seen Simon's mean and nasty side, the cruel streak, the Demon that came to him in his killing.

Nellie Jacks finally got the saloon back to a state of calm. It was calm anyway for a saloon with drunken cowboys and card players and the ever present piano music—some good, some bad. She joined Kate and Simon at their table.

"Simon, tell me, why can't you deal with people sensibly. You know, talk to them right, without the gunplay and such. Don't you think reasoning with them is a better way than instantly turning to violence?"

Simon took a drink straight from the bottle, not bothering to pour the whiskey into his glass. He took a long hard drink. Damn it Nellie; don't start this now, thought Simon. His mood shifted from light–hearted, to cold. He felt it, but he couldn't stop it. It was the Demon. *Can I come out and play?*

"Some men won't listen to reason, even when they are told no. And when they won't, then they need a little incentive so they'll go."

"So talk more to them Simon, it doesn't call for a gun!"

"Nell....to some people I am Able....to some I am Cain. I help those who are needy....to the predators I cause death and pain. To the downtrodden, the weak....I help them out of a jam....to the oppressors Nell....then I am what I am."

"You ought to be able to control it better than you do."

"It's in my blood....ever since the war it's been that way....I don't know how to control it....I fight it every day. But I can remember Nell....when you wanted me to kill....to avenge your man's death....up on that Tennessee hill!"

Nell looked at Simon with sad eyes. She wished that he would forget about that incident. She was certainly trying to.

"What happened up there was a different time and circumstance, Simon. That was war. This is just a peaceful saloon, for drinking, gambling and cavorting with the ladies. They don't come here to fight. Times have changed, Simon, and I have to."

"Being victimized, and the pain it causes can be like war....when it happens, then that's what men like me are for."

"I don't agree with that."

"Nell, if it weren't for men like me....lending a helping hand....the evil would come....and destroy the civilized man. The evil will come here someday....and its violence will be done....you will wish for someone like me....to stop it with a gun. This evil must be killed....rid forever from the land....what's wrong with saving an innocent, whenever we can?"

"Simon, I think maybe you're the evil!"

Nellie left the table and stormed off to the bar. Nellie was not afraid of Simon, but she was not comfortable having him in her saloon. He was hot–tempered, volatile, and above all—dangerous. He could kill a man with no more thought than most men would give to picking their teeth after a meal.

Simon had no reply. He took the rest of the bottle and went upstairs alone, leaving Kate and Nell to their own devices for the rest of the night.

The next evening Simon and Kate were sitting again at the same table at the back of the saloon, talking and drinking as they had the night before.

"Kate, are you working tonight, or you taking off?" asked Simon.

"I got to hustle me some money tonight Simon. So if someone comes along don't threaten to kill him or insult him or nothing like that. I haven't worked in two days because you have been here, but tonight, I need the money."

Simon removed twenty dollars from his pocket and laid it on the table. "Tell me something, Kate. You're not like the others I've met. What got you into this line of business? You don't seem the kind."

"Simon, it's like this. I can make more here in a week than I can in teaching school in three months. And I'm not like the rest of them, those you refer to, whoever they are. I pick and choose. Even the guy you thought was rough housing two nights past, the one you slapped upside the head, is a good customer of mine, and let me tell you something else, Simon. To put it in your words, I don't lay with the mean, the unclean, the drunken, or the obscene. Someday I'll have enough saved so I can afford my own place. Then I'll be really selective on who drinks from the nectar of my vine."

"Not the mean, the unclean, the drunken, or the obscene, did you hear what you said, Kate. That's a rhyme. So do those who talk in rhymes have a chance?"

"Nope, no way, I couldn't do it. I'm not whorin' for you, Simon. If we ever do anything like that, it won't be for money. And for now let's just leave it at that."

Big Legged Kate, she doesn't do the mean, the unclean, or the obscene.
She's saving for a place she'll own in due time.
Then she'll be selective on who drinks from the nectar of her vine.

The cowboy who Simon had encountered struggling with Kate in the hall two nights ago entered the saloon.

Simon saw him enter but did not recognize him. He had only seen him on the floor; face down, unconscious in a darkened hallway.

The man went to the bar and drank down three fast whiskies. He was studying Simon, weighing his chances. When the whiskey took hold and he finally got his courage. He grabbed an empty whiskey bottle and headed straight for Simon's table.

Simon was sitting at an angle to the bar and could not directly see the man approaching. Simon caught a reflection in his dark glasses of the fast approaching menace.

The man raised the bottle to strike Simon. "I owe you one, you son of a …"

Before the man could strike or finish his sentence, Simon ducked, reeled and viciously kicked the man just above his ankles. The man stumbled, then fell over a chair, and crashed head first into the wall. Instantly, Simon was on the man. Simon pressed his knee hard into the man's chest and took his forty–five and shoved up the man's nostril. "What you're breathing is forty–five lead....one wrong move....and off comes your head. You'll be best served to let this pass by....this isn't a good reason to die. Leave peacefully and you won't end up dead....if you understand me....nod your head."

The man nodded, very slowly. It was difficult for him to move his head with the gun in his nose. His nose had begun to bleed from the forty–five being shoved up his nostril. Simon hated that smell, that smell of blood. He didn't know what to do about it. When you shoot a man he bleeds.

Simon let the man up.

The man, shakily, walked toward the door, stopped half way and turned around to say something. Simon pointed his gun straight at the man's head. "Just go....go on out the door....I'm not going to play nice anymore."

The man turned and walked away.

Simon looked at Nellie.

She gave Simon a disgusted look and then turned and looked away.

"I guess she'd just let him....give me a scar on my other cheek....reckon that's what they mean in the Bible....just turn the other cheek?"

"I don't think that's what it means, Simon." Kate patted a chair next to her. Simon sat down.

"I hope he's a better lover than he is a fighter, Kate....if not you should find someone else to fill your slate."

"None of them are concerned about making me feel good. They are after one thing, and once it comes, off they're gone."

"I guess that says it all."

Simon knew he was wearing out his welcome at Nellie Jacks. Nellie was not friendly anymore. She was bitchy and surly.

Not long after the man had left, Kate and Simon had settled into a game of two–handed poker. They figured no one else wanted to sit at their table because they were afraid of Simon. Suddenly, the back door burst opened and there stood the cowboy again, with a gun. The gun was pointed at Simon.

Simon didn't move from his chair. He was looking straight at the barrel of the man's forty–five. Simon stared at man. The man's nose had caked blood on it from their previous encounter. His hair was messed and he looked frightful. He was sweating and was visibly nervous. The man never said a word, just stood there, wide–eyed and fidgety. He was so mad that he was almost crying. It was obvious to Simon the man was not accustomed to the prospect of having to kill a man or be killed himself.

Simon took control of the situation in the only manner he knew—to fight back or die trying. He slowly took off his dark glasses and revealed his, cold as ice, blue eyes. As he misdirected the man's attention by speaking to him, he moved the derringer to his left hand. Even though the man was pointing the gun at Simon, Simon knew the man was so mad he probably couldn't hit what he was shooting at, and Simon knew he was faster with the derringer than the man was with his finger.

"Now tell me....do you really want to do this....do you want to take the chance....on whether the hand is faster than the eye?"

The man said nothing. He made no move other than his shaking.

"Do us both a favor....just go back out the door and leave this be....then it won't be your time to die.

There was still no response from the man. No words, just his eyes darting back and forth in a nervous twitch.

"Oh, and just so you'll know....before you give it a go....I am a Demon in disguise."

As Simon spoke, slowly, very slowly, he moved the sawed–off shotgun from his side and raised it underneath the table to the killing level. As he spoke the last rhymes, he raised his left hand and pointed the derringer at the head of the cowboy.

"So now you have to choose....do you win or lose....go ahead, see if you can take home the prize."

Simon's talking in rhymes always seemed to unnerve, misdirect, his opponent's attention. Most had heard tell of his manner of speech, but actually hearing Simon in person was different. Even his voice changed into a low, rough, raspy sound.

Simon could see in the man's eyes and knew he was not a killer. The man was embarrassed and mad and sometimes that could lead a man to do something he would not normally do.

Nellie walked quickly into the back hallway and stepped between the maddened cowboy and the Rhymer. She faced the cowboy and gently took away his gun. She put her hands on his chest and pushed him backwards until he was out of the back door. She gently rubbed his head in an attempt to smooth his mussed hair. "Poor man, go on home, it's not worth all this. And please, don't come back here, Blackweller, not until he's gone. He'll kill you the next time he sees you, not a doubt in my mind. He's a cold dead killer, and I don't want your death on my conscience."

The man named Blackweller was still mad. "He did me wrong when he hit me in the head for no reason. He owes me, Nellie."

"Either stay away or all you're gonna get from a man like him is dead and buried."

"But, Nellie …"

"You men are all alike. You can't leave it alone. Tell you what. I'll get your gun and call the Rhymer outside. If you want to die this damn bad, then okay. But it isn't going to be in my place. He'll kill you, Blackweller, and then the ornery son of a bitch will spit venom in the holes his bullets make in your chest!"

Blackweller thought about it for a moment, and then finally gave in. "Okay, Nellie, for you, I'll go." Blackweller walked to his horse, mounted and rode away from the saloon towards the edge of town.

Simon was actually glad he did not have to kill the man. He really was not the type to waste lead on.

Nellie walked back into the saloon straight for Simon. She was mad. "Simon, you've only been here three days and I've already had more trouble than I've had in the past two years."

"You must be blind and can't see….he makes a fight twice….and you lay it off on me?"

"Simon, it's you. You draw it, like kindling draws a flame. You just sit and smolder, waiting to flare up into a full raging fire. You're an intemperate, hard case, cruel, mean son of a bitch. You could start a fight in an empty room. I can't deal with people like you anymore. Just leave, for the betterment of us all!"

Simon could not believe it. Nellie Jacks was getting soft. Like her man in the war, she didn't have the stomach for a ruckus. It made Simon wonder what Denzel Jacques was trying to flee for. Surely, he wasn't running home to a woman like Nellie, or whatever her name was. Some cannot handle the violence of the world, so they choose either to run away or to ignore the fact. He could fix the problem for her as far as having to deal with him. Simon said good–bye to Big Legged Kate. He kissed her on the cheek. It was the first kiss he had given Big Legged Kate. It was the only time he had touched her, since he had helped her from the floor and shook her hand the night they met. Simon left for Tascosa, in the Texas Panhandle.

As Simon walked away Kate waved good–bye to him.

Nellie turned to Kate. "There goes the devil himself."

"Did you ever think the devil would come in that disguise?"
"How's that, Kate?"
"Blond hair and blue eyes!"

A man came to Nellie Jacks, looking for me, not a roll in the hay.
The man had been a bit rough with Kate, and I defended her today.
He came back, pointing a gun, wanting revenge for me ruining his stay.
But in the end, cooler heads prevailed, saving his life for another roll, another day.
I probably would have only shot him in the arm, given my sensitivity and all.
I mean it's hard to kill a man, when he's so nervous he just stands and bawls.
Nellie intervened, she's gone soft now and she doesn't want me here anymore.
So I'm off to Tascosa. Came in by the front, thrown out through the back door.

In Tascosa, Texas, Simon did not find the town to be receptive, and he decided it was too dull. He had the mind to go back to New Mexico and see what he missed the first time. He also decided it was time he bought a new horse. He wasn't fond of the one he had purchased in Santa Fe. It was a little too skittish for his liking. He chose a big gray mare from the lot of about twenty horses. Simon decided on the gray mare when the owner told him the horse was gunshot trained, told him the horse wouldn't shy if a gun was fired when a man was sitting in the saddle. That was a trait Simon found useful in a horse. He made a fair trade, the gray for the Santa Fe horse. Simon saddled the big gray with the knife–marked saddle and headed back to the badlands of New Mexico.

-Into the Badlands-
Into the badlands go I ~ I hope I don't die.
I'm but a minute speck ~ over the landscape I trek.
I'll be best to behoove ~ don't make a false move.
Don't want to be food ~ for mama coyote and brood.
Scorpions, snakes and demons be ~ waiting for a slip from me.
I'll be cautious and slow ~ travel by the moon glow.
Ride across the rock and sand ~ to the other side of the land.
Why was the badlands created ~ who was it God hated?
Is this just a sample of hell ~ part of the Devil's hotel?
It takes something from one ~ the constant beat of the sun.
Each crossing you die a little more ~ it's never easier than before.
My flesh is further gone ~ but my spirit is ever strong.

I'll keep crossing 'till I die ~ never, ever really knowing why.
Into the badlands go I ~ eventually this is where I'll lie.
Won't be nothing to eat of my own ~ by then I'll only be skin and bone.

Chapter Three

Brock Deaton

Simon camped a few miles west of Fort Sumner, New Mexico. He had picked a nice area beside a fallen tree and next to a small pond he surmised was watering hole for the local cattle, and any other varmint that wanted to quench their thirst. It was a good place for him and his horse. Most of the land in this part of New Mexico was flat plains given the occasional small hill or knoll, mostly grass land. At times, one would cross a creek or two or find a watering place like the one he found.

He had finished making his fire when he heard the noise. He looked and saw six men coming over the hill riding hard and fast. Simon was staring into the sun. When he raised his hand to shield his eyes, he saw the men had raised their rifles. Simon did not move. He knew he was their target—but he was unsure why. He was out manned and had no chance if he attempted to defend himself.

The riders approached and held Simon at gunpoint. Without saying a word, they tied his hands and mounted him on his horse. The lead rider seemed to be the boss. He told Simon they were taking him to see a Mr. Harris back at the main ranch house. They talked to Simon on the way to the ranch and told him Mr. Harris, the owner, was not tolerant of cow thieves. They were taking him there so all could watch the hanging. The whole way Simon did not say anything. He was saving his speech for the owner. These cowboys were not going to let him go, even if he talked his best talk. Plus, he needed time to think and form a plan in case talking failed.

They finally arrived at the main ranch house. It was well into the night. Mr. Harris was awakened and came to meet the riders.

"Mr. Harris," the lead man said, "we caught this one camping just up north by the Ft. Sumner watering hole. I figured he might have something to do with our missing cows."

"Mister, I don't know who you are, but we don't take too kindly to strangers camping on our land without permission, especially in light of the fact that someone is stealing a lot of our cows and we've got all this trouble going on. You don't look like a rustler, but you do look like a bit like a hired gunman. You know anything about this? Have you seen anybody herding cattle while you were riding across my land? Anybody hire you go against us?"

"Mr. Harris, my name is Sublette, Simon Sublette. I'm just passing through, working my way down to Las Cruces. I haven't seen anybody, or any cattle herds. For that matter, I haven't seen one single cow. Check my camp; there were no signs of cow in my camp, no branding irons either. Check my gear; I don't have any marking irons."

"Jared, did you check his gear? Did any of you see any signs of cow at this man's camp?

"We didn't see anything," answered the man called Jarred. "We just figured we'd have you do the questioning and give him the once over."

"Someone untie his hands and get him some water. The way he's dressed, he doesn't look much like a cowman to me."

Simon spoke up. He was very careful not to talk in rhymes, although the Demon was near. He didn't want them to know who he really was. They might take unkind to having a coldhearted killer in their midst. "Mr. Harris, if you're satisfied with me, I would like to be on my way."

"I'm not satisfied yet. Do you know of a man named William Bonney?"

"No sir, I can't say I've ever heard of the name."

"Well, some call him Billy the Kid. Does that name do anything for you?"

"I heard mention of that in Tucumcari. I gave it no second thought."

"Well, he's behind some of our trouble. I could use a man like you to help us with him. What do you say?"

Simon considered the question for a moment then responded. "It's not my fight, and I choose to keep it that way. I guess I could help you find the rustlers though."

"And why would you do that?"

"Oh I don't know, reputation I suppose, and I could use a few dollars, if you're willing to pay. You know, one time back in Texas, we had this small band of rustlers. They mainly took only a few cows at a time so not to be noticed. They could move faster that way too. Now maybe your rustler's could be doing the same. I noticed when these men came after me; they made more noise than a band of mad Indians. If I was a rustler and heard this army coming, I'd high tail it before they could get to me. It might be easier for one or two men on patrol to catch the thieves." Simon shrugged his shoulders, "Just a thought."

Mr. Harris scratched his chin. "If you heard them coming, why didn't you run?"

"I had nothing to hide....didn't have any hides either. Only guilty men run....and....it was six guns to one. Plus I couldn't saddle in time."

Mr. Harris took off his hat and rubbed his fingers through his hair. "You might just have a good idea there, Mr. Sublette."

"I'd be glad to help. I'll prove I'm not one of them. Give me one man and I'll bring back the thieves....and your cows."

"Yeah, well I think you might be on to something, and I can always use an extra man, especially when he works for no pay. You know, Mr. Sublette, to prove yourself, it's got to be for free."

Simon didn't like it, but he nodded in agreement. "Even though it's a false accusation, I'll do what I have to do to show it is untrue."

"Jarred, pick us out a good man to go with Sublette."

Jarred Reeves, the foreman, spoke up, "What makes you think he won't kill who ever I pick and ride on anyway?"

Mr. Harris shot a mean glance towards Jarred. "If I thought that, Jarred, I'd kill him right now! Anyways, he doesn't seem the kind who would want me tracking him to the ends of the earth."

Jarred Reeves gave Mr. Harris a look like he did not agree with him. He obeyed the order and picked out this stocky built cowboy. The cowboy's name was Brock Deaton.

Simon noticed this Brock Deaton carried a gun, but Simon guessed it was only for snakes and the like. The snakes they were after did not crawl on their belly and hiss. This kind walked on two legs and shot hot lead when provoked. Simon quickly sized up Brock Deaton and decided he might be of help, but he would reserve judgment. Simon and the cowboy would go find the rustlers. It was the right thing to do.

We're out after the rustlers ~ I don't know if Brock Deaton is an able man.
I have my reservations about getting help from an ordinary cowhand.
I learned during our conservations that he was a central Texas lad.
He'd never been in a gunfight ~ fist fighting was the only experience he had.
He was a couple of years younger than me,
if he plays his cards right, many more birthdays he will see.

As the pair left the next morning, Jarred Reeves and Mr. Harris were on hand to bid them good–bye and good luck. When they were almost out of sight, Jarred turned to Mr. Harris. "It just occurred to me who that man Sublette is."

Mr. Harris looked at Jarred and raised an eyebrow.

"Ever heard the stories of a gunman that speaks in rhymes?" continued Jarred.

"I heard the stories."

"If you'll recall, the man who speaks in rhymes is named Simon Sublette. I reckon that man riding off with Brock is one and the same."

Mr. Harris replied, "So you figured it out. I knew last night when he gave his name, and answered me with a rhyme. That's why I asked about Bonney. And that's exactly why I let him go off with Brock. Everything I ever heard about him is that he is an honorable man, a mean sum–bitch, but honorable none the less. Brock's in good hands and I figured too that since he is the Rhymer, he's the best there is in a gunfight. Brock might even learn a thing or two. I wish them luck and a safe, successful journey. Let's get the rest to work. We're burning daylight."

"Think he's a match for Bonney, in case they run into him?"

"If what they say is true, he'd kill Bonney on the first heartbeat."

"That good, huh, well since they're headed south, think I'll take Clint with me and head north. We'll search up there then circle back east, two teams will be better than one. Anyway, who's to know if Brock and Sublette are headed in the right direction?"

"Okay, but be careful. You and Clint aren't gunmen like the one with Brock. If you see 'em, shoot first and kill 'em if you can, don't be trying to be no damn hero. We'll sort it all out later. Good foremen are hard to find. Besides, if I let something happen to you Cindy would never forgive me.

On the first night out, Simon asked Brock Deaton about his fighting experience? "Ever been in a gunfight, B.D.?"

"Nope, just a few scrapes when I was a kid."

"Ever shoot a gun? Were you ever in the army?"

"I was lucky. Didn't go to the war, but I've fired a lot of guns. Mostly hunting and all, I shot some deer up in the mountains, once bagged me a mountain lion. It's all the same, isn't it? Just point and pull the trigger?"

"Not quite the same. These deer we're after shoot back. You have to stand and aim with hot lead buzzing up your ass."

"Well, I guess we'll find out soon enough. Don't worry about it, I'll be okay."

"Maybe you will, maybe you won't. Just don't get in my way. If you haven't got the stomach for it lay down out of the way. If you freeze and your standing in my line the rustlers won't have to kill you, I will."

Brock looked deep into Simon's eyes, and he knew Simon meant what he said. He knew if he froze, he was a dead man, and it wouldn't make any difference which one killed him. But he would not freeze. He kept reminding himself of this every time he thought about finally catching up to the rustlers. He was preparing himself mentally.

"So why are you really helping us?" asked Brock.

"I'm not into accusations....especially when they aren't true. So to clear up any misconceptions....I'm here, doing what I do."

Since they had left the Harris ranch, they had not ridden fast enough to cause a dust trail. If anyone saw them, they probably would think the two were drifters on their way south. Simon, in his English waistcoat and long black topcoat, did not look like a man searching for rustlers.

Each night they found sheltered places to rest, but never made a fire. They made sure they called no attention to themselves. They hobbled the horses and got comfortable, as comfortable as one could get sitting on a blanket thrown on the rocks and ground.

Brock Deaton was rustling around in his saddlebags. "I'm so hungry I'm farting fresh air. Let's eat!"

Simon gave a chuckle. He had never heard of anyone being quite that hungry before. "I'm in. What we got, cold beans and jerked beef again?"

"Oh no, let's see here, we got cream chicken gravy, hot biscuits, fried chicken, ham, potatoes, fresh tomatoes and sweet corn. And a little brandy when we're done."

"You got a great imagination, B.D."

"Well, a man can wish now and again can't he?" Brock threw Simon a string of beef. He decided to save his beans for later.

"Where are you from, B.D.? Sounds to me like from somewhere in Texas or the south?"

"Grew up near Cleburne, Texas, born and raised."

"Why are you out here?"

"Don't know exactly, came out here on a lark. Just antsy I guess, how 'bout you, Simon?"

"Oh I guess I'm antsy too. Sometimes I just can't stay put. I got this voice calling me. Some think I'm running. Some think I'm crazy. I'm probably more crazy than anything."

"You from Texas?"

"Yeah, out near Marshall....but most all my kin died during the war....
nothing left for me there....nothing to go home for."

"I'm going back someday. I've been saving. I'm going back and have
me a little ranch someday."

"We had one near Marshall. I sold it after my mother died. Started
drifting around, only home is where I'm at. But it is nice for a man to
have a dream. There are a couple of good people you should look up when
you go back. Try a place in Sweetwater called the Palomino Palace and
ask for a man named Cordell Pitifore. Tell him I sent you. He might have
something for you. And another place is called Nellie Jacks, in Henrietta.
There's a fine woman there named Big Legged Kate. One of the best you'll
ever top. She'll rub you down and stand you up, if you know what I mean.
She's the finest of her kind, B. D."

"Big Legged Kate huh, what kind of name is that for a working
girl?"

"Oh, I gave her the moniker. She has the best pair of legs around. She's
a smallish woman but with legs larger than most for her size. Legs like she
was a dancer of some kind."

"I'll keep that in mind. What's your dream, Simon? Surely, a gunman
has some kind of a dream?"

"My dream will never come true. I can't go back and change the way I
am. That's what I dream about, for all of this never to have happened."

"Can't you just quit being a gunman? Ain't nobody twistin' your arm
is there? Hell, just walk away. After we get these rustlers, you and me, we'll
go to Fort Worth. Rustle us up some women and hallelujah the whole
damn town."

"Can't quit, can't change, B.D. It's like I'm cursed. There's something
in my blood, a poison, can't spit it out. I've tried but it won't cough up. And
then there are the others. They won't let guys like me retire. They find out
who I am, and they have to try me on. No, I'm afraid I am who I am."

"So what drives you? What keeps you reaching?"

"Peace, B.D., looking for peace, looking for the way to drive out
the Demon. Peace and a place where I could settle with a good woman,
somewhere where we can be left alone to enjoy our lives."

"Demon?! What in the hell are you talking about?"

Simon's voice changed to the low harsh voice of the Demon.

"The Demon....he's what I can't spit out....but he's kept me alive in tough
times no doubt. He comes to me in times of danger....kills coldhearted....
no remorse, no anger. I acquired him during the war."

Deaton stared at Simon for a moment, and then spoke.

"Tell me something, Simon, and be honest. Why haven't you cold jumped me and rode on away? This really ain't none of your business, ain't your fight."

Simon looked hard at Brock Deaton. It seemed, to Brock, like a very long time before Simon finally spoke.

"Every man casts a shadow, B.D.....mine's just darker than some.... but I must do this....it's something I can't run from. Everywhere we travel, we leave some of that shadow....some of ourselves behind....I don't want it ever said or rumored....that rustlers are my kind. This way I won't always be looking out for Reeves....or even you, B.D....nope, when this is over....I walk away clean and free."

"Kind of like honor among thieves?"

"I don't know what you mean by that. Gunmen and thieves aren't of the same ilk. Besides, there isn't any honor among thieves. That's an old wives tale. A thief is a thief. He'd steal from anyone. He'd steal his own mothers' egg money. What I'm saying is a man has a reputation....mine's for using a gun....but I haven't ever done anything or killed anybody.... that didn't deserve to be done. No one's going to say anything about the Rhymer that isn't true....I told Mr. Harris I'd bring back the rustlers and cows....and that's what I aim to do."

Brock Deaton looked at Simon with a little surprise and squint in his eyes. "So you're the man they call the Rhymer huh?"

"Yeah, that's me. I thought most people knew both of my names. Guess you didn't make the connection. Does it bother you to be with me now, now that you know?"

"No, no I didn't make the connection. You know when you hear those kinds of stories most times real names aren't passed along. Hell, some of them stories are damn hard to believe. I thought you were just made up. And no, it doesn't bother me either being with you."

"I am made up, by fate and circumstance. The real Simon James Sublette is in here somewhere, but it seems each day I lose more and more of me."

"I'll be damned. The Rhyming man is real and sitting right here, holy damn."

Brock offered Simon his hand and Simon took it in a strong, friendship handshake.

"It's good to know who you are, but contrary to what people say, I think you got integrity. Most gunfighters I've heard of would kill their own kin, if the price was right or just kill for no good reason."

"Well, maybe so, I have kin I think need killing sometimes, but it would be for a good reason. Let's get some sleep. We got some deer hunting to do tomorrow."

Simon rolled over away from Brock Deaton. He was not sleepy—just tired of talking. It took Brock a moment to realize what Simon meant when he referred to deer hunting.

Simon and Brock Deaton rose early the next morning and continued to track and hunt the rustlers. They were riding along looking for signs of the rustlers. Suddenly Simon stopped his horse dead in its tracks. He motioned for Brock to do the same. He sat motionless for a few minutes.

"Do you hear that, B.D.?"

"Don't hear a thing Simon, nothing except the wind."

"I hear them, B.D. Over there." Simon pointed to the northwest. Come on."

Simon and Brock rode north and west, not fast, but at a deliberate pace. Simon could hear the cows.

Brock wondered how Simon could hear the cows when he couldn't.

They rode until dusk. The cows were close, so were the men who took them. Simon could smell them. He thought maybe one of them was bleeding, had an open cut or something. If he wasn't bleeding now, thought Simon, he would be by morning.

The wind carried in a familiar smell, the smell of hot iron on cowhide. Simon caught the smell first. "B.D, do you smell something drifting in on the wind? I think our hunt for the rustlers has come to an end."

"Yeah, I smell it. Let's ride over and take 'em now!"

"Not yet, you stay here with the horses, try to keep them quiet. I'm going up to that ridge and see if I can spot their camp. I'll be back just after sundown. They'll be easier to spot when it's dark. It'll be easy to spot that fire."

Brock Deaton did not think twice about letting Simon go off alone. He'd been around him long enough to trust him, and he believed the Rhymer was a man of his word.

As Simon headed for the ridge, Brock made camp but did not make a fire. His and Simon's meal tonight was like all the other nights they had been on the trail, beef jerky, cold beans, hard biscuits and water. They both were growing tired of jerky, hard biscuits and beans. A vision came to Brock about the rustlers eating a hot beef steak and sitting next to a fire. The thought of it all made Brock mad.

Simon returned about an hour after sundown. "I spotted their camp. Best I can make out, there're five of them. Looks like they took about five to ten head. I was right about them being able to move fast. They killed one of the smaller beeves."

"I think they're gonna have a better supper than we're going too then."

"Oh, well, a man ought to eat a good meal for his last, don't you think?"

"That beef does smell good though, don't it? Smell's just like home cooking!"

"I'm telling you it does. You know, B. D.....you can get your fill of a woman....no matter how good looking....but you can never get your fill.... of good home cooking!"

Simon took a bottle of whiskey from his saddlebags, opened the top and took a long slow drink, then handed the bottle to Brock. Brock took a drink and wiped his mouth with his shirtsleeve.

"Damned if that ain't right, there's nothing like mama's cooking. Gosh–o–mighty–damn! My mama's cooking was damn fine eating. Hell, it still tasted good, even if you had to throw it up."

Simon laughed. He laughed almost too loudly. "They got food like that at the Harris's I bet?"

"Yeah they do. Mrs. Harris throws down a fine plate. Daughter isn't too bad, biscuits still a little hard. Course that ain't all she makes hard."

"Well, I guess bedding the daughter would be okay. You'd have to marry her, I suspect. If you didn't, Harris might kill you. Of course he might kill you anyway. Let you marry her to make her respectable, and then kill you....or hire someone like me to do it for him."

"Would you kill a man for something like that?"

"No, some others would, but I wouldn't. But I might kill the man who killed the man. Does that make sense?"

Deaton thought for a moment then replied. "It does to me, but it is starting to worry me some though, when I start to think like you."

"You just keep thinking like me....it'll serve you well....especially when we mix with those rustlers....and everything goes to hell. Keep thinking like that and we'll be okay....and we'll get our reward at the end of the day."

"Reward, what reward? There ain't no reward for this."

"Sure there is....rewards are awaiting at the Harris spread....home cooking for me....and a young lass for B.D.'s bed."

"Yeah, she's waiting for a bed all right, but it won't be mine. Jarred has his eye on her. I'm just a lowly cowhand. He's a foreman. Besides, I ain't marrying, and I ain't getting shot over a roll in the hay."

"Ever think that's why this Jarred fellow picked you, B.D....when he could've picked anyone to go with me. Maybe he thought you'd get killed in the fray....then he could have the girl 'cause you'd be out of the way?"

"Don't think so, Jarred ain't that smart. He's dumber than a hand full of hair. He's just got his nose stuck up Harris's ass that's all."

Both men took another drink from the whiskey bottle.

"Let me ask you something, B.D., you say you're not getting shot over a roll in the hay. So are you telling me you'll risk getting shot over a cow but not over a woman?"

Brock shook his head and laughed. "Hadn't thought about it like that. I think marrying worries me most. You can usually heal up from getting shot. I'm not sure about marrying. Anyway, if you kill a rustler no one seems to care much, but if someone gets killed over a woman then it's off to prison. You can steal a man's cow and get shot for it and nobody says too much. You can steal a man's wife or his daughter's virtue and if anyone gets shot, it's jail time. It doesn't seem right does it? I mean the wife and the daughter were willing right?"

"Well, the cows are willing too, but they don't know no better. They'll go along with whoever herds them."

Simon and Brock had passed the bottle back and forth several times. "Kind of makes you wonder about women don't it?"

"Yes it does, B.D., yes it does. But I haven't been around too many proper women in my adult life....mostly the whore type. Whores will damn sure go with whoever herds them. Proper women don't seem to me to be as willing. And it's been my experience that there are men who are always going to be trying to herd the strays. We can fight for the cows because they're stupid, but if a man asks and the woman says yes, then I say let them go. In my book, she isn't worth fighting for. I'm not fighting for a woman who wants me to do battle, and then she gets the winner. I mean, what the hell do I get in return, the same woman who wouldn't say no? Now if she says no and the man persists, then I'll fight for her, but the other way, huh uh, not me."

"Damn, here I go agreeing with you again. You're right. Women have got smarts; they can say no, a cow can't."

"That's right, B.D. But I'll tell you, I suspect that even if a woman is married, she still needs tending. It just comes to reason that if a man doesn't tend to his cows or his women, they're both subject to being herded by another man."

"Damned if that ain't right. Boy, this whiskey makes us smart don't it? But tell me, Simon, why just whores, why not some proper women?"

"I've only found one woman I could stand being around for more than three or four days. It didn't work out the way I wanted. Proper women are looking for a commitment. I can't offer that right now. I'm just looking for a brief stay in the hay. Anyway, once a man commits to a woman, it's that woman forever, and me, well, I kind of like having women I've never had before."

Brock shook his head in agreement to what Simon had said. "Why don't we go in now and get this over with. Hell, I could use me some fresh cooked steer."

"Look, B. D., there isn't any use in giving those thieving bastards an even chance. Right before first light we'll make our run....they'll still have sleep in their ears and eyes....they'll be dead and stinking before they can find their guns."

"I thought we were taking them back alive? I think that's what Mr. Harris wants."

"I told Mr. Harris I would find his rustlers and bring back his cattle. I never said one damned word about the rustlers being alive. Now get some sleep, you'll need it. I'll wake you when it's time."

Simon took another drink, so did Brock Deaton. Simon looked at Brock. Both were feeling the effects of the whiskey.

"There's some courage in that bottle, B.D....just don't pass over the line....if you drink too much....your brain won't recover in time."

Brock Deaton opened some beans and sat there. He couldn't eat. His stomach was not in any condition to handle food. It was getting close to the time when he would know if he could stand and fight, or as Simon put it, grovel and whine. He gave the beans to Simon. Simon's appetite was not affected at all.

"Tell me, Simon, how'd you come by that limp you got?"

"Frostbite, B.D. Mother Nature came and froze up two of my toes. The gangrene was sitting in so I took off my boot and braced myself with some whiskey. It was one of the hardest things I ever had to do, but I took my pistol and shot those two toes off!"

Brock Deaton looked at Simon. Simon finally grinned.

"You had me there for a minute, Simon, had me good."

"Well, part of it is true. I did lose them to frostbite. A Doc up in Fort Defiance cut them off for me. It does make a better story the way I embellish it a bit."

They could hear the sounds of the cattle and of voices coming from over the ridge behind them.

"Why do you think it is, Simon, that men do things like rustling, knowing that they'll eventually get caught and probably get hung? Do you think that, for some reason, they have a secret wish to die?"

"Well, it's hard to be good and earn a living in these times....there's a lot more money in being wrong....that's why heaven is only open for a short time, B.D.....but hell's open all night long."

"Maybe so, guess when we get to heaven we can ask the Almighty to explain it to us."

"Yeah, but in my case, I may have to ask the devil why."

"Think so? You're not all that bad, and I'm a pretty good judge of character, even half drunk. Even if all the stories I've heard are true, I never heard of a man going to hell for killing someone who deserved it, or in self defense. There's a lot of that in the Bible you know?"

"Time will tell, B.D., time will tell....will it be heaven....or will it be hell?"

Brock laid his head on his bed roll and tried to sleep. He knew Simon would not have to wake him in the morning. The anticipation of the events to come would keep him awake the rest of the night.

Simon waited. It was hard for him to sleep. His blood was getting anxious. He could feel it pounding in his temples. He could not rest well when the blood quickened in his veins and the Demon was near. He forced himself to rest. He knew being well rested was a good asset to have in a battle.

We caught them before daylight, surprised them right in their bed.
They put up a moderate fight and two of the five ended up dead.
Now as to having experience in gun fighting, Brock Deaton had no claim,
but when all hell broke loose, well, Brock Deaton sure was game.

Just before the morning sun gave them first light, Simon went to awaken Brock Deaton. Simon had finished saddling the horses and turned toward Brock's resting place.

Brock was already up and was washing his face in the cold morning water.

They walked their horses to the top of the ridge. It was there they mounted and rode swiftly into the rustler's camp. Brock Deaton was right alongside of Simon and did not falter when the gunplay started. Brock did not shy and he did not freeze. He stood his ground. It was over in a matter of minutes.

The two rustlers Simon shot were dead instantly. The other three threw up their hands in surrender. Simon wanted to kill them to save the trouble of dealing with them on the way back to the ranch. Herding cattle was one thing. Herding men was totally different. If he had been alone it would have been an easy decision. Being with Brock Deaton complicated the issue. Against his better judgment, he let Brock take them prisoner. Simon held his gun on the trio while Brock tied their hands and got them mounted on their horses for the ride back to the Harris ranch headquarters.

Simon talked to the three, as Brock did his work. "You sons of bitches, they almost hung me for this....when it was really your crime....I don't know why you do it....since you get caught and get hung every time. Now I'm thinking that you're going to end up....just like your two friends....but for justice sake....we'll take you back to the owner....and see if you can make amends."

Simon walked around to face one of the rustlers, so he could look him in the eye. The man certainly was ugly.

"Personally I think he's going to take your ugly ass out....and hang you from a lonely old tree....and you'll serve as a warning sign....for other rustlers to see. And you have to ask yourself the question....why for a cow did I have to die....well, when the rope snaps your neck....then you can ask the devil why?"

Brock Deaton looked at Simon. He stood and stared at him for a long time. He did not know quite what to think of a son of a bitch who talked in a rhyme and made it sound so natural.

"Hurry up, B.D. This is no time to tarry. What's a matter? Haven't you ever heard poetry before? What kind of schooling did they have back there in Texas anyway?" Simon looked at Brock and grinned.

Brock grabbed two extra large chunks of the fresh cooked cow ribs. He and Simon had a feast as they headed back to the main ranch.

Simon would have given the rustlers some meat, but he figured their stomachs were like B.D.'s was the night before. Besides, their hands were tied and Simon was not freeing any of them to eat. To hell with them, he thought, let them starve, it might save someone the time and effort of killing them later.

On the way back to the ranch, for two days Brock Deaton never did sleep.
Guess he didn't trust me or the rustlers ~ so all night, a watch he'd keep.

Simon's cavalier attitude about killing the rustlers bothered Brock Deaton. He had ridden beside Simon in the gun battle and had not flinched. He was proud of that, but he thought Simon could have somehow avoided the killing of the two men. He thought he had seen the ruthless side of the Rhymer, the side that enjoyed the killing. He wanted to get the other three back to Mr. Harris as he had said he would—alive. He just couldn't push it out of his mind that the Rhymer might suddenly decide to kill them—for no reason. In thinking this about Simon, his judge of character was flawed.

Simon sang to the rustlers as they rode back to the Harris ranch.

"Hangin' Tree oh Hangin' Tree, why do you call to me.

Hangin' Tree oh Hangin' Tree, why don't you just let me be?

Hangin' Tree oh Hangin' Tree, why do you waive your arm?

Hangin' Tree oh Hangin' Tree, please don't do me no harm."

The singing unnerved the rustlers. Was this man foretelling their future?

"Hangin' Tree oh Hangin' Tree, you whisper in my ear.

Hangin' Tree oh Hangin' Tree, you give me dread and fear.

Hangin' Tree oh Hangin' Tree, what was it you said.

Hangin' Tree oh Hangin' Tree, gonna make another dead?"

The words were bothering Brock Deaton too. He wanted to ask Simon to stop.

"Hangin' Tree oh Hangin' Tree, your limbs with no leaves.

Hangin' Tree oh Hangin' Tree, is it a part of you that grieves."

Simon stopped singing as the ranch came into view.

Mr. Harris, his wife, his daughter and several hands met us in the main yard.
Brock Deaton was dead tired, for the past twelve hours we'd been riding hard.
Then in a flurry of motion one of the rustlers got free.
I don't know how it happened. I just didn't see.
Brock Deaton and I were knocked from our horses, knocked to the ground.
When I got to my feet I saw that the rustlers had taken Brock Deaton down.

As Simon and Brock Deaton rode into the main yard one of the rustlers somehow got his hands free and jumped Brock Deaton. He knocked him from his horse, into Simon, resulting in a domino effect. Simon scrambled to his feet and through the settling dust could see that the freed rustler had Brock Deaton on the ground. The rustler was behind Brock holding a knife to his throat. Simon also noticed Brock's gun had fallen from its holster and was within reach of both Brock and the rustler holding him.

"Let us go or I'll cut 'im. He'll die right here and now. Cut them loose or I'll cut 'im.

Everyone had frozen ~ they weren't accustomed to violence I guessed, so I took over the situation, because killing is what I do best.

Everyone in the main yard, including Jarred Reeves, was frozen. Simon reacted quickly.

"There isn't going to be any negotiating....just you let the cowboy go....I know if you're set free....you'll kill him when you get to Mexico. So just go ahead and cut him now....cut the son of a bitch from ear to ear....but tell me something cow thief....then how are you going to get out of here?"

The rustler studied Simon's face to see if he was bluffing. Then for an instant the man relaxed.

When the man relaxed it was a signal for Simon. Simon placed a forty–five bullet in the man's right forehead and blew away his skull. Skin, bone and blood splattered on Brock Deaton's face.

Simon turned his attention to the other rustlers.

"That served him right....the cow thieving rat....can you imagine there's a mother somewhere....who'd love something like that?

Simon stuck out his hand and helped Brock to his feet. He rolled the dead man over onto his back with the toe of his boot.

"She was probably overjoyed....when birth she gave....reckon she'd shed a tear....if she knew how he went to his grave?"

The other rustlers, now scared to death, spurred their horses to run. Simon grabbed his sawed–off shotgun and fired, catching the nearest one in the chest.

Brock Deaton grabbed his pistol from the ground and shot the other one in the neck just below his left ear. Both men were dead, now lying in the main yard of the house. It took a few minutes to get their horses calmed down.

When Brock was knocked from his horse, Harris's daughter Cindy had turned and left for the safe confines of the house. Jarred Reeves had followed with her. He wasn't there to be of any assistance.

"Well, Mr. Harris, you might as well go ahead....and hang them up as a warning....I'm done here....I'll be leaving first thing in the morning."

Mr. Harris looked at Brock Deaton. He was a mess. He was dead tired. He had just escaped a date with the devil, and he had the rustler's blood and bones all over his face.

Brock wiped his face with his hands, and then wiped his hands on his pants. He looked back at Mr. Harris.

"Let the Rhymer go. He did what he said. We don't need him anymore. Probably ought to pay him something though, shouldn't be for free."

Mr. Harris nodded his head.

Mrs. Harris said with surprise, "Well I'll be. You're the Rhymer!"

Simon looked at Mr. Harris.

Mr. Harris looked at Simon and shrugged his shoulders.

Simon said, "I am one and the same....but you can just call me Simon ma'am....that's my Christian name."

Mr. Harris spoke, "I'm sorry about all this. If I had known early on you was the man called the Rhymer, I wouldn't have been so rude."

Simon knew Mr. Harris had just told a lie, but no one would know and it wasn't worth pursuing.

"You weren't in to who I was Mr. Harris....you were just in a hanging mood." At times Simon would make his sentences rhyme with those of others.

"Why don't you stay on for a while? We can show our gratitude better if you'll stay awhile. Stay and rest a spell," offered Mrs. Harris.

"No thanks, ma'am, I've had the notion for a while to go to seek my fortune in the Arizona territory. Guess I'll head that way."

"Better stay on, the pay is good. I could really use someone with your gun experience."

"Thanks for the offer. It's appreciated, but I'll be pushing on."

"In that case, I guess I had better give you a letter in case you cross onto the Etcheverry's land. They're four brothers and sometimes mean and impatient with strangers, especially in these times. If you run on to them, just show them this letter and then ride on until you're clear." Mr. Harris went into the house to pen the letter.

Simon and Brock Deaton washed themselves and sat down to a glorious feast prepared by Mrs. Harris and Cindy.

As Simon ate, he imagined Brock Deaton and Cindy Harris together in bed. He thought Brock might change his mind about getting shot at for a roll in the hay, since he'd finally gotten a taste of what killing was all about and how easy it was. Besides, Cindy Lou Harris was a damn fine looking woman, just like her mother. Simon thought if he were to stay, he might give it a try himself. Unlike Brock Deaton, Simon could kill Mr. Harris without giving it second notice.

Mrs. Harris offered Simon a really nice bed in the main house.

Simon chose to sleep in the bunkhouse instead.

Early the next morning he said good–bye to Mr. and Mrs. Harris. Cindy Lou was still sleeping. He shook Brock Deaton's hand and knew he had made a friend for life with the stocky cowboy from Cleburne, Texas. He hoped he would see him again someday.

I took my leave of the Harris family and bid Brock Deaton good–bye.
He shook my hand ~ he had that special look in his eye.
Somehow I knew our paths would cross again, in some future time.
I left Brock Deaton a note, I left him a Rhymer rhyme.

B.D.
When life deals you a cold hand ~ and it usually will.
Stand proud like we did ~ fight against the chill.
Friends are ready to come to your aide ~ that's why friendships are made.
If you ever need me again ~ just send for me my friend.
I'll heed the call. I think the two of us together ~ can take them all.
Simon, the Rhymer ~

As Simon was getting atop his horse Brock asked him, "Simon, this rhyming thing, do you have to think about it or does it just come natural?"

"B.D., you've heard tell of people who were great at the gift of making up wild tales and some people would say that person had kissed the Blarney Stone?"

Brock nodded his head. "Yeah, I've heard that."

"Well, it's been said by some that I have kissed the Rhyme Stone."

"Makes sense to me."

"Take care of yourself my friend."

"I hope you find what you're looking for. I think you deserve it.

Oh, and by the way, if you run across Billy Bonney, steer clear. He isn't anything but trouble."

"Oh, I don't think the Kid wants anything with me. You steer clear."

Brock Deaton nodded and grinned.

Lincoln, New Mexico

In Lincoln, I was playing cards.
Some cowboy was cussing loud, cussing each card he got.
The noise was starting to chafe me a bit,
I tried hard to ignore it, but the Demon did not.
My scar started to twitch as he got louder and louder.
One player said "Leave him be Simon. You'd just waste your powder."

"Hey cowboy," Simon spoke, in a loud voice, trying to get the man's attention.

The cowboy looked at Simon.

"Yeah you, do you think you could you hold it down some? We're trying to have some quiet while we play cards. How about you just leave the yelling be?"

The cowboy looked around the room as if to see who Simon was speaking to. "Who are you talking to?" the cowboy asked, shrugging his shoulders.

Simon pulled his gun and pointed it at the cowboy. "I'm talking to you. I don't see any other skunk butt, bad smelling, foul mouth in here. Do you?"

"Who the hell are you to be telling me what to do?" the cowboy replied, irritated.

Simon got out of his chair and walked straight to the man. The barrel of his pistol remained pointed at the man as he walked. Simon stopped two feet from the man and spoke in his low, raspy killing voice.

"I am he who talks in a rhyme.... and I kill shit heels from time to time."

The man stared blankly at Simon and did not respond.

"Killing you won't bother me one bit....I like watching shits like you suffer....your choice, get shot or quit." Simon smiled at the cowboy. "So what do you want to do....be quiet....or do I open a hole in you?"

The cowboy took a hard look at Simon. He looked in his eyes and knew what he'd better do. He said "Okay Rhymer, I didn't mean any harm. I was just in letting off some steam. Don't take offense." The man pushed back his chair from the table, stood, and left the saloon.

I backed it off. He left, and I let it rest.
He sure got polite with my gun pointed at his chest.

Why do trail hands get drunk, and loud, and cause so much unrest?
Why can't they get a bottle, spend the evening nuzzled in a woman's chest?

When it got around town in the gossip circles, what happened in the saloon, most everyone in Lincoln knew Simon as a gunman, probably for hire, and wanted him gone. They had had enough trouble with Billy the Kid during the brief Lincoln County War and wanted nothing to do with another of that ilk. Simon was unaware of the differences of each side of the Lincoln County dispute, other than what he learned from Brock Deaton. Lincoln wasn't friendly. He left hurriedly in the middle of the night. He didn't want any part of another man's fight, another in which he didn't know what he was fighting for.

Tularosa, New Mexico

I didn't see any sight of the Etcheverrys, guess it's just as well.
It probably saved one or the other of us, from going to hell.

Simon was not too comfortable in the environment he found in Tularosa. It was inhabited by too many criminal types and was a hiding place for outlaws from Sieto Rios, New Mexico. Sieto Rios was where most of the men came from that were for hire. Many of them had fought in the Lincoln County War. He had hunted, for bounty, these same types of men. Simon wondered how many of these men had a price on their head. With so many there, he was concerned about being shot in the back.

Some of the men in the town did not know how to react to Simon. He had a reputation both as a bounty hunter and as a flash, hot tempered killer for hire. Some wanted to kill him, but few dared to try.

In Tularosa, I killed a very young man today.
Why some persist in making a fight I really can't say.

Simon decided to leave after only two night's stay in Tularosa. He laughed at the thought of it—a place too tough for the Rhymer.

He was in the saloon having drinks for the last time. He was glad he had not run into any trouble. As he drank down his last drink a young man approached. He appeared to be a gunman, and he was extremely intoxicated.

"Hey, scar face, they tell me you're good with a gun. Personally, I don't think you can see worth a shit through them dark little glasses. I think your eyes is shot just like the rest of your body."

Damn Simon thought, I was hoping something like this wouldn't happen. "Leave me be, son. I have no quarrel with you."

"Well, I think you're a pegged legged, slop suckin' pig. A big fat yella pig with sores on it."

"Whatever you say is fine by me." Simon tried to leave.

The young gunman blocked his way. "What's a matta big bad Rhymin' man? Are you afraid of a little o' boy? Hell, I thought you were a gunfighter. Let's see what you got, less all them stories is lies."

Every eye in the saloon was now on the two. All activities, the gambling, the whoring and the piano playing came to a standstill.

Simon was aware of this, and he really did not want to fight. There was no way of telling how many allies the young boy had in the saloon waiting for Simon to make the first move. Maybe someone had put the boy up to this fight, so they could step in and kill Simon and make it legal. But then again, why would any of these men care about what was legal and what wasn't?

"You're right boy....it's all simply a rumor and a lie....I'll just be going now....and we'll let this pass by."

"You ain't going nowhere, old man. I'm gonna kill ya, then you can go to hell."

"Just let it go, son....this isn't something I'm going to do....I'm not making a fight with you."

"You got no choice, you yella haired sum bitch. I'm gonna draw and have you dead 'fore you can move your arm. I might even give you a scar on your other cheek 'fore I finally make ya gone. So what you gonna do 'bout it, yella rhymin' man."

Simon's scar turned blood red. The Demon awoke from deep in his soul, but he was still under control. Simon looked and saw that he could turn and go out the back door and not have to walk past the young, drunken gunman.

The boy continued to taunt Simon, kept calling him names. Simon turned to walk out the back door. As he turned, he heard the young man talking, but the Demon heard the rustling of a coat being moved and of a gun being drawn from its holster. Simon wished he had not heard the noise. The Demon did not care.

"Rhymin' man, you're yella, like a sack of fresh baby shit."

If the gunman had not of been so drunk he might have had a chance. When the Demon heard the rustle of the clothes and the movement of the gun, Simon instantly cocked the sawed–off shotgun, reeled and shot the young man in the stomach.

I tried to back down, but that mouth of his, he just wouldn't shut.
When I turned away, he drew his gun, and my sawed–off caught him in the gut.
When you shoot someone in the stomach, the sawed–off sure makes a mess,
but they won't get up again ~ there's some merit to that, I guess.

Simon went to the gunman He was still alive. Simon knelt down and took the young man's head in his arms. "All that cock strutting and crowing....doesn't do well in a fight son....you need to learn to be meaner minded....if you're going use a gun."

Simon looked around. No one else made a move. It was strange, as quickly as the saloon had become quiet when the young man picked the fight, at the same speed it returned to the normal din of bad piano music and men talking and cavorting with the women. It was almost as if the fight didn't happen.

He never had a chance to learn that gun fighting isn't fair.
He spit up some blood as his life slowly faded into the air.
Some will try to make a famous name no matter what you say.
I closed the young man's eyes as he passed away.

"Hope he's not kin to Olinger?" Simon said to no one in particular.

"Not to worry, he's not," replied the bartender.

"Who was he?"

"He was the youngest of the Taggett's. He was Jed Taggett."

"I guess he's got older brothers then?"

"Yeah he does, two brothers. They have a small place outside of town. They were always trying to keep Jed in line. I guess that won't be a problem for them anymore. You just saw to that."

"Only line Jed will be in now....is in a line of graves. When they come for him, tell them what happened. Tell them I tried to cut and run....but he wouldn't leave it be. It won't ease their hurting none....but maybe they won't come looking for me."

"I'll tell what I saw. I can't guarantee anything else. The rest is up to them."

I draw trouble like a horse draws a fly.
I've thought about it some and I don't know why.
Maybe it's my looks ~ or maybe my attitude,
or maybe there's some evil aura I exude.
I don't know what it is but it's like my skin.
I can shed it temporarily ~ but then it just grows back again.

Simon was glad he was part Cherokee. Having those extra sensory skills, like hearing the clothes rustle and the gun being removed from its holster, had kept him alive. Having the Demon helped too. Was the Demon his Cherokee side?

Simon thought about the rustler he'd shot with the sawed–off shotgun and about the young man in the saloon at Tularosa. A poem came to mind.

Suffering and Pain ~ from sawed–off came.
Flesh and blood were splattered into the air.

With the flesh gone ~ you can see to the bone.
What once was, now no longer there.

Body slumps to the floor ~ a life is no more.
Dead from another fight, that wasn't fair.

The trouble with all of this,
is now his family members will come to defend his name.
The barkeep said there are two brothers,
but hell, I guess they'll end up just the same.
That's the way I got started in this business ~ I killed one of a clan.
Once you do that you have to run or kill every last single man.
Hell if I'm going to have to fight a family for its honor,
I'd rather it not be for using a gun.
I'd rather it be for messing with the wife or daughter,
because to me, that's a lot more fun.
I'm avoiding all that fighting,
I'm going to make my fortune, and I'm going alone
I'm heading down to Arizona territory,
to a mining camp, a place called Tombstone.

Simon liked to sing at times as he rode along. It helped him to pass the time. For most songs Simon made up his own words.

"Bring me a woman ~ a woman so fair.
Bring me a woman with silken black hair.
Bring me a woman ~ a woman so fine.
Bring me a woman who wants to be mine."

"I met a woman down El Paso way.
She was my woman but only for a day.
I met a woman in O' San Antone.
I ran out of money and then she was gone.
I met a woman in Tascosa town.
She wanted to play but not settle down."

"Bring me a woman ~ a woman so fair.
Bring me a woman with silken black hair.
Bring me a woman ~ a woman so finc.
Bring me a woman who wants to be mine."

"I met a woman in Austin so sweet.
She charmed the boots right off my feet.
I met a woman from the city of Dallas.
She was soft but her heart was callous.
I met a woman on the Grande Rio.
She started out hot but then turned frio."

"Bring me a woman ~ one I don't care.
Bring me a woman with any color hair.
Bring me a woman ~ as gentle as a lamb.
Bring me a woman who'll take me as I am."

Thanksgiving Day

Simon left Tularosa early the next morning, right before the sun came up. He rode toward Lordsburg, New Mexico, to catch the train to Tucson, and then ride on to Tombstone. He left Tularosa with more money that he had arrived with—but that was the problem.

He had ridden only a few miles south of Tularosa and as he came around a rock outcropping, three men jumped him. Simon's first thought was that it was the Taggett brothers. As Simon reached for his guns, his horse, scared by the gunmen, reared and threw him backwards. He landed hard on the stony ground. As he fell, he clearly saw one man's face. It was a face he would not forget.

He landed hard on his right hip and then rolled down a small hill into a washed–out ravine. When he came to rest in the ravine, his head struck a rock, knocking him unconscious.

A bullet crashed into Simon's side—his body jumped from the impact.

"Guess he wasn't too damn tough after all, was he boys?" commented one of the attackers. They checked to see if Simon was moving and were satisfied he was dead. The three of them rode off with Simon's gray horse and his saddlebags full of money. They were certain he was dead. They should have checked closer. They would wish later wish they had.

I was leaving Tularosa when I was attacked without cause,
but this is a tough territory, and it is without laws.
My horse reared and I landed on my hip and my head.
They took my horse and my money and left me for dead.
Where I landed on my hip ~ it is sore from being bruised.
They didn't take my guns ~ soon they would be used.

Simon was awakened by something pulling, something biting his hand. What is it, Simon wondered? He slowly regained consciousness, and then when he opened his eyes he saw buzzards, those red headed, foul smelling buzzards. Simon hated those damned birds. One was biting at his hand, and one was pecking at the gunshot wound in the side of his waist. He waved his arms wildly and the buzzards flew away. He would have shot them, but he needed his ammunition for other foul smelling varmints.

No need to kill the buzzards, save the bullets for those men.
When I'm finished, they won't be able to ever bushwhack again.

The Demon spoke to him. *Attacked for money not hate, left for dead at hell's gate, they left you for goddamn buzzard bait.*

Simon sat up and saw he had been shot. Carefully, he moved his shirt and examined the wound. Luckily for him, the rifle bullet had only hit the fat part of the side of his waist and had not hit any muscle and did not do any major damage. It looked worse than it was. He removed his shirt, tore off one sleeve and made a makeshift bandage. He thought of Abigail.

Simon tried to stand up, but his right leg gave way. He had fallen hard on his hip, and it was bruised. He found a broken branch and made a makeshift cane. With the help of the cane, he finally managed to stand. He worked his way up and out of the ravine and to the top of the small hill. In the distance, he could see Tularosa. He started the long walk to the town, hampered by the sore hip, and the wound in his side. *Ignore the pain, you've had worse before. Find those men, I'll settle this score.* His limp was more pronounced than normal.

I walked back to Tularosa, through the scorpions, cactus and snakes.
If those men who attacked me are there, it will be their last mistake.
I thought about killing them with sawed–off, derringer and forty–five.
Then the Demon came to me and told me to take them alive.
He told me of his plan, for these three vile men, and he said it to me in a rhyme.
And it is fiendish ~ but it is a perfect punishment for the crime.

Simon limped into Tularosa just as the sun was setting. He was very tired. At first, he couldn't believe what he saw. He almost laughed. There, in front of the saloon, tied to the post was his gray mare. She was still wearing the knife scarred saddle. He was fond of the big gray mare. He was glad she was found, and that she was okay. He looked closely and saw his saddlebags still tied to the saddle. Quickly, he inspected the saddle bags was surprised. His money, all of it, was just as he had left it. He untied the mare from the post and led her down the alley to the rear of the saloon, so he could get away as fast as possible. There would be fewer men between him and the back door than if he went in the front door. He wondered just how stupid these men were, to leave the horse out front with the money still in the saddlebags. Simon removed a fresh shirt from his bags and slipped it on over the bandaged wound. Then he entered the saloon from the rear. He wasn't tired anymore.

I steeled myself for what came next, firmly I set my jaw.

All in the saloon were criminals ~ in this town without any law.
If they moved on me, Lynchburg would look like Sunday school.
The Demon was in control, he was ready to be ruthless and cruel.

Simon walked in the saloon through the back door. It took much too long, for those men inside the saloon, to realize who he was. It gave him the edge he needed.

One of the patrons suddenly recognized Simon and sprang from his chair and stood with his back against the front wall, near the door. Instantly, all noise stopped. The noise of the piano, the cards, and the trivial chatter, ceased. It got quiet, deadly quiet. One of the innocents later commented, "It was so quiet you could have heard a fly fart."

Their delay had given Simon enough time to locate the man whose face he would never forget—the face of the man he had seen as he was falling from his horse. Simon saw him at a corner table. Simon fixed his gaze on the man.

"You tried to kill the wrong guy....judgment time is here....it's time to die," Simon said, his cold–steel blue eyes stared at the man.

The man abruptly rose from his chair and ran toward the front door. As he ran he fired a shot at Simon.

When the man reached the swinging doors of the saloon, Simon's forty–five bullet caught him in the chest just under his left arm, piercing his lung, and killing him instantly. Simon kept the sawed–off shotgun and the forty–five trained on the others in the saloon as he walked to the man to see if he was dead.

When he reached the man, two other men jumped up from their table near the back door and ran out into the alley. No one else in the saloon made a move to stop Simon. They didn't want to risk being hit with a blast from the sawed–off shotgun.

Simon moved quickly to the alley. He saw the men on their horses. They were riding south.

I hadn't meant to kill any of the three, but one left me no choice.
He fired as he ran. My forty–five ended his life with a roar of its voice.
The other two ran, back towards from where we came.
I gave chase, I'm going to catch them and give them the same.
I gathered the big gray ~ headed south ~ I traveled deliberate, no haste.
I found them in Mesilla. They were holed up, in this whore–lady place.
They were both in bed, naked, with the same Mexican whore.

Finding them together was more than I could ask for.
I hit one in the throat and temporally snapping out his breath.
I knocked the other one out ~ it isn't time yet for their death.
No one said a word in that whore lady place down by the Mexican border.
Not in this territory where there is no law and not any order.

Simon had been in Mesilla, New Mexico, for two days when he finally got word where the two men might be. He heard talk they were down by the Mexican border in a whorehouse called the Casa de Blanco.

Simon found both men bedded down with the same Mexican whore, and they were easy to overcome. He rendered both men unconscious and with the help of a very scared whore, and the bartender of the Casa de Blanco, Simon tied the two men to their horses. He had a special treat for them.

Simon rode toward Lordsburg looking for the right place for his special punishment.

I found this perfect place ~ where no one could hear the screams.
God made it special for this purpose ~ or so it seems.
I spread them out and staked them to the ground,
and I made sure there was plenty of mean assed red ants around.
I staked them on the top of the mound. (Nice, Evil, Red Ants)
I killed myself a wild turkey and placed the carcass between the two.
To make sure the buzzards would come and do ~ what buzzards do.
I then sat on a hillside rock, gave thanks, and humbled to pray.
I cooked the turkey breast, slow, over a fire. I had nothing more to say.
I ate my feast as did the buzzards. It is 1880, Thanksgiving Day.

Scream you bastards, scream. Yell for all your might.
Scream you bastards, scream. No one to hear you tonight.
The ants crawling, and stinging, the buzzards biting ~ what glorious pain!
Greed, Fate and the Demon saw to it, you won't live to do this again.
All of our souls will rot in hell.

Lordsburg

I don't know what it is about some men and exactly what it is they seek.
And the trouble they cause for the people they perceive as weak.
I've had trouble about this scar and this foot of mine before.
Now there's another one a spitting up blood and lying on the floor.

Simon stopped in Lordsburg to catch the train to Tombstone. He stopped at the post office and sent a letter to Abigail. The letter told her he was going to try and settle in Tombstone. He wrote her telling her that good honest money could be made, and maybe this was the place he had been seeking. He wished her well and wrote he would write again after arrival in Tombstone.

He went to the saloon to spend his idle time before boarding the train for Tombstone. His foot hurt and he was limping more than usual because of the injury to his hip. When he walked in the door, the toe of his boot got caught on a loose board and he stumbled and fell. He was embarrassed.

"Don't look like this one needs any more whiskey to me." A voice said out of the dark of the dimly lit saloon. "Looks like he's already fell one too many times on that face of his. You boys ever saw anything this ugly before. I don't believe I ever seen me no scar faced, gimp leg before. We don't give out handouts in here boy. Take your crippled–up ass on outta here 'fore you get both legs busted up."

My mood was already bad, and I wasn't going to take his ridicule,
so I turned on the cowboy, hard and fast and I turned on him cruel.

It took a moment for Simon to get his saloon eyes. He found a chair and used it as a brace to help him stand up. Simon located the source of the cruel voice. It was coming from a man seated at the end of the bar. It didn't take long for the Demon to surface. Simon limped toward the man.

"You need to apologize for what you said....lesser comments have gotten a man dead." Simon smiled.

The man moved his coat to the side to reveal a gun.

With a twitch of his left arm, Simon's derringer was in his hand. It was a move he had perfected with hours and hours of practice. "So you want some gun play? Guess what....it's coming your way!" Without further warning Simon pulled the trigger on the derringer and shot the man in his knee. The derringer bullet shattered the man's kneecap.

The man cried out from the pain and fell instantly to the floor, grabbing at his knee.

"Think about it real hard shit heel....then when you're ready....tell me.... how does that feel?

The man, holding his wounded knee, cried out in pain again.

"Think about what you said....and now look at whose lame." Simon then shot the man in his other knee. The man's kneecaps were both a bloody mess. "Now do you want to call me another cruel name?"

Through the moaning and suffering, the words finally came.
They were choked with dread, and they were choked with pain.

The man said, "Mister, I didn't mean nuthin'. I was funnin'. I had no notion that you'd ever pull a gun."

"You moved your coat to reveal your gun....is that your idea of having fun? You ought to find something else that amuses you....I don't take to getting laughed at....unless I'm laughing too."

The man spoke, whimpered through clenched teeth, writhing in pain, "Now I'll be crippled forever, if I ever do heal." He paused, and then whispered, "I think I'd rather be dead."

"That suits me fine," Simon said. "And when you get to hell....maybe you can laugh at the devil....or perhaps, at his funny ears and pointed tail you can revel." Simon removed his forty–five from its holster. "But I don't think old Satan....is going to take it to well....have you ever thought about where you go....when you get killed in hell?"

Simon moved his forty–five to his hand, placing the derringer in its coat pocket. "Do you think it gets worse....the suffering and the pain....do you think the next level is worse....than from the one you came?"

The man looked up at Simon with pleading eyes.

Simon motioned for the bartender. The bartender came from behind the bar. "Take his gun from his holster, carefully, and lay it on his chest."

The bartender did as Simon requested. He took the man's gun from his holster and laid it on the man's chest.

Simon held his gun on the both them as the bartender did as he was told.

The bartender then went quickly back to his position behind the bar.

There were three paths the man could take. Simon would let him make his own choice. He could drop the gun, and lie in pain, or he could kill himself, or he would attempt to kill Simon. It was his choice. If he dropped the gun, Simon's intention was to walk away.

"So you have to ask yourself....why did I pick today to die....go ahead, kill yourself....and then you can ask the devil why." Simon smiled as he spoke the words.

The man, very carefully, took the gun and then ever so slowly moved it to his head, placing the gun barrel next to his temple. He gave a scared look. The look on the man's face told Simon he was going to pull the trigger and send himself to his maker. But then a smirk came to the man's face. Simon knew what that smirk meant. Instead of shooting himself, the crippled man made a move to shoot Simon.

Simon put a bullet between those pleading eyes.

To live as a cripple, or to die, it was his choice all along.
He chose the wrong one, and the forty–five sang its song.
Best leave me alone, if you don't want blood and bone
~ splattered on a dirty floor.
If its trouble you seek, for ridicule of the lame and weak
~ then from me, there's plenty more.

Simon looked at the other men in the saloon. There were two of them sitting at the same table near the back door. Simon saw them both turn their heads when he looked their way to avoid looking him in then the eye. They wanted none this trouble.

"Either one of you got a problem with this?" He approached their table. "He provoked me....calling me scarred and lame....one shouldn't take pleasure....from another man's pain!" Simon looked at the men with a hard stare. "I'm thinking both of you agree. Am I thinking right?"

Both men shook their head in agreement. What were they going to say? They thought it was either agree with him or end up like the loud mouth—dead.

Simon wrote out the sequence of events on a piece of paper and had both men make their mark. He didn't want any trouble later. The men were glad to sign the paper and be rid of this cold–hearted rhyme talking killer.

The bartender sat a shot glass of whiskey on the bar counter.

Simon saw this as a gesture of friendship. Simon drank down the whiskey.

The bartender poured another.

"You're Simon, the Rhyming Man, right?"

Simon nodded in agreement.

"You should know mister; there are two who are looking for you. I saw them at the livery this morning."

"Josh and Tanner Taggett is their name. Jed Taggett, the youngest, attacked me and he ended up dead. They want revenge. Perhaps I'll go sit in a dark corner....you go tell them I'm here....I'll shoot them in the head.... splinter them from ear to ear."

"I don't need any more trouble here. You better go."

"I wish they would think I was already dead. Then more senseless killing wouldn't have to be done."

"You need to hurry then. They are coming across the street as we speak."

Simon's head snapped to his right, and he saw the two men walking across the dusty street towards the saloon. He tipped his hat to the bartender, saying thanks for the tip. Hastily, he made for the back door of the saloon. He hoped he could get to the big gray mare before they saw him.

Simon had no way of knowing, but the bartender gave him the time he needed. He delayed the Taggett brothers long enough for Simon to escape.

The Taggett brothers entered the saloon. They spoke directly to the bartender when they saw the dead man on the floor. "We're looking for a man named Sublette. Some say he goes by the name the Rhymer."

The bartender motioned to the dead man on the floor.

Tanner Taggett went to inspect the man. After looking at him from different angles, Tanner spoke. "I don't think he's the one. I don't see a scar of any kind."

"Reckon that could be because he was shot in the face?" replied the bartender.

Josh Tanner looked at the two men at the table across the room. "You two know anything about this, did you hear anything?"

The bartender was looking hard at the men. Neither one of them wanted any trouble. One man spoke, "I heard the name mentioned that's all."

Josh and Tanner looked at one another. They looked at the dead man. Without saying a word they turned and left the saloon.

So I shot him in the head ~ left him for dead,
~ another passage in the life of he who talks in Rhyme.

Don't call me lame ~ or any other cruel name,
~ cause the Rhymer will kill you every single time.
They say only the good die young ~ wasn't true in his case.
You could see the cruelty and meanness by just looking into his face.
Besides, if only the good die young, then why am I not gone?
Why, I'm the sweetest thing a young lady would ever want to take home.
And am I not good? Most I've encountered say yea.
Then why the hell am I not dead today?

I was headed south ~ ran into the loud mouth,
~ then the Taggetts came along.
Me they sought ~ no battles fought,
~ escaped out the back door and was gone.
Would my reputation suffer from running from a fight?
They would have to be told it was not from fright.

Chapter Four

Tombstone

Simon was informed the train didn't go to Tombstone, Arizona. The train only went to Tucson. Tombstone was south and east of Tucson. The train stopped early and let Simon depart. He unloaded the big gray mare from the train, got the saddle in place, and then rode toward Tombstone. The countryside wasn't what he had imagined. He always thought of Arizona as being mostly a desert. The way to Tombstone, an oft used wagon trail, was not like that at all. There were plenty of trees, cottonwoods and others, and it surprised him. He figured he knew now why the Apache Indians had not wanted to leave.

Tombstone, there are only four or five hundred people in the whole town.
There are plenty of saloons and lots of mining companies around.
I got a job right off at a mining company as a security guard.
At night I play cards, drink with the easy women, and don't take life too hard.
Lots of gunplay here, the town as a whole is very rough.
Miners and cowboys mixing can make some saloons pretty tough.
I made friends with a man named Leslie, they call him Buckskin Frank.
He's ill tempered like me, we would make a dangerous pair, I think.
I'll just lie low ~ no trouble you know,
if need be, let them kid ~ keep the Demon hid.

Simon sent a letter to Abigail telling her she could write to him in care of the Cosmopolitan Hotel, Tombstone, Arizona.

Simon lived at the Cosmopolitan Hotel but preferred to play cards at the Grand Hotel's saloon. He left the Cosmopolitan's games to Buckskin Frank Leslie and the Earp brothers: Virgil, Wyatt, Morgan and Warren. Simon was friendly with Buckskin Frank, but kept him at an arm's length.

It was a Sunday and he was in the Grand Hotel. The time was a few minutes past noon. The poker game had started Saturday night and had carried into the next day. Only three players were left, and each was determined to stay in the game until he had taken all the money from the other two.

The day outside was sweltering. The temperature was near one hundred and fifteen. A new hand had just been dealt. Simon drew a straight flush. The betting went back and forth. Simon had his entire table stakes in the pot.

A loud, sharp voice came from the street. Someone was calling for one of the other players to come out and fight. The two yelled back and forth.

Simon couldn't let the man get up. Hell, if he got killed Simon might not win all the money lying in the middle of the table. Simon yelled out, "Hey! You out in the street....you shouldn't be fighting in this kind of heat."

The man in the street yelled back. "I ain't takin' no for an answer. I ain't goin' 'till I git what I come for."

Simon laid his cards on the table. He scooted his chair back from the table and stood. He motioned for the Swamper, the caretaker of the Grand Hotel, to watch his interest. Simon walked to the door of the saloon. He was careful; he did not want the man in the street to take a wild shot at him thinking he was George Johnson. Simon recognized the man. It was good it wasn't Frank Leslie.

"Jock, this is Simon Sublette speaking....go on home you old fool.... you're interrupting my poker game....come back tonight, and you can kill him when it's cool."

"Simon, I ain't lookin' to make a fight with you. I'm just lookin' to kill Johnson."

"He's busy. You can have him when I'm through with him. Now leave me to my peace."

"Ain't leaving Simon, you can have 'im back after he's dead."

"Jock, George can't finish this game if he's a dead man....I'm doing all of George's fighting until we're through playing this hand."

Simon stepped out into the heat on the front walk of the saloon. The summer heat in Tombstone was overwhelming at times, but Simon endured. Jock was not a gunfighter. This would be an easy task for Simon if it went the wrong way.

Jock knew this too. He turned and left, but he was still mad.

Simon returned to the table.

The Swamper gave Simon no indication that anyone had tampered with the table.

It would be ill advised for the other players to try to cheat Simon. They knew he would kill them for such a transgression. Simon found his cards as he had left them. The last cards of the hand were played. Simon's straight flush hand won the final hand of the game.

"I'm glad that's over," Simon said. "All this talk about fighting has made me tired. George, if I were you, I think I'd go out the back way with the Swamper. Jock is looking to kill you for some reason."

"Yeah and you made it worse. He wants the money I owe him, that or my hide, and you just took all my money. Want to loan it back to me?"

"Do you have anything you could sell me?"

"Naw, I ain't got nothing. That dried up mining hole done took all I owned."

"I'd sure hate to lose as good a poker player as you over some little spat about money. How much you need?"

"Just a couple of hundred would do it."

"That's a lot of money," Simon said as he handed George two hundred dollars from the money he had just won. "Now, George, I will kill you if you don't pay up. I won't be talked out of it like Jock was. You got anything at all to back this up?"

"Hell, Simon, all I got left that's worth something is my wife. But I don't think she'd take too kindly to being sold off for only two hundred dollars!"

"How much do you think it would take to make her happy?"

George looked at Simon and started grinning. "I don't know, Simon, she'd probably be the one pay you, just to get rid of me."

"No, tell me, George, how much you think it would take to buy your wife. How much would make her happy. I want to buy her, lock, stock and barrel. Right now, how much?"

"Simon, you're funning me. Most men would pay someone to take their wife, and here you are trying to buy mine. You're crazy."

George turned and started walking out of the saloon.

"Hey, George, don't forget you owe me two hundred. And don't go getting yourself all dead before I collect, or I might just have to go see the missus."

George Johnson headed out the back way accompanied by the Swamper. He spoke over his shoulder as he left. "If I see Jock, I'll tell him I owe you money too, and if he kills me then you'll be pissed and will probably come and kill him. Best insurance a man's got, owing Simon Sublette money."

George Johnson wasn't as dumb as Simon thought he was.

Simon left the Grand Hotel saloon and went to the Cosmopolitan. He needed some sleep after being up all night playing cards. Simon thought about George's wife. She was beautiful; one of the prettiest women in Tombstone, and Simon would have bought her, if allowed. But it wouldn't be for cooking and cleaning. Hell, he already had one of the Chinese women doing his chores. Maybe he needed to find a young, pretty Chinese girl to do another chore for him. He didn't know why he hadn't thought of that until now.

I've been here a few months ~ today, again, big trouble came.
I guess it's bound to happen, when you mix those seeking fortune and fame.
The City Marshal was killed last evening past. Virgil Earp is now the new law.
Cowboys aren't all too happy ~ I don't care, I get along with them all.
Virgil is now saying, that in Tombstone, you can't carry a sidearm.
He says he's tired of the Cowboys causing the innocent citizens harm.

Simon was sitting at his favorite table in the Grand Hotel saloon. He always sat with his back to the wall, facing the saloon door. It provided him with safety and with the best view of the entire saloon. Simon liked playing cards in the Grand Hotel. The women were okay, but none to his liking. The doves in the Grand Hotel were much too easy to suit Simon's taste. They would take on all comers, no matter how the men looked—or how they smelled. All doves are easy women, but some Simon knew, at least, showed some discretion, like Big Legged Kate. The ones in the Grand Hotel showed no discretion at all. Some of them would screw a dog if it showed up with two dollars.

Simon was sitting between George Johnson and Percy Jimcoat. A commotion began on the other side of the saloon. The poker players stopped the game to see what was happening. Suddenly, the whole place erupted into a brawl as miners and cowboys chose sides over some dispute. Simon picked up his money from the table and was walking to the back door to make his exit. He wanted nothing to do with this fracas. Someone yelled his name. As he turned, he was struck a glancing blow to his head by an empty whiskey bottle. The bottle hit him in the side of his face across his nose. The force of the blow knocked Simon to his knees, almost rendering him unconscious. He leaned backwards, against the wall and tried to clear his head. Even though his nose was broken, he could still smell the blood, and it was pouring, in a river, down the front of his shirt. Simon started to get up. As he rose to one knee he looked up and saw a man coming at him with a knife. Instinctively, Simon felt for his derringer—it was not there. On the floor, next to his feet, was the broken whiskey bottle that had smashed his face. Simon grabbed the bottle by the neck and when the man lunged at him, Simon slashed the man's throat. The man fell, head first, into Simon's chest, hurling both men to the floor among the dirt and the whiskey and blood. The dead man's blood gushed forth onto Simon's already soaked shirt. It was too much for Simon—he vomited.

The Earp brothers came and brought the melee to an end. The man Simon killed was the single fatality. Percy had escaped with only a couple of cuts and bruises. Johnson had hid behind the bar.

Virgil Earp took Simon to jail. A doctor was called to tend to Simon's broken nose. Virgil made Simon spend the night in jail.

He did not like it one bit. Twice during the evening Simon awoke out of breath and in a sweat. The nightmare that haunted him sometimes in his dreams had returned.

The next morning Percy and George came and spoke on Simon's behalf. They related the facts of the fight to Virgil. Percy and George told their story and said the Swamper would also vouch for the fact that the man came at Simon with a knife and that if Simon had not defended himself, he would have been killed instead.

"If what you two say is true, then I can rule in self defense. Only thing puzzling me is why he came at you with a knife. If he wanted you dead why didn't he shoot you?" Virgil asked Simon.

"You're the one that took the guns out of play, you tell me. Maybe it wasn't planned and he saw it as an opportunity."

"The man you killed is one of Ringo's friends. It could be they want you out of the way for some reason. Maybe they thought you'd join up with us, since you and Wyatt did that stint together in Dodge?"

"Don't know, but if they're thinking that way they're wrong. Can I go now? I need to get some fresh clothes. The smell on these is making me sick?

"Just watch your back, Sublette. If Ringo is involved in this, he won't let it slide. If he comes to town and some of the others are with him, it could go rough on you. Sign on with me and you can help us get rid of that kind of trash."

"Virgil, I didn't come here....to be part of a feud between warring factions....let me wear my guns....and I'll take care of my own action."

"Suit yourself, but you aren't wearing a gun. You know the law."

"Your law, not mine, just you keep the guns off Ringo and Curley Bill and the rest of the Cowboys. If you don't there'll be a big fight someday and this town's going to get shot all to hell."

Simon and Percy left for the Cosmopolitan Hotel.

George went to his house to get Simon some fresh clothes.

George Johnson came to the Cosmopolitan and brought Simon the clothes. "Simon, try these. The little missus said for me to fetch yours, and she would try to clean 'em best she could. Here, this came for you too." Johnson laid a letter on the table. The letter was from Abigail Sweeney.

It made Simon happy. "Thanks, George, it's appreciated."

"There's something else, Simon." George began to fidget. He lowered his head and would not look at Simon.

"What is it, George?"

"Well, people have been talking. I uh, don't know how to say this right."

"Just say it and get it over with."

"I don't want any trouble with you, you being a friend and all."

"What the hell are you talking about, George?"

"It's just that I don't think my wife ought to be talking to you like she does, her being married and all."

Simon was appreciative of what George had done for him, but he was not in the mood for this petty behavior. His nose hurt and so did his foot. His attitude became somewhat surly.

"If you don't want her talking to me, George, then cut out her goddamn tongue."

George looked at Simon, knew it was hopeless, shrugged his shoulders and left.

The conversation put Simon in a real bad mood. As he bathed and dressed, his anger increased. To hell with the law and with the Earp brothers he said aloud. Simon got his derringer and strapped it to his arm—never again would he walk the streets of Tombstone unarmed. He fashioned a special holster for his forty–five. It allowed it to stay hidden until needed. Simon had a good mind to turn the Demon loose. Get his pistol, the sawed–off shotgun and go to the Oriental and kill every one of the Cowboys he saw. He could take Ringo and Curley Bill and the Earps, too, if necessary. He knew he could, the Demon told him so.

Simon told Buckskin Frank of the incident in the saloon. It was Frank's opinion they should go and be rid of Ringo and friends.

That's the trouble with not being armed.
Hell, I had to use a broken bottle to cause a death.
Fighting with your fist is much too ghastly.
You have to get close enough to smell their rotten breath.
The cowboys come to town, get liquored up and shoot without warning.
Here in Tombstone, there's a dead man in the street every single morning.
Virgil ruled self–defense ~ fined me for fighting then let me go.
He told me to be careful, the one I killed was a friend of "Johnny Ringo."
Buckskin Frank said we should be rid of Ringo and friends.
I told him it was good with me, just say when.

Doc Holiday is here, he's mean, and fast enough to cover their back,
~ as long as it doesn't come during his coughing attack.
I've been watching Holiday, he's walking death,
~ sometimes his cough is so bad, he almost chokes to death.

Simon had heard all the rumors and stories regarding Doc Holiday. It was told he was an expert marksman and cool mannered in a fight. He was from the south and was slowly dying of the consumption. Most were afraid of him just on reputation alone. Holiday's illness made him extremely dangerous. He did not care if he lived or died.

Simon watched Holiday closely. Terrible coughing spells would come over him. It seemed, to Simon, that at times Doc would almost choke to death. It occurred to Simon that if Holiday were his sworn enemy, he would attack during one of Doc's coughing spells. He'd be easy to kill then. Simon wondered why the gang called the Cowboys, did not do the same. Maybe they really were afraid of the Earp brothers.

Simon opened the letter from Abigail. It brightened his spirits. She was considering a change. Fort Defiance held nothing for her. She had decided she didn't want to be an army wife like her mother and move around from fort to fort. She still wanted to settle down. Simon never lost hope. If only he was the one who could settle down.

A few weeks after the saloon fight, Simon and Percy were standing at the bar in the Grand Hotel. The Grand Hotel saloon was like most hotel saloons, a large square room with a long bar on one side. Sometimes the bar was in an L shape. Most times it was a simple, long, straight bar. The Grand Hotel bar was more of a straight bar with small wings.

A man, slender of build and with blood shot red eyes, came through the front door. The Demon sensed something wrong. *Evil is near, death is nigh, ready the derringer, shoot for the eye.*

Percy confirmed the fact, getting Simon's attention by gently nudging him with his elbow. Percy whispered to Simon, "In the flesh, Johnny Ringo."

Simon had seen Ringo before, but never at close range. His senses came to their full awareness. The Demon came to his scar. He rubbed the coat sleeve of his left arm. The derringer was in place, ready, wanting to be called to action. The derringer and the Demon called to him, *Simon, make the move with your arm....let me come out and do Ringo some harm.*

Ringo walked to the end of the bar nearest the door and ordered a whiskey. Simon did not take his eyes from this man who he heard had killed Petey Joe Tyree, and who he heard was also going to kill Simon if he ever got the chance. Simon and Ringo never spoke. Ringo had a couple of whiskies and left. The whole time Ringo drank, he never took his eyes from Simon. It was a staring contest between two cold–hearted killers. Simon could smell the blood in the air.

The tension eased in the hotel when Ringo left. The atmosphere returned to normal. One of the hotel girls came and stood between Simon and Percy.

"Come on Simon, let's me and you mix it a little."

"No thanks. I'm busy. Go bother someone else."

Percy patted her on the butt.

She turned and looked at Percy.

Percy gave her a smile, "Later hon', I'm visitin' with Simon right now."

This particular lady of the evening was the one the miners called Bam Ma'am. She gave up on Simon and went to another table. Percy patted her on the butt again as she walked away.

"Simon you never do have anything to do with the women. Is there something wrong with you? How come you don't ever take one of them girls up and give 'er a poke?"

"You go ahead, not me. Tell me something though. How the hell could you do it with someone with a name like Bam Ma'am? Damn Percy, she got that name for a reason you know!"

Percy shrugged his shoulders. A motion indicating he didn't know why he did such a thing. It always felt good he thought.

"To me most of these women are just like milk buckets....cowboys and miners squirt in them, and then push them aside until they need them again. I'm just not interested in a woman like that. I like my women with a little more snap in her garters than that. When I go for the bacon, I want the sizzle too. Some romance never hurt anyone. When I see the right one I'll let you know."

"Damn Simon I didn't know someone with a face like yours could be so particular."

"Face may be scarred Percy, and my morals a touch....but not my mind....don't need women of that ilk....they're not my kind. You keep on dipping your wick in that kind of trough....and someday your manhood is going to fall off! I tell you Percy....that poison pu....is going be the death of you."

"Maybe so, but at least I'll die doing something I like."

After Ringo came into the Grand Hotel that day, Simon began to study him He was sizing up his enemy. Over the next few weeks, Simon came to the conclusion that Ringo was an alcoholic. He was drunk most of the time, sometimes to the point of embarrassing himself. Simon did not know what the fuss, or fear, over Johnny Ringo was all about. Hell, he could kill Ringo anytime he wanted. With the bad blood between Holiday and Ringo, Simon wondered why Holiday had not killed him by now. He had the protection of the Earp brothers, what else did he need? Maybe he was waiting for Buckskin Frank to do the deed.

Ringo wasn't pretty to look at. He had one of those faces that made you want to slap him when you saw him. Simon grew up, and went to school in Texas, with some kids who had faces the same as Ringo's face. That red eyed, red nose, down in the dumps face like kids have when they are sick with a severe cold. Simon called it a red–eyed–pissy–face. Every time you saw them, you wanted to slap the hell out of them. Ringo looked like that and he was a grown man.

On more than one occasion, Simon heard Ringo and his Cowboy friends plotting to kill Holiday and the Earp brothers. Simon made an observation—when trouble started Johnny Ringo was conveniently nowhere to be found. Simon wondered if this was a coincidence, or if it was planned. Was Ringo's reputation merely a bluff, was he over hyped? Was he all bravado? Was Johnny Ringo a coward?

Simon wanted to kill Ringo for the death of Petey Joe Tyree, and because he was one of those red–eyed–pissy–faced men—but he never got the right chance. There was definitely a war brewing between the Cowboys and the Earp brothers. Simon knew if he stayed, somehow, he would be drawn into the battle. There would be no more wars for Simon. He decided to leave even though George Johnson still owed him two hundred dollars. He would not stay in Tombstone for two hundred dollars and possibly get involved in a war. There was not enough money in the entire world to get him to stay and fight.

Simon told George Johnson he was going to Nogales and to send him his money the first chance he got. He also asked George to send any letters that might come for him at the Cosmopolitan Hotel. He said he would be beholding. Simon left Tombstone.

There's plenty of blood in the air ~ I think there's going to be a war.
I can feel it in my neck hair ~ I'm leaving before I have to settle some score.
I'm not getting mixed up in what the Earp's and Holiday are going to do.
I'm leaving ~ it isn't my trouble and I'm keeping it that way too.
I'm riding over to Nogales, south of Tucson, on the Mexican border.
It's in the Santa Cruz Valley. Will I find peace there, perhaps law and order?

Tumacacori, Arizona

Simon rode west out of Tombstone across the open, rolling Arizona plains. He rode with no particular destination. He rode due west and through a small valley, eventually finding the green, tree lined, Santa Cruz River. He came across the town of Tubac, which was mostly uninhabited at the time. Tubac did not interest Simon. He then turned south and rode towards Nogales. He rode until he came upon the old vacant Spanish Mission of Tumacacori. The Apache Indians had driven all of the settlers out of this area with their constant raiding. It was near night fall when Simon arrived at the mission. Behind the main mission building, Simon found adequate shelter for him and the big gray mare. He decided to stay here. There weren't any people around, making for plenty of peace and quiet. It was close to the river and he could catch some fish to eat.

After settling into his new home, Simon explored the surrounding countryside. Just to the north of the mission Simon found a quaint, quiet, Mexican cantina. The building looked to be as old as the mission. The cantina was located near the river and about one mile north of the mission.

This little cantina here, Madera's, close to the old mission, is a nice safe haven.
I can't see much of my scar anymore ~ my face is now unshaven.
I can get to Nogales later on, here life is slow, easy and free.
It's a good place to reflect, maybe I can figure out what is wrong with me.

Madera's Cantina had a bar, a few rickety tables and chairs, and a dirt floor. The bar was on the right immediately as you entered its only door. The door could not be opened without hitting the end of the bar. The bar was built in an L shape. At the end of the bar was an opening leading to a storage room and a small kitchen. The opening had a Mexican blanket attached to the top with ropes. The blanket was red with crosses made of gold, blue and white thread. It was quite a contrast to the rest of the room. Simon thought the blanket was beautiful.

Everyday Simon went to the Madera's Cantina to drink whiskey. Simon stood out like a sore thumb in this little Mexican village, but it did not take long for him to become friends with the Mexican locals. And it did not take but a few times for the Mexican locals to get Simon to switch to their favorite drinks, Tequila and Mescal. He preferred the Tequila over the Mescal. To him the Mescal had a dirt taste to it. He had to be careful when he drank Tequila or Mescal because sometimes he lost control. Simon didn't like being out of control. On occasion, the drink made him hallucinate.

Some of the Mexican locals had never seen a man with yellow hair and fair skin before. Simon's ice blue eyes also caused more than a few stares, especially from the senoritas.

Of particular interest to Simon was the daughter of the man who owned the cantina. Her name was Melina Madera. Eventually, Melina and Simon became much more than friends.

A beautiful señorita came to share my bed last night.
We rolled for hours and made each other right.
Such a beautiful body she had, highlighted by the glow of the candlelight.

When Simon and Melina enjoyed each other's company, Melina would go with Simon to the old mission at Tumacacori. She was not completely comfortable with how her father felt about her and Simon. It was one thing to sleep with a man out of wedlock, quite another to be doing it with a gringo. Nonetheless, Simon got along rather well with Melina's father, Carlos Madera.

Carlos and Melina would travel to Nogales for flour, beans, cured meat and tequila for the cantina. The trip was a three day affair and was made every six weeks or so. Simon was invited to go with them. Carlos brought the wagon to the front of the cantina. He was wearing his best clothes, black pants and a vest with many colors of thread sewed in, and a white shirt with tie. He wore a large brimmed, high crowned hat. The brim of the hat was trimmed in red and black braid. Simon had seen this hat on some of the cowboys in Tombstone. It was different than most hats men wore at the time.

Simon smiled at Carlos. "Nice hat, señor."

"Si, tan galán."

"Ten gallon?" said Simon mispronouncing the Mexican word.

"Si, tan galán."

Simon looked at Melina, "I think you father has it wrong. I don't believe that hat will hold ten gallons of anything."

"Oh no, my Simone, it's not ten gallon, you say it wrong." Melina said the word slower, emphasizing the Spanish enunciation. "It is tan galán. In Spanish it means 'So Elegant'. He is trying to tell you it is an elegant hat."

"Oh," said Simon. He looked at Carlos, "Si, tan galán."

We go sometimes for supplies and tequila down to Mexico.
They have a name for my kind down there, they call us "Pistolero."
I've got it made here, peaceful, serene, no trail–hands or lead slinging,
but for some reason I'm getting restless ~ I wonder what the future is bringing
I tried on some of the Mexican clothing, including a nice tan galán hat.
Carlos and Melina laughed at me, so I guess I won't be dressing like that.

When Simon went to Nogales was the only time he carried his weapons. He had no need of them in the cantina. But he felt differently in Mexico. He was easy for the locals to identify as a gunman. Simon always wore his forty–five on his waist, never on his leg as most others did. He learned in the war that the pistol was easier to use and more convenient at his waist than tied to his leg, especially when sitting down. Being on a wagon, a horse or a chair, he had learned he could draw the weapon twice as fast when carried in this manner.

Goddamn nose, it takes it upon its self to start to bleed,
it doesn't last long, but it's a distraction I don't need.
It starts now and then, ever since that Tombstone cowboy started the trouble.
I wish he wasn't dead already, so I could give him back double.
It's nice here and I have time to think and time to reflect.
I drink and swear too much, I should stop, but won't I suspect.
When you call a man a son of a bich, if another word gets substituted,
then the meaning of what you're trying to convey gets diluted.

Pencil writing is better than with a pen,
and I'll never spill the ink bottle again.
It's raining hard today, can't fish, Melina is not here.
I'm lying in my bed, too much time on my hands, I fear.
I've been thinking on this. What is the world's greatest driving force?
I've thought about money, power, the will to survive and sex of course.
I've seen extremely rich men risk all in pursuit of sharing a bed.
Some lost it all ~ the women got the money ~ and some ended up dead.
I've seen men of politics lose their integrity, when a woman cast her spell.

They lose their influence, and when it comes, their future you can foretell.
I've seen cowhands, stand to give their life for the right to a soiled dove.
To their own determent, they will risk all, for a chance of meaningless love.
It's curious I guess, sex might just be the most powerful force in life,
but I've also seen that this isn't satisfied just because a man's got a wife.
I guess it may be true what was said by Big Legged Kate.
"Most women do it for love. Men do it cause they're driven to fornicate."
Women are mystical creatures, with mystical powers; they weave spells on us men
~ I don't doubt it.
What else could bleed for five days without getting sewed up,
~ and live to tell about it.
I recollect another dove that said the reason some men resort to gunplay,
is because our sex is short, so we had to prove our manhood in another way.
Well, I don't know who she'd been with but I damn sure proved her wrong.
I drank a lot of whiskey, I put her in a sweat ~ and ~ I took all night long.
Rain quit ~ nothing else left to write, it's just as well.
I'm going over to Madera's and drink a spell.

When Simon got to Madera's Cantina Melina was waiting for him at the front door. She had his supper of fish, cabbage and tortillas, waiting along with a full bottle of tequila and some fresh, sweet Mexican "limons." Simon preferred the Mexican limons rather than limes or lemons. They tasted sweeter and did not have as much acid as their American counterparts.

"My Simone, where you been all day? I have been lonely here in the rain waiting for you."

Melina came up to Simon and gave him a very passionate kiss. When the kiss was over Simon looked over at Carlos. Simon did not want a stomach full of buck shot from the shotgun Melina's father kept behind the bar. Simon was glad Carlos did not make any sign of disapproval.

"I was at the mission, writing, and waiting for the rain to stop. I would have come earlier, but I didn't think you'd want me all soaking wet."

"Oh no, I like the way the rain makes the air smell clean. It might make you smell clean too, my Simone." Melina gave Simon a mischievous smile. "What were you writing about that kept you away so long? Let me see?"

Simon told Melina what he had written in his journal. He told her about the doves and about how he had come to the conclusion sex was the most driving force in life.

"Are men really like that, Simone?" Melina asked.

Melina had not been around enough other men to know. She was lucky. She was a young, pretty girl working in a cantina but had been spared the actions the doves had to endure who worked in saloons. Probably, because of that shotgun old man Madera kept behind the bar.

"Sure they are. If you'd of ever traveled outside of this valley you'd know it to be true. Some men are like an old bull. When they get an indication the female is interested, they'll walk through a fence or drown crossing a river just so they can mount that cow. Hell, you've seen that before, haven't you?"

"Simone, I've never seen a bull do that before. But then I haven't been around cows all that much. There's not too many of them here to watch."

"Shoot, we should get us some. There is plenty of water and grass for them to eat. But I tell you, it's true. I've seen cowboys stand and fight over a soiled dove....just for a few minutes of meaningless love. Look at us, Melina. We risk your father's wrath, so we can be together. At anytime he could get that shot gun and kill me.

"Would you fight for me, my Simone?" said Melina, batting her eyes at him, puckering her lips, flirting with him.

"I'll fight for you, Melina, but I won't fight over you. If you ever pit me against another man for your love then you can have the other man."

Simon's face was growing red. He swallowed a mouthful of the tequila.

"But now if some no good molests you or harms you in any way, then he'll be in for a lot of trouble."

"My Simone, my Simone, you act so mean, but you just a big fuzzy bear. You shouldn't get so angry. Here eat this." Melina put a Chile pepper to Simon's lips. "When you're hot you should always eat something hot. It'll cool you down. This little Chile pepper here will make you cold like the winter!"

"So I'm supposed to eat this hell fire hot pepper to cool down?"

"Yes, my Simone, it will move the burn from your brain to your belly. You can drink something to fix the burn in your belly. It's hard to fix the burn in your brain."

Simon took the Chile pepper into his mouth. He bit down hard; the pepper's juice brought the liquid heat and put his mouth ablaze. Simon chewed the pepper a few times and swallowed. Tears came to his eyes. Quickly, he took a mouth full of Tequila. He swished it around in his mouth trying to kill the pain. He swallowed and quickly took another mouth full of the Tequila.

"Mighty fine pepper Melina, I think I can feel ice icicles forming now."

Simon was grinning. Melina and Carlos were laughing. Simon was sweating profusely.

Simon took in another mouth full of tequila. With this large gulp of Tequila, he also took in the worm. He swished the worm back and forth in his mouth, and then bit into it and finally swallowed. "Yep, right fine Chile pepper and a damn fine worm to boot, what more could a man ask for?"

Melina was right in what she had said. With the burning in his mouth and stomach, Simon did not have time to think about being mad. Simon ate another Chile pepper—he needed more pain.

Melina knew it would be a good night later in the evening.

Simon knew it would be a good night later too. The Demon told him that if he had someone to kill at this very moment, it would make the end to a perfect day. *Simon, Simon, I have an itch, can't you find me a rotten son of a bitch?* The Demon surfacing bothered him. Why was he thinking this way? He had come to this place to escape the violence. Maybe he was going crazy, here, now!

Tequila, more Tequila for the pain,
for the tooth or the toe ~ numbs the same.
Tip the bottle high, suck up the worm,
roll it in your mouth ~ feel it squirm.

Melina rubbed Simon's thigh and whispered in his ear. "I'm like the Chile pepper too, mi Simone. Bite me and I will be hot for you!"

Simon took Melina's hand and quickly went towards the old mission. They only made it half way.

My body moved against hers ~ hers against mine.
We lay entangled ~ for the longest of time.
Her lips tasted of Tequila and lime, her sweat, salty sweet.

She was something delicious. She was good enough to eat.
What one would desire ~ the other would not decline.
We were exhausted and spent ~ when the sun decided to shine.

It was a wonderful night of drinking and sex. They were both wild, like crazed animals—uninhibited. Simon didn't know a woman could be like that. All the women he knew before were either reserved or a prostitute. The prostitute's only desire was for you to get your business done as soon as possible.

Simon was glad he wasn't awakened by the nightmare as he had been the evening before. That night, he screamed. He screamed loud enough to awaken Melina. She screamed also, later they laughed about it. Simon never did explain the dream to her.

Later the next day Simon was helping Carlos Madera with some of the chores when a rider came in with the news about the gunfight in Tombstone. The rider showed them the copy of the Tombstone Epitaph and the related story. The date on headline was October 26, 1881.

Simon, Carlos and the rider shared a bottle of Tequila. The rider also related the story about Billy the Kid being killed in Fort Sumner, by a sheriff named Pat Garrett. Garrett killed him in July of the same year.

Simon thought 1881 wasn't a good year for some on the other side of the law. He was glad he was out of touch.

"There's a cowboy who worked at the Harris Ranch, name is Brock Deaton. Have you heard anything about him, about being killed or anything?"

"No, I can't say I ever heard his name mentioned. Is he a friend of yours?"

"Little bit, just curious, nothing else."

The rider finished his Tequila and left.

Simon was worried about his friend, Brock Deaton. Evidently, Brock was more to Simon than he thought. He usually did not worry about anyone but himself.

A rider came in, told about Tombstone and the shootout in Fremont Street.
The Earp brothers, Holiday and the Cowboys finally got to meet.
Now a full war's in place, in the wake of the aftermath.
Wonder what happened to Ringo, wonder if he finally felt Doc's wrath.
I'm glad I left ~ I'm glad I chose not to fight, but to run.
It's really peaceful here not having to worry about using a gun.

Folks went to Tombstone to seek their fortune. The undertaker's making a mint.
Every single day he has a new customer, who's been hell or heaven sent.

Simon had visited the rock hard piece of land they used for a graveyard in Tombstone. They called it Boot Hill. Most of the graves were piled high with rocks. He had not thought much about the graveyard until now.

Boot Hill

"Ground's too hard to dig too deep.
Pile on them rocks, pile them on steep.
Ain't no headstone to mark the grave.
Some died cowardly ~ some died brave."

As Simon was listening to the rider, something stirred in his blood. What was calling him, why did he have this urge to go? He wished someone could tell him. He was truly beginning to wonder if he was going crazy. He sat and wrote in his diary.

When I heard the story, it called me again. Soon I'll have to leave.
It'll be in the spring, and it's not right, but I have no choice I believe.
Most men would kill to have it like this. It would be a dream to fulfill,
but I'm leaving next spring ~ I guess ~ going off to satisfy my urge to kill.
I've got free whiskey, good food, a good woman and more.
What is it tugging at me ~ what could a sane man ask for?
I wonder about my sanity some ~ I feel like I'm standing on its ledge.
I fight it every day ~ hoping the evil doesn't come and push me over the edge.
When it comes over me, it seems like I'm not in my body anymore.
I'm acutely aware of everybody and everything and what's more.
It's like there's one of me standing on the side directing the action at hand.
And then when it's over, I come back to my body and become a single man.
Now this talent isn't learned, I don't think it's an inherited trait.
I wonder sometimes if my fate was to stand at the Devil's gate.
I guess when I die ~I'll just ask the son of a bich why.

Simon thought about his own funeral. Would he be tossed in a ditch somewhere, or thrown in a makeshift, hand dug grave, and crudely covered with dirt? Or would he get a glorious send off like the men in Tombstone? Would he get a funeral parade in that big black funeral hearse pulled by those six beautiful horses? Both carriage and horses would be shining in the sun as they moved slowly down the street taking the departed to their final resting place. Simon had seen it three or four times and each time it was a marvel to him. As Simon thought about it, he scratched out a poem.

The Black Moriah

Black Moriah, they call the hearse Black Moriah,
it is sinister as it rolls down the street,
the only way you can get a ride on Moriah,
is when you become graveyard meat.

The horse walks at a very slow pace,
many tears are cried and cried,
the mourners follow Moriah along,
and pray for those inside.

Get along Moriah,
the women are weeping way to long,
they stand on the side of the street,
and chant the funeral song.

Moriah, get those lifeless,
on down to their resting place,
the graveyard critters are a waiting,
in a few weeks there'll be no trace.

In the summer heat, it sparkles,
and glistens in black,
and those inside leave,
and they never come back.

Moriah, though you do glisten,
and shine in your blackened sheen,
the world is better off,
when you remain unseen.

In all of its sinister splendor,
bedecked in ornaments of silver and gold,
Moriah never saw a smiling face,
and a happy story it never told.

Simon finished the poem. He often wondered how things like this came into his head. Perhaps they came from the Demon, maybe he thought, egotistically, he was talented. He laughed at the thought. At the bottom of the page, he drew a rough sketch of a funeral hearse with skull and crossbones on the side.

Simon enjoyed several months of quiet, serene solitude, sharing his time between his humble dwellings at the old Mission Tumacacori and at Madera's Cantina. There was something at Madera's Cantina that fascinated Simon. On the roof of a side building Carlos used for storage sat a large cistern. Carlos had fashioned a pipe and a spigot to the side, near the bottom, of the cistern. A man, or woman, could turn on the spigot, stand under the stream of water and bathe themselves. He first saw Carlos do it. Then one day he saw Melina. He wondered if Carlos had ever seen Melina stand under the spigot and bathe herself.

A cistern on a roof, fitted with a pipe and spigot, turn it on,
and the water came running out, making the dirt all gone.
It was ingenious, one of the most curious things I've ever seen.
A man didn't have to lie down in a tub, to get his body clean.

Simon was able to stay with Melina longer than most women he had met, but he always looked forward to his time away from her. Sometimes he would stay away for three to four days. He hunted on occasion and spent a lot of time fishing the Santa Cruz River, never really caring if he caught a fish or not. The valley here was lush and green, much like the valley leading into Tombstone. On rare occasions, Simon would venture to Nogales alone. Each time he went to Nogales, he sent Abigail a letter writing her about how nice and peaceful it was. He told her he might have found his place.

She had written back saying she was happy for him. She wrote she was going to move to Fort Sumner for better employment and better surroundings. She wrote she would send him her new post address.

Simon never went to Tucson or ventured east of the Madera Valley. The Earp brothers' private war, against Sheriff Behan and the Cowboys, was in full force and was lasting quite a long time. Simon wanted to be nowhere near it. If he would not go and help Brock Deaton, he was damn sure wouldn't go and help the Earp brothers. Besides, Wyatt and his brothers, along with Doc Holiday, were outnumbered. Simon figured it was only a matter of time before they lost or were forced out of Arizona. However, he did have to admit, from the stories being passed along; the Earp brothers and Doc Holiday were giving Behan and the Cowboys one hell of a battle.

Simon had written a letter to George Johnson inquiring on Johnson's intention of paying him the two hundred dollars. A letter was returned, and it told Simon that George Johnson had been wrongly hanged. They had written a poem on George's headstone. 'He was right, we was wrong, but we hung him and now he's gone.' So much for the two hundred dollars thought Simon. Oh well, he had spent more on less in some of his other dealings. He wondered about Johnson's pretty wife—maybe she would like to repay him.

Simon played cards some with the Mexican locals. They had come to accept the fair skinned, yellow hair man with the southern accent and his way of talking. Simon knew a few words in Spanish. He had learned them from Melina or from the profanity uttered by one of the locals when they would lose a poker hand. Simon thought he could stay here forever, living in peace and not doing a damn thing. So far, he had been successful in keeping the voice inside, the Demon, from leading him away. Occasionally, he would get the itch to move on. He hated it when that feeling came over him. He fought the urge to move on. Every day it seemed to get stronger, but so far he was winning.

Simon's urge to leave, his stirring blood, was becoming more urgent as each week passed. The meanness, the evil of his coldhearted killing sense, was now lying just below the surface. Why couldn't that evil stay away and let Simon live in peace?

That evil, that eeriness that came over him when the killing Demon came, showed its ugly head to Carlos and Melina, briefly, for the first time one evening at the cantina. Neither one of them fully realized what they had seen, but they suspected.

It felt good to Simon, but he was mad about it.

The day it happened, Simon and Carlos Madera left the cantina about mid–morning. They had taken a bottle of Mescal and walked to the river on the pretext of going fishing.

Melina knew they had gone only to drink and to be lazy. The fishing was their excuse.

Just before dusk the men slowly ascended the gradual slope from the river to the cantina. They had no idea of what was going on inside the quaint, quiet, cantina.

They both entered the door, still telling the same lies and stories they had told all day while they attempted to drink the fish onto the banks of the river. Neither one had gotten their fishing line wet. But their tongues were plenty wet from the Mescal.

A tall, well built, man was in the bar. He spoke to Simon and Carlos when they walked in. "Well, glad to see there are some men here about. Thought maybe it was gonna just be me and this split–tail sen–yur–rita here for the rest of the night. She's a fine one though. Just like I like 'em, small and hot."

Neither Simon nor Carlos answered the man.

"Yes sir, I sure nuff like my meskin women, how 'bout you mister; you're a white man, you like the brown eyes too?"

Simon looked at the man. He stared hard and then removed his small dark glasses. "Can't rightly say," Simon's scar twitched, his baby blue eyes, his icy stare never left the man's face.

"You mean you hang around here and ain't topped this little pepper yet? Is everything all right about you?"

Simon broke his stare when Carlos walked behind the bar. Simon then went into the small room behind the bar to put away the fishing poles. He could hear the man talking as he stored the equipment. He got his guns, from behind a sack of beans, and came back out of the room.

"Hey old man," the stranger yelled at Carlos. "As long as you're back there, get me some more fire water. I want to be just right when I give this pepper my full intention."

Melina took the drink to the man's table. He grabbed her hand and with a twisting force spun her around, sitting her in his lap.

"You know what I like most 'bout these pepper women. You don't even have to warm 'em up. They're all self greasing."

The man then tried to kiss Melina. Instantly, she took her free hand and hit the man squarely in the nose. The blow brought blood.

Simon's scar twitched. He could smell the blood—the Demon could too. *This is going to be fun, let's hoot him with the little gun.*

Melina moved off of the man's lap and kicked him on his shin. The kick, or the nosebleed, did not seem to faze the man in the least.

"Hot damn, a fighter. I like 'em like that. Let's get naked and wrestle!"

Melina wrestled herself free from the man's grip and fled to safety behind the bar, next to Simon.

"I think that's enough of that kind of talk," said Simon. Then he smiled. It was the smile many dead men had seen before. But they only got to see it once. And none of them knew what the smile meant.

"Yeah, says who?"

The Demon, the Rhymer, came to Simon. He raised his left arm to show the man the derringer.

"I say so and so does the Sweet Pea." Simon was still smiling.

The man took a quick glance at the derringer.

"If you didn't have that gun, I'd get up and whip your ass." The man then smiled back at Simon.

"Maybe yea....maybe nay....but you'll never know....your problem is.... is that I do have it....and if you don't want it, you better go."

"Easy talk for a coward," the man said.

Simon laid the derringer on the top of the bar. He motioned with his finger for the man to come.

The man rose from his chair and came at Simon. He threw the first punch with his right hand.

Simon deftly ducked the punch and with his left hand crashed a forceful blow to the left side of the man's stomach, just below the rib cage. Simon thought he felt the lower rib crack.

The man fell backward.

Simon then hit him in the temple knocking the man to the floor. "Had enough....or do you still think you're tough?"

The man lay for a moment gathering his breath. "Why's a white man takin' up for some peppers?"

Simon's scar twitched, violently. He picked up the derringer from the bar top and pointed it at the man's head. "Sweet Pea is talking to me.... can you could hear it?"

The man looked up at Simon and frowned.

"It's saying....your finger is on the trigger Simon....give it a twitch.... let's shoot the foul mouth....let's kill the son of a bitch."

The man slowly stood from the floor, raised his hands above his head, and started to back away toward the door. "Your name be Sublette, Simon Sublette?"

Simon did not answer.

"It's been told you were dead."

"Just wishful thinking on some peoples part....you going to do something stupid....or are you going to be smart? What you're looking at is pure flesh and bone....it's time to die....or time to be gone!"

The man stepped to the door and reached for the handle. As he did, Carlos stuck his shotgun, the one he kept behind the bar to use for times like this, to the man's cheek. He spoke, in his broken English.

"Senor, thees ere ess Swee' Pea's lil' brother, it talks too, muy fuerte. Eef ever these eyes of mine stare on you more, lil' brother will kill your ass!"

Carlos backed the man out of the door and held the shotgun on him until he mounted his horse and rode away.

Simon wished his horse was here and ready to go so he could follow the man and kill him. He wanted to kill him, oh, he wanted to kill him real badly, but he did not want Melina to see that side of him.

"Simone, how did that gringo know of you? You made him afraid."

Simon thought hard about how to answer Melina. After a long silence, and a large drink of Tequila, he finally spoke. "In my past, in other places.... when I was near....some men died....others were in fear. I was hoping my trouble would not follow me here. Some believe me to be coldhearted....a killer with no remorse. I tell you honestly....that is not me of course. I'm sorry my trouble found its way to you....I must decide now, what I am to do. You are safe from them....I don't know about me....we'll sleep on it tonight....tomorrow we will see."

With that said Simon excused himself. He told Melina and her father that he was tired and was going to bed at the mission. He went to the mission, got his rifle, and kept a watch until morning. He wanted to make sure the man did not double back and attempt to kill them in their sleep. Something told him not to ever be without all his weapons again. That something was the Demon inside and the voice who was calling him.

"Papa, did you see the look in my Simone's eyes. He looked like he would have enjoyed killing that man."

"Si, Melina, your Simone, I think he has El Diablo in his soul."

A blasphemer came to break the peace ~ he was sent away by my gun.
He might return for his revenge ~ he might choose not to run.
Some like him will come back ~ return in the dark of night.
Then kill us as we sleep ~ thinking, they are setting things right.
From a vantage I stood watch ~ from here I could make the kill.
But would it be for our protection, or would it be for the thrill?
With this matter, the Demon was completely in control.
My blood is running quick and hot ~ is this what makes me whole?

The Hair Takers

Simon tried to keep the Demon at bay, tried to keep it hid from Melina, but it had finally happened. It was something he hoped would never happen again. His hope was short lived. The Demon was a powerful entity.

Then they came. Bounty hunters, hunting Indians for their scalps, stopped in at Madera's Cantina one afternoon. Simon called them Hair Takers. It was a day Simon was glad he was at Madera's Cantina, and he was glad he had his weapons. It was a day Melina and Carlos were more than happy he was at the cantina. These Hair Takers were rogue Mexicans and white trash, like some of those from Sieto Rios. And some of them were from Texas. They were low–life men, scraped from the bottom of the lowest barrel. They scalped Indians and sold the scalps to the Mexican government for the bounty. The Mexican government only wanted the Apache hair—but who would know the difference? If they couldn't find enough Indians to feed their sickness, they resorted to killing Mexicans. Some even killed whites if their hair was dark. With the hair cut from the head how could anyone tell? It could be any Indian's hair—or maybe— even Mexican hair.

It is funny how fate works, three riders came into Madera's Cantina evening past.
They came to drink and brag, not knowing this day would be their last.
When they first came in I was keenly aware they looked a little tough,
and I knew that the more they drank, the more they would get rough.
I guessed that they had been to Mexico, selling the Indian hair.
These three were dangerous. My senses told me best to beware.
I stood at the end of the bar. I just wanted to stay out of their way.
I wasn't interested in their way of living or anything they had to say.
They grabbed Melina, slapped her butt as she waited their table,
but she could handle herself, in those matters, she is quite able.
The more they drank, the one I guessed to be the leader got real loud.
I guess about killing and scalping Indians, he's quite proud.

Simon's blood quickened as he listened to the men talk. A thought came to him as his blood grew hotter and hotter. The Demon was coming again, just under the surface it was there, screaming to be let loose, but it was not time yet. *I'm in your fingers, Simon, feel the blood run, I'm in your fingers, Simon, let me feel your gun.*

*"The peace finally broken ~ with obscene words spoken,
the blood rises hot ~ whether I like it or not!"*

The one doing most of the talking, the bragging, would raise his voice each time he talked. He wanted to make sure everyone heard what he had to say. He was foul mouthed and would curse and make insults about Blacks and Mexicans, and especially about Indians.

Simon did not look in their direction and he tried not to listen to their conversation, but the Demon was listening—and waiting. Simon noticed, out of the corner of his eye, that each time the braggart would insult someone he would look straight at Simon. It occurred to Simon that the braggart was, for some egotistical reason, attempting to provoke him. Was it because Simon was the only man in the cantina at the time? To be safe Simon reached behind the bar and got his sawed–off shotgun. It was the most destructive weapon he used. It killed fast and in a wide pattern. He kept it out of sight just behind his right leg. The sawed–off shotgun called to the Demon. The Demon called to Simon. *Let me loose Simon.... say something in rhyme, let's kill the bragging tongue....let me loose Simon, I'll get it done.* The sawed–off shotgun felt good resting in Simon's right hand. The wait for the Demon was over. He was here now. Although Simon tried to fight it, the Demon made Simon feel warm. The man was going to get his wish but it would be more than he bargained for. He had succeeded in provoking Simon—and the Demon.

The braggart spoke loudly again, looking directly at Simon.

It made Simon's killing juices flow.

"Now take them goddamned Texicans," the braggart said, "I ain't ever, in my whole life, run a crossed anythin' lower than a goddamned Texican. A sorry assed Meskin ain't even that low."

Simon surprised them when he spoke. "I might be from Texas, so might be my friends....want to retract what you said....and make amends?"

The braggart looked at Simon, sizing him, to see if he was a real threat. "There are three of us and only one of you, so piss off, unless you are expecting help?"

"I don't need much help, just me, myself and I," Simon raised his eyebrows and shrugged his shoulders, "and of course there is always the Demon....he helps us make vile men die."

Simon knew it was now time. He was going to kill the braggart and his two companions. As he was talking, he slowly, with his left hand removed his small dark glasses and looked straight at the braggart with his icy stare. Then he smiled. The braggart saw Simon's eyes, and at that moment he knew who Simon was. His face went flush like he had seen a ghost. Before any of the three could move, Simon raised the sawed–off shotgun and turned loose hell.

The notion came over me to kill these three,
dump the bodies on the road for everyone to see.
When I looked at the braggart straight on ~ he showed his surprise.
His expression changed ~ when he saw his tombstone in my eyes.
I started the madness, to rid the land of these vile men.
The sawed–off caught one in the face, he never left his chair.
It killed a second one, where his chest was, now nothing was there.
The Braggart dove behind an upturned table, a shot had busted his arm.
I was between him and the door, he couldn't leave
~ and~ I meant to do him more harm.

Simon had shot the one man in the face, instantly killing him. The man died never leaving his chair. With just a slight movement of the sawed–off shotgun Simon tried to kill the braggart but the braggart's reflexes were fast. Simon missed but instead caught the second man in the chest, splattering him against the back wall. The braggart was trying to find some place to hide. A bullet from Simon's derringer struck the braggart as he scrambled behind a table that had been over turned.

Simon knew that the shot hit the braggart and that the bullet might have broken his arm. There was no way he could leave without having to face his judgment day. "Think about it hair taker....there's more where that came from....and from where I stand....you're the low life piece of scum. I've seen better....come out of a fresh pile of cow....so tell me hair taker.... what do you think of us now?"

Slowly, the braggart stood, revealing a bloody, shattered gun arm. "What the hell was that all about?"

"It's about coming in here....insulting people....committing the cardinal sin....it's about waking up the Demon....getting him mad....it's about killing you and your friends."

"Hold off mister, let's talk this over, let's work something out."

"You know....your kind judges other people....by the actions of a few.... if I had it my way....somehow, I'd kill every goddamn one of you. You're awfully tough acting when you're in a pack....but when you're standing alone....a streak of yellow runs down your back. You and your kind....you sons of bitches make me sick....I'm not sure if I'm going to kill you slow.... or if I'm going to kill you quick."

The braggart studied Simon. He knew he had crossed paths with a dangerous man, and that he was in serious trouble. He was thinking hard on how he was going to get out of this mess and be on his way.

Simon continued. He was toying with the man like a cat toying with a mouse. "Maybe I should shoot you....get you close to your last breath.... then let Melina here scalp you....and we'll all laugh while you bleed to death."

"Wait a minute, I got plenty of money in that bag, and I'll share it with you, just let me go."

At that exact instant, the one Simon shot in the face, fell out of his chair. Simon walked over and looked at him. "He should have been shot in the face long before now....I think it did something for him, don't you.... made him better looking somehow?"

Simon then looked back at the braggart. "You yellow backs....you're a sorry lot....you're going to die today....and you don't even know if I'm a Texan or not."

While Simon was talking, Melina had eased her way around the dead bodies, slowly she reached down and got the braggart's saddlebags full of money and ran out the door. On her way out the door, she spat on the one lying on the floor.

The braggart said, "Let me go. You got my money. Look mister, I'm sorry for the things I said."

"Are you really sorry?"

The braggart nodded but did not speak.

"You come in here hurting people....saying foul things to cause a fight....then you think by saying you're sorry....that it makes everything right?"

"I am sorry mister, please, let me go."

"I'm sorry too." Simon looked at the braggart.

The braggart smiled like he thought Simon was going to let him go.

When Simon saw him smile, he shot him in the stomach. The man reeled backwards, slammed against the wall, then crumpled to his knees and fell on top of his dead friend.

You know there's something about standing here, drinking, with gun in hand, and having total control over the life or death of another man. Not king of the day, but king of this moment and how it went.

King to all involved ~ master of those whose life was spent.
Killing these hair taking yellow backs is just like squashing bugs,
put them under your boot and grind.
And then when you're finished, the world has lost nothing,
it pays you no never mind.
And like squashing bugs, it isn't all that much fun.
You don't even want to take credit ~ after the killing's been done.

Melina had now seen Simon's hot streak of temper. She'd seen small flashes before, but this one scared her. She had no idea that Simon could be so cold and ruthless. He had fired on the men without warning.

Simon used the incident as his excuse to leave and to satisfy his yearning to be on the go again. Simon told Melina it was for the best. He told her the story of the shooting would get around, and others would come and try to make a reputation. He said it was best if he was not around to bring trouble to her and her family.

Melina did not agree with him nor did she understand. She thought Simon should stay and give them protection. Deep down though, she knew Simon was leaving and nothing she could say would stop him. Something else was causing him to go, and she wasn't sure what it was. Something was in his blood she thought, and he was restless. She could not comprehend what this unseen force was. This thing, whatever it was, a thing with which she could not compete, was calling her man. She tried not to cry when he left.

Melina finally saw my true trade, and I told her I must go,
but there are three less malcontents selling Indian hair down in Mexico.
I tried to explain to Melina, but she just can't understand
that I'll never be worth nothing ~ because I'm a gun fighting man.
I guess I was born a gunfighter ~ born to the gun,
and it's that destiny that keeps me on the run.
My occupation is one that needs to be done alone.
Melina is a hell of a lot safer staying at home.
I told Melina that I'd be back, but in her eyes she knew I was lying.
I rode off and didn't look back ~ I knew Melina would be crying.
I made camp toward Nogales and I sit here poking the fire and its red–hot embers.
I know I don't fit into the normal society ~ I am not a good society member.
A feeling of being trapped was causing some dissatisfaction.

Domesticated life and I don't mix well ~ I need the action.
I like being alone, I take pleasure from the solitude.
I don't want a steady woman ~ I'll go find one when I get in the mood.
But I guess, in my character a little cowardice I can detect.
I want no responsibility, and I want no one else to protect.

Johnny Ringo

Fate came calling again, came to satisfy my thirst.
When it comes another man always gets the worst.
I rode south to Nogales, posted a letter to Abigail,
told her I was leaving, would write soon, and I was well.
I then rode towards Bisbee, then turned north to New Mexico,
when I crossed paths at Turkey Creek with none other than Johnny Ringo.

Simon rode south of Madera's Cantina, past the Tumacacori Mission, to Nogales. He posted a letter to Abigail telling her he was moving back toward New Mexico with the intention to end up in Texas. He had chosen this path south and then over to Bisbee to avoid going to Tucson or Tombstone. There were still troubles between the Earp brothers and others. Simon wished to skirt that trouble.

Simon thought about Abigail and how she wanted a man to settle down. He knew it would never be him. He was given that choice at Madera's Cantina, and it wasn't enough to hold him. He had lived mostly in peace, until the incident with the Hair Takers. He had an easy life, hunting and fishing. And he had a good woman who would take care of him in good times and bad, and the sex was incredible. Isn't that what most men look for, an easy life and a good woman? But other men didn't have the Demon. Was it the Demon's fault? The Demon had protected Simon in times of trouble, but it had also caused him unrest in times of peace. Simon needed a way to get rid of the Demon then perhaps he could settle down to a normal life.

Simon was riding along at a leisurely pace when he happened to see a man sitting underneath a tree near the banks of Turkey Creek. It was July, and it was damned hot. The man had his boots off and was rubbing his foot. It was mid–afternoon, when the sun was at its hottest. Simon could not avoid the man so he rode towards him to greet him. He was surprised when he saw the man's face. It was Johnny Ringo, red–eyed–pissy–faced Johnny Ringo, killer of Petey Joe Tyree. Simon knew he would find out how good Ringo was with a gun, and it would be soon.

"Well, I'll be goddamned, the poet. I heard you'd left this territory. Tucked tail and run like a scared dog," said Ringo as Simon approached.

Simon dismounted and slowly walked toward Ringo. "A scared dog can't hunt....and here I am."

"I imagined all the stories I'd heard about you being a gunman were lies. Buckskin Frank, now there's a gunman, but you, I don't know." Ringo rose from his sitting position and leaned against the tree, barefooted.

"Shouldn't believe everything you hear. Should only believe what you see."

"Also heard you snuck up on my friend, like a coward, and slashed his throat from behind. To this day just can't keep from thinking about it." Ringo stood away from the tree not taking his eyes from Simon. "Your hair's yellow, I thought maybe your spine was too."

"How do you want to do this, Johnny boy....what do you want to do? Your gang's not here for protection....it's just me and you."

It never crossed Ringo's mind that he could not kill Simon. He never considered Simon was as good as they said.

"Ever heard of a boy named Petey Joe Tyree from Texas? He was just a simple minded boy....and a friend of mine....I heard you killed him.... just to be passing time."

"Yeah, so what, I've killed lots in my time."

"Not face to face I suspect. They shouldn't let people like you breed.... they should cut your balls off....and stop your seed. It takes a real low life son of a bitch....to kill for no reason....to kill a young boy....just for the pleasing!"

"Piss on you Rhymer, you sweet talkin' son of a bitch. I'll kill you the same way, and then leave you here to squirm, dying in the dirt."

Simon's blood was hot and fast. He could feel the twitch come to his scar. The Demon was in his eye. He left the derringer in its hiding place. Killing Ringo with the derringer would have been too easy. With a small twitch of the arm, the derringer would flash into his left hand and Ringo would be dead. No, not this time, Simon was going to take Ringo head on, just to show him he was as good as the stories had told, and to show Ringo he was a second rate gun man at best.

"Let's get to it Ringo, let's see what you're made of."

Their eyes locked on each other, fingers dancing just above the handles of their guns, each waiting for the other to make a move.

Simon spoke the last words Johnny Ringo would ever hear. "Christmas in July....what a treat....never thought it would come true. I thought I'd never get the gift....of getting to kill you."

Then we did the gunfighters dance ~ eyes locked in a killing trance,
fingers moving like a spiders prance ~ just waiting for the chance.
Waiting, waiting for a hint ~ from the eye comes the glint,

then the bullets are sent ~ and another life is spent.
Ringo was a bit too slow ~ but not me.
I shot him in the head ~ he slumped against the tree.
I always had heard Ringo was fast,
guess not ~ he breathed his last.
Gasping his last ~ how sweet the sound!
I once was lost ~ but now I'm found.

When my blood runs hot and fast, I can feel it just under my skin.
When the Quickening comes, I know I'm going to kill again.
If Ringo had looked deep into my eyes,
he would have seen the Demon in disguise.
Damn I seem a happier man now with the killing running through my veins.
I think the driving force in my life is blowing out another man's brains.
It doesn't really matter that I killed Ringo today,
the locals will just blame it on Frank, or Earp, or Doc Holiday.
Or it may appear to some that the way he died,
was he sat under that tree and committed suicide.

When Simon shot Johnny Ringo he walked to him as he slumped against the tree. Ringo was dead but Simon spoke to him anyway. "You give and you get....tell the devil you were shit!"

To date, Johnny Ringo was the only man Simon had ever stood face to face and had given an even chance. Why? Just to show Ringo he wasn't worth a damn and to prove he was only a chicken–shit, second–rate gunman.

He wouldn't do it again. No other man would get that chance, unless some strange circumstance prevailed. He should have killed Ringo as soon as he saw him leaning against the tree, but then that would have been too easy.

The Tombstone Epitaph reported on finding Johnny Ringo, dead, underneath the cottonwood tree, on the banks of Turkey Creek. It was reported he had a .45 caliber Colt clenched in his right hand and a bullet hole in his head. The coroner's report stated the death was "supposedly" a suicide. Others speculated it must have been a murder. And those others blamed Wyatt Earp and Doc Holiday.

Simon rode north.

Mountain Red and Cortez Snow Horse

I picked up a wanted poster ~ Mountain Red, Wanted Dead or Alive.
Maybe this is something on which my sadistic mind can thrive.
Five hundred dollars is a lot of money, but I'd have to bring in all four.
I've packed my weapons and enough jerked beef for a week or more.
Mountain Red and bunch, killed a rancher, his wife ~ kidnapped a young girl.
What his kind might do to her sours my stomach, makes my neck hair curl.
They had just been released from prison when they went on their spree.
Why they picked on the rancher instead of a bank, or stage, is beyond me.
They say Red is of Irish descent, he has this long flowing red mane.
He weighs in at almost three hundred, that's how he got his name.
I guess some Arizona lawman also has his job to do.
I have to outsmart him. I need the action ~ and the money too.
Three days I've been out, I finally cut their trail and I got a hint,
that the girl is still alive, I could tell by her horse's hoof print.

Simon made camp at the edge of some trees near a small bluff. There was a small creek just below the bluff. He couldn't hear any movement, other than the wind rustling the trees, and the rush of water from a creek. His senses, his Indian blood, told him that someone was near. And then with his superior peripheral vision, he caught a glimpse, for only a fraction of a second, of a movement. Someone was in the trees, but he couldn't see them or hear them. Simon went about his business, as if he was unaware of being watched. He moved the sawed–off shotgun into position, to his right hand, unseen behind his horse. Even though the gray mare was gunshot trained, he worried she might bolt and run from the extra noise a shotgun would make. He didn't want, or need, the aggravation of chasing her down. With his left hand, he crudely tied the reins over the branch of a tree.

He saw the movement again, but as before, he heard nothing. Quickly, Simon laid the sawed–off shotgun over the saddle, keeping the horse between him and whoever was in the trees. "I don't know who you are, but you better come out. This sawed–off here speaks in wide voice when it gets angry, and I'm going to let it start talking at the count of three."

Slowly, a man appeared from the trees. He was an Indian, a Navajo, Simon suspected. He carried no weapons except for a knife at his waist. The man posed no immediate threat to Simon.

Simon watched the Navajo closely. As the Indian came around to

Simon's side, Simon moved the sawed–off shotgun from where it rested on the saddle and kept it between him and the Indian.

"Indian, I am he....who talks in rhymes....and I hunt for money....those who commit crimes. Now tell me who are you....who makes no sound.... when he walks on leaves....fallen on the ground?"

The Indian continued to walk toward Simon. The Indian knew who Simon was.

"I have heard of the one who speaks with the singing tongue. The tellers of tales have spoken of you. I am Snow Horse of the Navajo. I am tracking some men, one a Navajo breed, that kidnapped a young white girl."

The Indian's English was excellent. He was an educated man.

"I'm tracking them too. I didn't think Navajos hunted men for money."

"The money offered is of no concern. I am sent to kill the one who is of Navajo and Mexican seed, the one who rapes women and who is the stealer of babies. My tribe does not like to be involved with the white crime. No other trouble we seek, this Navajo must die by my hands."

"They're all alike....kill them all if you want. Just give me the one.... whose hair is red like the flame....he's the one I have come for....I believe you know his name."

"I know you have come to kill for the gold. I come to kill for the Navajo honor. You can have all but the one I am sent for. He will stay so the bugs and animals can eat his soul."

"It is fine with me." Simon crossed over and took Snow Horse's hand. Their pact was made. Simon liked Snow Horse. Snow Horse would have liked the way Simon had killed and left Murdock McKenzie in the trees near Fairplay, Colorado, or maybe the way he had left Ringo, dead slumped underneath the tree. The bugs could have eaten their souls too.

A Navajo has joined me. He says one of them is a Navajo, Mexican breed.
He's been sent to kill him ~ this kind of trouble the Navajos don't need.
The Navajos name is Cortez Snow Horse, he's been sent to stand by my side.
He wants no reward, just the breed that has damaged the Navajo pride.
Snow Horse is a big man, even bigger than me,
and perhaps, he's the prettiest man I ever did see.
His features are bold and striking, not one mark can be seen,
and his raven black hair has this silken sheen.
He's something to behold, this young Navajo warrior man,

sitting atop that pure white horse with his size and his skin so tan.
Cortez Snow Horse is, as Carols Madera would say, tan galán!

As they camped that night, Simon thought back to Tombstone. It was one tough town with every vice a man could think of, and openly available to all comers. He had heard about the new Bird Cage Theater and some of the escapades that had happened since he had left Tombstone. He had been lucky and had avoided two wars. He preferred to keep his fighting more on a one to one, or one to two or maybe three.

"I'm sometimes amazed,
and sometime dazed,
at the decadence of Tombstone."

"If you had money to be burned,
and for whiskey and women yearned,
then that was the right place to go wrong."

Simon and Snow Horse tracked Mountain Red and his cohorts. It was nearing mid–afternoon on the second day when they found them. They followed them silently and out of eyesight until darkness came.

We have them in sight. Cortez Snow Horse can track a horse on solid rock.
We're setting our trap ~ at first light they're in for quite a shock.
Snow Horse left camp on a mission, no doubt he will succeed.
When he came back, he said he'd caught and killed the Navajo, Mexican breed.

Snow Horse left Simon at the camp after they had settled the horses. He had gone over the rocks and slipped through the trees, and just as he had when Simon had first met him, Snow Horse made no noise when he walked. He was gone until after midnight. When Snow Horse returned, he told Simon he had killed the half–breed Navajo.

"I'm glad to see you're back. Did you scout the camp?"

"Yes, Singing Tongue, come and I will show you. I found the one who rapes women and who is the stealer of babies. He was lying in his bed asleep, dreaming of the hereafter. I pulled his head back by his hair and let him see my face. Before he could scream, I cut his throat and let his soul mix with the dirt."

Simon gave Snow Horse a hard stare. "Why didn't you just kill all of them and save me the trouble? It would have been all right with me if you had made them dead. I could go collect the bodies in the morning."

"Some were awake and I had no weapon but the knife. My killing is done. I will help you rescue the girl to bring honor to the Navajo."

Simon thought it incredible that someone was awake in the camp and Snow Horse had been able to kill the Navajo breed without being detected. He was glad Snow Horse considered him a friend.

As he had done in the past, Simon made his plan to attack Mountain Red at the first light of the morning.

Snow Horse showed Simon the way to the camp. They were making a silent entry when Simon's horse stumbled, loosening a rock, causing it to crash into the trees, waking Mountain Red and the others.

Mountain Red quickly rubbed the sleep from his eyes and sprang into action. He ran over to where the half–breed was sleeping and tried to wake him. He kicked him in the side. The breed's body rolled on to its back, but the head did not move. Snow Horse had entirely severed the half–breed's head when he had cut his throat.

"Holy Jesus, what the hell, God O Mighty!" screamed Mountain Red as he saw the half–breed was dead. He stumbled backwards in fright. He yelled at the other two to get up and get moving. He ran to where the girl was sleeping, grabbed her by the arm and ran toward a ravine.

When Simon saw that Mountain Red was awake and that the element of surprise had been lost, he took dead aim and fired his rifle at one of the men, catching him in the hip. The man fell sideways into the fire and rolled to his side with his shirt on fire. Simon rode up to the man, towering over him sitting atop his horse.

"Tell me....why is it you want to die?" All the man could see was the hole in the end of Simon's rifle. Before he could answer Simon said, "Go to hell....and ask the devil why." Simon shot him in the head killing him instantly.

Snow Horse caught the other one on foot and killed him with his knife.

That left only Mountain Red to deal with. Both Simon and Snow Horse turned and saw Mountain Red running for his life. He had let go of the girl. She was of no consequence to him now. Red's only concern was that he saved his own life.

"Get the girl. I'll get Red," said Simon.

Simon rode fast toward Mountain Red. Simon caught up with him and used his horse to knock him into a ravine. When Mountain Red landed, he twisted his arm and his gun hand. Simon dismounted, stood at the edge of the ravine to face Mountain Red.

Red was trying to get to his gun with his other hand.

Simon spoke to Red and Red knew that his case was hopeless. "Red, you dumb son of a bitch....fresh out of prison and you do something where you have to die....I don't understand....while you're still alive, could you tell me why?"

Mountain Red started to grin, almost laughing. "I ain't gonna die. It's back to trial for me."

"Nope....wrong again Mountain Red....molest a child, you get no trial....you just get dead!"

Mountain Red recognized Simon. "Now Rhymer … "

He now recognized me, he grinned, and he drew his last breath.
My bullet splattered his head and sent him to his death.
I almost considered taking him alive, back for trial,
until he started laughing, with that shit–eating smile.
I brought Mountain Red's body from out of the ravine.
Snow Horse had the girl, she was unharmed, though a bit unclean.

Simon and Snow Horse used a rope and their horses to haul Mountain Red from the ravine. They gathered the other two bodies from the campsite and tied them to their horses for the journey to the nearest town, Holbrook, Arizona. They left the half–breed, with his head nearly severed from his body, where Snow Horse had killed him. As they rode out of Mountain Red's camp Simon noticed the ants and bugs had already discovered the feast and had began to devour his flesh—and his soul.

They sense the smell, then signal the others.
And scurry around with all their little bug brothers.
It's such a fine feast, it will last for days and weeks.
And then they will have to scurry about, another to seek.

They reached Holbrook, Arizona, and took the decaying bodies to the undertaker for keeping, and then went to the local marshal's office. They told the marshal their story. The marshal sent for the girl's only kin, her aunt.

Simon went with the marshal to identify the bodies, so he could collect the reward.

The marshal looked at the bodies, comparing them to the wanted poster. "No way you could have brought them in alive, huh?"

Simon looked at the marshal and frowned. "If you wanted them alive, you should have put it in the print. I only did what was on the poster. Isn't this what the poster meant?" Simon waved his arms at the men and then smiled at the marshal.

The marshal was about to say something but was interrupted by a deputy telling him the girl's aunt had arrived.

Simon and the marshal went back to the marshal's office.

The aunt was there, holding the girl in her arms, and they hugged for a long time. The aunt looked toward Simon and Snow Horse, "I can't thank you enough. I thought I'd never see her again, neither did anybody else. To thank you properly, I need to know your names."

Simon started to speak but Snow Horse responded first. His answer startled Simon.

"He is the one who talks in rhymes, hunts for money those who commit crimes. I am he who makes no sound, when walking on leaves fallen on the ground."

Simon, stunned, said nothing.

With that said Cortez Snow Horse turned toward the door and left the marshal's office. He got on this horse and began his ride out of town.

Simon went outside and watched him ride away.

Snow Horse stopped at the top of a small rise just outside of town, turned to see Simon watching and waved good–bye.

The girl, her aunt and the marshal joined Simon outside. The young girl said, "You've got real names. Please tell me to whom I owe my life?"

Simon pointed to Snow Horse and said, "He is the great warrior of the Navajo nation of course....remember, forever young lady....you were saved by none other....than Cortez Snow Horse!"

Snow Horse then turned and rode away.

The girl looked at Simon. "And you, kind sir, what is your name?"

"As for me....my name is of no mind....it is better not to know anything....about men of my kind."

The aunt, after hearing Simon speak, knew he was the one people called the Rhymer. She had heard of him in gossip. Until now, she had never considered such a person actually existed. But he was here, in person, and the rescuer of her niece. She wanted to think that he did it to save an innocent little girl, but she thought it was mainly for the money. If she had known Simon better, she would have known that he did it for both reasons. The aunt or the girl did not say anymore. They left the building in silence.

Simon guessed he would be required to wait for a time to collect the reward money. He inquired about lodging and the saloon.

The marshal, and the town, did not want Simon to tarry any longer than necessary. The marshal convinced the bank to advance the reward money to Simon so he could be gone from their city. The bank would be reimbursed when the reward came in.

The banker was more than willing to make the advance knowing of Simon's reputation for drawing trouble.

Old Mountain Red ~ he lays dead,
his partners are sucking up dirt.
Snow Horse and I ~ we're alive of course,
and the girl was returned unhurt.
We returned the girl safe, gave her over to her aunt.
The girl and I understand what happened but most people can't.
I was paid today, some town people were happy, some were not.
They think us gunfighters and bounty hunters are a part of the Devil's lot.
I'm heading east, I'm thinking about maybe going back home.
Maybe back there I can find my peace, at the place where I started wrong.

Simon went to the marshal's office the next morning to get the reward money. The marshal handed him an envelope. Simon opened it and counted the money.

"You're short, Peck, half the money's missing."

"The Indian is due his half. Since he didn't want it we decided to keep it for the town. Maybe pass it on to the girl."

Simon's anger flashed. "Pass it to the girl or to yourself? So who was it decided....to take half my pay....did you really think I'd sit for that....then be on my way?"

"That's what Sidney and I decided. He's the one advancing the money. Feel lucky you got what you did. It is done and over."

Simon grinned, a sinister grin. "If you believe that....then you got shit for a brain....I want what I got coming....for my time and my pain."

Marshal Peck shrugged his shoulders and started to walk away. Simon grabbed Peck by the collar of the shirt and violently threw him against the corner of the room. The force of the blow knocked him to the floor. Simon removed Peck's revolver from its holster and threw it on the table. The derringer flashed to Simon's hand and he stuck it in Peck's eye.

"I did what was asked....something you didn't do....I saved the girl's life....now all the money is payable and due."

"If you hadn't got involved, the Indian would have done it for free."

"Snow Horse was only interested in but one....for the rest....I got the job done. He only wanted to kill the breed....he gave me all the reward.... to satisfy my need. I want my money....or I'll poke a hole in your brain with this little toy....if I get cheated on this Peck....this town will think Mountain Red was a goddamned choir boy."

Peck was scared of Simon and what he had heard he could do. He was shaking and he was starting to sweat. "Okay, okay, I'll go talk to Sidney and see what he says."

Simon pulled Peck to his feet. And then threw him against the wall. Peck's head slammed hard into the wall.

"We'll go together....you're not leaving my sight....you're my insurance.... you're going to see to it that fat–assed, chair–sitting son of a bitch makes things right."

Simon grabbed Peck by the arm and shoved him out of the door. As they walked by his horse Simon got his sawed–off shotgun. "Mess with me, Peck, and you won't have to be worried about this town and how I leave it....you won't live long enough to see it."

He walked behind Peck to Sidney's house with the sawed–off shotgun cocked and ready. At the end of the street they reached the banker's house. They walked on to the front porch and knocked on the door. Sidney's wife answered.

"Good morning ma'am," said Peck, tipping his hat. "We need to see Sidney."

"Good morning, Mr. Peck, this is a surprise. He's having his breakfast just now. Can this wait?" She spoke to Peck but her eyes were fixed on Simon.

Simon put the sawed–off shotgun against Peck's back and gave it a gentle shove.

Peck took the cue. "No ma'am, it can't. It's urgent. We need to see him now."

"Oh, Sidney," his wife called out. "Mr. Peck and some other man are here to see you. They say it's urgent. I'll keep your breakfast warm."

It took a few minutes for Sidney to come to the door. The delay added to Simon's irritation. When he saw Simon, he went white.

"Sidney, the Rhymer here wants the rest of the money, the other half," said Peck nervously.

"It's the Indian's money, we all agreed," replied Sidney nervously.

Simon stepped to the side of Peck aiming the sawed–off shotgun at Sidney.

"Then go get it....I'll take him his share....get the other half....that'll make us square."

"Today is Sunday, the bank is closed."

"Locks don't know what day it is....your key still fits the door....I'm tired of excuses....go get what I came for."

"Now ..." Sidney started to speak.

Simon stuck the sawed–off shotgun against the screen door.

"There isn't any now to it....it's either the money or your life....and be quick about it....Peck and I will sit with your wife."

"You wouldn't kill me right here in my own home."

Simon grinned. The Demon flashed his face and his scar twitched.

"That's exactly what I mean....you got ten seconds....or I'll splatter you right through the screen."

Simon whispered to Sidney as he came out of the house.

"I don't know if you care for Peck but I will kill your wife....come back quickly and alone....and I'll spare her life. If you know my reputation.... you know I don't lie. Any tricks or anything funny....and both of them will die!"

Sidney got his coat, went to the bank to get the money.

Simon, Peck and Sidney's wife sat on the porch and had coffee as they waited. It was nice, thought Simon, to drink coffee from a porcelain cup instead of a mug made of tin.

Sidney returned with the money. He placed an envelope in front of Simon. Simon made the men stand back to back with their hands clasped together, and he had Sidney's wife count the proceeds of the envelope. The money was all there.

"Go into the house and stay there until I leave....come out and the town will have a marshal and a banker to grieve."

It really made Simon mad. People say they will pay for a job well done, but once it is accomplished, they do not want to keep their end of the bargain. Goddamned sons of bitches he thought. He hated people like them. The sort that thinks they can make some arbitrary decision affecting someone's life, and it will be accepted without question. It went against his grain, almost enough to make him want to kill them. He thought about going against his word and coming back at night and killing the both of them. If he did he would be like them, and then he would have to hate himself. Every incidence like this made Simon trust the human race a little less. The world would be a lot better, and there would be less conflict, if people would simply honor their word.

As Simon was leaving Holbrook, he passed by the church. They were having their Sunday morning services. Simon knew the banker and his wife weren't in attendance. He wondered if anyone would miss them. The congregation was singing "Amazing Grace." It was one of Simon's favorite hymns. It was also his mother's favorite, and she used to hum the song while she was working around the house or out in the garden. Simon stopped, took off his hat, dismounted and knelt on one knee.

Simon thought of his mother, his brother—and—he thought he heard his daddy call. He thought he saw him standing on the steps of the church. He spoke aloud as if his father were there.

"Daddy, I kept my promise....I sent McKenzie to rot in hell....whether I'll ever get to see you again....only time will tell. I heard the angels sing today....among them your voice....I'd join you right now....if I had my choice. But Jesus might take issue....with some of my actions....and send me to hell....out of dissatisfaction. I'll work on it Daddy....the best I can.... you and Mama and William....put in a good word with the man. Damn Daddy, you know, this isn't fair....the talks we used to have I sorely miss.... tell William hello....and give Mamma a kiss. I'll talk to you later, Daddy, Amen."

It was Simon's way of praying. It was a strange prayer, but then Simon was a strange, complex man.

A mist came to his eyes. He was glad no one else saw him—but if they did—to hell with them—he didn't give a damn. And if they said something or made fun of him—he would just kill them. He said amen out loud again.

Time moved slowly, it had been less than a month since he had left

Madera's Cantina. Simon decided to go to Albuquerque, New Mexico. On his way to Albuquerque, Simon had plenty of time to reflect and time to write. Simon thought about freedom, and when the whiskey would take hold and free his mind, about his friend, Boyce, the Rooster Man.

Freedom is to do and say and at a moment's notice to pick up and go.
Freedom and the 'Quickening' are what's been calling I know.
The Demon and the 'Quickening' are one and the same.
They are both evil and quick—tempered killers by any name.
I guess because I can go when and where I please that I'm free,
But it's not so, because of this force that keeps tugging on me.
Now as far a true freedom goes, I'd say that most people really ain't,
There's always some boundary, always some kind of constraint.
Like if you want to run away to a boat and sail the open sea,
Your constraint is having the money to pay the Captain his sailing fee.
So who is really free ~ the wealthy ~ I tend to think not.
Aren't they bound by their love of money and trying to protect all they got.
You see, there's always some rule, constraint that keeps people inside the fence.
Now every single day that passes, those rules, constraints, get more dense.
We still have our freedom of thought, and they can't fence in our souls.
But now across the land, for passage, we have to pay a toll.
The freedom to roam, explore, to live off the land,
the rules are changing, and I'm told it's coming in a four wire strand.
Fences or not ~ most of us live in an invisible cage,
and the life we live is just playing a role on our own stage.
The size of that cage is of each person's own creation.
The life we choose to live determines the cage's size and its formation.

I wondered about my old friend, the Rooster, Boyce.
If I can see someone first when I get home, he'll be my first choice.
But I heard he was living with a Medicine Woman in Comanche land.
The Indian's think he's crazed, they call him "White Chicken Man."
The Indians say he's possessed, the eternal spirits he can evoke.
When he is either drunken on whiskey or numbed by the Indian smoke.
I heard from another he ran guns to the Indians and was serving time.
Makes no matter ~ he's still a friend of mine.
I don't care if he runs around naked living in a tepee,

or if he's in some dung hole jail you see.
It won't taint his image. My memories of him can't be changed.
I'll always remember the Rooster the way he was,
not what they say he is or anything they say he does,
I refuse to believe anything bad, even though he may be deranged.

Albuquerque, New Mexico

Simon rode into Albuquerque and found a small cantina near the train station. In front of the cantina was something Simon had never seen before. There was a man, smartly dressed in coat and string tie—and he had a monkey with him. The monkey was tethered to a music box resting on a pole. The monkey had a small red cup in his hand. The man would turn a handle on the music box and the monkey would hop around and people passing by would sometimes drop coins into the small red cup. When a coin was put into the small red cup the monkey would jump on top of the music box, reach into the cup grabbing the coin, and then give it to the man. The man would then remove his bowler hat and let it roll down his sleeve in thanks.

Simon was sure it took many hours of practice to perfect the hat trick. The same amount of time it took Simon to perfect the movement of his hand to retrieve the derringer. Simon gave the man and the monkey two coins just to see the trick twice. Simon later learned the man was called an "organ grinder."

It was in the cantina he heard about the Taggett brothers. It was strange to him they were still asking about him after all the years had passed since he killed their younger brother, Jed.

Simon did not really want to meet the Taggett brothers. He did not want to cross their path and be confronted. He knew nothing about them, but he knew they fostered a hate and had done so for many years. Simon knew if he ever met them, it would bring nothing good. Simon was not afraid—he simply wanted to avoid this confrontation. His mood was sour, and if they came face to face, he would surely kill them both.

I learned today, Josh and Tanner Taggett are still trying to find me.
They have wasted many years seeking my destruction, will it ever be?
I killed that boy in Tularosa ~ he was their brother Jed.
It is best we never meet, someone will just end up dead.
Sometimes this manliness ~ this eye for an eye ~ is taken too far,
especially after several hours of drinking in some old bar.

Simon sat in a corner of the cantina enjoying a drink, in solitude. Albuquerque was different than the wild and sinful Tombstone. Things had changed in New Mexico in the years he had been gone. The East was coming to the West. Simon was not sure about all the changes. He felt crowded and estranged, and he had only been here a few hours. However, Simon had a feeling the Easterners and the Eastern way would never come to the West, unless men like him killed the vermin and made it safe.

The Tequila was good here, but the Tequila at Madera's was more to Simon's taste. He had not realized until now that there could be different tastes in Tequila. Melina's cooking was better tasting, too, better than this local fare, but then hell, who was he to complain.

Our society is getting soft ~ hell, just take a look.
A cowboy makes less than someone writing numbers in a book.
People who don't know the ways of the land are making the rules.
Characters like me don't fit in ~ I find it hard to deal with those fools.
To my way of thinking, the East is trying to impose their ways on the West,
and I'm not sure that for all concerned that this is best.
The land and the people are rugged and still pretty raw,
and I don't think that it can be governed by the Eastern law.
Maybe this is a result of the North winning the war,
but I prefer the life and the ways as they were before.
I guess the powers that be, will always continue to try,
but the hardiness of the land and people will never die.
Maybe someday it'll become civilized ~ damned if I know.
I don't think I'll live to see it ~ it's coming way too slow.
But I do think that if the western ways are to become citified.
It'll come from hands like mine ~ not from those who are sissified.
Hell, sometimes I just ramble on with these things that I've said.
No one will ever read this journal ,but writing it does clear my head.

Simon found a hotel away from the train station. As he walked down the hotel steps one evening, two riders came down the street. Their horses appeared to have been ridden long and hard. The two riders were Wyatt Earp and Doc Holiday. They rode past the hotel toward the nearest cantina.

I ran into Doc Holiday and Wyatt Earp.

They rode into Albuquerque today.
Their horses were tired and beat.
They looked like they had come a long way.
Wyatt told me that I'd left Tombstone too early,
that I had missed all the fun.
I replied that it must not be all that good,
it looks like you boys are on the run.
That comment seemed to wrinkle Doc.
His brow furrowed and he gave me a glare,
but with the mood I'm in he shouldn't mess with me,
and I said so with my stare.
Anyway, Holiday's no match for me,
I'm not a cowhand who is drunk and who is slow.
Wyatt told Doc it was of no matter and Doc let it go.
They both were tired, hungry and in bad need of rest.
I bade them goodnight, and for the future, wished them my best.

Simon noticed, as he was having his brief encounter with Doc and Wyatt, there was another man standing nearby who was staring at them and eavesdropping.

As Wyatt and Doc departed from Simon's company the man approached them and began rapidly talking. He was quickly brushed aside by the pair; Doc called him a foul name.

The man, being rejected, turned and chased after Simon. "Mister, mister, wait up, I need to talk to you," the man said as he ran after Simon.

Simon stopped and turned to wait for the small man. He was dressed in a formal suit and necktie. The man's shirt and necktie were the same color, and Simon thought it strange. He had not seen that sort of attire before. The man carried a rather large leather satchel. The satchel seemed too big for the little man.

"What is it you want from me?" inquired Simon.

"I couldn't help but over hearing your conversation with Wyatt Earp and Doc Holiday. You're acquainted with them, aren't you?"

"I guess one could say that, sort of. Acquaintances only, what's it to you?"

"You were in Tombstone with them weren't you?"

Simon studied the man for a moment. "Yeah, I was in Tombstone, lots of men were in Tombstone."

"What was it like, with all of those rowdies and all of that shooting?"

"Want to know? Go there yourself....plenty of riches still waiting for the man with enough nerve. Go to the Bird Cage Theater. Anything your heart desires is waiting for you there. Whiskey, loose women, gambling, killing, the Mexican smoke, just take your pick."

"No, I'm not talking about that. I want to know what it's like to be in a gun fight."

Simon did not know why he was tolerating this impish little man. "I'm thirsty....I think and talk better....having a whiskey or two....how 'bout you?"

"Yeah, uh, sure, fine with me, I don't drink, but I'll get you one."

Simon and the small little man went across the street to the nearest saloon and settled into a corner table.

The man told Simon his name was J. Patrick Fleckleman. He told him he was a writer for a magazine in New York City, and he was doing stories on the wildness and wickedness of the West. He was especially interested in gun fights like the one that had happened in Tombstone near the O. K. Corral. J. Patrick ordered them some whiskey. "Now, tell me about the gun fight."

Simon thought, what the hell, won't hurt anything to talk, and drink free, for a short spell. "All of them are done the same way. Two factions agree to meet....they get their guns and get in the street. The fighting is done in the heat of the sun....and with the cold steel of the gun."

Simon was becoming dramatic. He was now talking in a harsh, hushed whisper, much the same voice the Demon used when he was nearing a kill. "The scent in the air is blood and death....women hide, men hold their breath. Then the gun is taken from where it rests....and shoots a hole in some man's chest."

J. Patrick was mesmerized with Simon's manner of speaking. He was writing Simon's words as fast as his small fingers would allow. He had Simon pause on occasion to allow himself to catch up.

"Gun powder is the smell in the smoke....a forty–five or a shotgun spoke. The loser's blood forms in a pool....it's the juice of the gunfighter's tool. A man dies....the grim reaper won't wait....when one of the factions shoots straight. From the body, the soul is bled....you see....there is the lucky one....and then the other is the dead!"

J. Patrick was transcribing as fast as he could. He finished, sat back, relaxed and re–read what he had just written. It was then that he realized what he had written was a poem. J. Patrick looked at Simon. "Oh my God, Jesus Christ, hell, I should have known. You're Rhymin' Simon, aren't you? I recognize you now."

Simon reached over and grabbed J. Patrick's hand and crushed his fingers against the pencil he was holding. "Book Man, get it straight....that isn't my name....Mr. Sublette will do fine....if it's all the same."

The words were soft that Simon spoke to the writer but the look he gave him was cold and hard. Simon's crushing grip was beginning to hurt J. Patrick's hand.

"I apologize. Sorry I called you by that name, my mistake. I heard you didn't like it. It won't happen again."

"No it won't, Book Man, no it won't."

Simon motioned to the bartender for more whiskey to be delivered. "Write this down so it can be read....calling me Rhyming Simon....is a good way to end up dead."

"You really are the poet then, aren't you?"

"No, really I'm a prophet....a soothsayer....a fortuneteller. I can tell your future....by looking in your eyes....I can look deep into a man's heart and soul....and I can predict if he lives, or if he dies."

Simon took off his dark glasses revealing his penetrating eyes. "Now look at me, Book Man, tell me what you see. Do you live or do you die.... do you see yourself walking out of here....or do you see your death in my eye?" Even though Simon was only putting him on, he tried to give J. Patrick his hardest stare.

J. Patrick swallowed hard, and then he too ordered a whiskey and had his first drink ever. He was scared and nervous, but he was not leaving now. He was so scared the harshness of the whiskey did not make him gasp. Danger or not, this was what he came for. If he couldn't get a direct story from Earp or Holiday the Rhymer would do just fine. Anyway, rumor had it the Rhymer had killed more men than Holiday and Earp combined.

Simon finally eased his hold on J. Patrick's hand.

J. Patrick shook his hand, as if he were shaking out the pain Simon had caused. "I think I will take my leave with my papers in hand, and tell the story of my encounter with the Rhyming Man." He gave Simon his best smile. He knew he had made a rhyme. J. Patrick took his handkerchief and wiped his face. He gave Simon a smile.

Simon then smiled too, and relaxed.

"Tell me about Tombstone, Mr. Sublette."

"I wasn't there when the fighting took place....the happening's, I can't tell....all I know is that the Earp's and Holiday....sent the Clanton's to hell."

J. Patrick's face expression dropped in disappointment. Simon took J. Patrick's tablet and wrote the following.

Tombstone

Blood in the air ~ citizens beware.
A feud is brewing ~ both sides a stewing.
Earp's ready to fight ~ Ike Clanton drank all night.
Johnny Ringo is away ~ the Earps joined by Doc Holiday.
Out on Fremont Street ~ the Earps, Doc and the Clanton's meet.
McLaurys joined in the fray ~ both lost their life that day.
Right beside the house of Fly ~ hot bullets came flying by.
Frank and Tom McLaury, Billy Clanton dead.
Virgil and Morgan Earp bled.
Feud didn't stop here ~ Virgil ambushed later in the year.
Morgan shot in the back ~ Stillwell found dead on railway track.
Ringo later found dead ~ someone shot him in the head.
Killer not known even today ~ was it suicide, Earp or Holiday.
Doc and Wyatt fled the scene ~ escaped Sheriff Behan's scheme.
Got money to be burned? ~ For the ladies you yearned.
Like whiskey and song ~ it's the right place to go wrong.
The town was sinful, bad to the bone.
Want to die? Go to Tombstone!

The Rhymer
Simon Sublette

Simon pushed the tablet back to J. Patrick. That's all he had to say on the matter. Simon thanked J. Patrick for the whiskey and for the conversation, and then got up and left the saloon.

Mississippi Jim Bob

I saw an old friend today ~ his name is Mississippi Jim Bob.
I first ran into him in Dodge, when we were working the same job.
He's not a gunfighter ~ he's just a gambler by trade.
I saw him over by the cantina ~ he was standing in the shade.

Jim Bob Purcell was a red headed, half Cajun, half something else, from Louisiana, but told everyone he was from Mississippi. No one knew why he was running from the law. Some said he had done a stint of running guns to the Indians. He also claimed he had a law degree, but the only law Jim Bob practiced, was law that fit his situation at the moment. Simon called him Mississippi Jim Bob.

Mississippi Jim Bob traveled with his cousins, Ollie Gerald and Rudy Tom. Mississippi Jim Bob, Ollie Gerald and Rudy Tom were mainly gamblers and hucksters looking for easy money.

Simon waved and went to greet his old acquaintance.

"Mississippi, it's good to see you again....tell me, just how in the hell have you been?"

Mississippi grinned from ear to ear. He was looking around, nervously, looking back and forth, like he didn't want anyone to see him.

"Hey, Si—mone, keep it quiet I'm on the run again."

"I should have known, it is just like old times, isn't it?"

"You ought to know. Hey, Si—mone, don't know if you know it or not but two feller's named Taggett are askin' about, inquirin' as to your whereabouts. We seen 'em 'bout a week ago over near La Mesilla, they sure got a hankerin' to find ya, Si—mone. What'd ya do, steal their sister's virginity or somethin'?"

"Yeah, I heard. They were here a few days back, but the trouble is for their brother not their sister."

"Whoo—whee, Si—mone, didn't know you cared for little boys?" Mississippi said as he laughed.

Simon started laughing. Mississippi always did make Simon laugh. "Mississippi, you have a devious mind. Their brother was young....skunk drunk....and on the losing end of a conversation with my sawed—off. I tried to back it off....but for him, killing me was all that mattered....so for some whiskey—caused wrong thinking....he got himself all splattered."

"Well, maybe that's right. But them Taggetts, now they aim to kill ya, Si—mone. Me and Rudy Tom told 'em we saw ya in Tascosa; thought they went that way, guess not. I was hopin' they had, and then maybe you'd owe us one."

"Like I said, they were here a couple of days ago. They're like most of us though, they get their jaw set on something then they're hell bent to get it done. The Taggett's think they want to tangle with me but they really don't. They shouldn't let this pretty angelic face of mine fool them. If they bite my ass, I might drag them to death. I might not let them go, and they will get hurt....they'll just end up like their brother, face down, bleeding on the dirt."

"Maybe, maybe so, they sure looked meaner than hell to me. Might just meet your match, Si–mone, maybe you want me and Rudy Tom to plant 'em for ya. They wouldn't be expectin' it from us. Shoot, we could walk right up to 'em, and pop, they'd be dead."

"Nah, let it pass. They're just farmers. Where are Rudy Tom and Ollie Gerald anyway?"

"I brought Rudy Tom over to the depot a while ago to fetch us some tickets for Reno. We're gettin' outta here first thing in the mornin'. Now as for Ollie Gerald, he's dead. He took a knife down in Sonora. Some meskin carved him over a woman. Shoot you know, we'd kinda like to find the greasy no good tortilla eater 'cept me and Rudy Tom was drunk, and laid up, and no one would tell us who done it. We got someone to be suspicious about, but you know Si–mone, knowin' Ollie Gerald like I did, he probably had it comin'. But listen, I might need your kind of help. Me and Rudy Tom got a real mean 'un a chasin' us. I'll buy us a drink and tell ya about it."

Simon and Mississippi went into the cantina. Simon told Mississippi about Tombstone, Melina, the Earp brothers, Doc Holiday and the Hair Takers. He also made sure Mississippi Jim Bob understood that not all Mexicans were greasers—or tortilla eaters. He was stern about it.

Mississippi knew not to say that again. Mississippi was about the tell Simon the story of the man who was trailing him and Rudy Tom but was interrupted when Rudy Tom come in.

Simon saw Rudy Tom enter the saloon, and he also saw that a very large, sinister looking man followed behind.

The man walked up to Mississippi. Mississippi knew the man.

Simon guessed that this was the man looking for Mississippi and Rudy Tom. Mississippi had a right to be concerned. This was one large, mean looking man. Simon stepped from behind Mississippi, so he could have a free firing lane if it became necessary. Simon motioned the derringer into his left hand and laid his left hand on the bar. The derringer was in full view.

"Purcell, when people lie to me and cheat me, I don't take to it so well." The large man spoke, looking directing at Mississippi, ignoring Simon and the derringer. "And you're a lying, cheating, no–good lowlife son–of–a–pig–shitting–bitch if ever one was born to a woman. I want my money back, or I'm going to take me some lily white Cajun–assed hide for payment."

Mississippi moved his hand toward his gun. "Get outta my face, cockroach. You knew the risk going in. It was a fair deal. Me and Rudy Tom lost our money, too, but we ain't lookin' to kill someone for it. Grow up. You and the bankers you work for are all the same. You'll give us money as long as you think you get a piece of the action and can collect some interest. You thought it was a good deal going in but when it turns sour you still want your profit. You ain't risk takers. You're worse than train robbers. You, of all people, should know that sometimes bidness deals don't work out. Now git on outta here and save your skin, your wife wouldn't want ya comin' home without all of that purty hair of yours, would she?"

In the middle of Mississippi's speech, the man noticed Simon and the derringer. He continued to look at Simon until Mississippi finished talking. Somehow the man knew who Simon was. One wrong move and the man knew he was dead. The man never said another word. He stood there for a moment, then turned and left.

"Well, Simon, guess I showed him, didn't I?"

"Yeah, Mississippi, you showed him, showed him good." Simon grinned. "But why did you call him cockroach? Most men would have called him a son of a bitch or the son of a whore but not the cockroach!"

"Cause he's so low he is a cockroach or worse. Besides Simon, you know I ain't given much to cussin'."

"How much did you take him for?"

"Not enough to risk gettin' killed over, just enough for me and Rudy Tom to get to Reno, get us into the gold minin' bidness."

"Are you prospecting for real or you just setting up camp so you can do some stealing?"

"Minin' is minin'. Nobody ever wrote it down that a man had to use a shovel. Me and Rudy Tom just found another way of diggin' that's all. Anyway what we gonna do is become gold speculators. We gonna buy it for one price and sell it for another. Shoot Si–mone you ought a come and go with us. We could cut you in for ten percent."

"Ten percent, it looks like a third to me."

"A third, no way, we like you Si—mone but we thought of it first. Nope, bidness is bidness and a third is horse shit."

Evidently, Mississippi did not think saying horse shit was cussing. Simon started laughing.

Mississippi always makes me laugh, I didn't want to see him go.
The next morning I put Mississippi on the stage, the one bound for Reno.
Mississippi said he preferred the company of the ladies who are painted.
Even though they're a little rough, and used, and a little tainted.
He said, "For the short time I'm with them, I'm perfect and can do no wrong,
and then when I'm tired of them, you can just leave and be alone.
You can gamble your money and can have whiskey to drink,
and you don't have to worry about being told what to think.
You see a marrying woman wants you to stop gambling and drinking,
and more often than not, she'll be telling you what you should be thinking.
And your needs they'll no longer serve.
I think that a woman's ring finger has a special nerve.
When a man says I do, with that gold band, that nerve gets cut.
Because then they say I don't and their legs go shut.
I guess I agree with him, but hell, I can't be tending a wife.
They'd just end up dead trying to live my kind of life.

I bought me a new great coat today and also a waistcoat for a vest.
I don't care for a vest too much ~ the waistcoat always did serve me best.
I also got me a new white shirt and a fancy string tie.
These are fine clothes, nice enough to be buried in when I die.

Simon was awakened, scared awake actually, from his sleep that night by a nightmare. The same nightmare he had been having for years. He thought that maybe, just maybe, writing it down might clear it from his head and be gone forever.

The Nightmare

They handcuffed me and threw me into a cell.
Being in Yuma prison is surely the same as being in hell.
The rats run across your boots, and the roaches and bugs run up your leg.
Men go insane from the solitude ~ they lay in the floor and beg.
The wailing of the lost souls puts my sanity at stake.
As I pace the dirt floor, I wonder just when my mind will break.
Now I see a crack above the window, from which I can flee.
If I can kick that window loose then I can be free.
I beat and kick that crack with hands and feet bloody ~ finally it comes loose.
I step through to the other side, right into a hangman's noose.
My neck is stretched thin, and I can feel it about to break.
Then suddenly and gladly, I finally awake.
Dreams seem real and sometimes can be quite hellish.
This one keeps coming back ~ it will again ~ a thought I don't relish.

While Simon was in Albuquerque, he received a telegram from Mr. Harris, the man who owned the big ranch near Ft. Sumner, New Mexico. Mr. Harris wanted Simon to come and do some work for him. Simon wondered about Brock Deaton and where fate had finally taken him. It did not take Simon long to leave Albuquerque. He would ask Mr. Harris, when he got to the ranch, how he came to find him in Albuquerque.

Fort Sumner, New Mexico

Being alone, the solitude is good, but the longer you're on the trail,
lonesome tends to take its toll, and your thoughts turn to the female.
My mind wanders to Melina Madera. She's a special woman you know.
The only thing I can figure out is that she has more fire down below.
Then there is Abigail, but I didn't know her in a carnal way,
but something about her, keeps me wanting to see her some day.
She said she was going to Ft. Sumner, perhaps she will be there.
I hope she's doing well, for her good health, I still care.

The Taggett brothers rode into Albuquerque today, while I was riding out.
Guess we'll cross someday ~ to that, I now have no doubt.
Most men just can't leave the revenge alone,
and in their craze, it matters not right or wrong.
I'm over by the Texas ~ New Mexico border to work a little for an old client.
He wants an escort for his wife and daughter, and he wants someone reliant.
They're to travel through some rough land on their way to visit a sick friend
I have done work for Mr. Harris before, and he has sent for me again.

Simon arrived in Ft. Sumner and was in the Redondo saloon waiting for the Harris women, Mrs. Harris and her daughter, Cindy, to arrive. Simon was to escort the women to Tascosa, Texas. He inquired of the bartender to the whereabouts of Miss Abigail Sweeney, a nurse. No one in the saloon had heard of her. While Simon was making his inquiry, a man carrying a gun came into the saloon, walked to Simon's table and spoke.

"You here to compete for the Harris escort job?"

"No, I am not."

"I heard you were."

"There isn't anything to compete for."

"Sure there is. I saw the ladies. They are on their way."

Simon studied the man's face. "You hear wrong....now leave me alone."

"I need that job, mister."

"I've been hired. It's settled."

"Well, that may be true, but if you don't show, well, then Mr. Harris would need to hire another man, now wouldn't he?"

"And what in God's good name could cause me not to show?"

"I could cause that," the man said.

Simon did not move from his chair. He moved the derringer into its killing position and at the same time moved his coat to the side revealing his forty–five. Revealing his forty–five to the man was only for show—and distraction. Simon would shoot him with the derringer.

"Tell me, mister, whoever you are. Are you a gunfighter?"

"I make a living like that some. A man's got to eat."

"You know, Shooter Man, lying on a dirty floor bleeding....don't sound like food to me....that's all you're going to get here....dead is all you're getting from me."

The man weighed his position carefully, and then slowly backed away and left.

Simon finished his drink real slow. Simon knew the gunman would be back, the fighting and poison were in his blood. He left his derringer in position.

It was only a short time until the gunman walked back in the door. "I just had to come back. I can't leave 'till this is settled."

"Yeah, I know. It's always the same for our kind....it's the poison....it confuses the mind. It settles in behind your eyes....gets under the skin.... you can't be rid of it....can't be normal....ever again." As he had done before, Simon moved his coat to the side to reveal his forty–five. "So tell me, Shooter Man....why is it you want to die....should I send you to hell.... so you can ask the devil why?"

The gunman knew who Simon was, and for a brief second let a flash of fear cross his face. It was the gunman's moment of truth. He could either continue, or he could turn and walk out the place.

When the fears hits, it sends a bolt of reality up the spine.
A man can either deal with it, or he can grovel and whine.
The man smiled, the dead man's smile, how many times had I seen it before?
My bullet crashed through his chest and then his body crashed to the floor.
These fights can be avoided. Another human life doesn't need to go to waste.
But the poison sets in, and some men won't spit it out, once they get a taste.
I collected Mrs. Harris and daughter ~ the undertaker collected his fee.
Mrs. Harris was happy to see the Rhymer, the town was glad to be rid of me.

Another man burned ~ another lesson not learned.

The gunman never had a chance. Simon shot him with his derringer and left the saloon with the man lying, dying, on the floor.

Simon found the Harris women and they departed immediately for a ranch near Tascosa, Texas. Simon learned Mr. Harris was sick, or he would have made the trip himself.

Mrs. Harris told Simon she was afraid Mr. Harris was dying. Mrs. Harris told him Jarred Reeves had been killed by one of Billy the Kid's gang.

Simon asked about Brock Deaton and was told Brock had been involved in fighting with some other rustlers but survived and had left the Harris ranch over a year ago.

Mrs. Harris told Simon she thought Brock Deaton had gone to somewhere near Sweetwater, Texas.

Simon asked them about Abigail. He was surprised and happy when they said they knew of this lady named Abigail Sweeney. She had worked in the infirmary and once attended to Mr. Harris for his illness, but she wasn't there anymore.

Simon was fearful he had lost track of Abigail.

As Simon and the Harris women were nearing the edge of town. the pot bellied constable of Ft. Sumner finally came to the saloon.

The dead gunman was being attended to by the coroner.

"What happened here?" asked the constable.

A saloon girl spoke before the coroner could answer. "Sir, that man layin' on the floor dead …"

"Yeah, what about him?" the constable interrupted.

"Well, he picked a fight with this other man. He talked funny."

"Who talked funny, this one?"

"No, the other man, the man that shot this one."

"How you mean, talked funny?"

"His sentences, you know. They rhymed, like poetry of some kind."

"What do you mean, rhymed?" the constable asked, excitably.

"After he'd shot 'im, he walked over to us and said, all the kings' horses and all the kings' men, won't ever put him together again."

"Was he a stocky feller, with a big scar on his cheek?"

"Yeah, yeah, stocky, with a scar, that's him, you know him?"

"And he talked in rhymes?"

"Sure enough," the girl said as she and the others nodded in agreement.

"The Rhymer, shit!" the constable said as he swallowed hard and let out a big sigh. He took off his hat and wiped his brow, he was nervous. "Damn, where is he now?"

"He left with two women in a buckboard, headed out of town to the east."

"Good riddance." The constable did not relish having to confront the Rhymer in person. He certainly didn't want to arrest him. If he was leaving town, it was okay by him.

"You know what else?"

"What's that?"

"That funny talkin' feller didn't even draw his gun. He had one hid in his other hand. That poor feller layin' on the floor didn't even have a chance."

"They never do."

The moment of truth, that moment tells no lies.
To me, that's the moment when another man dies.
It's the moment when you finally realize,
that you get one more breath before you finally close your eyes.
And some say that right before you die, you see your life and how you spent it.
All of your years flash before your eyes in just a single minute.

Simon wondered about what he had just written. He heard many times that your life flashes in front of your eyes as you are about die. He thought maybe those he had sent to their grave were too busy trying to figure out how to stay alive rather than have time to think about how their entire life was spent.

Chapter Five

Texas Sweet Talk

I delivered them unharmed ~ the whole way charmed,
by both daughter and mother.
The work was o.k. ~ so was the pay,
but it's not what I'd druther.
I'm not the sort to dally about and make idle talk with their kind.
I headed to the nearest saloon for whiskey, a perhaps a stimulus for my mind.
I'm fresh back to Texas ~ the air here sure is clean and sweet.
A most handsome young lady was the first person I happened to meet.

The trip from Ft. Sumner to Tascosa took most part of a week. There were some Indians and bandits that roamed the plains of eastern New Mexico and the panhandle of Texas requiring Simon to stay alert, especially after the sun set for the day. Simon was not comfortable with the small talk the women engaged in during the evening. Their talk and their subject matter were, at times, foreign to Simon. He tried his best though and was polite throughout the whole trip. Simon lacked the proper education to be conversationally literate about some subjects they discussed. Most of Simon's education came from listening and learning in the saloons and his encounters with people from different places and cultures across the country. Simon liked his women less frilly, just a bit rougher, although Abigail wasn't on the rough side, but she certainly was different than the Harris women. He used his guard duty as an excuse to evade the talk, going off into the night to be alone. He was glad, though he did not show it, when they finally arrived at Tascosa and he delivered the Harris women to their destination, the X-Bar-T ranch. Simon noticed something he had not seen before—fences made of wire with barbs.

As soon as Simon saw to the delivery of the Harris women to the ranch, he rode to the town of Tascosa and checked into the town's only hotel. Down the street from the hotel, toward the red light district, was the Equity saloon. Tied in front of the saloon were several horses. Simon presumed they belonged to cowboys from the surrounding ranches. The last thing he wanted was a run in with some over served cowboy. He saw another saloon next door to the hotel. He went there to have his first drink of whiskey in several days. He could imagine the feel of the whiskey burning his throat as he walked across the dusty alley and up the stairs. He stood outside the door, with his eyes closed for a few moments before he entered. He wanted his eyes to adjust to the dim light as quickly as possible.

Simon quickly opened his eyes and dashed around the corner. Much to his surprise, the saloon was bright and airy. It wasn't like any saloon he had been in before. This saloon was more like a hotel lobby. It had several windows on each wall decorated with curtains. The curtains were drawn open and the windows were raised. The clean fresh air was gently blowing into the saloon. The curtains were softly swaying in the breeze. The saloon was clean and smelled good, not like most saloons he had frequented. The air smelled cleaner, sweeter to Simon this particular day. He could not put his finger on why, but it just did.

Simon looked around and most of the people in the saloon were fashionably dressed. Simon, in his dirty range clothes, was out of place. Simon wondered if there was a funeral or wedding going on in town because most all the patrons were dressed in what he called "Sunday clothes." Sunday clothes, suits and ties for the men, pretty full slipped dresses for the women. He was embarrassed with his clothes, dusty and dirty from the trip. He went back outside, and using his hat, he rapidly dusted his coat and pants, and then went back inside. He was as presentable as he could get. He considered getting a bath, but the desire for the whiskey overruled the bath.

Simon found a table in a back corner, out of the way. It suited him to be as less noticeable as possible. He ordered a bottle of whiskey, the saloon's finest brand. He deserved it after the trip he just made. And he could afford the expensive brand with the money he was paid. Sitting at the table next to him was a young, pretty woman. He had not noticed her when he selected his table. It would have made his choice much easier if he had seen her. He didn't notice her until after he had ordered his bottle of whiskey. Simon had a couple of drinks. While he drank he wondered what a woman, alone, was doing in a saloon, unless she was a working girl. It wasn't proper for a young woman to be in a saloon by herself. Eventually, he struck up a conversation with the woman.

"Ma'am, you know. I couldn't help but notice …"

The woman looked Simon's way.

"That you're pretty good looking....for a woman." Simon smiled, his charming smile—not his killing smile. And then Simon chuckled. He was suddenly euphoric. Ah, he thought, is it the clean air, the pretty woman, or both?

The woman smiled back. It was one of those fake, courteous smiles. "Really, what a comment to make, how flattering. What are you cowboy, a sheep lover?"

When Simon heard her voice, he almost melted. It was one of those voices you hear that only comes from women of the south. Her voice was a deep, Texas, southern accent. He had not heard a voice like that in so long. He almost jumped out of his chair. He picked up his glass and bottle, and without asking, left his table and sat down at her table.

"Or maybe you're a horse lover," she continued still smiling. "Oh no, I got it, you must be one of those men who likes other men!"

"Well where I been....sheep would've been better than some of the women....and I do like my horse. But I'm not into men or boys....no, when it comes right down to it....I still prefer a soft woman, of course."

"That's comforting. Where is this place you've been that sheep are better than women? Sounds like a real southern lady could make a good living there?"

"Ever heard of Tombstone, in the Arizona territory?"

"Just in idle talk, is that where it is?"

Simon nodded his head yes.

"No thanks. I heard that place is dreadful, just rocks and stickers."

"Well, it's somewhat different than that, but it is a rough town. You might describe some of the citizen's demeanors as rocks and stickers."

Simon and the woman continued the small talk and became very friendly. The woman would lean over to Simon, put her hand on his leg and whisper small talk in his ear. Simon was becoming aroused and his blood was beginning to run hot. The woman was in the same state of mind.

"You know, sir. I don't know what kind of lady you think I am, but we've been sitting here carrying on, and we haven't even been introduced."

Simon put his arm around the woman's shoulders and gently kissed her cheek. "My name's Sublette, Simon Sublette....and your voice, well, I haven't heard any like it in, I don't remember when. I've never heard a voice as sweet as yours....in all the places I have been."

She whispered in my ear ~ God it was good to hear the accent again.
I don't know if it was the voice ~ or the words ~ that gave chills to my skin.
She talked sweetly ~ and real low in that Southern accent.
Instantly from cold to hot is how my blood went.

The woman slightly pulled away from Simon. She blinked, slowly, several times. "Well, I'll be snookered. You're Rhymin' Simon, aren't you? Well pull up my skirt and spank my bottom. I heard all about you. Those stories they tell about you, are they true?"

She whispered "You're Rhymin' Simon. I've heard all the all that's been told."
When she said it, I became chilled ~ it made my hot turn cold.
I don't like that name ~ I can't figure why it gives me the chill.
It is grating to my nerves ~ I can't get used to it, never will.
It's a state of mind. That's sad, a silly name making me so mad.

Simon grabbed the woman's hair, slowly he pulled her head back and brought her face close to his, and then he pulled her hair hard enough she could feel the pain.

"You can call me The Rhymer....or Poet....or Simon....it all means the same....but I just don't cotton....to the Rhymin' Simon name."

The woman stuck out her tongue and lightly licked Simon's lips. She was slightly afraid of Simon at this moment, but she was not going to let him know of her fear.

Simon eased the hold on her hair but kept her face close to his. "Talk some more Texas Sweet Talk....it's been a while....talk sweet to me....make the Rhymer smile."

From that moment on, the woman only called him Simon. Eventually, she and Simon took a room upstairs—the whole time she never quit smiling.

Simon enjoyed a few good evenings with the woman. He gave her the name, Texas Sweet Talk. Her given name was Caroline Endryl.

One evening, while she slept, Simon was unable to get to sleep. He got up and went downstairs and found a late night card game.

It was just after dawn ~ it was just me and the barkeep.
I was having one last whiskey ~ before heading up to get some sleep.
I was at the end of the bar ~ the one closest to the back door.
Experience taught this best ~ I could see the entire floor.

"Give me one more Jones, and then I'll be out of your way."

The doors to the saloon opened and two men quickly stepped inside with their weapons drawn. One of the Taggett brothers pointed his gun toward Simon.

Simon knew who they were.

Tanner Taggett said, "We finally found you, you bastard, after all these years."

"Yeah, I guess we finally meet." Simon answered. "Which one are you?"

"I'm Tanner Taggett, this here is Josh." Tanner said pointing to his brother Josh.

Simon knew the faces of Tanner and Josh Taggett. He had seen them many times before. Now he could put the names to the faces. Simon could see Tanner was nervous and had begun to fret. The Taggett brothers, Tanner and Josh, thought Simon, finally, here, for real. The Demon surfaced but for some reason stayed calm. The Demon would wait and see how they wanted to play out the hand.

Josh said, "You gunned down our little brother, then rode away. Me and Tanner want satisfaction right here and now."

"You're a long way from Tularosa. Why haven't you spit this out by now? It's been years since it happened."

Neither of the Taggett brothers responded.

"Let me tell you how that fight was really done....I'd turned my back to leave....when your brother pulled his gun. I tried to avoid it....tried best I could....didn't the barkeep tell you....said he would."

Again there was no response from the Taggett brothers.

"I had to shoot back....or be killed in that fight....your brother was skunk drunk....he wouldn't listen to what was right."

Josh said, "It doesn't make no never mind how that fight happened, you know that. We have to kill you just so we can save face. We've been hunting you a long time."

"Why don't you go back home....and lay claim for my death....tell everyone in Tularosa you took my final breath. You can claim I groveled, begged not to die....save your name, say each one shot me in an eye."

Tanner and Josh quickly exchanged glances. They were weighing their chances.

"And another thing my friend....I promise I won't ever go to that part of your country again. I want to end this right now....one way or the other. You can leave unharmed....or you both can join your little brother."

Simon moved the derringer into his left hand. His being at the end of the bar obscured his hands from the Taggett brothers' view. They had no idea that Simon had taken his forty–five from its holster.

Simon stepped from behind the bar revealing his drawn weapon, pointing it at Tanner's stomach. "Now look, you've probably lost all you own....with the hunting and tracking me down....do you want to lose your life too....and then be planted in foreign ground?"

The Taggett brothers looked back and forth to each other. This was not how they had expected for this to happen. Neither of them thought it would be this hard to kill a man. They also had not thought about taking him on face to face. They thought he might run and they could shoot him while he was running. Someone had given them the wrong word on Simon Sublette.

"The barkeep will sign a paper....telling your people what is true. He'll vouch for the fact you killed the Rhymer....tell them it was a fair fight too. Jones, write the words."

"So tell me....do you really want to die?" Simon paused to let them think about it, and then said, "Think about it....why not back on off....and just let it pass on by?"

I watched their eyes as they carefully weighed the consequences.
Reality went to their head, and they came to their senses.

The Taggett brothers quickly agreed with Simon. They took the paper Jones had written, quickly read it, and then slowly walked backwards to the door.

"I won't speak to you any more in a rhyme....if I see you again....I'll kill you....both at the same time."

Jones went to the door and watched the Taggett brothers get on their horses and ride west towards New Mexico. "That was a good thing you did, Rhymer, letting them boys live like that. Reckon why they chased you for so long then didn't want to fight?"

"Fighting wouldn't have changed anything. They're just regular people and it was easy for them to back off, with no witnesses and all. I don't know why....they come after me like they do....they should know they can't kill me....hell, Jones....there was only two."

Simon smiled at Jones and drank down his last drink.

Jones smiled also.

"They'll go home now....and claim they sent me to my grave....that way their lives....and their honor they can save."

Simon started up the stairs to rejoin the warmth of Sweet Talk in bed.

He paused and turned toward Jones. "That was a good thing you did too, Jones, writing the paper for them."

He continued up the stars and without looking back at Jones said, "I tell you Jones....some get brave and get killing on their mind....but then lose their nerve....when they finally have to face one of my kind."

What normal, sane man wouldn't, thought Jones.

I paid Jones to guard my room, I needed my sleep.
Guys like me have to be careful of the company we keep.
I feel better now that I got a good night's rest.
What happened yesterday morn was for the best.
~

Texas Sweet Talk and I boarded the Fort Worth train at noon.
With her along on board ~ it will get there way too soon.
The train chugged, chugged along, singing its working song.
Train, Train, take us away from this town,
The Rhymer and the Sweet Talk are Fort Worth bound.

Simon and Texas Sweet Talk rode the train from Tascosa to Fort Worth. Sweet Talk eventually got around to asking Simon about some of his encounters. She asked about how he came to talk in rhymes and about the gunman in Fort Sumner and the confrontation with the Taggett brothers.

Simon told her about some of his escapades, all though he omitted a few, and how he had slowly built a reputation. He did not tell her about Johnny Ringo. He wanted the blame for that killing to remain secret. He told her about the beginning, being shot in the face, and about losing his toes. He told her of the poison that takes hold of men who live by the gun and how they are compelled to prove their manhood and how it gets in the way of sane thinking. That kind of thinking almost got the Taggett brothers killed. Even if they know your reputation is that of a cold dead killer, some still try to make a name. He explained it to her as they sit sipping champagne one evening on the train.

"You know, Sweet Talk....a man like me can't live on his reputation.... even for a day....it'd be nice if when they learned your name....they'd be fearful and just go away. When they come you must prove yourself....

you have to make a stand....all the disbelievers....have to find out if the reputation fits the man."

The bubbly liquor helped free Simon's tongue.

"Just like the man in Fort Sumner, they're willing to risk all....not heeding what's known for a fact....they still seek your defeat....it's remarkable how some men act. But experience has taught me....that the disbelievers always fall short....I win and they lose....and the coroner has another obituary to report. Some will still try....even though they've seen me in action....I think the devil is somehow....getting some sort of satisfaction."

Idle time on the train,
sipping whiskey, drinking champagne,
from the killing ~ a refrain
Sex with Caroline Endryl,
fuels the heat, satisfies the will,
for the duration ~ the only thrill.

Simon and Texas Sweet Talk spent a few days in Fort Worth. They spent their time dining in fine places and drinking in the saloons. They only ventured once into Fort Worth's Hells Half Acre.

Hell's Half Acre was located on the south of town, covering about four square blocks, and contained Fort Worth's "red–light district." Hell's Half Acre was an aggregation of one and two story saloons, dance halls and bawdy houses, with an occasional empty lot. There were also a few legitimate businesses. It got started being the first place cowboys saw when they drove the herds of cattle to the railway. Only those looking for trouble or excitement ventured into the Acre. The train station was located on the south end of the Acre. It was Sweet Talk's first exposure, walking through the Acre to find suitable accommodations.

It was a quiet time for Simon and a grand time for Texas Sweet Talk. Sweet Talk spent her days promenading the streets of Fort Worth, window shopping in the fancy stores. Simon mostly slept during the day and spent the evenings with Sweet Talk. It was peaceful in Fort Worth for Simon.

Caroline thought they could settle here and find legitimate employment. She mentioned it to Simon one evening over dinner.

"A legitimate job, now I wonder what that would be for me. A dry goods clerk I am not....working at a foundry is way too hot. Guess I could work in a hotel....go running every time someone rang a bell."

"I'm sure we could find something. For me, I would be just fine in a dress shop. I found one. The lady told me she needed some help."

"My temperament, for now, isn't suited for these civilized folks, so working here and settling down, no, it's not the right time. You could go to Nellie Jacks. A woman like you could make more money with her than with a dress shop."

"Maybe I don't want that kind of life."

"My opinion is you should make all you can while you have your looks. You can find you a rich man later and then be a wife. I have things I must do and people I must see....a legit job isn't in the cards for me."

The argument was useless and Caroline discontinued the discussion.

Simon did not tell Caroline that he had enough money that he did not need to work, not now, maybe not ever. Simon was a frugal man and did not allow himself many luxuries. He had the money from the sale of the family farm and had never touched the proceeds. He had made it a practice to save half of each bounty he had collected. He lived on the rest and on payments for services performed. In some people's terms, Simon James Sublette was a rich man.

Texas Sweet Talk told Simon about a high stakes poker game she had heard being discussed and thought it might something he would like. She said it was run by some cardsharp and he was sending everyone to the poor house.

Simon asked Sweet Talk to find out more about the game. It might be of some interest to him.

Sweet Talk told Simon the next day that the man doing all the winning was called Calico, but the game had folded. For some reason, this man named Calico had taken his winnings, and most of Fort Worth's money, and had left town.

The name sounded familiar, but Simon couldn't quite put his finger on it. Simon knew why Calico had left Fort Worth in a hurry. Some called him the Calico Kid. He knew Calico was somehow cheating these people out of their money.

Texas Sweet Talk was curled up in Simon's arms. It was just at daybreak. They lay naked on the bed with the sheets drawn back. The morning breeze gently cooled their bodies after they had enjoyed rigorous pre–dawn sex.

"Simon, I've decided you're right about what you've been saying. I'm going to Nellie Jacks to work. When can we leave?"

"I'm not going with you. I've got other things I have to do."

"You mean to go see those men friends of yours?"

"Yeah, I told them I'd drop in first chance I got."

"What you mean is you'd rather spend time with them than with me?"

"No, what I mean is, I told someone I'd do something, and I plan to do just that. Besides, Nellie doesn't care much for me."

"That's not much of an excuse."

"Why is it you women have to make something out of nothing?" Simon rolled over, got out of bed, washed his face, and began to put on his clothes.

"I'm not making a big deal. Let me go with you?"

"No. I'm going on horseback and you don't ride, remember? Go on to Nellie's and I'll meet up with you later."

"When, how much later?"

"Hell, I don't know? Later, that's all!" Simon was becoming irritated.

"If that's the way you feel, don't bother." Texas Sweet Talk was getting mad. "You want to go hang around a bunch of foul mouthed, bad breathed, cow shit smelling men instead of a sweet talking, sweet smelling woman, then go on."

"Are you ragging my ass for a reason....or are you just ragging to find it pleasing?"

"I'm not ragging your ass, Simon. You'll come crawling back when you want something sweet, but don't tarry too long, love. I might find me another man by then."

"There aren't any strings on you Sweet Talk....do whatever you need to do....do you think you can find another man to satisfy like I do? You know when you've had the best....it's hard to find another who can stand the test."

"Is that right? It works out both ways, I would imagine."

"Yep, when you've had the best is hard to find any better. It's what my dear old daddy used to say....anyway."

"So what do you do when you're out on the trail by yourself? Don't you get lonely?"

"That's what I like about it, the solitude. I just find me a nice piece of ground, make a fire, and sit back and listen to nature, have a drink or two. It's serene, peaceful, one of the simple pleasures in life."

Simon sat down on the edge of the bed and gave Sweet Talk a kiss, and then left.

Texas Sweet Talk sat up in bed to watch Simon leave. She knew Simon was a hard case, but she was beginning to fall in love with him. She also thought that he would only be gone a couple of weeks.

Texas Sweet Talk moved on ~ I decided to move on too.
The Palomino Palace is a good place for me ~ and what I like to do.
Do I think I will find my peace in one of these bawdy saloons?
Would perhaps one of them have a "peace and quiet" room?
Instead of being only a place of cheap whiskey and games of chance,
and parlaying with women for pay, in a meaningless horizontal dance.
I don't believe one would find Proper women of any sort.
One who is like your mother, on whom you could call and court?
The places I'm drawn to, only the rowdy and lustful congregate.
It must be my visceral appetite I am trying to sate.
Maybe in Sweetwater I could go to a social, drink milk or sweet tea,
and meet a fine young lass who would bring a healing light to me.
The Demon would have to stay hidden ~ not do those things forbidden.

Palomino Palace

Simon rode into Sweetwater, Texas. He arrived a few minutes after noon. The smells of the dinners cooking in the hotels, saloons and homes were pleasing. He was hungry. He could hear an anvil ringing. It was making a rhythmical sound. He heard someone singing to the beat of the pounding on the anvil. The sun was at its highest point of the day, beating down on the dry parched street with hot daggers. The heat was coming from both directions. It was being belched up from the hard packed sand and dirt of the street, and rained down in razor sharp spears bouncing off the tin roofs of the buildings. A slight breeze was blowing making the air almost bearable. It was a Wednesday and few people were about. The heat kept most off the streets. They were inside for protection. There were other sounds coming from the street. The sounds of a rolling wagons and a dog barking was mixed with the sounds of the anvil and the singing. The anvil and the singing could be heard clear to the edge of the town.

"Mammy's little baby loves short'nin', short'nin'
Mammy's little baby loves short'nin' bread.
Three little fellers ~ lyin' in bed
two was sick ~ an' the other most dead
sent for the doctor ~ the doctor said
feed those chillun on short'nin' bread.
Mammy's little baby loves short'nin', short'nin'
Mammy's little baby loves short'nin' bread"

Simon rode past the saloon, the sheriff's office and on to the livery stable. The ringing of the anvil and the singing continued. The closer he got to the livery, the louder the singing and the louder the beat of the anvil became. The singing was in perfect time with the ringing of the anvil. The ringing of the anvil was like a drummers beat.

"When them chillun ~ sick in da bed
heard that talk ~ 'bout short'nin' bread
popped up well ~ and dance and sing
skippin' 'round ~ cut the pigeon wing
Mammy's little baby loves short'nin', short'nin'
Mammy's little baby loves short'nin' bread.
So put on the skillet, slip on the led
Mammy's gwine to make a little short'nin' bread

that ain't all ~ she's gwine to do
Mammy's gwine to make some coffee too."

Simon halted his horse in front of the livery and dismounted. He could see the blacksmith in the shadows of the stable. Simon removed the sawed–off shotgun from the saddle. He hobbled around for a few minute or two, stretching his legs and trying to get some feeling to come to his right foot. The singing continued. The source of the pounding on the anvil and the singing came from the blacksmith.

"Mammy's little baby loves short'nin', short'nin'
Mammy's little baby loves short'nin' bread.
I slip in the kitchen ~ raised the led
stole me a mess of that short'nin' bread.
I wunk at the gal ~ then I said
baby how'd ya like some short'nin' bread
Mammy's little baby loves short'nin', short'nin'
Mammy's little baby loves short'nin' bread"

Simon limped through the door. The blacksmith continued the pounding, his forging of a horseshoe. As Simon came near, the blacksmith pounded the horseshoe harder and harder, in time with his singing. He hit the horseshoe like he was sending a warning to any man invading his territory.

"Caught me with the skillet ~ caught me with the led
caught me with the gal makin' short'nin' bread
six months fo' the skillet ~ six months fo' the led
six months in jail fo' stealin' short'nin' bread.
Mammy's little baby loves short'nin' bread
Mammy's little baby loves short'nin' bread."

Simon could see that the blacksmith was a large black man. Simon couldn't guess his age, but he was older than Simon. His hair was almost white, a salt and pepper color, and Simon could see he was strong and fit. As the blacksmith sang the last chorus, he slammed the hammer on the anvil with an evil–force, and stood there with the hammer in his hand, staring at Simon.

Simon nodded his head, his way of greeting the blacksmith.

"You need somethin' here mista?" the man asked.

"You got a name, Short'nin' Bread?"

"Yes sur, peoples call me Tandy."

"I kind of like Short'nin' Bread better."

"Don't bother me none, been called worse."

"My name is Simon. I might be here a spell. Can you take good care of that big gray outside?"

"That's my job Mista, yes sur for sure. I'll take right good care of her for ya."

Tandy stood there, magnificent, his muscles rippling and swelling from the hard work. His skin glistened with the sweat caused by the summer heat, and his labor.

"Well, kiss my ass. I'd think my eyes were lying to me if they weren't my own. This is unbelievable."

"What's that Brock?" asked Cordell Pitifore.

"Hide the women, lock up the children, warn all the men, and call the sheriff."

"What the hell are you talking about, has the sun cooked what little brain you got?"

"No, I'm not half baked at all. You won't believe it Cordell, but Simon Sublette just rode into town."

"Bullshit, it can't be. They say he was killed up in Tascosa! You shouldn't try to joke about something like that with an old man. Are you crazy?"

"I'm not crazy, but the town may get that way. I'm not kidding either. No bullshit, it's him, come here and see for yourself."

"What?"

Cordell walked to the door where Brock was standing. "Are you sure about that, that it's him?"

"You know any other big, yellow haired, man who wears a waistcoat vest, a long black coat, has a scar from mouth to ear, walks with a limp and carries a sawed–off shotgun for a side arm?"

Cordell took out his handkerchief and wiped his forehead. "No, can't say I do. Sure sounds like the Rhymer to me."

Cordell looked out the door of the saloon and saw that it was Simon.

"God help us all," he said. "Yeah, it's him all right, in the flesh. He looks to be hot, mean and nasty. I wonder what he is doing here."

"Simon's always mean and nasty, unless you're a woman, then he's just nasty."

Cordell shook his head in agreement.

"Reckon it's a social call, or he's come killing?" asked Brock.

"Don't know. If he's come to kill someone, I wonder who it might be."

"Better go and get him and bring him over before we have to put on our Sunday's and go to some poor soul's funeral."

"He looks like he's put on a little weight to me."

"Are you going to tell him?"

"Not me. I didn't get up this morning aiming to do something stupid to ruin my day."

Simon was still in the shadows inside the livery talking to Tandy Ledbetter when Brock Deaton approached. "Simon, you old cuss, it's Brock Deaton."

Simon turned to see his friend. A smile covered his face wrinkling the corners of his eyes. "Brock Deaton, gosh all mighty damn, it's good to see you again. I'll be." Simon shook Brock's hand. "Thought maybe one of them Bonney boys had killed you....or some rustler had done you in. I was over in Fort Sumner. I asked around. Nobody knew."

"Naw, Bonney and his pals never bothered me. Mr. Harris chased him off, and I didn't see him much after that. And I haven't chased many rustlers since we did a few years back. Any ways, we just hang 'em here soon as we catch 'em. Not much sense spending any more time with 'em than we have too. You taught me that."

"Hang 'em high....stretch 'em until they die. Hell of a lot less messy, isn't it?"

"Mr. Brock," interrupted Tandy, "is this the Simon feller you told me 'bout?"

Brock Deaton nodded his head in agreement.

"This here–a, this be the Rhymin' man?"

Brock patted Simon on the shoulder. "The one and the same Tandy, take good care of him would you?"

"Sure thing, Mr. Brock, I'll take right nice care of Mr. Simon." Tandy laid down the hammer and offered his hand to Simon. "It's good to know ya, Mr. Simon. Heard all 'bout you from Mr. Brock, I heard all them other stories too. Anything else I kin do fo' ya besides the gray?" Tandy didn't know why but he took an instant liking to Simon.

When Simon took Tandy's hand, he marveled at its size. He could feel Tandy's strength. He did not want to have Tandy Ledbetter take a hold of him, in anger, for any reason.

"Well, uh, yeah, if you don't mind. After you feed and water the gray, if it is okay with you, you could take my things over to the hotel and tell them I'll be along directly. I'm going to get a little food and have a drink with Brock here first."

"Yes sur. Tandy will take right good care of Mr. Simon, yeah he will."

Simon turned to leave then turned back to Tandy Ledbetter. "You sing right nice, Short'nin' Bread."

Tandy grinned and waived to them as Brock and Simon walked out of the livery stable.

"Come on. Simon. I'll buy us a drink, there's someone wanting to see you."

"Hope it's a friendly someone. I'm not much in the mood for a fight. I never did like fighting on an empty stomach."

"Hungry huh, you fartin' fresh air?"

Simon had not thought of that expression, or heard it again, since he'd been with Brock Deaton in New Mexico chasing those rustlers. Simon grinned. "No, I ate so much dirt on the trail, I'm fartin' dust clouds."

Brock Deaton laughed.

"I am hungry though, so hungry I could eat a week old dead skunk."

"That's pretty damn hungry, Simon."

"That's real hungry, damn near had to do it once back in Virginia. Where's the food."

"Come on, let's go see him and get some ham and a beer."

"I can sit still for the food and beer, but I'm not into having any company. I'm tired. I need sleep as much as I need the food."

Simon and Brock Deaton walked toward the saloon.

"Where have you been all these years anyway?" asked Brock.

"I went to Tombstone....but the town was too tough....spent the rest in church....'till it got too rough."

"You in a church, I would not have guessed it. It must have been some kind of church."

"It was, but I thinned the congregation some....we differed on a political view....the sawed–off preached the sermon....so here I am with you."

"Didn't know you were into religion and politics?"

Simon smiled. "Oh yeah, you should know, B.D.....there's more here than just this scarred face....they bad mouthed Texans as a whole....so I put them in their resting place."

"Killed a man for cussing Texans?"

"Yes, I did, and I felt better for it."

"Did you kill him hard?"

"Yeah, I did. I killed him....killed all of them, rock hard dead."

For some reason, Brock got really mad. "Goddamned people, why can't they judge a man for what's done instead of for where he's from?"

"Some do....some don't....some let it pass....I won't."

"Wish I had been there."

"Me too....you could have killed a few."

Brock nodded his head.

"Next time I'll just lame them and bring them to you, and you can have a go."

"Deal's a deal."

Simon and Brock Deaton reached the steps leading up to the saloon.

Simon looked up as he started up the steps, the sign above the door read, *PALOMINO PALACE.* The lettering was bold, dark red, and highlighted in yellow. This was the place Cordell Pitifore mentioned when they were in Santa Fe.

They went through the doors. The saloon was dimly lit. Both Simon and Brock Deaton had trouble focusing coming from the harsh sunlight to the darkened saloon. This was the one thing Simon disliked about coming into a saloon's front door during the day light hours—momentarily—until he got his saloon eyes—he could not see, and he was vulnerable. He preferred to come in the back way, enter by the hall, that way his eyes could adjust by the time he entered the main room.

"You be Simon Sublette, the Rhymin' man?" a voice from the dark asked, in a surly tone.

Simon did not recognize the voice. Was it an enemy, someone looking to do harm? A subtle move of his left hand and the derringer was ready. He could not see clearly yet, but he did not panic. It was not his nature. He had trained all his senses to locate a man by the direction from where his voice came, but he preferred to buy time until his eyes adjusted.

"Excuse me. I didn't catch what you said. Who are you looking for?"

"I asked if you are the Rhymer, you know, the man who talks in rhymes?"

Simon could now make out the shape of a man. It was the man from where the voice came. Simon could not tell if the man was holding a gun. Simon whispered, "B.D., can you see anything? Can you see who's talking to us?"

Brock Deaton heard the hammers on the shotgun cock into firing position. Shit, thought Brock, Simon is going to kill Cordell if I don't act fast.

"It's okay, Simon. Ease off those hammers. The voice is an old friend of yours from Santa Fe. He isn't armed. He's just funning you a bit. You remember Cordell Pitifore don't you?"

Finally, Simon had his saloon eyes and could see. The man's face on who he had fixed his attention was Cordell Pitifore. Simon looked around. Cordell, Brock Deaton and Simon were the only people in the saloon.

Simon laid the sawed–off shotgun across his chest and eased off the hammers. "Goddamn, Cordell, I was fixing to apply some buckshot to your torso. You shouldn't prank on me like that, me being jumpy like I am."

"You're as jumpy as a lizard on a hot rock I'd say."

"How have you been anyway?"

"I've been fine. You wouldn't have killed me Simon. I would have talked to you long enough for you to get your saloon eyes. I wasn't going get in no conversation with that sawed–off of yours. I know how you are, saw for myself."

"That's good to know." Simon grinned.

Simon looked around. The Palomino Palace was built almost exactly like the Grand Hotel in Tombstone. The Palace was larger, had a bigger bar and the furniture was better. The Palomino Place would be considered a plush establishment no matter its location.

"Simon, B.D. and I have been hearing stories 'bout you. We've been curious of late. We sure are glad to see you all in one piece. What have you been up too, anyway? We heard a couple of brothers killed you in Tascosa a few weeks back."

"They did kill me, I'm a ghost now and I've been doing the same old thing, Cordell. A cat doesn't change his spots. You know me....left alone.... won't do any wrong. I chase easy money....faithless women....and try to stay out of the rain....and, on occasion....I have a little whiskey for my pain. Speaking of such, I'll buy us a drink."

"Nope, drinks are on me. What are you doing in our part of the country?"

Cordell got a bottle of whiskey from behind the bar. He, Simon and Brock Deaton sat at a table facing the front door.

"Just got to missing Texas, I guess. I thought I'd check you out and see if Aurora had sent us any money."

"She probably would have if she knew how to write." Both men laughed.

Simon drank down his first glass of whiskey and poured a second. The burn in his throat felt good. He could feel the warmth of the whiskey in his empty stomach.

"Got anything a man can eat, Cordell? I'm starved. B.D. calls it farting fresh air."

"Sure thing," said Cordell and then left for the kitchen to make Simon a sandwich.

"Missed Texas did you? Is that the reason you're here?" asked Brock curiously.

Simon nodded in agreement. It pleased him to be back on home soil.

"Same thing for me....finally had to come back home."

"You know, B.D. I've traveled pretty much far and wide....and every where I've been....I've carried Texas inside. I feel it deep down in my bones....and I guess it finally called me home."

"There's something about it, isn't there? Always something special about being home, any home, one place or another for some, but it is Texas for us."

Simon raised the tenor of his voice slightly and raised his glass in a toast, "Texas. To me the sky seems bluer....the air smells cleaner....the women are sweeter....but, unfortunately the men are meaner!"

"Amen to that," exclaimed Brock.

Cordell returned with the sandwich he made for Simon.

It was Simon's favorite sandwich. Sour dough bread, mustard, a generous portion of fresh cured ham, finished with lettuce, tomatoes, pickles and onions. Simon ate wolfishly.

"What do you think of my place here, Simon?" Cordell inquired, after Simon finished eating.

Simon looked around, and motioned with his hands, "This all yours?"

"All of it is mine, lock stock and barrel. I came here when I left Santa Fe and bought the place. Told you I was going to, remember?"

"I remember. I'd heard in passing that you had done it. I actually came to see it for myself. I never expected to find B.D. here of all places."

"That isn't all, Simon," spoke Brock Deaton, "Old Cordell's done gone and got himself elected mayor too."

Simon looked at Brock and frowned. "Are you pulling my leg?"

"Nope, Cordell is the mayor and head of the town council."

"Damn, Cordell, that's like getting a license to steal. I guess you didn't tell them about your sordid past when you were doing your campaign speaking, did you?"

Cordell started laughing.

"Did you tell them 'bout Santa Fe? Do they know you're friends with someone like me?"

Cordell did not get to answer. At that moment Tandy Ledbetter walked into the saloon. "Mr. Simon, Mr. Simon. I done all ya said. They's got a room holdin' fo' ya o'er to the hotel. Now, if you's need anythin', anythin' at all, you just call old Tandy here. Yes sur, I do's it all. I shoe horses, I mends saddles and leathas, shine boots, clean guns, gets things most peoples don't even know we's got, yes sur, I do's it all."

Simon looked at Tandy Ledbetter. Tandy had a smile on his face wider than the state of Texas. Some called it grinning from ear to ear. Simon looked at Tandy's hands again. Each one of Tandy's hands was bigger than Simon's two hands together. Damn Tandy had big hands.

"You do's it all huh?" said Simon.

"Yes sur. I've done everthin' there be to do Mr. Simon, everthin' there be, uh huh, sure nuff."

"Everything, Short'nin' Bread?"

Cordell and Brock became concerned, concerned for Tandy, especially when Simon called him Short'nin' Bread. They both had seen Simon in action and neither one knew how he felt about blacks. Tandy stood silent for a few moments. Then he spoke.

"Well, Mr. Simon, I done everthin' there is I guess, 'cept bed another man, screw a dog or a baby chicken!"

Everyone broke out laughing, even Simon. Simon stopped laughing and looked back at Tandy. "You ever bed a white woman, Short'nin' Bread?" As he spoke, an evil smile came to his face.

Tandy became nervous. "Why you wants to know, Mr. Simon?"

Cordell and Brock remained silent. By the looks on their faces, they both were quickly calculating what they would do if Tandy gave the wrong answer.

Brock was watching Simon's hands, and especially his scar. His derringer hand was holding his whiskey glass.

Simon did not answer Tandy's question.

Cordell and Brock were still concerned, and they were very nervous.

Tandy was uneasy, and Simon knew it. "Ever kill a man?" Simon asked.

Brock shuffled uneasily in his chair.

Cordell rose from the table and went behind the bar.

Both men were studying Simon, looking for a tell–tale sign he was about to turn into the Rhymer. Simon did not seem to be mad. His face was calm and his scar had not started to twitch, as it did when Simon's blood ran hot and his Demon surfaced.

Tandy looked Simon straight in the eye. "Yes sur, back durin' the war. Kilt a couple in the line of duty."

"Fight for the blue coats?"

"Yes sur, Mr. Simon, shore nuff, in the Carolinas, and Virginia."

"Virginia, did you happen to fight in a battle at Saltville?"

"Uh, yes sur, you know about Saltville?"

"Yes, yes I do. You are a brave and lucky man Short'nin' Bread. Those all you ever killed, just those in the war? You ever kill one up close and watch him squirm and bleed on the ground?" Simon drank another shot of whiskey and refilled the glass.

"Oh, yeah, well, afta the war when I was a free man, this man called me a sorry no good nigger."

Cordell cringed. He was hoping Tandy would not tell Simon this story. There were things Cordell did not know about Simon, and he certainly did not know how he would react to Tandy's story.

"Now I am black and to some that's bein' a nigger, even hera in Texas, but I ain't sorry 'n' no good. Nuh, uh. I works hard for everthings I got. No sur, ain't nobody callin' me sorry 'n' no good. So I put black all over that white man's ass. I took holdt of him wid these big old hands of mine and I choked that bad mouthin' piece of shit white trash 'till he was bug eyed. Yeah sur, his gaw–damned eyes popped right outta his head. He looked jest like a head squashed frog. If I'd of had time, I would of laughed. But that's when I left and came here with Mr. Mc….huh….Mr. Fendley."

As Tandy was relating the story to Simon another man entered the saloon and stood at the bar next to Cordell. Cordell was glad he came.

Simon studied the man standing next to Cordell as Tandy talked.

When Tandy finished and before Simon could speak the man introduced himself.

"Mr. Sublette, I'm the Mr. Fendley that Tandy refers to, Moses Fendley. I'm the local sheriff."

Moses approached the table and offered his hand to Simon. They shook in greeting.

"Is everyone in this town running from something?" asked Simon.

"Everybody's running from something, Mr. Sublette, aren't they? Most people are just running from themselves. Why do you ask?"

"Well, there was a McFinley in the Carolinas that ran into some trouble. A sheriff, Mac McFinley, he had to leave for killing the wrong man. You wouldn't be that man would you?"

"No, I believe McFinley would be Irish wouldn't it? No Irish here, it's just a coincidence. My name is pronounced FEND–LY, like friendly, spelled F,E,N,D,L,E,Y."

Simon's senses told him Moses Fendley was probably, in fact, the McFinley he had heard about. Tandy had almost confirmed it with his slip.

Moses reasoned Simon had caught the inference, but he had this suspicion that his secret would be safe with a man like Simon. For some odd reason, instantly, despite Simon's reputation, Mac McFinley, alias Fendley, liked Simon. For some reason, he trusted this man who was fast to kill and slow to ask why.

Simon's attention was no longer on Tandy Ledbetter.

Tandy turned his back to Simon and walked toward the saloon door. Suddenly, he stopped and turned to face Simon again. "Mr. Simon, just so's you'll know." Tandy began to sing and to do a little dance.

> "All white women love short'nin', short'nin'
> all white women love short'nin' bread.
> Loves it dark, loves it in bed
> all white women loves short'nin' bread.
> Just like the size, of this big old hand
> they loves the size, of the Tandy man.
> All white women love short'nin', short'nin'
> all white women love short'nin' bread."

When he was finished singing, Tandy started laughing, and he laughed hard.

Simon smiled, and then he too, started laughing. They all laughed. Simon liked Tandy Ledbetter, even if he was a blue coat, even if he was black. It would not be a good idea for anyone to say anything about the color of Tandy's skin while Simon was near.

"Hey, Tandy," said Simon.

"Yes sur, Mr. Simon"

"That man you killed, that bad mouthing piece of shit white trash got what was right."

Tandy smiled and left, singing his new version of Short'nin' Bread as he shuffled back to his unfinished work on the anvil.

Simon finished his whiskey. "I'm tired. Thanks for the hospitality, but I have to get me some sleep. I'll see you later in the evening." Simon left for the hotel.

Moses walked with him. "Simon, I know all about your reputation. I trust you'll be a gentleman while you're here, I got no problem with you or what you do, but this is how I want it. If anything comes up, let me handle it. It'll be better for you, me and everyone that way."

"No problem. Give my regards to the Mc....huh....Fendleys in the Carolinas."

"I'll do just that. Just keep your hands on the cards and the women and off your guns, and we'll be just fine. Can I count on you for that?"

Simon looked at Moses, looked him in the eyes. "You have my word."

Moses sensed he could count on Simon to keep his promise.

Simon went to the hotel to rest. His room, on the second floor, was facing the street. He always liked a room with a window facing the street, but without a balcony access. Simon asked the hotel clerk to come to his room and take his clothes to be cleaned. They could be cleaned while he slept. After the clerk left with his clothes, Simon closed the shades to the outside windows. He took the chair and propped it under the door knob, bracing it tightly. If anyone was coming in, he wanted ample warning. He stood the sawed–off shotgun next to the bed. He put his forty–five on the pillow beside his head. He lay down to sleep. It had been three days, since he slept last. He hoped he did not dream.

Simon was aroused from his sleep, rudely, by someone knocking on his door. On natural reflex he reached for the sawed–off shotgun and, without sitting up, aimed the gun at the door.

"Who the hell's making all that noise?" he said angrily.

"It's me, Mr. Sublette, the hotel clerk. I got your clothes cleaned best I could, and it's time for you to get up, just like you asked."

Slowly, painfully, Simon arose from the bed. Reluctantly, Simon removed the chair, slightly opened the door and took his clothes. Simon ordered a hot bath.

After the bath, Simon dressed in his freshly cleaned clothes and then went down stairs to the dining room. He stopped at the front desk and handed the hotel clerk a gold coin. "You keep taking care of me the way you have been and you and I will get along just fine."

The clerk nodded his thanks. He would certainly take care of Mr. Sublette. He had never seen twenty dollars before, let alone held it in his hands.

Simon went to the dining room and ate heartily, a big steak, cornbread, and buttermilk to coat the stomach. There was nothing better in Simon's opinion to coat the stomach than buttermilk. He knew he could not stay up half the night drinking and carousing on an empty stomach.

Simon left the hotel and walked toward the Palomino Palace. He met Tandy Ledbetter in the street.

"Going to the Palace, Tandy?"

"Yes sur, there's a card game I'm fancying. You gonna play too?"

"No, I think I'll just drink and visit with the natives, check out the ladies."

"Best be careful of the one named Lettie."

"Why, is she dangerous or something?"

"She be a she—whore—witch."

"A she—whore—witch?" Simon laughed.

"Yep, yes sur, a she—whore—witch. She can do things to a man that ain't even been thought of before!"

"Well, if that's the case, I'm gonna let her try on me."

"You be brave Mr. Simon. You sure enough be brave."

They walked into the Palace together.

I was going into the Palomino Palace, and a man says,
"I wouldn't go in there if I was you. The cards are cold and the women are too."
It sounded like the house was having a good run at the table,
and if he was telling the truth, Pitifore needed to hire a new stable.

Simon and Tandy walked into the Palomino Palace. The first one they saw was Cordell Pitifore.

"Well, look what the cat done drug in. I thought you might sleep around the clock. Come here, Simon, and I'll introduce you to some of my friends."

Tandy greeted Cordell and then walked past the long bar to a private room where the card game was to be played. Cordell had added this room for playing cards so the participants could have privacy while playing and not be bothered by whatever was happening in the general saloon.

Simon and Cordell only took two steps when Simon overheard a man at the table nearest him speak to his companions.

"See, I told you it was Rhymin' Simon. I don't believe it's safe in here right now for decent folks."

Simon stopped and spoke to Cordell. "Excuse me for a moment, Cordell. I think I'll stop and visit here for a spell." Simon took a vacant chair from an adjacent table and slid it next to man who made the comment and sat down. He shook the man's hand. "Gentlemen, just so you won't make the same mistake twice. My name is not Rhymin' Simon. Mr. Sublette will do quite nice." Simon tipped his hat to all at the table in greeting.

When Simon spoke to the man, face to face, he could tell it unnerved him. The man rose from his chair to leave. Simon, ever so gently, placed his hand on the man's shoulder sitting him back in his chair.

Cordell then spoke to the man and the others at the table. "Why don't you just keep quiet? There's no need to agitate anyone here. Let's all drink and enjoy."

"It is okay, Cordell," spoke Simon, "Go ahead men, finish your whiskey....then I'll buy us some more....then you can tell me....what decent folks would even come in here for."

Simon looked at Cordell and smiled, "Mr. Pitifore, a bottle of your finest, if you please, for me and my new friends here.

"Now that you know my name....which one of you Christians is going to explain? I need to be learned in your ways....just what is the definition of decent folks these days?"

Well all those men were silent. None knew quite what to think.
I took the whiskey bottle and poured each one of those Christians a drink.

"Is it being well dressed, honest, prim and proper....is religion involved to some degree....think about the definition of the word....and then, please tell me."

Cordell and the bartender arrived with the whiskey and fresh glasses. This premium bottle of whiskey would taste better if not mixed with the house brand The Palace served. Cordell poured each man a shot, and then poured himself one as well.

"I think you Christians came for what I came for....to get a snoot full of whiskey....and maybe a slat rattle with a whore."

190

None of the men answered.

Cordell scoured all the tables at The Palace looking for Lettie. She was his best girl. And just like the whiskey Simon ordered, she was premium too. "Where the hell is Lettie when you need her? I need her to help me out," he said to the bartender.

The bartender shrugged his shoulders to say he didn't know. Cordell left to find her.

Simon continued, as he served the men another shot of the premium whiskey, "You must have talked to my daddy....before they killed him and put him in the ground....he said if you marry a smart looking woman.... you won't have a reason to go to town."

Simon poured all the men another drink. He made sure they had a full glass and drank one each time he did. They knew not to refuse....and they all were afraid to talk.

"You know, Christians....most men seek their own level....some tend to rise above it all and have honor....some go to the devil. If I was to kill you right now....would you go to heaven or would you go to hell?" Simon paused, no one said a word. He continued. "And while they're kicking the dirt on your face....what words would the preacher man have to tell?"

Simon poured himself another shot of the premium whiskey. He did not refill the other men's glasses.

"Would he say the good words....or would he say something bad.... especially if the preacher man....knew of all the whores you'd had?"

Simon laughed and then said, "Don't you just love it when a good rhyme comes together?" Simon then turned to the man who had originally spoken. Simon motioned for him to come near. The man leaned over close to Simon. Close enough to smell the whiskey on his breath.

"So don't talk to me....about who are decent folks and who ain't.... unless you're above reproach....unless you're some kind of saint. And about how good you Christians are....I don't want to hear it....and as far as being decent folks....you shits aren't even near it."

Simon pushed the man away. Simon rose from his chair and stood over the man. "Now tell me, Christian, do you love Jesus? Have you been saved? On Sunday do you get on your knees and pray?"

The man jumped from his chair and quickly made for the door, getting away from Simon as fast as he could.

Simon yelled after him, "Do you go to church and repent....get forgiveness for your Wednesday night stray?"

Another man at the table, using the distraction, left his chair and followed, he didn't finish his last drink. Two men remained at the table.

Simon returned to his chair. Simon looked at the other men and grinned.

One of the men finally spoke to Simon. "Mr. Sublette, we aren't like him. Hell, most of us don't even like the bastard. We wonder sometimes why we even drink with him."

"You ought to pick your friends better. People are going to think you're all the same, you keep his company, might get his name."

He isn't anything but a hypocrite.
Preach the good word but then don't live by his belief.
I think his kind should be strung up ~ just like a damn horse thief.

Cordell found Lettie. "Come quick, I need your help. Simon's got some citizens cornered and I'm afraid they'll say something wrong, and he'll kill the whole damned lot of 'em. Come with me."

Cordell got a couple of the other girls and, along with Lettie, took them to where Simon was sitting as the two men ran from the saloon. Everything was calm and peaceful when Cordell returned with the girls.

"Girls, I want you to meet a friend of mine, this is Simon Sublette. We know each other from back in Santa Fe. Now just so you'll all know, he is known as the Rhymer, and a fair warning, don't call him Rhymin' Simon. It might cost you some of your pretty features."

All the stable girls were pretty but the one called Lettie was the best.
I'd get to know her a lot better later on was what I guessed.
The she-whore-witch Tandy said ~ hope she's like that in bed.

Simon removed his hat to greet the girls. His forehead was whiter than the rest of his face. His was like most men's forehead who spent time in the sun wearing a large hat. The exposed parts of the face were tanned. The forehead wasn't.

"Where's B.D., Cordell, I thought he'd be here tonight."

"He's at the ranch. He's sweet on a woman out that way. I'm surprised he didn't tell you. He said to tell you he'd see you in a couple of days. He said to stay until he got back."

"Trying to settle down is he?"

"I guess it might come to that, terrible shame though with all the fineness I got in here."

"Terrible shame indeed, Cordell, it looks like you have everything a man would need."

Cordell told Simon that Brock Deaton would come into town only on the weekends. During the week, he had to make a living working on the ranch. On some occasions, he would come to town for supplies. That was how Simon happened to catch him there on a Wednesday.

Simon turned attention to the ladies. The one named Lettie won his full focus. She was the best–proportioned woman he had ever seen, from her eyebrows down to her toes. She was perfect. She was absolutely beautiful. Simon thought she could have been anything she wanted or had anything she wanted, but here she was, in a saloon, a prostitute. Why had she not found one of these rich, powerful ranchers, or politicians, and married well? Life's full of strange choices. He wondered why she had made this one, but for now he wasn't complaining.

"Bitch, wolf, bitch," Simon said under his breath when he saw her. He was momentarily taken aback. Was what he felt? Fear, or was it intimidation? He did not know but he was uncomfortable with the feeling. He did not know if he could lie with a woman like Lettie. For some reason, he did not feel worthy. He somehow felt inferior. He felt she would be in control. The feeling of inferiority and weakness passed when she sat down in his lap.

"Simon Sublette, the gun fighting poet, you know a man in dark glasses does something for me." With her finger Lettie began to rub Simon's chest, in a slow circular motion. "What you say me and you get some champagne and go off by ourselves and leave the riffraff to each other?"

Simon looked into Lettie's eyes. Lettie had great eyes. She could have robbed a bank with those eyes. Simon was sure she was going to rob him, but he did not care.

"I could sit still for that. Do you know if Cordell has champagne?"

"He does, some of that French kind. I had him get some from Kansas City, just for special occasions and special people."

"I can't think of anything more special than us."

Simon asked the bartender to bring them some of the imported French champagne. He and Lettie headed toward the upstairs where they could be more comfortable and private. As Simon walked past Cordell, Cordell said, "That'll cure what ails you."

"Damned if it won't," Simon concurred, not taking his eyes off the backside of Lettie's beautiful body. Her backside moved even better when she walked up the stairs. Such a lovely motion thought Simon. He could hardly wait until he could feel the motion for himself.

You know a good hot bath and a rub down, sure make a man feel good.
A man should do this every time the notion strikes, if he could.
There's something special about feeling good and being clean.
I think if I could do it enough ~ I might be inclined, to be less mean.

Simon would learn that Lettie was from Kansas City and that she had left there after a mysterious fire had destroyed her place of business. Simon also learned that she had been a strip tease dancer in an upscale nightclub while in Kansas City. Her stage name was K. C. Strip. Simon thought she was much more tender, and juicy, than any K.C. Strip steak he had ever had.

During the entire incident, no one noticed Sheriff Fendley standing in the shadows in the back hallway. He left when Lettie sat down in Simon's lap.

Johnny Calico

Simon had wanted to check in on the card game when he was in the Palomino Palace. With the interference by the Christians, and then his introduction to Lettie, he had not had time to ask Cordell, or Tandy about the game. After a few nights with Lettie, even as skilled as she was in the art of pleasure, Simon was ready for some other kind of entertainment. There were many hours in the day to enjoy oneself.

When he did finally ask Tandy about the card game, he learned this man, Johnny Calico, the one Texas Sweet Talk had mentioned in Fort Worth, was in town and winning most of the card games. When he heard the name, Simon's senses were alerted.

I'm in the Palomino Palace and to me it's the same old scene.
It's me, Cordell Pitifore and Lettie, the bar room queen.
There's also the music, the drinkers and gamblers in a high stakes card game,
A card slick is taking them real good ~ Johnny Calico is his name.
I heard of this man before, I heard it from Texas Sweet Talk.
The Calico Kid cleaned Ft. Worth ~ then suddenly took a walk.

Simon went to the private room to study the game, and to study this Johnny Calico from a distance. When he entered the room, he saw the large card table. Tandy Ledbetter was seated directly across the table from this man dressed in a dark blue suit, fancy shirt and string tie. He wore no hat. Simon assumed this man was the one named Johnny Calico. Then Simon saw the man's face. Simon's blood rushed in his veins. The hair on his neck bristled. Son of a bitch! The derringer, moved on its own, and without call, instantly into his left hand and the Demon sprang from his resting place. The man dressed in the dark blue suit, fancy shirt and string tie, sitting across from Tandy Ledbetter, this Johnny Calico, the Calico Kid, was none other than Ian Calcough. Suddenly it all made perfect sense. Ian changed his name to get away from the stigma of Saltville. Simon knew he was right. Just like he knew he had a large scar on his cheek—and it was twitching.

Simon quickly got his emotions under control. He sent the Demon to rest for now. There would be better time and place to deal with Calcough, or Calico, than here. He needed time to think about how and when the Calico Kid would meet his end. He was going to turn and leave unnoticed, but Tandy gave him away.

"Mr. Simon, you be playing wid us tonight?"

When Calico heard Simon's name he slowly looked up from his shuffling of the cards and stared at Simon for a moment. He didn't speak and he had no panic on his face. He knew it was Simon Sublette. The same Simon Sublette as from the guerrilla war squad they had served in during the Civil War, even though now Simon had this nasty scar on his cheek. Calico knew Simon's past, and his current reputation, but he didn't show any concern. Calico thought he was colder and more ruthless than Simon. With his right leg, he reached over and slid a chair away from the table indicating there was a place for Simon at the game.

Simon didn't greet Calico but instead answered Tandy. "Not tonight, perhaps later, I might watch for a bit."

Calico returned to his shuffling of the cards. He was good at the task, a professional. He had great fingers.

Simon watched for a while. He noticed that for most part Calico lost when the betting was small. However, when the betting got heavy, and the money was high, Calico always seemed to get just the right card. He had seen that before. In the makeshift games they played sometimes in the army. There always seemed to be someone with a card hidden somewhere. Maybe Calico was doing the same.

Simon debated if he should tell Fendley about Ian Calcough. Maybe Fendley could kill him and make it legal.

"Cordell, you ever studied that game?" Simon asked Cordell when he caught him alone the next day.

"No, not much, I only know that Calico fellow has been on a good run, cleaned out most people who've sat down. Tandy said he was slicker than a boiled onion."

"Something isn't right, Cordell....I can feel it in the hairs on my neck.... think I'll go sit in....I think something is wrong with that deck."

"Yeah, now that you mention it, I kind of feel it too. You think he's cheating somehow?"

"I don't rightly know, but a man can't get a card on demand.... something doesn't set well about this Calico man."

"He's just too damn lucky, isn't he? I'll cover you. If you need any money I'll be there."

"If the game is on the up and up, I'll be okay....but if it's not then Calico may have seen his last day."

Oh shit, thought Cordell, here we go again. Cordell had trusted Simon before when he had one of his gut feelings. He was going to trust him now.

Simon told Cordell who and what Calico was.

Simon had his plan. If Calico was cheating the players then it would be a perfectly good reason to be rid of him forever.

We played draw poker and I stayed pretty even for a while.
Then a pot started building ~ I noticed on Calico's face there was a smile.
The stakes were high ~ all folded but me, the others had to go.
Now the game was down to me and the sharp ~ Johnny Calico.
Calico didn't know. I came to set things right.
Calico didn't know. A Demon was hidden in plain sight.

The money on the table was substantial. Simon called Calico's bet and then raised the bet again.

Johnny Calico opened his coat real slow, reached in and removed a large roll of money.

Simon looked at the roll of money and knew it must have been over a thousand in cash.

As Calico closed his coat, something fluttered to the floor, and it caught Simon's eye. The item, whatever it was, landed on the floor beneath Calico's chair.

Simon saw it and so did Cordell Pitifore. At first Simon thought it was a plain piece of paper, but then he saw it was an Ace of Spades. It had the same markings as the deck they were using. Simon and Cordell now knew how he had been so lucky and how everyone else had been losing. When the card fell, it landed near the front of Calico's chair. Neither Simon nor Cordell said anything; they just let it lay there.

He had the same poker face I seen before, and I kept looking into his eyes,
to see if he was holding good cards, or if he was just holding lies.

Johnny Calico called Simon's bet and raised the bet again. He then moved his hand toward the watch pocket in his vest.

Simon now knew this was how he exchanged the cards. Calico was polished in this move, this sleight of hand.

Just as Simon was polished in moving his derringer to his left hand— as he just did.

Panic, briefly, flashed across Calico's face.
The card he reached for was not in its usual place.

Simon called Calico's bet and raised the bet once more. Calico took a look at his cards. It was the first look at his hand since he had removed the money from his coat. His demeanor finally changed.

Calico was good, real good, but Simon noticed the slight change in Calico's face. It was a flash, a brief flash, but it conveyed concern.

Quietly, Simon said, "Calico, I think what you're looking for....is lying on the floor." Simon smiled.

Calico studied Simon's face and his smile. He had seen the smile before. He knew what it meant. Then, slowly, very slowly, he looked under the chair. When he saw the card he flinched. His face drained of all color. It was as if he had seen a ghost. As he raised his eyes from the floor, he saw Simon's derringer in his left hand, under the table. It was aimed at his stomach and the hammer was cocked. He could also see Simon's finger twitching back and forth. If he could have heard the Demon talking to the finger he would have heard, *Come on Simon, give me a squeeze, let me kill him, let me please!'*

The Ace was on the floor ~ a deck only has four, never five.
Since it was me, Calico knew he wouldn't get out of this game alive.

Johnny Calico looked up from under the table, grinned at Simon and shoved all his money to the middle of the table. "Too rich for me, I fold!"

Fendley had been watching from the door and knew what Simon wanted to do, so he intervened and said, "Calico, you're a lucky man. I'm going to let you leave this town alive. There's a stage leaving for El Paso early in the morning. Have your cheating ass on it. If not, the Rhymer here is going to be writing you a graveyard sonnet. Now, give me all you got and get."

Johnny Calico got up from his chair, laid his roll of money on the table, took one last drink, and started to leave.

"Leave the money belt too, Calcough....then you can go," spoke Simon.

Ian Calcough, the Calico Kid, hurriedly left the Palomino Palace.

Simon was disappointed Fendley did not let him kill Calico right then.

They certainly had good reason according to Simon's way of thinking. Simon did not know why Fendley would wish a card cheat on the citizens of El Paso?

"Why'd you let him walk for?"

"We got our money back, didn't we? Card cheating isn't any reason to lose a life," said Cordell.

"Is with me, besides, I bet we didn't get all the money."

"Well, yeah, you and John Wesley would kill a man if he farted wrong. It's our town and our place, so I'm asking you to let it be. You exposed him, caused him shame. I'll wire El Paso and let them know he's headed that way," spoke Fendley.

"What if he gets off the stage before El Paso?"

"Isn't my problem, Simon. I can't protect the whole world from card cheats or from themselves. A man sitting down to a table ought to pay enough attention for himself. So just let it go. Okay?"

"I can protect them."

I'm asking you as a friend."

I took the poker pot and Cordell took Calico's stash.
He said he'd return the money to those who'd been swindled of their cash.

As the conversation finished, Lettie came to Simon's side with a magnum of champagne. They went upstairs. It was good, but Simon couldn't get his mind off of Calico.

Fendley did make one mistake that night. He didn't put Calico in jail to wait for the stage.

Calico waited in the alley behind the hotel. He had been waiting in ambush for Simon and Cordell, to kill them and get his money back. He was naïve enough to believe he could defeat Simon one on one. He had always believed he was better than Simon when they served together, and he still believed that way. He was of the belief no one could beat him in a fight, man to man. Now was his chance to prove it. Cordell didn't concern him whatsoever. When they didn't come, he reasoned they both had stayed in the hotel with one of the girls. He knew exactly where Simon would be. With the one called Lettie. He would sneak up the back stairs and kill the both of them, get his money and leave town as fast as possible.

Simon lay in Lettie's bed, awake, thinking. He could not sleep but he didn't know why. Usually he didn't have trouble sleeping. He was lucky he couldn't sleep this night. It was the Demon, it saved his life. He heard the stairs creak with the weight of a man. The groaning piece of wood called to the Demon. *A killer is coming to take you in the night....better rise and arm yourself for the fight.*

Simon knew who was coming, the same man as had come that night in Saltville and killed those helpless men. Simon wasn't like those men. Simon had the Demon. He was ready when Calico slowly opened the door to Lettie's room. As Simon was about pull the trigger to fire his gun, someone jumped Calico from behind. As they fell into the room they crashed into Simon knocking him backwards. One of the hard boot heels stomped on Simon's bad foot. The three men struggled against each other. Simon could not get his gun free. Simon recognized one of the men from his voice.

"You cheatin' white son of a bitch. I'm gonna kill your card switchin' ass! Take my money, now take my fists!"

It was Tandy Ledbetter's voice. Damn, thought Simon.

The three continued to struggle. Then somehow, suddenly Calico got free. He rose to his feet and ran out of the room.

"Tandy, get your ass off of me," said Simon as he pushed Tandy to the side. Then he rose to his feet and helped Tandy stand.

"Lettie, stay put. I'll be right back. I've got to get Tandy home."

Lettie was too scared to leave the room.

Tandy and Simon went as quickly and silently as they could to Calico's hotel. They saw him enter the back door. They waited in the alley, in the darkest place they could find. It didn't take long. Calico slowly emerged from the hotel's back door. He stuck his head out of the door like a turtle coming out of a shell. When he got all the way into the alley, to Simon's surprise, Tandy jumped Calico again.

Calico drew his gun but Simon's reaction was too quick for him to shoot Tandy. Simon knocked the gun out of Calico's hand. Calico was no match for the muscular Tandy, even with his special training. Tandy gave him a severe beating. Simon thought he was going to beat him to death but for some reason Tandy stopped. As Tandy was about to walk away, Calico drew a knife. Simon moved Tandy out of the way just in time. When Calico attacked, Simon threw Tandy aside, grabbed Calico's hand, twisted it violently, and shoved the knife into Calico's heart. He died slowly, but not painfully enough for Simon. He died knowing there WAS a man he could not defeat—Tandy Ledbetter.

Simon took the card that had fallen from Calico's coat, the Ace of Spades, and placed it on Calico's chest. Simon picked up Calico's saddlebags and pitched them to Tandy. Tandy and Simon left the alley and the dead Calico, having never spoken to each other. Some would say this was murder. Simon would say it was justified.

Fendley went to get him the next morning but Calico wasn't there.
He was still lying in the alley ~ and ~ he wasn't breathing any air.
That Ace of Spades, his death card, was lying on his chest.
There was a note on the card that had brought Calico to his final rest.
It read, "With this card he cheated many an innocent man,
his fall came when it fell from his hand."
Fendley ruled it a suicide, but how he died was never clear.
Cordell gave me that Ace of Spades and I kept it as a souvenir.
Now Fendley and Cordell won't say, but from others it can be sworn.
That Poetic Justice is what killed Calico that early morn.

Murdock and Calcough, killed by my own hand.
Destroyed by the one they created, the Rhyming Man.

Simon came down from Lettie's room about mid morning. Cordell was waiting. Cordell handed Simon the Ace of Spades he had found laying on Calico's chest.

"I thought you might want this. I found it on Calico this morning."

"Did you get him on the stage?"

"You know damn well I didn't. Found him dead in the alley behind the hotel this morning. I took that card off his body before I called Moses over. I asked you to let it go."

"Don't blame me. Lots of men in this town had more reasons to see him dead than me. If you want the truth ask Lettie."

"I'm not blaming you, Simon. Don't have too. You did it as sure as I know I'm fat and white. I can't prove it except for that card, but you did it all right."

"Okay, Cordell, I did it. It served him right. A man like Calico....as slick as he was....would just cause more suffering and pain....if he were let go."

"Maybe I should have shot him. I don't know. But you know with sons of bitches like him. You would have to shoot him in the back, and then Moses would have been pissed."

"Now, Cordell, you know me. I'd have figured a way. The real reason he's dead is he attacked Tandy with that knife you found sticking in his chest. It only makes sense....it was self defense."

"Tandy, what did he do? Go to get his money back?"

"It was something like that. How is Moses on this anyway?"

"He thinks someone who'd lost some money might have tried to take some back, and they fought about it and Calico lost. He doesn't really care who did it, if you know what I mean. It sounds like that's what actually happened. He called it a suicide. He's protecting you, isn't he? Are you holding on Moses, Simon?"

"Not me, Cordell. He must hate card cheaters too."

Moses will protect me, we have gotten quite friendly.
He came over from the Carolinas ~ his real name is Moses McFinley.
He keeps a low profile ~ he doesn't want anyone asking of his past.
I'm the only one here who knows of where he was sheriff last.
In the Carolinas, he was sheriff and one night was making a round,
when he saw a man running from a store, and he gunned that man down.
The town's people were going to hang him, but he escaped out the back door.
You see the man he shot down, was in fact, the owner of the store.
He landed here and instilled himself as an honest man, good with a gun.
He knows I'll cause no trouble. That I'll leave as soon as my business is done.
~

Ian Calcough, the Calico Kid, by another name.
He was eliminated from life, over a crooked card game.
Sins not cleansed, wounds not healed.
Murderer of innocents, fate forever sealed.

Moses Fendley found Simon at his hotel eating his supper. He told Simon he had talked to Lettie and Tandy. He was satisfied the death of Calico was in self defense and he thanked Simon for being there to protect Tandy. He also told Simon the towns people were glad too, especially all those who had lost money.

Simon told Moses who Calico really was and why the town was lucky to be rid of him. "Ian was a natural born killer of men....if we had not killed him in the alley....he would have come for us again. He was no match for

Tandy until he pulled the knife. It was a necessity....at that time....for me to end his life."

Simon waited for Moses to eat his supper and then the two went for a private encounter with Lettie and a young lady named Tammy McFree.

The Rooster

Simon was in the Palomino Palace early in the afternoon sitting with Brock Deaton and Lettie.

Brock wasn't comfortable sitting with Lettie given her profession and the fact he was betrothed.

Simon had just finished telling Brock the story of Ian Calcough and was about to ask Brock about his woman. He remembered Brock once told him he would never marry. Simon wondered about this woman who could change his mind. He didn't get to ask. They were interrupted by a voice coming from a man entering the front door.

"Simon, Simon Sublette, is that really you?"

When Simon heard the voice, it sent a chill up his spine. Simon would have known that voice anywhere. He looked at the man and he was right. Walking toward their table was his childhood friend, Boyce, the Rooster. Simon rose from his chair, walked up to the Rooster and gave him a bear hug.

"Rooster, man, good gosh almighty, what in the world are you doing way out here? You want to get a chair and join us? Lettie, B.D., this is a child hood friend of mine, Rooster Nutt."

Rooster was looking around like a man possessed. He seemed scared about something.

"Oh no Simon, don't sit down. We got to hurry. We gotta get the hell outta here and fast. The man called the Rhymer is comin', and he'll kill us if he sees us."

Simon laughed. "Rooster, Rooster, calm down, calm down. There's no reason to be afraid. I'll get us something to drink. We can relax. We're safe here."

"Hell no, Simon, he'll come in and start drinkin', and then he'll get mad, and 'cite some poetic verse, and then kill ever one he sees."

"Poetic like....tell me Rooster....why is it you want to die....do you want to go to hell....so you can ask the devil why?"

Rooster took the bottle of whiskey on the table, turned it up and took a long, hard drink. He drank almost a fifth of the bottle. He wiped his mouth with his shirtsleeve. He paused for a moment, and then he did the same thing again.

"Damn, Simon, you've seen 'im in action ain't ya?"

"Calm down, Rooster....you're a good friend of mine....and I must confess....I am the man who talks in rhyme!"

A look came to Rooster's face. It was one of divine revelation. He started walking around the room in his chicken walk. He was strutting around the saloon, carrying the whiskey bottle, flapping his arms like a chicken and bobbing his head back and forth. He stopped strutting right in front of Simon, long enough to take a drink and then said, "I'll be damned. I'll be damned." After he finished talking, he crowed like a cock in the morning.

He took a few more struts then said, "It's hard to understand. It's hard to understand." He took another strut around the saloon, and then took another long drink. "My Simon, my Simon, my–o–my, is the Rhymer Man."

He made several trips around the saloon, strutting, drinking, crowing, and saying the same thing. "I'll be damned. I'll be damned. It's hard to understand. It's hard to understand. My Simon, my Simon, is the Rhymer Man." He put on quite a show for the saloon patrons, but only a few of them laughed. It could have been they were afraid.

Brock Deaton laughed as did Lettie. They weren't scared by Simon or by Rooster.

Again he strutted back to where Simon was standing and said "I'll be damned, Simon. You crazy son of a bitch, you're as far off center as me." The whiskey bottle Rooster was drinking from was almost empty.

"Maybe, depends on the view, but I can't say I disagree."

Simon excused himself from Lettie and Brock. He would talk to Brock about his lady friend at a later time. He needed to spend some time with his friend. Simon drank that evening with Boyce Nutt, the Rooster. As they sat and talked Simon, knew that Boyce was in deep trouble mentally and was becoming insane. The whiskey and the Indian/Mexican smoke had already taken their toll on his brain.

Several times during the evening Boyce would rub himself from his head to his legs in a furious manner.

"Rooster, what the hell's that all about?"

"It's the ants Simon. They get on me and it's hard to get 'em off. They are drivin' me crazy."

"I can see that they are. Let's go to bed, you can sleep in my room tonight."

"Can't sleep in a bed, Simon, beds are full of ants. Don't you know that's why they call them ant beds?"

Only a crazy person would think of something like that thought Simon. He could not get Boyce to leave the saloon. Simon got him a couple of blankets and made him a bed in the private card room. Simon could not stand to see his friend like this. He hoped Cordell knew of places that could help people like Boyce.

Rooster wanted to sleep, propped up against the wall, sitting on the floor.l
His mind was crazed ~ he wasn't good for anything anymore.
I made him a bed, but comfort he would not find.
He was beyond my help. He needed the mental doctor kind,
or maybe, in Boyce's case, a single bullet to the head.
He told me he knew he was crazed, he needed to be dead.
But it won't be from my hand ~ not from this man.

Simon asked Cordell if there were somewhere they could send Boyce, some place for the mentally disabled. Cordell knew of a place. He said he would get Moses, and they would take care of the Rooster, since he was a friend of Simon's. Simon didn't care where he went as long as he was cared for.

The next morning, Simon helped Cordell load Boyce into the back of a wagon. The local doctor had given Boyce some medicine to help him sleep. They were going to move him to a state run hospital in Austin, The Texas State Lunatic Asylum.

It was a long trip from Sweetwater to Austin. Simon paid the driver handsomely for the trip. He also made sure the attendant had plenty of the tranquilizing medicine for Boyce. Simon watched until the wagon cleared the horizon.

As he was turning to go to the Palace, the man who ran the telegraph office brought him a wire.

Simon read the message, and then went to find Cordell. He told him he would be leaving with the next morning sun.

"Cordell, a man has sent for me to help him with a family problem. He's made a generous offer, one hard to turn from. I can use it to help Boyce. I'm leaving in the morning."

"Where are you headed?" asked Cordell, being nosey.

"Up north a bit, up near Tascosa, there are some bandits, perhaps splintered Comancheros, bad trouble."

"Yeah, we're starting to see a few of those here, bad folks to deal with, the Comancheros. They are being hired by some of the fencers."

"They're rotten sons of bitches all right, the worse kind. Listen if I don't see B.D. before I go, tell him good–bye for me, would you?"

"I can do that, anything else?"

"No, tell B.D, when I clear all this up, I'll be back. I have some things to do, and then I'll come to see you tonight. When you need money for Boyce, let me know how much."

"It's a state run place. I don't think it costs any money, but if it does I'll let you know when you get back. Simon, this family up north, would it be anybody I might know?"

"Do you know a Joshua Ravenwood?"

"Ravenwood, Joshua Ravenwood, and yeah, I know the name, English fellow, from Boston, but I never met the man. He owns most of the land around Tascosa. It's one of the largest ranches in Texas."

"He's the one that sent for me. He needs some of my special talents."

"Reckon how he heard of you, and how he knew where you were?"

"I can't rightly say," said Simon as he turned and went to prepare for his trip to the X–Bar–T ranch.

Comancheros was a general name given, in this part of Texas, to rouge bands of misfits and outlaws. They would do most anything for money. They had no conscience and raped, plundered and killed with no remorse. Ian Calcough would have been a great Comanchero, except he liked to work alone. A lot of these men were left over from the war and knew no other way of making their way in the world. The original Comancheros were mostly bands of Mexican nationals who traded with the Comanche Indians. That is how they got their name. In the beginning, they were peaceful people. The remnants were not.

Simon spent one last night with Lettie, and told her he was leaving.

His leaving did not bother Lettie. She knew it would come to that some day. Another would come along to fill her bed and buy her champagne. He might not be as generous as Simon, but he would come along. And knowing Simon, he would be back in due time.

The next morning Simon gathered his things from the hotel and went to the livery stable to get his horse.

Tandy was there and already had the gray horse saddled and ready to go.

"Short'nin' Bread, how much do I owe you?"

"It's on me. You don't owes me nuthin," said Tandy.

"No way am I not paying. Man's got to make a living, can't make it giving it away."

"Na sur, you took all the blame for the Calico man. People's ain't even lookin' my way and I appreciate it."

"Didn't take any blame. Hell, Short'nin' Bread, Calico was killed in self–defense. Didn't you hear Moses say that's how he died?"

Tandy shook his head back and forth.

"What the hell were you doing up there anyway?"

"He took most my savin's wid his cheatin'. I got's it back, from the saddlebags, but when it was happenin', it caused me great grief and pain. For a while there, just thinkin' 'bout everthin' I ever worked for bein' gone, 'caused to me think 'bout killin' my own self. I was worried folks wuld call me sorry and no good, and it wuld da been true too, this time, so I went to kill him on gen'ral principle. What 'bout you?"

"I heard him sneaking up the stairs. He was going to kill and rob me to get his money back....and do no telling what to Lettie. I'm just glad he chose me instead of Cordell. I know some folks in El Paso where he was headed. And the ones I know would have done just like you. They would have sat down with Calico and played cards. And he would have cheated them. I saved them the trouble." Simon smiled at Tandy. "Plus, I liked it. I have wanted to kill him for years."

"For those things he did in the war, like Saltville?"

"Saltville....and places not mentioned."

Tandy slammed the anvil, hard, with his hammer. "Sum–bitch no good white piece of shit trash." He slammed the anvil a second time.

Simon gave Tandy what he thought was a fair price plus a little bonus. He stepped into the stirrup and rose atop the gray horse. "Short'nin' Bread, take care, I should be back soon. If you ever need anything, anything at all, you let me know. I'll help if I can."

Simon started singing.

"All white women love Short'nin', Short'nin'
All white women love Short'nin' Bread.
Three young women ~ a lyin' in bed
two of 'em sick ~ the other most dead
sent for the doctor ~ the doctor said
give them women some Short'nin' Bread.
When them women a lyin' in bed
heard that talk 'bout Short'nin' Bread
popped up well ~ then dance and sing
eyes wide open at the size of that thing.

All white women love Short'nin', Short'nin'
    all white women love Short'nin' Bread."

Simon started laughing. "Yes sir....if you want to be serviced....just give old 'Short'nin Bread a call....'cause he do's it....he do's it all." Simon was laughing hard when he rode off, so was Tandy Ledbetter.

Moses saw Simon riding out of town. He asked Cordell, "Where's Simon off to?"

"Someone needed killing. They sent for Simon."

"Good choice."

"Damned if it ain't."

Joshua Ravenwood

Simon followed the instructions in the wire and went to a saloon on the north side of the main street in Tascosa, Texas, and waited.

An affluent looking gentleman walked into the saloon.
He was looking for me I'd bet.
He said, "I'm looking for the man who talks in rhyme,
the one they call Simon Sublette."
Before I could move this man in overalls, a farmer,
walked over and stepped in.
I thought to myself ~ hell I must have a twin.

The affluent gentleman's name was Joshua Ravenwood. He had sent the wire, but Simon did not expect him to come in person. Simon thought Mr. Ravenwood would send one of his hired hands to explain the details of what Simon was to do.

Why this man was stepping in, I didn't hear him mention.
I approached Ravenwood's table with deadly intention.
Another incident like the so–called gunman in Fort Sumner came to mind.
Why do amateurs in these matters even dare to cross my kind.

Simon approached the table where the two men were sitting. He touched the brim of his hat with his right hand in greeting.

"Are you Joshua Ravenwood?" Simon asked, ignoring the other man.

"Yes, I am Joshua Ravenwood," the gentleman, dressed in suit and tie, answered looking up at Simon.

Simon took a quick look at the other man. He was dressed in work overalls, a soiled shirt. His hat was sun baked and stained with sweat. He was an older man and he had a kind face. It was the kind of face a person could like on the first meeting.

Both men saw Simon's scar twitch.

Simon looked at Ravenwood's face. "Mister Ravenwood, this other man I don't know....I'll leave it up to you....on how this might go. I don't know what name he gave....but the name you seek is mine....I am Sublette....he who speaks in rhyme."

Joshua rose from the table. So did the other man.

The man offered his hand to Simon and said, "Rhymer, I'm Carl Boyd.

I don't mean to butt in, but I knew you were coming and I need money for my wife and children. We ain't had food in days. I want to help you do what you got to do."

Simon looked at the farmer. He understood the farmer had not represented himself as Simon. He knew a man would do what was necessary to survive, sometimes at grave risk, and to feed his family. Simon shook the farmer's hand.

Joshua Ravenwood looked startled.

Simon addressed Mr. Boyd. "It's okay. I know about doing without.... and I know hunger by his first name....in your place....I would've done the same. Wait outside until I'm through....then I'll see if there's something we can do."

Mr. Boyd agreed, left the saloon, and stood by the back door. He was such a lucky man. Lucky Simon hadn't shot him for a simple misunderstanding.

Ravenwood shook Simon's hand. "When I first saw that farmer, I couldn't imagine the stories I had heard about the Rhymer were true. He certainly didn't look like a bounty hunter. Anyway none I had seen before. And then he explained himself."

"Poor man, he meant no harm....the hunger has gone to his head.... but if he was looking to hunt bounty for you....he would have ended up dead."

"Well, that may be the case. What I want you to do, it is quite dangerous and some men have already died."

"Why did you send for me?"

"Have you ever encountered a man named William Jefferson?"

Simon thought hard. A wrinkle came to his forehead as he thought. "Perhaps, the only name that comes to mind is a William Zachary Jefferson from Kansas. I believe he was one of Quantrill's Raiders."

"That's the same man I refer to. Have you ever heard of Willie Patch Eye?"

Simon nodded. "Yeah, now there's a miserable low life son of a bitch if one ever existed."

"Mr. Sublette, Patch Eye and Jefferson are one and the same. He and his bunch of so called Comancheros raided our convoy between the rail station at Tascosa and my ranch headquarters. My son and daughter and I were on that convoy. They killed two of my drivers and took my daughter. Simon, she was barely sixteen." Ravenwood's voice broke when he spoke of his daughter. He composed himself. "For some reason, they left my son and me alone. I guessed it was probably for a ransom later on. The ransom demand didn't come. I hired this man, recommended to me, E.J. Pilgrim. I hired him to try and get my daughter back, but he never returned. I guess they killed him."

Simon could feel his blood beginning to rise. "You sent E.J. Pilgrim, alone, to fetch the lass? With all due respect, Mister Ravenwood....Pilgrim couldn't make a welt on a good gunman's ass. I'm surprised, given his demeanor, he even would consider going after Patch Eye. He hasn't come back?"

"No, I have not seen him again."

"I doubt he ever went to find her. He's the type that takes the money and runs."

Ravenwood gave Simon a surprised look.

"If he really went then he's dead no doubt. I believe you under estimated Patch Eye, and his abilities. And, no doubt, you gave too much credit to E. J. Pilgrim. Two things one shouldn't do in matters such as these."

"It's may be too late now though, it's been seven months."

"That's a long time for a young girl to be in their hands. It's irrelevant anyway. One man can't do it....there is no doubt....it'd take a whole army.... to go in and get her out. I don't mean to sound cold, but one girl isn't worth that much blood. If she is alive, she would probably get killed during the fighting anyway. Patch Eye and his bunch are mean sum bitches, better off left alone."

"There is still something I want you to do. What I sent for you to do."

"Hell, Mr. Ravenwood....just put a scorpion down your pants....or lie naked in a bed of red ants....you'd be better off than dealing with their kind. Rape, plunder and pillage....burning, stealing and killage....is all they got on their mind!"

Ravenwood thought, well, they are right; the son of a bitch does talk in rhymes.

"Mr. Sublette, I've checked around and what everyone tells me is when it comes to pure killing, you are the most heartless and cold son of a bitch in the world." Ravenwood looked cautiously at Simon.

Simon's expression did not change. How could he get mad for a man speaking the truth?

"I think, that maybe, you are the only one, who would understand what I'm about to say. They say you have been to hell, seen the devil in person. They say you have been tempered by the heat of hell fire and damnation."

Simon raised his eyebrows, sipped a drink of whiskey and slowly nodded his head. His killing smile came to his face. Damn, he was being described perfectly.

"You see, Mr. Sublette, I don't want you to bring her back. I want you to go find them, and if she is still alive, kill her and let her suffer no more." Ravenwood stopped and poured himself and Simon a drink. "If you were to, somehow miraculously, bring her back she would just suffer the whisperings and ridicule of the town. She could never have a normal life or settle down and have a family. Who would have a woman soiled by the Comancheros? What man would ever marry a girl with that curse upon her?"

Simon studied Ravenwood for a moment. He knew he was serious. "You could sell the ranch go back east. Not likely anyone back there would find out."

"In this day and age, I think they would find out somehow. It would only take one loose tongue. I moved here for a reason, and I'm staying."

"Is she not worth the try, not worth the chance it could happen?"

"I don't have to justify myself to you or any other man. Besides, like you said, if she is alive, they might kill her anyway. I'm not paying you for your thoughts or advice. Are you taking the offer or not?"

"Why don't I just go get her....then stay awhile and linger....and kill all those sons of bitches....that make fun and point the finger?"

Ravenwood studied Simon. His conclusion was Simon was mean—minded and coldhearted. It scared him somewhat. "That's an idea, Mr. Sublette, but even if you could save her, as good as you are at your trade, it still wouldn't ease her pain. Anyway, I don't think you could kill the whole town."

The Demon came to Simon. *Maybe we could....maybe we couldn't....but set me loose....inflict the pain....we could kill them by the thousands....until our salvation came.*

"What makes you think I won't do what I suspect E.J. Pilgrim did, take your money and be on my way?"

"Mr. Sublette, I made a mistake with Pilgrim. I admit it. Those people I asked, when I inquired on you, told me that even though you are the way you are, and do what you do, you have never lost your honor. They all say you do what is agreed to. I have no reservations."

Simon stood and shook Ravenwood's hand in agreement. "Some sort of employment for Mr. Boyd would be part of my pay."

"I can do that," Ravenwood said, "And if you get a chance at Willie Patch Eye, kill him too, to even the score a little."

Simon stood and replied. "May kill him....may kill more....could end up being a ..." Simon paused, and then grinned his killing smile again, "a somewhat pleasant chore!"

As Simon agreed to Ravenwood's terms, he knew what he had to do. He had to do what he did back in the war. Create a diversion to give him enough time to kill the girl, if in fact, he found her alive. If she was already dead, was he to keep the money anyway?

Simon met Mr. Boyd in the alley behind the saloon. Simon told him to go to Mr. Ravenwood's ranch and there would be a job waiting for him.

The man was shocked Simon had done him this favor, especially a favor of this magnitude—a job at the X-Bar-T ranch. In his gratitude he mentioned he had some dynamite. He told Simon if needed help, he would be glad to go along.

Simon didn't want the man's help, but he did take the dynamite.

A farmer, Carl Boyd, almost got in my way, he didn't have the poison in his eye.
He was half crazed from hunger, and wanted to be my ally.
I'll find them. If she is alive, I will end her misery, from the pain, set her free.
Mr. Boyd got a job at Ravenwoods ranch, as part of my fee.
Mr. Boyd had dynamite, I'd need all he could seek.
Those Comancheros probably hadn't seen hell before,
but if it became necessary they might get a peek.
I told Mr. Boyd to stay at home, they would kill him,
maybe skin him and eat him, one could never tell.
But he would end up dead and before they killed him,
they would make his every breath~ a living hell.
He had a wife and children at home, no need for him to die.
I have nothing but the Demon ~ and we have cravings to satisfy.

Comancheros

Ten days out, below this stand of trees, I found the Comancheros campsite.
They had posted a guard ~ silently he lost the fight.
I killed him with hands and knife ~ not to make any noise
I didn't want to arouse any of those other, nasty, nasty boys.

Simon spotted the Comanchero guard from a distance. He dismounted and walked the last few hundred yards toward the guard. When he got within a hundred yards, Simon stopped and took off his right boot. He limped up to the guard. The guard had his rifle aimed at Simon as he approached the man. When Simon got close, he sat down on the ground and started rubbing his foot, the foot with the two toes missing.

"Sorry to bother you partner, damn foot's killing me. I think two of my toes fell off I've walked so far."

Simon removed his sock to reveal the foot with the two toes missing. Simon started shaking the sock like he was trying to get the two missing toes to fall from the sock. The Comanchero guard bent over to look at Simon's foot. He had never seen a man with two toes missing. Perhaps he believed maybe two of Simon's toes actually had fallen off. It was a mistake to get that close to Simon to see the foot—Simon cut his throat.

Knife through the throat ~ like a knife through butter.
Blood rushed to meet dirt ~ not one sound did he utter.
I put on the dead man's hat ~and when someone looked my way.
I gave them a wave to tell them he was still there, so to say.
I saw no sign of a girl, just tents and a makeshift corral with a horse or two.
I waited until dark when they would get drunk ~ to do what I had to do.
Nightfall, campfire aglow, ~ whiskey a flow,
Willie Patch Eye brought the girl out and tied her to a tree.
I sighted my Sharps, it was an easy shot, finger on the trigger,
but then the Demon gave another plan to me.

Simon studied the camp. He was on one side of the Canadian River and the camp was on the other. His vantage point was on a small hill rising away from the river. The camp was next to a large stand of cottonwood trees. There was a fallen tree, now stripped of all its leaves. It was a beautiful place to make camp. Simon liked it. He would like it better if was not occupied by Willie Patch Eye's bunch of murderous thieves. The men were using the fallen log as a place to sit. At one point Simon counted seven men sitting on that log.

Simon hated Comancheros. Simon had brought the dynamite with the idea he would create a diversion with the explosions, kill the girl, and then escape quietly during the confusion. This way they would be stunned and shocked and not chase after him. After he had seen the campsite, and where it was located across the river, he didn't think his plan would work. With the river between him and the camp he couldn't get close enough to use the dynamite. It was now his intention to wait until they all were drunk on stolen whiskey, then kill the girl and ride away fast before they could follow. He sat and waited for darkness to come.

He and the Demon thought about different scenarios, like he did in the war when he was planning a guerrilla attack. *The girl is going to die anyway, let's kill every single man. Let's kill as many of those low—life, thieving, sorry, foul smelling, sons of bitches we can.* The Demon, speaking to Simon, made him remember something he and Calcough did one time to some Union soldiers. The dead Comanchero and his horse were something Simon could use. The guard turned out to be a bonus for his plan. Simon lifted the dead man onto his horse and tied him securely to the saddle. He found a long piece of tree limb and stuck it in the man's pants and secured it across his back to help hold him upright. He put a rope around the man's neck and tied it backwards on the saddle to keep him from slumping forward. He took all the dynamite he had gotten from the farmer and placed it in strategic positions on the horse and around the dead man's body. As he'd been trained to do, he carefully estimated the distance to the camp and then made the fuse. He estimated the length of the fuse, and the burn rate, required to explode the dynamite at the exact moment the horse and rider would reach the camp. He hoped he wasn't wrong. There wasn't enough water flowing in this section of the river to slow the horse. He took a deep breath and then he sent the horse galloping toward the camp. When the Comancheros grabbed the horse's reins to slow him down, the fuse was still burning. Simon had calculated wrong. Quickly he sent a bullet from his Sharps rifle and when it crashed into the dynamite all hell broke loose.

As the horse drew near I heard one say, "Es okay, es jes Ramone."
He was right ~ but in a few minutes they'd all be gone.
They all gathered around, then they spotted the dynamite.
I made the fuse too long, I moved quickly to make it right.
I raised the Sharps and made the shot, I was perfect I could tell.

It struck the dynamite tied to the man, and blew them all to hell.
It made one hell of an explosion ~ death and destruction was wrought.
I rode fast across the river ~ to finish what the dynamite had not.

When the dynamite on the horse exploded one of the packets of explosive near the rear of the horse was dislodged and it landed in the campfire. It caused a huge blast killing several men. Simon rode as fast as he could to the camp. Some of the Comancheros were still alive. He was shooting atop his horse in a full gallop. When he crossed the river, he dismounted in a rush and shot one in the face with the sawed–off shotgun. Another of them rose up, and before Simon saw him, shot and wounded Simon in the thigh. He stumbled, but managed to kill the shooter before he could fire again. Then Simon started killing those still alive.

Simon found the one called Willie Patch Eye. His face was a bloody mess caused by the explosion.

He had gotten the name Patch Eye during the war when he was wounded, lost the sight of his eye, and begin wearing a patch.

Simon reached down, grabbed Patch Eye's hair and pulled his head back so he could see Simon's face.

"Patch Eye, I am the Rhymer....I wanted you to know who brought you to your end....I sent the death to you....tied there to your friend. The suffering of others is over....from the hands of your kind....I'd like to hurt you some more....but I don't have the time."

Willie Patch Eye tried to say something, but he could not speak. He had bitten his tongue in half when the blast hit his face.

Simon stood and yelled, "I am the Rhymer....I bring hell fire and damnation....make your peace....I'm bringing you your salvation!"

Simon put his gun point blank to Patch Eye's good eye. "Willie Patch Eye....take a deep breath....it's time to die." Then he pulled the trigger. "No need to ask the devil....you already know why!"

Very quickly, and methodically, he went to all the Comancheros, and to make sure they were dead, he shot them each in the head. He counted thirteen. To move as fast as possible and not have to take time to reload, he used the Comanchero's weapons to kill each one. When one weapon became empty, he grabbed another. The explosion and fight lasted less than five minutes.

After he made sure all were dead, Simon went to the body of Willie Patch Eye and grabbed the eye patch from his face. He had accomplished what a thousand Union soldiers never could. He killed William Zachary Jefferson. Simon took the scalp from William Jefferson.

I found the girl. She was one hell of a mess, beaten, scared out of her mind.
I pointed my gun at her, but I couldn't do it. I guess I'm really not that kind.
The girl had lost her mind, she was in shock ~ I'd tell Ravenwood a lie.
I didn't know at the time what to do with her ~ but she didn't deserve to die.

Simon pointed his gun at the young girl's head and looked at her face. Her face was dirty and bruised. He held her face in his hands. She was covered with some of the men's blood, skin, and bone from the blast. Simon saw bruising on the exposed portions of her legs. Simon knew she had been through something unimaginable, and it had lasted seven months. How was she still alive? The blast had knocked her unconscious, but she was not hurt otherwise. A sudden image of his mother flashed through Simon's mind. This girl could have been Simon's sister. She looked like Simon's mother when his mother was a young girl. With the image of his mother in his mind, Simon could not kill the Ravenwood girl. He untied her, found some blankets and gently laid her on the ground. He took another piece of a blanket, wetted it in the river, and washed her face.

Simon found the Comancheros war chest. He opened the box and looked inside. There was a lot of money, taken by ill gains, in that chest. Well, it was his now, and he did not feel bad about it. How was he to know where it came from or where to return it? Simon grabbed a bedroll from one of the dead men. He went to each man and took anything he deemed valuable. He took ammunition, some more dynamite, pistols, rifles, ammunition belts and holsters. He did not take any of the men's boots. Another man shouldn't wear a dead man's boots, especially a murder's boots. They were haunted and would only bring bad tidings. He searched each man's pockets and took what he found. There were small amounts of money, some rings, some watches and other miscellaneous trinkets. He secured all of his findings into the bedroll. Simon picked out the best horse, a black and white paint. He took one of the Comancheros saddles and saddled the horse. He tied the bedroll and war chest to the saddle. He gathered the remaining horses and bound them together so he could lead them as one. He then placed the girl on the horse with the commandeered bounty. They rode across the river and away from the X-Bar-T ranch.

Simon had no intention to bury the men. He didn't have a shovel. If he had a shovel it wouldn't matter, he wouldn't waste the effort. *Such a feast, for the ants and beast and buzzards, have a good time, complements of the man who talks in rhyme.*

They rode until the sun came up. Simon then reassessed their position.

Simon decided to give the takings from the dead men to the young Miss Ravenwood. She could live quite a long time on that amount of money. She would have to be nursed back to health, and that would cost. Simon had his killing fee. It was ample. So he decided the money in the chest was for the girl. She had certainly earned it, in a sick, cruel sort of way. He would sell off the contents of the bedroll and use that money to help the Rooster.

Nellie Jacks' Longhorn Saloon was the only place Simon could think of right now. Nellie might not welcome him there, but she owed him a favor, and taking on the girl and nursing her back to health would make them even. It wouldn't cost Nellie anything—just a little time and care.

You know what's funny, as those Comancheros raided across the land.
Bet they never figured that they ever would be killed by a dead man.
All the way to Nellie Jacks she just hummed this song.
It sounded like Amazing Grace, but I could be wrong.
I got her a horse, from the Comancheros, so double we wouldn't have to ride.
Every night she fell asleep never leaving my side.

Blonde little girl ~ so innocent to the world.
Comancheros. An aberration of all mankind.
Renegade Mexicans, Indians and whites ~ the worst one can find.

Simon and the girl rode as long as they physically could each day. Simon wanted to get to Nellie Jacks as soon as possible. Simon sang as he rode.

"Swing low sweet chariot, comin' for to carry me home
Swing low sweet chariot, comin' for to carry me home
She once was lost, but now she's found,
Comin' for to carry me home
Saved her from the hellish ground,

Swing low sweet chariot swing.
Swing low sweet chariot, comin' for to carry me home
Swing low sweet chariot, comin' for to carry me home
Takin' her to see my ladies,
Comin' for to carry me home
Shot the dynamite, sent 'em to Hades,
Swing low sweet chariot swing.
Swing low sweet chariot, comin' for to carry me home
Swing low sweet chariot, comin' for to carry me home."

Simon and the girl made camp each day as the sun disappeared over the western horizon. He would kill a rabbit or squirrel or wild chicken for them to eat. He would roast it over a big warm fire. Each night he would make a bed for the girl close to him and the fire. Each morning he woke up with the girl sleeping at his side. Simon tried to talk to her, but she would only hum the song that sounded like "Amazing Grace." After a few nights Simon decided that it was "Amazing Grace" and would lightly sing it as the girl hummed.

Simon knew he could not take care of the girl. He needed to get her to Nellie's as fast as he could. He decided they would not stop again to rest or camp until they reached Nellie Jacks' Longhorn Saloon.

'Poor little Jenny Sue' thought Simon. There it was again. The thought of his mother, Jennifer Suzanne was his mother's name. His daddy called his mother Jenny Sue. Simon liked it.

Simon stopped in Wichita Falls and sent Ravenwood a telegram. He also sent a letter with the eye patch and scalp enclosed.

The telegram read:

"My deal with you is done. A young girl went to heaven today and you'll be glad to know, Patch Eye and twelve others went the other way. His eye patch and scalp was sent by letter, I hope you feel better." The Rhymer.

Simon bought them a hot meal before continuing to Henrietta and Nellie Jacks.

Jennie Sue Simon

Simon and the Ravenwood girl finally arrived at Nellie Jacks. Luckily, for Simon, Nellie was not there, but Big Legged Kate and Texas Sweet Talk were.

When Simon rode into town with the girl, and leading twelve horses, it caused a commotion.

Both Kate and Caroline ran to the door of the saloon to see what the commotion was about. They saw him and the girl coming. When they rode past the saloon, Caroline could see they were dead tired and were covered with the dirt and grime from the trail. When she saw them Texas Sweet Talk thought, *'A pole cat would not drag home something this bad.'* He was not a sight for sore eyes. What in the world had Simon gotten into now?

Simon rode to the livery and dismounted. When he hit the ground, his right foot gave way. He fell to the ground. His missing toes were really bothering him, after having been in the saddle so long, and the wound to his thigh hurt like hell. The wound began to bleed again. He couldn't feel it, but he could smell it. Slowly, he got to his feet using his horse for a brace. After he got some feeling in his right foot, he went to the girl and gently lifted her from her horse. The weight of her body, as small as she was, caused white pain daggers to shoot to his head. *Damned Comancheros, if it wasn't such a long ride I would go shoot them all again.* He had to pause for a moment to get his strength and to fight off the pain. He told himself the pain did not matter. He endured and had brought her to safety. His leg and foot hurt so much that it brought tears to his eyes. No one could see the tears though because of his dark glasses.

The girl would not leave Simon's side. She put her arms around his waist and laid her head on his chest. He worked around her so he could tie the string of horses to a post.

The livery stable owner came quickly and took the string to the corral.

Kate and Caroline caught up with them. Caroline spoke first.

"What's going on here, Simon? What have you got yourself into now? Who's the girl? Where'd you get her? And why in the H E double L haven't you written?" said Sweet Talk, not bothering to say hello first.

"That's an awful lot of questions for someone as tired and thirsty as I am," said Simon in an irritated voice. "Get us something to drink, would you?"

The livery owner brought them some water.

Simon and Jenny Sue drank the water and asked for more.

Kate got close enough to smell Simon and the girl, and it was bad. The days of being on the trail and sleeping on the ground without bathing made him and the girl two randy people.

"Damn, Simon," said Kate, "you smell like you need to be left alone."

"Long, hard ride, tough circumstances."

"Well, why didn't ya?" asked Sweet Talk.

"Why didn't I what?"

"Write, you know, paper and pen, like you write your poems."

"You know Sweet Talk. The goddamned mail runs both ways! Give it a rest." Simon gave Sweet Talk a look that wasn't pleasant.

Caroline noticed Simon was bleeding. He would need his wounds tended to later, but first, she wanted some answers.

"Who is she Simon?" Sweet Talk asked as she surveyed the girl. She wasn't giving it a rest, no matter how many mean expressions Simon gave her.

Simon's scar twitched and turned red, Kate noticed. Caroline did not. He started to say something but Kate interrupted and saved Caroline from an embarrassing situation. "Caroline, let's get them bathed, fed and rested. And then Simon can give us the details and how he came to find this girl." With that said, Kate took Simon by the arm and in turn, Simon took the girl's hand in his, and they went to the hotel to be bathed and fed.

Before they left the livery, Simon asked the owner to untie the bedroll and the chest, along with his saddlebags from the horses and bring them to the hotel.

Simon got two rooms at the hotel. Simon removed his clothes and sent them to be cleaned.

The girl's clothes could not be saved. They were worn and ragged. They could purchase new undergarments and a dress when needed. For now, she could wear hand me downs.

Kate went with the girl to tend to her cuts and bruises. She bathed the girl and carefully cleaned the cuts and applied medicine and bandages. The local doctor examined her. She finally fell to sleep after Simon came and sat beside her bed. Kate had to stay with the girl as she slept. She refused to sleep alone.

The doctor told him he had seen some men in fights before, but he had never seen anyone beat up as much as Jenny Sue. Simon was glad he had saved her. He was really proud that he had been lucky enough to kill all the Comancheros. The Demon had done well. Simon finally got a long hot bath. The doctor cleaned and dressed his bleeding leg from the bullet wound.

Simon and the girl slept through the rest of that day and through the night. The following morning, during breakfast at the saloon, Simon explained and answered their questions.

"I need for you to take care of her. With her past you needn't be concerned....Nellie owes me a favor....now that favor's being returned."

"We need more than that," said Sweet Talk, still being persistent as she was the day before.

Simon was irritated with Caroline. Did she think she owned him? He did need their help, so, for now, he tolerated her brashness.

"I took her from some Comancheros....they were just dying to set her free....got all blown up about it....blown all to hell you see. She's in shock and about half dead....she needs nursing....and lots of time resting in bed."

"Simon, if we're going to keep her and nurse her, we got a right to know. You're not just going dump her here and then be off again. That isn't fair to Caroline and me. Nellie owes you. We don't."

Simon drank down a glass of water, and then went behind the bar and got a bottle of whiskey. He poured himself a drink.

Caroline saw Simon's mood was bad. She could tell by the manner of his talk and the fact he was drinking whiskey for breakfast. She would not push her case any further. She also knew there must have been one hell of a fight for the girl.

He took off his glasses and stared at Kate and Sweet Talk.

That stare, that damned killing stare, those cold icy blue eyes—his scar twitching—and his words—sent a chill up their spine.

Simon was holding the girl's hand when he spoke. He began to stroke her long blonde hair. His voice carried his most chilling tone.

"This blonde little girl....innocent to the world....was thrown head first into the bowels of hell." Simon took a sip of his whiskey. "The dirty, surly beast....came and had its feast....the horror was greater, than she can ever tell. She endured the pain....until I finally came....and her peace was finally found. She suffered the sin....God, in time....will make her whole again.... and someday she'll be glory bound."

The Rhymer was in full voice and animation. His eyes were glazed like they were when he was about to kill.

"So I slew the dirty, surly beast....blew him north, south, west and east....those not blown up I killed with my forty–five. I slew the whole mangy lot....sent them to hell where it's hot....none of the thirteen, not a single mangy one did survive."

"Good gosh o mighty damn, Simon," Kate said in a soft whisper.

"Her daddy wanted her to suffer no more....sent me to do the evil chore....sent me to make Jenny Sue dead." He took another sip of the whiskey. "But when it got right down to it....I just couldn't do it....so I brought her here instead. So never let it be said that of the innocent I am a slayer....I'm only a soft hearted gunfighter....who at times is a rhyme sayer." Simon then drank down the rest of the glass of whiskey.

Kate said, "Jenny Sue? Is that really her name, Simon?"

"Yeah it is, Jenny Sue Simon. She's my niece if anyone wants to know."

Sweet Talk said, "What's gonna happen if her pa learns she's not dead? That you didn't really kill her?"

"Who is going to tell him, you?" Simon poured another drink, took a small sip of whiskey and swished it in his mouth before swallowing. He licked his lips and then made a smacking sound.

Caroline did not reply to his question.

Simon looked directly at Caroline. "You know as well as I, it's not what you do that matters....it's what people think you do. Rumor, idle chatter, and what's said....that is what is held true. She's been dead to him. Ever since she was taken....he killed her in his mind, all kinship forsaken. If she does regain her memory and remembers all....then it's up to her to make the call. He thinks they will suffer from the ridicule, knowing how so called decent folks can be so cruel. She could go back to her father....maybe be his niece....maybe that way....they could somehow live in peace." Simon paused for a moment, and then said, "Those Comancheros kidnapped her. Goddamned heathens, for seven months they raped her, and beat her. She survived. She is a tough girl. We owe her the chance to recover."

Both Kate and Caroline sat speechless.

Simon spoke softly to Jenny Sue and coaxed her to go to Kate.

He went to the hotel room, removed the war chest and brought it to Sweet Talk. "There's plenty of money in that chest....to care for her quite a spell....she might come around, might not....one can't ever tell. I will tell you both....there is something you can do....and hold this to be true." Simon's face flushed, his scar was bright red and it twitched. His voice quivered. "Don't let anyone ever touch her....not a single time....the person who does....well, the last words they'll hear, will be a rhyme."

Kate and Caroline could see Simon was not kidding. They both saw the Demon in his face. They knew he was not a man to make idle threats. They now knew intentions for Jenny Sue Simon.

Both Kate and Caroline know she can do washing, ironing, any simple chore.
They also know that Jenny Sue was never to become a whore.

Nellie Jack was out of town so it was okay for Simon to stay around, at least until she got back.

~ Barkeep ~
The whiskey is my friend,
so pour it again.
Don't be stingy ~ pour it deep.
You can feel its heat,
plum down to your feet
That whiskey glow is hard to keep.
Finally, it thickens your tongue
makes your brain numb,
then you crawl off somewhere to sleep.

Ivory Joe

I was in Nellie Jacks' Longhorn Saloon,
it was cold and pouring down rain.
I was sitting with Big Legged Kate and Texas Sweet Talk,
and having some whiskey for my pain.
Where my toes are missing sure hurts when it gets damp and cold,
Texas Sweet Talk said it was a sure sign that I was just getting old.
Business was slow and we were just sitting around chewing the fat,
when this young man came over and interrupted our private little chat.

Simon, Kate and Texas Sweet Talk were having a drink together at the back corner table in Nellie Jacks. Simon had his chair leaned backwards, against the wall. His hurt leg and foot were lying across the seat of another chair.

A young man came in out of the rain and took a position, standing at the bar. He was the only other person in the bar besides Simon, Kate, Texas Sweet Talk and the bartender.

"Looks like it's going to be a slow night, with this rain and all," said Simon, nonchalantly.

"Yeah, we're the only one's here except for the guy at the bar. Look at that sum–bitch–greasy little bastard," said Kate with a slight amount of disgust in her voice.

Simon gave the man at the bar a cursory look. He looked like some other cowboys who had spent a week working cows and did not bother to wash off the manure before he came to town. That was why Simon called them shit–heels. They never took the time to clean it from their boots.

"I don't mind long hair on a man," continued Kate, "but least they ought to keep it clean."

Texas Sweet Talk added her opinion. "Why should he clean his hair–don't clean nothing else. He's been in before. He's a randy son of a bitch from head to toe. He's a trouble maker too."

"Want my gun to walk over and kill him?" asked Simon rather casually.

"No. I think I'll just go over and whip his never wiped ass."

Simon and Sweet Talk chuckled. As they were finishing their conversation, the young man approached their table. He was well on his way to being intoxicated. He must have had some whiskey somewhere else to get this drunk in such a short time. Simon could smell him as he approached, he could smell the cow and the cheap whiskey. Simon's nose flared. He thought Kate and Sweet Talk could smell him too.

"You whores need to trade up, take on a young buck. I can do more for ya than this scar face broken down old man can do."

Kate and Sweet Talk looked up from their drinks. Neither one had a reply. Neither did Simon. They knew Simon would reply in time. The man had just crossed the line into death and self–destruction, and he didn't even know it. They both knew they could stop Simon, but they also knew they would not. They didn't like this man and had trouble with him in the past. He had slapped Sweet Talk once but she hadn't told anyone.

"Come on," he motioned with his arms. "Get up bitches, let's go and do what you whores are supposed to do. And when we're finished you can say that old Ivory Joe gave you the best bucking of your life."

Well, now there's a new one, thought Simon. He had heard it called a lot of things before, but never had he heard it call a bucking. Simon took a sip of his drink, smiled, and said, "Either one of you ladies ever been bucked before? Go on, get on up there and give the boy what for."

Texas Sweet Talk said, "No, thanks, I'm passing on the bucking, go find someone else."

Big Legged Kate spoke. "Ivory Joe, huh, I didn't know ivory was brown, did ya'll. Get on outta here, get the hell outta my face and away from this table."

When Kate said that, Ivory Joe got unruly. He started calling the girls foul names and cursing to Simon. The madder he got, the nastier and louder he became.

Simon finally spoke up.

Kate and Sweet Talk wondered why he had tolerated the man this long.

"Hey, hey, hey, Joe, why don't you calm down? There will be another time and place, just not tonight."

"Back off, mister, there are places you shouldn't be sticking your face. And one of those places is in my business." The cowboy paused, took another drink from the bottle he held in his right hand, and then added, "You broke down, kink legged, scar faced, piece of shit."

The 'Quickening' came to Simon's blood. Killing this one was going to be fun. The man named Ivory Joe had no idea of what he had released. Simon began to laugh.

Kate and Sweet Talk both saw Simon's scar twitch. They knew what he was going to do, but, unlike Nellie Jack, they did not care. They wanted him to kill Ivory Joe.

"Hell, I know who you are, the gunfighter that talks in rhymes. You think I'm scared? You know, I know another poet. She's a sissy friend of mine. All the poets I know, they all wear ballerina tights and frilly lace, so why don't you just get up and priss on outta here."

Kate and Sweet Talk were watching Simon. They knew he was like a rattlesnake, except he did not rattle. They knew anytime now he would strike.

Simon quit laughing, and then smiled at the man called Ivory Joe. It was his killing smile.

The girls could not wait.

Simon thought before he killed this loud mouth, he would make him suffer a while. The Demon wanted to toy with the man.

"You're just funning me, aren't you, Ivory Joe? Anyway that's what I presume....but don't crowd me too much....'cause tonight, I don't have the room."

Ivory Joe said, "On second thought, maybe I should just kill ya and get it over with for good."

Simon took off his glasses. His eyes were ice cold and glazed. He looked at Ivory Joe and said, "You know, you ought to know somebody that could!"

Then he made the move, something he should not have done.
He made the fatal mistake of moving his hand toward his gun.
He couldn't draw, the bottle in his hand got in the way.
It was going to be a bad end, for him, to a cold rainy day.
I never left my chair, the whole time it had been there in my fist.
My derringer came alive and my shot shattered his right wrist.
With the second shot I blew off the lobe of his ear.
He fell to his knees in pain, his outcome was now quite clear.

Ivory Joe grabbed his ear; it hurt worse than his broken wrist. He writhed in pain. The bottle had fallen to the floor and shattered.

"Kind of ruins your day, don't it?" spoke Simon.

"That ain't fair. You sneak shot me."

"Fair," Simon laughed, "hell, foul mouth, it's going to get worse.... it been a long time since I've satisfied my thirst. You're an irreverent and blasphemous young man....only place for you to go is to the devil's land."

Ivory Joe obviously was in a great deal of pain. Simon took a drink of whiskey.

"You provoked me and attacked me for no cause....being fair with you gives me no pause."

Ivory Joe sat backwards onto the broken glass of the bottle and the spilled whiskey.

"You are a foul man....and of cow shit you reek. You interrupted our quiet evening....with your loudness and the filth you speak. You owe the ladies an apology....and the money for a night....you didn't come here for sex....you just came to fight."

Ivory Joe started to squirm.

"Hell, I thought you were tough....I've known women who'd make you a disgrace....see this scar here....a woman put that mark on my face." Simon pointed to his scar with the derringer. "You know, Ivory Joe....as a gunfighter, you're not worthy of the name....you're just a low life coward.... who came in looking for fame."

Ivory Joe was trying to crawl away, trying to get behind the bar. It was a long crawl.

"Most of your brains must have run down your daddy's leg....deprived you of your wits....hell, I'd bet whatever gave you birth....didn't even have tits."

Both women laughed.

Simon poured himself another whiskey. He motioned for Kate and Sweet Talk to rejoin him at the table.

"So tell me, Ivory Joe, should I get my tights and lace....and do you the devil's dance? Do you want me to pirouette around the room....so you'll have an even chance?"

Ivory Joe was now trying to crawl faster toward the bar.

"Now, tell me foul mouth....just why is it you picked tonight to die.... do you want to see the devil....and ask him why?"

Ivory Joe looked up at Simon. "To hell with you, you and your whores too, you can all go to hell."

"I've already been to hell....but I didn't take to it much....there's no one down there to kill....and it's a bit hot to the touch."

Simon kicked Ivory Joe's gun over next to his good hand. "Go ahead foul mouth....claim the right to be the killer of the Rhyming Man."

Ivory Joe knew the derringer was spent. He went for his gun thinking he could get to it before Simon could draw—he guessed wrong. Simon drew his forty–five and blew away his left hand.

Ivory Joe reeled from the pain.

Simon chuckled. "Guys like you just don't learn....you keep coming for more....but look at you now foul mouth....all shot to hell and lying there on the floor."

Kate said angrily, "Simon, he shouldn't have talked to me and Sweet Talk mean like he did. Let's cut off his balls and feed 'em to the pigs."

Simon looked over at Kate. She was mad as hell. He laid his gun on the table and smiled. He reached over and poured himself another drink of whiskey.

Kate shoved back her chair, grabbed the gun and walked to Ivory Joe and said, "When you get to hell, you son of a bitch, tell the devil a whore sent you there."

Kate then shot Ivory Joe in his privates. He let out a loud yell. "OK, Ivory Joe, now who you gonna give a bucking to?" Before he could answer her question, she shot him in the head. Kate DeLauro had finally finished what the man called Ivory Joe had begun.

The fact Kate killed Ivory Joe was fine with Simon—he had had his pleasure.

The county sheriff would be less inclined to arrest someone for the killing if it came from Kate or Caroline. He didn't know how Nellie Jacks would react.

The sheriff came the next day, after the rain stopped, and analyzed the situation. He had Simon, Kate, Caroline and the bartender all present for his questioning.

"Rhymer, did you have anything to do with this?"

Texas Sweet Talk spoke up for him. "Hell no, sheriff, the lazy bastard never left his chair. He just sat there like a lump on a log. He didn't do a damned thing!"

Kate and Sweet Talk told the sheriff their version of the story. The bartender, knowing it would not have served his best interest to disagree, confirmed what was said.

The sheriff said, "Well, Ivory Joe probably deserved it. He was kind of a mean sort. I had some trouble with him in Wichita Falls. I'm ruling a justifiable killing."

Ivory Joe, Ivory Joe, didn't you know?
If you mess with the Demon you're going to get burned.
Ivory Joe, Ivory Joe, didn't you know?
There's no fury like a woman spurned.

Ivory Joe, a foul mouth, thought he was a stud.
He now lies in a pool of whiskey, glass and blood.
He can't buck anyone any more. He's dead on the floor,
sent to Hell for blaspheming, for cussing a whore.

Away went the rain and I drank away my pain,
I awoke in Sweet Talk's bed.
My missing toe didn't hurt any more,
the whiskey moved the pain from foot to head.

Send me more to fuel my flame!
I am he who kills the evil ~ The Demon is my name.

Chapter Six

The Home Land

I got back to my homeland today,
few know I'm here ~ it is better that way.
I went to where I grew up, sat up on the rise.
I see the cemetery, mama's grave. It brings tears to my eyes.
It's been a many a year and the old home place doesn't look the same.
The memories are still there, they're the reason I came.
Looking down at that old home place gets me to thinking,
and the thought's come freely, especially since I have been drinking.
I close my eyes and see me and Wes and Boyce running and falling,
and if I listen really hard I still can hear my Mama calling.
I can see us hunting and fishing. For mischief, we certainly had a knack.
You know, it's too bad that we can never go back.
The evening chill is coming. I'm warned by my missing toe.
Guess I had better get on the gray, and again, be on the go.

Simon untied the big gray horse and led him down a slight incline and then up to a knoll that over looked his former home. The small cemetery where his mother was buried was now surrounded by a white picket fence. The new owner must have added it, he surmised. He went to the cemetery and found his mother's grave. He picked some wild flowers along the way, some yellow and some red. He placed the flowers on his mother's grave near her headstone. He sat beside the headstone and wrote a letter. Later that evening, he would write the same words in his diary. As he finished the letter, he realized it was February fourteenth. It was Valentine's Day.

Valentine's Day was Simon's mother's favorite day. He decided to stay the evening in the cemetery with his mother. He went to his horse to get his bedroll. On the way back, he removed his boots as he walked across the cemetery to his mother's grave.

As he sat and wrote, he gently chewed on the stem of a yellow wild flower. He liked the taste of the small flowers. He liked the taste of the native grass. Simon was at peace for now and if he died right now, it would be the right place—lying beside his mother. If only his father and brother were here, too.

The Demon told him not to be so melancholy.

Dear Mama,
I hope you're not too disappointed in your youngest son.
I tried to save Daddy and William, but I failed, I didn't get it done.
I tried Mama. I'd have taken the bullets for them, you know I would.
I would have traded places with either of them, if only I could.
I know you wanted me to come home and be a farmer or teacher,
and that you had big hopes of William being a preacher.
Mama, don't judge me too harshly, not all the doings were mine.
I wonder if somehow, perhaps I was born under a bad sign.
I'm sorry, Mama, that I sold the place we all called home.
I didn't start that feud ~ but then I couldn't leave it alone.
Mama, I'll probably never see you and Daddy and William again.
My fate seems to always be violent, and I've lived too much in sin.
The evil, and the demons have come, and they have taken their toll.
So pray for me Mama ~ maybe God, will have mercy on my soul.
Love, Simon.

Simon folded the note and placed it under his mother's headstone. A tear gently rolled down his cheek—God how he loved his mother.

As he sat engulfed by the memories of all things that had passed, the gentle air of the evening and the native smells and sounds brought another poem to him.

Bare as birth ~ I have walked the hallowed earth.
I have felt the souls ~ through thin naked soles,
and felt the matter less energy soak my brain,
like warm soft drops of a summer rain.
The feeling brought thoughts of my own demise.
Oh yes! I heard the unfit cries
of those who shunned the religious well
and drank naught ~ and now face hell.
If the afterlife is glorious and gold
and all is true for countless stories told
that we will stand with generations past and all we knew,
those taken by the ravages of time and those by another slew.
Then why be so earthly stubborn ~ why wait?
Why not go now, to stand at the pearly gate?
Why fight so hard to remain earth bound,

why not answer the angels trumpet sound?
I laid down on fresh hallowed earth ~ still bare as birth,
seeking wisdom from good and bad ~ of all those who had
passed through the veil and went before
and I heard ~ what in heaven's name ~ are you waiting for?

I went into town, and I find it hard to believe what I'm being told.
My friend Wes has taken to graft, killing, raping and stealing gold.
I'm no saint but I never forced anyone to do what they didn't want to do.
I'm going to go find out for myself, if what they say is really true.
I can find him, I'm leaving tonight, it shouldn't be too long a jaunt.
I know all of his favorite places, I know the places he used to haunt.
What has darkened his soul? What made him fall?
What made a man lower himself who once stood so tall?
The Rooster, now Wes, if it's true what a shame.
All along I thought it would be me who'd go insane.
It is hard to understand the robbing and killing and the sodomy and rape.
What the hell caused him to get in this kind of a scrape?

Simon rode into Marshall, Texas to purchase supplies, and the first person he saw was J.T. Johnson, the sheriff. Simon was surprised to find J.T. was still holding the office. It had been almost seventeen years since they last saw each other.

They greeted each with enthusiasm.

J.T. called him into his office, walked to his desk, opened the bottom drawer, removed an envelope, and handed it to Simon.

Simon saw the envelope was addressed to The Nutt Family, General Delivery, Postmaster, Marshall, Texas. He saw it was from the Texas State Lunatic Asylum. He opened the letter and read, "Dear Mr. & Mrs. Nutt. We are regretful to inform you about your son, Boyce Bruce Nutt. He passed away last evening in his sleep. It should be a comfort to you to know he was at peace here and enjoyed many good days. Sincerely, Dr. Amos T. Brackett." The letter was dated December 24, 1883. It had only been a few months ago.

"We found this in Mrs. Nutt's things when she passed. We wouldn't have known otherwise."

"She must have passed pretty quickly after Boyce died. This letter is only a few months old."

"Yeah, it was strange. Mr. Nutt was kicked in the head by a mule last summer and died. And then she gets this letter, and I guess it was more than she could take. They found her New Years Day, dead on the front porch in her church clothes."

Then J.T. began to tell him things that Simon had a hard time believing. J.T. told him Wes had become the sheriff when he retired. Then Wes lost control and went crazy, so he had to come back and be sheriff again.

"Is all you told me true, even the things about the young girl?" Simon asked J.T. Johnson.

"Ask anyone, Simon. Wes has gone crazy or something. The son of a bitch is a certified lunatic. He's my son and I need to kill him. That's how bad it is. We've hunted for him but haven't had any luck so far. It seems he's always one step ahead of us."

"I'll find him, but I sure hope you're wrong," said Simon sternly. "If you are, I pity the sons of bitches who have been making the trash talk."

"Just so you'll know, he took my name, after I finally married his mother. He goes by Wes Johnson now."

Simon thought of the old broken down cabin at the lake, by the trees and brush where he and the Rooster and Wes used to sneak off to and go fishing. That was where he would go first. Few people knew of the place. It was pretty well dilapidated and hidden from sight.

Simon gathered his supplies from the general store and waited until early morning to ride out of town. He rode in a different direction than where the old cabin was located. He wanted to make sure he wasn't being followed. After a while, Simon changed directions. He now rode toward the lake cabin. Simon approached the cabin cautiously. He couldn't see anyone, but there was a horse tied to a tree in the back of the shack. It was the time in the morning after the sun first shows itself over the eastern horizon.

"Wes, Wes Johnson. It's me Simon, Simon Sublette."

Simon only heard the sound of the water gently lapping at the lake's shore. There were the tweets of some morning birds and the shriek of a Mocking bird.

"Wes, I know you're in there. I saw your horse out back. It's only me, Wes. Nobody else is with me. I'm alone."

Wes finally spoke. "Leave, Simon, this ain't any concern of yours. This is a private matter."

"I'm not here to make a fight with you, Wes. I haven't seen you in a hundred years. I just thought we might visit 'bout old times. See if there's any way I can be of help."

"Only way you can help, Simon, is to go away. No reason you got to get mixed up in this."

"I'm coming in, Wes. Just don't shoot damn it. I only want to talk to you."

Simon walked, slowly, to the ramshackle cabin and went inside. He had not prepared himself for what he saw. Wes' face was hollow and shrunken. He had not shaved or combed his hair in weeks—he probably hadn't bathed either. He was wide eyed with the craziness going on in his head. To Simon, he looked like some sort of devil, not like the childhood friend he remembered. It flashed to his mind that he looked a lot like Boyce had looked, when he was at the end.

"Damn, Wes, don't guess I have to ask how you have been."

"The Rhymin' Simon, you have done gone and got yourself quite a reputation."

Simon flinched at the words but let it pass. He hated that moniker. "You look like you've been through hell."

"I've been to hell and back, how about you?"

"I spent a cold day in hell once. Is all J.T. told me true? The killing, stealing, raping a young girl, that doesn't sound like you."

"Killing, yeah, I have killed some. I stole some things too, so I could eat. Rape, wasn't me."

"What happened to you, Wes....you used to walk so tall....what bent you over and made you start to crawl?"

"I started to drink a bit, it turned into a lot. Then, as a town drunk, they started laughing at me. Simon, they say I lost my nerve, said I was afraid of a fight. They said I couldn't do my job. They laughed so hard and long it took my pride. Then they got together and fired me. I straightened myself out but afterwards, everywhere I went people would point their fingers at me and whisper behind my back. And they laughed at me, and they called me a washed up drunk. It finally got to me, drove me crazy, so I have been shutting them up the only way I know how. They're not laughing now. Oh hell no, could you smell their fear when you were in town? Those that laughed the hardest, I sent to suck dirt. They can't laugh much when they got a mouthful of grave dirt, can they? You know. You've sent a lot of 'em to the graveyard. The rest are scared to death just waiting for me to come."

"So you didn't rape a fourteen year old girl and sodomize another woman?"

"Never did such, Simon, goddamned blaspheming heathens. That's why they have to die. I'll show 'em sodomy. I'll shove this forty five up their ass and blow their guts outta their goddamn noses."

Wes wiped his face with his handkerchief. He had broken out in a generous sweat. Then he started to laugh, a nervous crazy laugh. "Anyway, Simon, you can't rape the willing. Hell, it's so bad they're blaming anything that happens on me. If the wind blows too hard, or the crops fail, or if it gets a might hot, they get up a posse and here the holier than thou sons of bitches come. Let's get old Wes. It's all they think about, just getting old Wes, bastards." He laughed the nervous crazy laugh again. "That girl, she followed me around for months begging for it. So she finally got it. All I did was give her what she asked for."

"Some think that's a little young, Wes."

"Hell, Simon, you have seen them younger than that working the houses. You've probably had some that young yourself. You might have known it, might not have. I think a girl should get what she wants, no matter the age. Don't tell me you never did it."

"There's some merit to that I guess....but that isn't enough reason to hold the town hostage. I thought about killing a whole town once, considered it strongly, can't say it's out of the question yet, but it is insane."

"It isn't that, Simon. It's the laughter. I can't stand anyone laughing at me. I can hear them in my sleep, laughing and pointing their bony little fingers at me. It's drivin' me crazy. Every day that goes by it gets worse, and I get to thinking that I'd be better off dead."

"You and me, we are crazy. I've thought about killing myself. You ever give it a thought?" asked Simon.

"You know I've tried to do it myself, but I couldn't get my finger to move."

Simon thought about the Rooster. He was here now with his other childhood friend and he had gone crazy, too. Simon blamed his craziness on the Demon, but somehow he kept it in control. Was it the water they drank as kids? Was it playing in the graveyard that time? What was driving them over the edge? The three of them, all crazy!

"People making fun of you isn't a reason to go off killing them."

"Well, ain't you one to talk. Look what you do when someone calls you Rhymin' Simon." Wes laughed. "Look what you did to the Henrys, and all they did was put a little scar on your face. These here scarred my mind and my soul. They cut my heart out and made me eat it."

"This isn't right, Wes. You have to figure a way to end this."

"What the hell do you mean, Simon? I heard tell you killed some just because they made fun of your limp or made some remark about that scar of yours."

"That was different."

"Yeah, how do you figure?"

"They were low life, Wes, trash that talked trash. They weren't good for nothing but dying. They were put here just so someone like me could kill them. They wanted to die. They weren't innocent, law abiding common folks. Besides they were armed and they all had a chance. These people don't."

"They own guns, they have been warned. They had better be carrying."

"You got your jaw set on this, don't you?"

"Yeah I do, can't argue me down another road either."

They both stood in silence for a few minutes. Wes finally spoke.

"Let's go fishing, Simon, wade right out in the water like we used to."

Simon and Wes took off their boots, got some fishing poles and waded out into the water. The water was cold in February. They cast their lines near some weeds and rocks.

"Wes, why don't you leave, go hide in Missouri. They won't find you there."

"I'm not leaving, Simon. I'm going to kill every last one of those heartless, laughing heathens....every man, woman, child, dog and cat, and their birds if they own one."

Simon actually laughed at Wes's comment. He hadn't ever thought about killing someone's bird.

"Just like my old pal Simon did to the Henrys. Then I'm going to town and burn the son of a bitch to the ground and then I'm going run naked through the ashes and piss in the town well."

Simon laughed again. "You can't do that, Wes."

"Well, the only way to stop me is for them to kill me." Then Wes turned and looked at Simon. "Or until you kill me. That's why you came, isn't it. Everyone else is a goddamned coward, especially that chicken shit J.T. My own birth father, he wouldn't say shit if he had a mouth full. He never said one word to help me."

"I came to help you, Wes. There's the place Rooster went to that can help."

"Well, I'm damn sure not going to a lunatic asylum and end up like Rooster."

Simon looked at Wes. He wondered how he knew. Simon knew, deep down, down in his soul, if Wes went to Austin, he would end up dead just like the Rooster. And he would suffer the whole time he was there. The people in Austin would never cure him.

Then Wes started to cry. Damn Simon hated it when grown men cried. Even though he had done it before too, he still hated it.

Wes was really sobbing hard now. He was squatting in the lake with his head buried in his hands. Suddenly, he stopped, rose up and looked coldly at Simon. He had a gun pointed at Simon's face. "I know you're here to do it for them, but I'm not ready yet."

Simon froze momentarily. He looked into Wes's eyes, and they were the eyes of a crazy man. Simon saw Wes's finger move. Wes, his childhood was actually going to kill him. Instinctively, Simon whipped his fishing pole into Wes' face and the shot from Wes' gun went harmlessly into the air. Wes lost his grip on the gun. Instantly, Wes removed a knife from his belt and lunged at Simon. Simon jumped aside and shot Wes with the derringer. He died as he was falling into the water.

Wes cast his line ~ for the last time.
A Mocking bird shrieked again.
I said good–bye to my childhood friend.
Nightmares no more, no longer taunted.
It wasn't the way for him to go, it wasn't what I wanted.

Simon carried his childhood friend's body back to the cabin and buried him in the dirt floor. Then he set the cabin on fire. That's what he would have wanted if it had been the other way. Having to do what he did, the killing of Wes was something that would haunt Simon for the rest of his days.

He made his way back to town. He needed to tell J.T. but he didn't know how—or what to say.

I felt sorry for my old friend. I knew why he wanted to die.
The Devil had stolen his soul ~ when he gets to hell he can ask him why.
Wes and I went fishing, I was the only one who returned.

The town only knew he was dead, how he died was never learned.
"The suffering and evil are no more
~ after all, what is a friend for."

Let It Go
There's no future in the past,
especially if a life or love comes to an end.
You must ease your mind,
and give yourself time to mend.

There will be some tearful pain,
but don't let the sorrow multiply.
You must make peace with yourself,
and find a way to say the final good—bye.

Memories are all you can hold now,
remembering their good deeds is best.
Because you can't change the past,
and sad thoughts must be put to rest.

The only future in the past,
is from experience and a lesson to learn.
The past is gone and cannot be changed,
you can't go back, you can never return.

You must get on with living ~ end that chapter,
and let a new ones begin.
And they won't be in it,
the life ~ or ~ love ~ that came to an end.

Rhymer

Scofield

I morn Wes every day, except for the end he was truly a good man.
But now there's something else that's gotten out of hand.
I served side by side in the war with the man who owns the general store.
I learned today he was killed in Louisiana, for mistreating a whore.
It's a bold face lie, in the war, he lost his abilities to do such acts.
Whoever is doing this lying, and for some reason, covering up the facts.
All I want is to be told the truth, told to me face to face.
I want to look him in the eye, the man who sent him to his resting place.
I'm going to get the body ~ for a proper burial ~ and his soul to save.
If I find he is a lying son of a whore, he will get his own grave.
The sheriff sent a telegram telling them I am on my way.
They know the Rhymer is coming ~ and there might be hell to pay.
It reminds me of Revelations. He rode a pale horse, and Death was his name,
and what follows him is Hell. Well, I'm bringing the same.

"I sent the wire. They know you're coming. I told 'em you'd fetch Clifford's body and be gone. I think that's the best way," J.T. said.

"How in hell could you believe the story they told?"

"I don't believe it, Simon, but what can I do? I got no authority over there. Hell, it's in another state."

"What about the federal marshal, what'd he say?"

"He's in cahoots with the local sheriff. He says he's convinced it was handled correctly. The man who done the killing is a well respected businessman. He says the matter is shut."

"That's bullshit, J.T. and you know it. You may not have any jurisdiction over there, but I do."

"You think you can go anywhere you want and do your bidding. They have laws in Louisiana. They aren't going to be as lenient as me."

"What law have I broken here where you need to be lenient me with me?"

"Well, there are the rumors about Wes. I hear a new one every day."

Simon laughed. "I think I'll start the next one. I think I'll tell them I sent Wes to Austin, to the nut house, and he has escaped. That'll get them to talking, now won't it? What they need to talk about is what kind of medal they are going to pin on me for saving their pansy asses! How can it be a crime if he was wanted?"

J.T. pushed back his hat revealing more of his face. "None I guess. But be careful, Simon. He's a powerful businessman. The federal marshal ain't gonna take kindly to you shooting up the town."

"Well, federal marshals can be bought and paid for too, can't they?"

"I 'spect so."

"If that's the case, then the corrupt son of a bitch can just get dead too with the rest of them."

The man who killed him owns a local saloon and is held with respect.
I'm going to have trouble getting to him is what I suspect.
I also learned he beat him to death, and he did it for no reason.
He was drunk, and he did it, because he thought it was pleasin'.
I'm going to find this man, and not take no for an answer.
My break came in another saloon when I befriended this dancer.

Simon went to Shreveport, Louisiana, retrieved Clifford's body from the undertaker and had it shipped home by train. He wired the sheriff, J.T., and told him he was staying for a few days. As he left the telegraph office, the sheriff and the marshal approached him.

"Why didn't you leave with the body?"

Simon studied the men. He saw the badges pinned to their shirts. The one with the marshal's badge was the one who had spoken. "A dead man doesn't make for good company on a train ride," said Simon, guessing why they were asking.

"What business do you have here? We don't want your kind to loiter."

"My kind, tell me, what is my kind, I'd like to know."

"A coldhearted killer, that's the kind we're referring to. We got the wire from your sheriff. We don't want you here. You're not wanted for anything as far as we know and let's keep it that way. There's still time to get on that train."

"Gentlemen, let me make this very plain....dead, in a box, is the only way I'm getting on that train!"

The three stood and stared at each other deciding what to do.

Simon broke the silence. "Either of you two up to it?" he said, and then he smiled at them.

"What is the reason you're risking arrest to stay?" asked the marshal.

"I seek the absolute truth about the death of Clifford Caldwell. The circumstance didn't ring true with me. His name has been soiled. If it is the actual truth, so be it....if not then I want to clear it."

"The absolute truth, as you say, is he was in a whore house and didn't get his way. He was drunk, pulled a knife and went after one of the girls. It cost him his life."

"Clifford wasn't capable of such things. I knew him well."

"That may be the case, but men do strange, uncharacteristic things when they get away from home. I think that was the case with your friend. There is still time to get on that train." The marshal was persistent.

"I was with Clifford many times away from home. Not once did he exhibit any such notions. And as far as being in a whore house looking for sex, that part is absolutely untrue. He was chaste....and deeply religious. He was shot in the privates during a battle in Virginia and they had to remove his testicles. He couldn't have screwed a whore if you held a gun to his head. So why don't you reopen your investigation and find the real truth?"

"The matter is shut with us. Go home," the sheriff said stiffly.

"I'm not in that box yet. If either of you are game....I'm at the Jefferson....I'm registered under my name." Simon turned and left the two men standing in front of the telegraph office.

Simon calculated they would send an assassin to be rid of him. He didn't check into the Jefferson Hotel. Instead, he went to the Shreveport's red light district, St. Paul's Bottoms, to find a safer place and where he could buy protection.

The Demon and I have decided, to kill them all, all Clifford's killer's friends.
The sheriff, the marshal, any other abettors, the vileness must be cleansed.
If this is proved to be a cover up, those involved, for their lives they should fear.
What I did to the Henry's will be trivial, to what I will do here.
If they issue warrants for my arrest, then I will flee.
Mexico is a safe place, I'll take Melina with me.
They will send men, but they had better send more than a few.
They are naïve and have no idea what a man like me can do.

"He doesn't care does he, that you're a federal marshal?"

"He's dangerous, just like Drummond."

"Why didn't you kill right on the spot?" said the sheriff, irritated.

"Too many witnesses, we have to do this so it's in our favor. Tell Scofield to keep a low profile until we get it handled."

"Let's kill him at the hotel then bury him where no one would ever find him. They're building some new places down by the river. We can make him part of one of the foundations."

"Okay, get it done, but I don't want any reports. Nothing sent to J.T. It'll be as if he completely vanished."

"It'll take a lot of money to make someone completely disappear. Do you want to use Drummond?"

"I don't know where he is, and I don't want to wait. Besides, he isn't very discreet at times with his business, and we need to do this quietly. I'm sure Mr. Scofield will contribute whatever is necessary."

Simon had no luck in finding the man named Scofield, the man who killed Clifford Caldwell. Scofield was in hiding and the town's people, none of them, were talking. Finally, one evening late he got lucky. Simon was in a saloon on the far edge of town. He was approached by one of the girls who danced in the saloon stage show.

"Simon, come here but be quiet."

Simon stood close to the woman and bent down so she could talk in a whisper.

"I was with one of Scofield's men earlier. He sure was bragging 'bout how they'd kept him hid out."

"Did he tell you where he is hiding?"

"No, but he did say that Scofield was going to be in his saloon 'round midnight tonight, to count his money. Even though his friends hide him out and lie for him, he still doesn't trust them with his money."

"Thanks, I'll do something for you sometime."

"You can do something for me now. Just kill him. He hurt me once. Then we're even."

"Kill him? Oh my dear, it will be my pleasure."

"Oh, and by the way, his men always play poker in the private room in the back. They'll know exactly where he is."

His cronies always played poker in the same private room.
So I waited for the proper moment to unleash my doom.
I quietly opened the door and stuck the sawed–off in the first man's ear.
Their eyes got as big silver dollars, you could smell their fear.
I think he soiled his pants. He will never ever be the same.
That man, in whose ear, my sawed–off took aim.

Simon quietly said, "I am the Rhymer....and when I speak in verse.... the next ride most men get....is in the back of a hearse. I want Scofield now....and get him fast....or there is going to be one hell of a blast. I'm in no mood for trifling....your answers better be true....or I'll come back and kill you....and kill your families, too."

Simon shoved the shotgun a little harder into the man's ear. "Now get those jaws loose or die in place....licking this man's brains off your face."

One of Scofield's men at the back of the room pointed his thumb to the sky towards the upstairs. Simon knew where he meant without ever looking up.

"Gentlemen, I know your faces....and if I see any of you before first light....I won't hesitate....I'll kill you on first sight."

This was one of those fights that wasn't going to be fought fair.
I backed out of the room and quietly went up Scofield's back stair.
When I opened his door, Scofield had the look of a coyote in his eyes.
He never expected me to come and he showed his surprise.
I slapped him across his head with my gun and took him down.
Then I carried him to my horse and we rode out of town.

Simon, slowly, carefully tried the door knob; he was surprised—it wasn't locked. Quickly, he was inside the room facing Scofield. Before Scofield could move, Simon hit him with the butt end of the sawed–off shotgun, rendering him unconscious. Hurriedly, Simon got all of Scofield's money, clothes and personal belongings, packed them in a bag, threw Scofield over his shoulder and went down the back stairs. No one saw him leave. He was right in his guess about Scofield's friends. They would lie and cheat for him—but they would not die for him.

Simon took the money, clothes and other items from the room to make it appear Scofield left town, and in a hurry. He wanted to make it look like Scofield decided to leave until the danger from the Rhymer passed. Simon did not see anyone from the room below as him and Scofield rode away from Shreveport.

The further I rode and thought about it, the madder I got.
To take advantage of an unarmed storekeeper makes my blood run hot.
I wanted this one to suffer, for a quick death I had no desire.
I wrapped his body and hands and feet in some of that new kind of wire.

This place I had stopped was nasty and we were all alone,
and I horse drug the son of a bich until most of his skin was gone.
They would hunt for us, how hard and how long one couldn't say.
How much loyalty did his money buy, for a month, a week or a day?

Simon took Scofield to another place he and Rooster and Wes used to play as kids. It was totally uninhabited and a place a person would not go on purpose, unless of course you are teen–aged boys looking for mischief.

"Now you know how it feels to be on the other end, when a man is just killing for the pleasure. The same way you killed the storekeeper, Clifford."

"He was beating up a whore, ruining my property."

"You forgot to check his pants Scofield....the yanks blew his balls in the war....what would a man like that....want with some old whore"

Scofield squirmed against the barbed wire.

"I heard you killed him....just to show you could....and that you laughed....the whole saloon laughed....while you proved your manhood."

"You heard wrong. It wasn't like that. I'll pay you to let me go. I have plenty of money."

"Congratulations, I got plenty too....look at all this money I took from you."

"You've had your revenge, now let me go."

"You aren't going anywhere but to hell....I'm going to kill you, but when, I can't tell. I want you to suffer like Clifford did. I heard it took three days for him to reach his end....and no one in that miserable goddamned town of yours came to help him."

"Go ahead then. Kill me and get it over with."

"I think not. I'm going to hurt you bad....it might even drive you mad. I might even let the buzzards come and thrive....might let them eat out your eyes while you're still alive." Simon thought about doing Scofield like he had those done those men back outside of Mesilla, New Mexico. But they died too quick. Dying too quick was too good for Scofield.

He begged for me to kill him, he wanted to end the suffering and die.
But I wasn't ready to do it quickly, wasn't time for him to ask the Devil why.
I poured some whiskey on his wounds and listened to him yell.
Two more days passed before I sent him to hell.
I know they are hunting for us, but this place they'll never find.

I wonder what they think now, what they think of my kind.
For his end, a bullet from his own gun splattered his head
I have to run now because the law will want me dead.
If not for the barbed wire, a suicide is how he died.
I don't think they'll ever find his body, not this place and how I hid it.
The creatures and rot will take hold and they can never prove I did it.
But I don't mind running, not from their kind of law,
but they better keep a vigil at night, I might come back and kill them all.
Before they could realize ~ I'd come in the Demon's disguise,
and kill them with the sawed– off, derringer and forty–five.
They better watch every night ~ just in case I might,
because none of them, not a single one, would survive.

Simon finished his burial of Scofield. If anyone ever found him, it would be from dumb luck. He was in a place where the buzzards would not know he was dead. When he left Scofield's tomb, not a trace was left behind. Not a single thing that would show that anyone had ever been there before. He rode back toward Marshall. He stopped at the burned down shack where Wes was buried and cleaned himself beside the lake. When he rode into Marshall, he didn't look like a man who had spent four days in the wilderness without bathing.

He didn't know how this would work out. He could run to New Mexico or Arizona. Secretly, he did not think the law would come for him. He suspected the corrupt federal marshal might. They would have to find Scofield's body to prove anything against him. And he was sure this federal marshal didn't want another lawman involved, one that could uncover his corruptness.

This might just be the time to kill a whole damn town. Maybe he had killed Wes too soon. He and Wes could have turned loose their destruction, and then both would be satisfied.

Jedediah Drummond

J.T. went to Simon's room above the Marshall Mercantile. It was a strange place to stay, but the Caldwell family insisted when Simon returned and cleared Clifford's name. They offered the room free of charge as an act of gratitude.

The federal marshal from Shreveport came to speak to Simon about the disappearance of John Scofield and was at J.T.'s office.

"People tell me you kidnapped Scofield from his office above the saloon. They said you rode off with him on horseback. He hasn't been seen or heard from since."

"I didn't ride anywhere with Scofield, got any witnesses?"

"Not at this time, but I want to know your involvement."

"None here, I spoke with him in his office, and he told me the truth about Clifford. He told me he really wasn't in a whore house and never threatened any of the girls. He said the real argument was over some money Clifford thought Scofield owed him on some imported whiskey he bought. He said Clifford pulled a gun. They wrestled, and Clifford got shot. That worked for me, so I left."

"Then why did he tell me about the whores?"

"Easier to explain I guess. I don't know. Maybe you should ask him the next time you see him."

"No one has seen him since you were there that night. Someone cleaned out all his things. It appears as if he left town, but I think you forced him. If I can ever prove it, I'll be coming for you, Mr. Sublette. I would arrest you right now, but I have no concrete proof, only hearsay. No one will sign a statement. My gut instincts tell me you killed him and buried him somewhere."

"You must have eaten some bad crawfish if your gut is telling you something like that. J.T. will vouch for me."

The federal marshal left without hearing a word from J.T. Johnson.

Two days later Simon overheard the telegraph operator's comments. "What in the world is he doing coming here, we'd better tell J.T." The telegraph operator was excited—and nervous.

What was it that would get them this upset? Simon followed the operator to J.T.'s office.

"This just came in, J.T. Better look it over, might be trouble."

J.T. read the telegram. "I'll be damned. Thanks, Dan."

The telegraph operator left and Simon walked in. "From the look on your face it looks like bad news, J.T. I overheard. What's in that wire that's got Dan so upset?"

J.T. handed Simon the telegram. It was from a sheriff in Missouri. It said for everyone to be on the alert, the notorious killer, Jedediah Drummond, was headed toward East Texas.

Damn he'd be here soon, they have hired them an assassin.
I got lucky and got wind of it just in passin'.
The name gave me a chill ~ it was Jedediah Drummond.
Folks around here haven't ever seen bad ~ but he is coming.

"Damn, Simon, this could have been better news. Reckon why he's coming here?"

"He's coming after me, I suspect. I think he's coming to collect my dead body."

"This wouldn't have something to do with this Scofield fellow, would it? Did you kill him, Simon?"

"You heard what I told that marshal. Why ask again? And besides, that marshal is corrupt and you know it. That story they made of about Clifford was all fabricated."

"I know, but he still thinks you killed him. He just can't prove it. Maybe he's sending Drummond to do what he can't, being a lawman and all."

"Let them think what they want to. They probably did hire him to kill me, just thinking I did in Scofield. Has his body turned up?"

"No, Scofield ain't surfaced yet, dead or alive."

"I think he's just somewhere where people can't find him. Maybe he saw the light....the wrong he'd done....perhaps something scared him out of his skin....and he decided to run. You know he murdered Clifford....just for fun and all....then stood behind a lie....and was protected by their law."

"Yeah, I know. I know. You keep telling me. Far as I'm concerned the matter is closed. And I haven't said so, but thanks for helping out with Wes. I didn't want to have to do it, since he was my son."

"Wes was a good man....did a lot for this town....but when you drink as much as he did....it'll finally take you down."

"There's a reward for Wes, Simon. How do you want the money?"

Simon almost slapped J.T. "You can take that reward and shove it up your ass, J.T.!"

Simon thought for a moment. "Give it to the church. Give it in my mama's name. And make damn sure they get the money too." Simon turned and left. He was mad. One more word from J.T. and the town might be looking for another sheriff.

J. T. had been afraid of Wes. Even though he was Wes's father, he hardly ever spoke to the man or helped him out.

Simon thought as he was leaving, Wes was right; J.T. is a chicken shit. J. T. wouldn't say shit even if he had to swallow a whole mouth full.

Simon now knew. The federal marshal didn't arrest him for a reason. No need to arrest him. They didn't want to put him in jail. They wanted to kill him. They hired themselves a killer, Jedediah Drummond, to settle the score.

He is the meanest man that I've ever heard tell.
They say he's been everywhere killing ~ except to hell.
He's given to wickedness and is of a most evil sort.
He once burned down and killed a whole town, I heard report.
He is known to shoot blacks and china men ~ just to see the color they bleed,
and to kill innocent men and women just to hear them plead.
They say he killed his ma and pa and sisters and brothers,
and they say he's been known to eat the flesh of others.
Now he isn't coming to visit or to hear me talk in rhyme.
He's been hired to take a life ~ and that life is mine.
He doesn't fair fight and is known to shoot in the back.
I'm not waiting for him to come ~ as always I'm going on the attack.
He's mean enough all right and they say he has no fear.
I suspect that's cause no one's ever really gave him a scare.

Simon waited for each train to arrive. He chose a spot a few miles outside of town to watch the train approach. His suspicion was Drummond would halt the train and depart before the train reached the depot. When the train did not stop early, he would follow it until it reached the depot and inspect each passenger to see if any of them matched the description of Drummond.

Simon's suspicion was turned out to be true. One evening seven days after he first read the telegram, the train came to an early halt and a lone man disembarked. It was late at night. Simon knew the man must be Drummond, but he couldn't be sure. His blood raced. He could kill him in an instant, but if it wasn't Drummond he would be in big trouble. More trouble than he wanted. He approached carefully, silently. He got close enough to see Jedediah Drummond, in the flesh.

I put my gun to his head, I cocked the hammer, and he heard me click it.
If he'd never been to hell ~ then I'd just bought him a ticket.
I should have killed him outright, like all the others I had tracked.
A mistake on my part, he moved so fast I had little time to react.
Why I did it escapes me, is the Demon leaving me be?

"Drummond, this doesn't need to happen, just get back on that train and go back to where you crawled out from under."

Drummond didn't move, but he spoke, "Go to hell!"

"I'll be glad to oblige you....if you really want to dance....but think it over long and hard....to see if it's worth the chance."

Simon made a deadly mistake. He didn't pull the trigger.

Drummond didn't say a word. Then suddenly, Drummond's elbow crashed into Simon's face.

He was quicker and stronger than Simon had anticipated. Simon's gun roared into the night catching Drummond in the shoulder.

Drummond fell to the ground and rolled to his right. Another flash came from a gun, but it was not from Simon's gun. It was from Drummond. The shot hit Simon in the calf of his leg, above the left ankle. Drummond fired again catching Simon just above the knee in the fat part of his thigh. It was a grazing blow, not penetrating the muscle. Simon was struck twice more, but with his blood afire and with the Demon along side, he felt no pain.

Simon fired his remaining bullets at Drummond, three of them. He was sure he hit him somewhere. It was hard to tell in the dark.

Both men emptied their guns at each other. The pain and wounds inflicted would have been too much for most men, but not for these two. The adrenalin wouldn't let them feel the pain. The pain would come much later for the survivor.

When he ran out of bullets, Simon threw his gun at Drummond striking him in the mouth, breaking a tooth and temporarily stunning him. Then Simon jumped on Drummond and they fought in the dirt. Drummond was stronger than Simon, but Simon was more skilled in fighting hand to hand—thanks to the army. Many punches were thrown and the men kicked each other viciously. Both men were bleeding from their mouth and nose. They wrestled and struggled in a life and death dance. They fell into a large rock, and if there had been a witness, they would have heard the breath of both men being expelled from the blow. At one point in the fight, Drummond had almost bitten off one on Simon's ear lobes. In the life and death struggle, both men had drawn their knives. Simon got a cut on this right check from just below the eye down to his chin. Drummond finally got on top of Simon. Each man had a hold of the other's wrists, struggling, trying to stab the other to death.

Simon summoned all the strength he could find—he raised his leg and got it positioned over Drummond's head. Finally, with a grunt and all his strength, using his powerful leg muscles, he dislodged Drummond, knocking him backwards. Drummond's head hit the railway track dazing him for a second. It was the second Simon needed. He took his knife and shoved it into Drummond's ear, killing him instantly.

"I'm sending you to hell, Drummond....to the devil's den....and when I get to hell....I'm going to kill you again."

With those words, the fight was over. Simon was lucky, very lucky indeed.

It was bare fist and knives, I got the upper hand and my knife took its toll.
I shoved it deep in his ear ~ Hell opened up and swallowed him whole.

Simon rolled off the body of Drummond and lay next to him in the dirt. He laid his head on the railroad track. The cold steel of the track felt good on the back of his neck. He was breathing heavily. His wounds began to ache. The pain was coming rapidly. He was lucky. Most of his wounds were only flesh wounds. He thought he had been hurt worse than this before, but he couldn't remember where. He made some make shift bandages and tied them to the wounds. He lifted Drummond's body to his horse. It took him a while, with most of his strength gone, to get in the body in position. He would rest as he rode. He rode toward the town that had hired this assassin. Simon thought they might want a report on the outcome. The report would be so much better first hand and in person.

Simon left his knife sticking out of Jedediah Drummond's ear. With the blood covering his face, coming from his ears, nose and mouth the man was not something pleasant to look at. Just for good measure, Simon poked out Drummond's eyes. He wanted everyone in the town to see what happened when the Rhymer Man turned the Demon loose. Simon took Drummond's knife to replace his own. Drummond's was a better knife than his. Drummond's knife had an ivory handle.

I hung the body on the bridge ~ most of my strength it took.
I wanted everyone in that town to get a damn good look.
I had poked out his eyes and pinned a note on his coat.
I meant every last word of the rhyme that I wrote.

"Here is your hired assassin, He wasn't up to the chore.
This ends it right here, don't send any more.
I asked him to leave but for some reason he didn't hear.
I guess there must have been something stuck in his ear.
There is no one left, I've killed all who have come to kill me.
So those that hired him, leave this state and I'll leave you be.
I have the wire with the names of those who hired this man.
Leave me be, or the proper authorities will find this in their hand.
I'm an intemperate son of a bich and those I touch die.
I send them to hell so they can ask the Devil why.
Hellfire killing is in my blood so do take heed.
Pack up your families and leave now with due speed.
I will come again soon, to kill those who remain.
I have a thirst for bloodletting and I am insane.
I will come shrouded in shadows, on a hot breath of wind.
For those who caused this trouble ~ their lives will end."

I have no plans to go back but they'll never know.
I just want to heal good and proper, so I can go.

Simon was a mess and his gunshot wounds began to take their toll. With his left leg now shot all to hell he would probably have a limp in it also. He thought maybe if he limped on both legs it would look like he was walking normal. Simon laughed thinking about it—double limp, walk normal. If that was the case, maybe he owed Jedediah Drummond some thanks. The money he took from Drummond would more than pay for his rehabilitation.

Good–bye to the Home Place

It took Simon longer than usual to ride back to Marshall. He was in great pain. With the help of J.T, he rested and nursed his wounds. He knew he was going to leave as soon as he felt in full repair. He did not know where he was going, but he was leaving. Too many bad memories lingered in this town.

I have one last friend here ~ he's a reverent, religious type of person.
He puts up with my temper and with all my cursing.
He says he sees more good in me that he does bad.
I told him I needed to buy some eye glasses just like the ones he had.
But what he sees, I guess, comes from the Almighty on High.
He sees a lot more with his heart than he does with his eye.

Simon sat at his regular table in the back of the local saloon. He was healing fast. His face now looked worse than before, with the tiny red knife mark on his right cheek courtesy of Drummond. It would heal eventually and would not leave a scar, but it would take a while. He noticed for the first time, as he was shaving, that he had teeth marks on his ear. He didn't remember being bit on the ear. He counted himself lucky that Drummond did not bite off his ear. The bite marks would fade, too, in time.

Everyone in the town respected Simon, some from fear, some who knew him as a tough man fighting for what he believed was right. All gave him a wide berth. The killing of the likes of Jedediah Drummond was making him into a local legend. He sat and drank and wrote in his diary the Jedediah Drummond story. He knew how lucky he was to have won that fight.

I've mostly been alone in the things that I've done, kept my separation.
My only allies were the Demon, my guns and my reputation.
Some say I don't ride alone, that death is my passenger.
They say when the Grim Reaper calls, I am his messenger.
To me, I champion women and children ~ make right things done wrong.
I've never taken anyone undeserving ~ against injustice, I've stood strong.
I have ridden through the canyons and valleys in the midst of death.
Of those Devils encountered, I'm the only one who still draws a breath.

I have looked the Devil in the eye ~ the red blood is his wine.
I've been through hell and back ~ I am of the gunfighters design.
I have faced down many killers, and I have faced down death.
I have stood in the furnace and withstood the demon's fiery breath.
And though that fiery breath touched me, it harmed me not.
At times that breath was cold. At times it was white hot.
You break out in a sweat, but it chills you to the bone.
Your blood runs both hot and cold and the fear is never gone.
The Devil comes along side and licks you with his flame.
He expects you to crumble and quiver at the trumpet of his name.
But you look the Devil in the face and you don't ask him why.
You defeat his evilness and you spit in his red flamed eye.
Then you stand on the brink ~ you shudder ~ you almost went to hell.
But you have faced down the Devil ~ it's another story to tell.
Someday someone will come and put me to my final rest.
So far I've been lucky in my fighting ~ somehow I've been blessed.

Simon got a letter from Melina. Brock Deaton had forwarded it to him. In the letter, it said that her father and her brother were killed in Nogales. Melina wrote and asked for Simon to come back and help her with the cantina. It came to Simon that this was where he would go. He had a couple of other places to stop at along the way, Fort Worth for some relaxation and then the Palomino Palace.

He went to the post office and sent Melina his reply.

Maybe I should take up with Melina, become an honest man.
Go on back to Tumacacori, maybe ~ while I still can.
I remember when I first saw Melina, like none I'd ever seen before.
Prettier than any woman, be they proper or be they whore.
When I first saw her ~ she was near ~ maybe five or six feet,
and even from there I could feel her body heat.
Crow black silken hair and ruby red lips,
fire in her eyes, melon chest, and the slimmest of hips.

Simon was in his room above the Mercantile. It was late and he was lying in bed thinking about if, and when, he should make the trip to see Melina. There was a knock at his door. Instinctively, he reached for his gun. The door opened and there stood Jolene Caldwell, Clifford's daughter.

She had been born to Clifford and his wife before the war. Jolene was a beautiful young lady in her early twenties. Jolene's mother ran away with some drifter when Clifford returned from the war and she learned of his affliction.

Simon started to say something, but Jolene put her finger to her lips telling him to not say anything. She walked to his desk and blew out the flame in the lamp. The only light filling the room was the light of the moon. Jolene slowly removed her dress and undergarments. She then pulled away the bedcovers and joined Simon.

"I never did get to thank you proper," she whispered in his ear, "for what you did for my dad. There are not too many men like you anymore who would do what you did."

Simon didn't know how to react. Accept her generosity or turn her away. The warmth of her body and the smell of her skin made it an easy decision. Jolene wasn't skilled in the art of love making, like the others Simon had been with, but she made up for her shortcoming with enthusiasm. Jolene was a very supple woman. She upheld the reputation of the female in honorable fashion.

In the heat of night she came to set things right,
and who am I to turn her away.
By the light of the moon, the bedsprings sang a tune,
but it is not enough reason to stay.

Simon was awakened by a cock crowing and a cool breeze blowing across his naked body. Jolene was not in his bed. Simon washed himself and then gathered his belongings from his room. He went down the stairs and found Jolene behind the store counter.

"I brought you some of your father's things. I got them when I went to get him, his watch and boots, and there's some money there for you, too."

Simon handed Jolene the watch and boots. He had placed the money he had taken from Scofield in one of the boots. He kept the money he had taken from Drummond. The money Drummond had received to kill Simon.

"I don't know how to thank you, Mr. Sublette." She stood on the tips of her toes and kissed Simon on the cheek. It was as if nothing had happened the evening before.

"I've already had the best thanks a man could ever get. Take care of yourself, Jolene. If you need me, J.T. will know where I can be reached."

"Mr. Sublette?"

"Yes."

"Did you know my mama?'

"Yeah, well, sort of, I only met her in passing, why?"

"I'd like to find her, talk to her, and tell her about Daddy."

"I get around a bit. I'll keep watch."

"Thanks." Jolene then gave Simon a hard hug.

For a moment, Simon didn't know if she was going to let go.

Simon left the Mercantile. For the life of him he could not remember the face, not one feature, of Maudie Caldwell.

West Bound Again

Simon walked off the front porch of the mercantile and turned toward the livery stable.

"Mr. Sublette, wait up."

Simon looked and saw a stranger approaching. He saw the man was not carrying a gun. He was relieved.

"J.T., the sheriff, told me I could find you here. I'd mentioned, in passing, to him, about this place called Nellie Jacks and he said you would want to know."

"What about Nellie's," Simon said with concern in his voice.

"Well, I was there about a month ago. That woman Nellie, the sheriff said you'd know her; well, she got herself killed by a shooter. He was beating some girl, and she tried to stop him, but he wouldn't listen to reason and just turned and shot her dead cold."

Simon's face turned cold. His scar twitched. "Was the girl this shooter was beating, was it a young girl?"

"Nah, it wasn't a young one, hell. I didn't see no young ones while I was there."

It relieved Simon to know that Jenny Sue was not involved. "Was it the one they call Sweet Talk, or Big Legged Kate?"

"No, wasn't them, one of them others, didn't catch her name. And you know what else, Mr. Sublette, that one called Big Legged Kate, damn finest I have ever seen. Whoo—wee what she could do! Knew more tricks than a fast cow dog in a small pen."

"Sounds like Kate to me. Thanks for the information." Simon tipped his hat and started to mount his horse. He had a shooter to find.

The man turned and walked away.

As he watched the man leave, he noticed J.T. walking toward him waving a piece of paper.

"Simon, I didn't get to say goodbye. I guess you got the news about Nellie Jacks?"

"Yeah, he found me, told me about it. Do you need something important? I need to be on my way. I have people to see and things to do."

"They found the shooter, Simon. Rangers tracked him down and killed him."

"Are you sure about that?"

"Yep, it's right here in this telegram. It just came across the wire. I guess they saved you the trouble?"

"Sounds like it, don't it?"

"Tell me something, Simon, I've know you a long time, ever since you were a kid. You were always rambunctious, but you weren't mean or nothing. What made you like you are, you know, how is it a man finds it so easy to kill and....and....it doesn't....and it doesn't bother him at night?" J.T. stuttered.

Simon stared hard at J.T, stared long enough to make J.T. uncomfortable. "Just lucky, I guess," he finally said, and then turned to go.

J.T. scratched his head and pulled an envelope from this vest.

"Here's a telegram addressed to you. It came with the other wire."

Damn thought Simon, I hope it's not more bad news. I'm tired of bad news coming. Every telegram I get something bad has happened or is going to happen. Simon read the wire.

"Dear Simon. Nellie Jacks has been killed by a gunman. Jenny Sue and I and Kate are fine. Come soon." It was sent by Caroline.

Simon wondered if Nellie Jacks had her 'Moment of Truth' before she died. Probably not, he thought, knowing her she was too busy trying to talk the gunman out of killing her to see her life pass before her eyes.

The day Simon rode out of Marshall, the train arrived from Shreveport. It carried a coffin. Inside the coffin was the body of Jedediah Drummond. There was a note attached. It read, "I believe this belongs to Simon Sublette. It's over and done. The matter is shut."

There was a reward for the killing of Drummond. J.T. didn't know if he would tell Simon. J.T. was thinking about collecting the reward money for himself. He sat in his chair and thought about it hard and weighed the consequence of what Simon would do if he found out about the reward and he wasn't the one to collect. J.T. reckoned Simon might call on the Texas Rangers to make sure they actually found the killer of Nellie Jacks and learn of the reward. Having to face the Rhymer about any issue was not something J.T found pleasant. It was the Rhymer's rightful money. J.T. made the right choice. He decided to stay alive. He went to the telegraph office and sent a telegram to the Texas Rangers in Ft. Worth telling them that Simon had killed Jedediah Drummond but had failed to collect the reward. The telegram said if Simon Sublette was seen to please have him wire and collect the proceeds.

Simon considered stopping in Fort Worth at the Texas Rangers Headquarters, but that would only delay his seeing Jenny Sue. He needed to see for himself she was okay and unharmed.

Simon rode past Fort Worth and arrived at Nellie Jacks' Longhorn

Saloon. He rode to the back of the building to tie his horse. It was mid–afternoon and he wanted to enter by the back hallway. As he entered the alley behind Nellie Jacks, he saw Jenny Sue. A man had her by the arm, and she was trying to get loose. Quickly, Simon dismounted and went to Jenny Sue's aid.

"Hey you, let go of the child!" said Simon as he hurried down the alley.

"Who says?" the man said angrily.

The evilness of the Demon appeared. The Demon's voice was harsh. "Simon says."

"To hell you say. I'm just gettin' a little kiss. Anyways, who the hell are you to be bothering me."

Jenny Sue saw that it was Simon and was glad it was not just some other cowboy. She spoke first. Simon had never heard her voice before; it was deep, raspy, like it was sore. It almost sounded as if the Demon had possessed her. Simon smiled.

"He is the one who talks in rhyme, protector of the old, the feeble, the lame, the weak, protector of the disfigured, the deformed, the young and the meek. He kills vile men like you. I think he's gonna kill you today."

The man looked at Simon and raised an eyebrow. He could see Simon's face up close. He saw a devil of a man. He saw the huge scar on his left cheek and the new red thin line on his right cheek running from his eye almost to his chin. He saw that Simon's large scar was flushed red. He saw it was twitching. He also saw Simon's forty–five pointed straight at his left eye.

Simon cocked the forty–five. The Demon made his finger twitch. The sawed–off shotgun was mad because it was still on the horse. Simon answered the man's question. "Who am I? Can't you see my wings? I'm your Arch Angel....and I've come to take you home....unless you go down this alley....and leave the child alone. I will kill you, shit heel....then you can ask the devil why....that for trying to kiss a child....that you had to die."

He turned to look at me ~ all he saw was the killing steel in his nose.
He ran on down the alley ~ to live again, is what he chose.

Jenny Sue said, "Uncle Si, glad you came by."

"I am too, Jenny Sue. I'm glad I showed up when I did....isn't any sense in a man mistreating a kid. Are you okay?"

"I'm fine. He didn't hurt me. He just tore my dress."

"We'll get you a new one tomorrow, my treat, maybe a pretty blue one."

Jenny Sue smiled. She was glad to see Simon. She was happier than anyone could imagine.

"Where are Kate and Caroline?"

"They're inside somewhere, probably drinking."

"They drink a lot, do they?"

"Might as well, isn't much else to do in a town like this on a Sunday afternoon."

"Pretty girl like you ought to be out on a picnic or something."

"Can't, they won't let me go anywhere or do anything."

"Would you like to do that, go on a picnic?"

"Oh, that would really be fun."

Simon got a spare derringer from his saddlebags and handed it to Jenny Sue. "This is in case Uncle Si can't come by....next time, you shoot the vile men....you make them die."

"Will you teach me, Uncle Si?"

"It'd be a pleasure, wouldn't leave it to anyone else. We'll go on a picnic, rustle up some old cans and have some target practice."

Jenny Sue smiled again. She was happy Simon—and the Rhymer—was here.

Jenny Sue looked at me. I knew simple she was no more,
but no one would know the difference, she liked her life ~ and ~
she knew what the derringer was for.
I should have killed him right then.
He'll get full of whiskey and he'll come back again.
I'd like to see his face, when he tries to lift that skirt,
and Jenny Sue uses the derringer, to give him a powerful hurt.
I told her to shoot him in the privates, that's where those men have their pride,
then he could hold on to what he loved most ~ as he died.

"Let's go find them drunks," Simon said.

Simon and Jenny Sue found Kate and Texas Sweet Talk sitting at his favorite back table. They were laughing and carrying on, and both were pretty drunk.

Texas Sweet Talk jumped up when she saw Simon. "Goddamn, Simon

Sublette, the Rhymin' man, I heard talk you was gettin' bigger than life, killed old Jed Drumstick. Hell, you look the same size to me, 'less they're talkin' 'bout somethin' else." She gave Kate a wink and they both laughed hard.

"Don't think you should talk like that with Jenny here. She'll learn fast enough, no need to speed it up." Simon shot Sweet Talk a hard look. "Some drunk tore her dress sleeve; we need to get her a new one."

"Look, Jenny Sue, there's a clean dress up at the house. Why don't you go change? We'll be 'long directly. We need to talk some business with Simon. We'll take you shoppin' tomorrow and get that new dress," said Kate.

"No need, Uncle Si has already promised me a new dress."

"Uncle Si, huh? Go on and get changed," said Sweet Talk.

"I don't want to go. I want to say here and talk to Uncle Si."

Texas Sweet Talk said firmly, "Go on ahead now, Jenny. We'll only be a minute or two." She moved her arms to shoo Jenny away.

Jenny Sue let out a gasp of air. It frustrated her not to get to be close to Simon. She whirled around angrily and left.

Texas Sweet Talk looked at Simon's face. She saw the new mark on his cheek and the still present bite marks on his ear.

"Damn, Simon, looks like you were sent for but didn't go."

"I went....but he wished he hadn't of sent."

"Guess you got our telegram, 'bout Nellie."

"Yeah, I came as soon as I read it. Took a while for you to send it, must have been busy."

"We had lots to do and no one was harmed, guess we should have sent it sooner."

"I dropped everything and came here to see if everything was okay. I ride in and I see some shit heel cowboy trying to molest Jenny in the alley. Are you watching after her like you said?"

"Look, Simon, we're tryin' hard, but we can't shadow her every damn minute. She's a right smart lookin' young lady. Men are gonna pay her attention, and as long as she's here, in this place, sometimes it's gonna be a shit heel. It's time she learned to take care of herself," Kate said. Her voice told Simon that she was irritated.

"Just 'cause a chicken has wings don't mean it can fly."

"Bull shit," said Sweet Talk. "She's got snap in her garters. She'll be just fine."

"Maybe so, but I'll make sure. I'll get her some insurance. Just make sure she has a place to eat and sleep. How's her money holding out?"

"It's still all there. We ain't touched a dime."

"I hear you girls took over this place when Nellie got killed"

"Damn sure did, she left papers. What do you think about the improvements?"

Simon looked around. He was surprised. Kate and Caroline had cleaned up the place, added some new window coverings and furniture. The saloon looked damned near respectable. "Looks good, so why don't I have some whiskey already?"

"We ain't into whiskey. We're drinkin' champagne. We're gettin' uppity now that we're property owners."

"I'm in. I'll have some champagne....just to ease my pain....and maybe later some soft flesh....to ease my brain."

Texas Sweet Talk raised her eyebrows.

Kate didn't acknowledge his last comment. Kate poured Simon a glass of champagne. "There's one more thing Simon. We bought that big house down at the end of town, the white one with the wraparound porch and the picket fence. We're living there now, thinkin' 'bout turnin' it into a boarding house. What do you think?"

"Good idea, a boarding house should make some good money."

"We thought so, but we need some money to fix it up proper. If we make Jenny Sue a partner and let her run it for us, can we use some of the money she has?"

"It sounds okay to me. It'd be a better place to finish growing up than a saloon. I'll talk to her tomorrow." A look came on Simon's face like he remembered something he had forgotten. "If you're going to run a boarding house, take a look at this. It could be a welcome attraction."

Simon reached into his coast pocket and removed a piece of paper. He handed the women a drawing of the stand–up bath he had seen at Madera's Cantina. He had added a few things, such as a privacy fence, so it could be used without embarrassment. It was one of the most amazing things he had ever seen. That and Lettie's naked body.

"We're glad you approve! That makes us happy. Hell, Simon, if you weren't Sweet Talk's man I might finally give you a taste of what it's really all about."

Texas Sweet Talk looked at Kate and smiled. "When you've already had the best, Kate, it's hard to get any better, right, Simon?" They all laughed.

"Simon says, two on one....could be fun."

Caroline slapped him on his arm.

"When did you get into liking champagne? Thought you were a straight whiskey man?" asked Kate.

"It's my refined side, Kate....my kinder state. Hell, I might become a gentleman....if given the chance....I might mend my ways....and hell....I might even learn to dance.

"We believed everything you said 'till now. Did the champagne already get to your head?"

"Might buy me a shirt with some of that lace....I even heard there's a doctor, who can fix my face."

"There ain't that much money in the whole damned state," remarked Sweet Talk, and held up her glass to toast the comment.

They all laughed again. The three drank well into the night, too long to suit Jenny Sue. They never did come along directly.

Simon ended up in bed, at the saloon, with Sweet Talk. He would not go to the house the women had bought because Jenny Sue was there. He would not sleep with Texas Sweet Talk in that house, or any place where Jenny Sue was near.

Late into the night, Caroline awoke and rolled over in bed, Simon was not there. At first it startled her. She got out of bed and went to look for him. She did not have a robe or any bedclothes—they were at the house. She looked around and saw Simon's shirt. She slipped it on to cover herself. She could smell Simon on the shirt. The smell pleased her. She walked down the stairs and found Simon, naked, sitting cross–legged, Indian style, in the middle of the saloon floor. He had a bottle of whiskey between his legs. "Simon," she called, but he gave no answer. "Simon, what are you doing?"

Simon did not move. Caroline walked to where she could face him. "Simon, it's Caroline, what are you doing? Are you okay?"

Simon looked up at Caroline. "I'm having a conversation with my daddy."

"Simon, dear, your daddy is dead."

"Yeah, and that's why it is a private conversation, so leave."

"But, Simon ..."

Simon interrupted her. The look on his face scared her.

"Leave Caroline, you don't want to be able to hear both sides of this, do you?"

She saw Simon's look was hard and cruel. It was a direct threat, and she took it as such. She went back to bed. Why was he such a hard man? She wished she could find out and help soften him some. At least he had finally called her by her real name. There might be hope yet.

Later he came to bed. Almost instantly he fell into a deep sleep.

Caroline Endryl could not sleep. She sat at a small table beside the bed and wrote a poem. She thought about the hell that Simon must have gone through in the fight with Drummond. She thought about Simon killing Drummond. When the poem was finished, she slipped it into Simon's diary. Maybe he would find it and read it sometime.

Lover or Killer
I lay beside him, silently watching the rhythm of his sleep.
This lover of mine who I sometimes hate.
What images walk in his dreams as he cries and moans?
Am I here to witness his final fate?

As before—our bodies form as one.
He stirs that hunger that heaves.
That reaches, deep down, to the bottom of my soul.
And it's never sated because he always leaves.

At times he stares and drifts to another place.
Why does he come to me, time after time?
Where does the one man begin—the other end?
My lover, who at times, speaks in a rhyme.

Sometimes his rhymes are filled with cold–hearted hate.
He is a notorious gunfighter of the west.
Walking, talking in the best and worst of times.
He is a stranger who can find no rest.

If I awake beside the killer, what would be my fate?
Would the gentle touch still be there?
Or would I cringe in fear at the look in those cold eyes?
Would I feel arms around me that could not care?

Who really knows the one, who beside me lies.
Could he be perhaps, a soul taker from the devil's land?
Is this my lover who just killed with cold blooded hate?

Or is he simply the gentleman I know, the Rhymer Man?

Caroline Endryl
Texas Sweet Talk

The next morning Simon came down from the room where he and Caroline spent the night. When he got up that morning Caroline wasn't there. He figured she had gone to the house for the rest of the night and to bathe and change clothes.

He walked down the street towards the big white house at the end of town, the one the women now owned. He had not paid any attention to the house before. He saw it had two stories. It had a wraparound porch on two sides of the house. It was painted white except for the window shutters. The shutters were a pale blue color. It was an attractive house to Simon's eye. It appeared to be well built from the outside. A window facing Simon was open and a blue gingham curtain fluttered with the morning breeze.

He was going to find Jenny Sue and buy her that new dress he promised. Half way to the house he saw all three of the women walking toward town.

Jenny Sue ran ahead to greet Simon.

"Caroline, do you notice anything different about Simon?" asked Kate.

"You mean old Fire and Ice. I can't see much, he's dressed the same as always. Why?"

"He's not limping much this morning."

"Oh yeah, I can see that now that you mention it. It must have been all that cure all I rubbed on him last night."

"Cure all?"

"That's what Simon calls it. He says some feline varmint will cure damn near anything that ails a man."

"Feline varmint, is that what he calls it?"

"Beats me, but that's what he calls it."

"Worked on him."

"Worked on me too."

"What's with the fire and ice comment?'

"He's hot blooded and coldhearted, Kate, both in his killing and his loving. He can be sweet and loving but then there is a cold spot in his soul. I got the nerve to ask him about it about once."

"What did he say about it?"

"I think this is how he said it." She lowered her voice and tried to speak in a rough, harsh tone like Simon did at times. "I try to keep it hidden.... pain and death are all it gives....it's where the Demon lives."

Kate laughed at the imitation Caroline did of Simon's voice. "Guess he meant the killing Demon, huh?"

"Guess so."

Finally, they caught up to Simon and Jenny Sue.

"Good morning, ladies, anyone care to go spend some ill gotten gains?"

"We're all going. The house is the limit, and the Rhymer is buying," said Caroline.

Jenny Sue had her arm locked into Simon's. They turned and walked in front of the Kate and Caroline and went to the general store. Simon bought Jenny Sue three new dresses of her choice. He also bought her a nice pair of riding pants, a blouse and a hat. In a way, Simon thought of her as his niece.

After the trio finished their shopping, Jenny Sue changed into her new pants, blouse and hat. She and Simon left for their picnic.

Kate and Caroline went to the saloon to tend to business.

Jenny Sue and Simon rode out to the river and found a nice secluded place where Simon could teach her how to use the derringer. It didn't take long—she seemed a natural. With practice her aim would improve, but she could hit a man at close range. Simon thought she had been taught some basics previously, probably by her father.

"That part was easy. I think I'm ready for something bigger. Can I try your forty–five, Uncle Si?"

"I think the derringer is all you'll ever need."

"But I might want to kill someone farther away than this little toy will reach."

Simon looked her in a different manner. What was she thinking?

"Maybe so, Jenny, but my advice is, don't get into it. It isn't worth it." Simon paused for a moment. "Jenny, you know I'm not your uncle don't you? You know there is no blood relation?"

"Mr. Sublette, I know exactly who you are and what you are. You were, and are, my salvation, and I truly love you for that. You resurrected me from a hell and gave me life. More importantly, I know who I am. I know my real name is not Jenny Sue. For the time being, I prefer to remain just plain old simple–minded Jenny Sue Simon. Being this way serves my purpose for now. I know what happened, and what you did. I remember everything, even my daddy. I know the whole story. I might forgive him someday, and I might not. But, I will never forget. Right now, if I saw him, I'd kill him."

Goddamn Kate and Caroline, was Simon's first thought. She must have overheard them talking about it. Why couldn't they keep their mouths shut?

"Sometimes I have bad dreams about it, but I'm doing okay with it. When the time comes, I'll become Rebecca Anne Ravenwood again, but not now."

Rebecca Anne Ravenwood, Simon liked that name. He hadn't known her real name until this very moment.

"Kate and Caroline bought that house wanting to fix it up into a boarding house. They want you as a partner. They want to use some of your money to make the place more presentable and fancy. I told them it was your call."

"Jenny Sue will talk to them about it. Come on, Uncle Si, let's shoot some more."

She took his forty–five, took aim, and shot a twig off of a branch.

Simon smiled. He was a happy man. He finished eating a chicken leg, he then threw the bone into the air, flipped his derringer to his hand and shot the bone into pieces. It was a lucky shot but he wasn't going to tell Jenny Sue.

Simon was sitting at the back table in Nellie Jacks. He saw Caroline come down the stairs. She and the man named Blackweller approached the table at the same time. She came from the stairs, and Blackweller came from the back door. Simon saw him coming. He noticed that the man was not carrying a gun and he was glad.

"You're the man I had a run in with before, ain't ya?"

"Guilty," Simon answered. "What can I do for you?"

"Well, I'm gonna be in here tonight drinkin' and choistin' a girl or two. And you know sometimes I get a bit rowdy, but it's all in fun. So please, when it happens, don't come and bust my head or nuthin', okay? I don't want to be lookin' over my shoulder all night while I'm tryin' to have me some fun."

"It's fine with me Blackweller. If I hear a scream....make sure it's one of pleasure....know what I mean?"

Blackweller tipped his hat and left.

Caroline said. "What the hell was that all about, askin' your permission to have fun with the girls?"

"That's how Kate and I met. He was rough housing her and I busted his head."

"Oh yeah, she told me about it, she said you still owed her one for that."

"Hey barkeep, more whiskey here," said the man who, a day earlier, had tried to kiss Jenny Sue. He was standing on the far side of the saloon at the bar.

Simon had not yet seen him.

The bartender took a bottle of the house brand whiskey, a clean glass, and placed them on the bar in front of the man. He noticed the man staring at someone in the corner of the bar. "You're looking at someone hard and mean, Wood. Anybody I know?"

"See that big, ugly, sum–bitch over there in the corner."

"You mean the one talking with Sweet Talk."

"Yeah, that's him, the one wearing them funny glasses, someone ought to learn that boy some manners."

"That gonna be you?"

"Maybe."

"Better think twice, Wood. That's Simon Sublette, the one called the Rhymer. He's the one that killed Jedediah Drummond. He, stuck a knife in his ear, poked out his eyes and sucked out his brains. You'd be better off to go out back, on that hill, and grab a rattlesnake and try to teach it not to bite than you would be to take hold of him."

"Is that right?" Wood said questioning what the bartender just said.

"Wood, let me tell you something, you could survive the snake bite. You won't survive him."

"He still ought to be taught," said Wood, continuing to stare at Simon.

"Go ahead then. It'll take dying to get it done."

After Wood had a couple of more drinks, he said, "So you're telling me that man is the Rhymer, huh, in the flesh?"

"For real, all blood and guts and meaner than the devil, they say he killed his best friend too. He killed him in a squabble over a fishing pole."

"Why ain't he in jail for it? Was it for a just cause?"

"Ain't no just cause for killing your best friend, and an argument over a fishing pole ain't good reason either. He's just a coldhearted, ruthless, devil–eyed, mean, son of a bitch. That's all."

"I wondered why he talked so funny."

"Yeah, sometimes he talks funny. But, Wood....he don't kill funny!"

The man named Wood thought about it, finished his whiskey and headed for the front door.

Simon saw him leaving and recognized him as the man in the alley who had tried to kiss Jenny Sue.

Wood shot a glance toward Simon and momentarily their eyes locked.

Simon puckered his lips and blew Wood a kiss. Both men knew it was a promise; it was a kiss of death.

Caroline saw the exchange between the two men. "What was that all about?"

"Nothing much really, it's that I'm his arch angel.... I promised to take him home....just letting him know I'm watching....that's he's not alone."

"Guess I don't understand, but then there's a lot about you I don't understand, like last night, Simon."

Simon's mood went silent. He poured himself a drink. He offered one to Caroline.

She took it and drank it down to help her courage. Simon gave her his full attention.

"I know you've been dealt some hard blows, but hell, Simon, who around here hasn't. You're just having a harder time letting it go than the rest of us. We heard about you killing your friend, Wes. Want to talk about it?"

"Really now, tell me, who is spreading that kind of talk?"

"Simon, you're getting famous, people talk about you a lot."

Simon looked at Caroline. Simon decided to tell her. What the hell he thought. There was no harm in telling. The church in Marshall received a nice donation in his mother's name. The proceeds came from the reward money for Wes.

"He called me Rhymin' Simon. You know how I feel about that." Simon smiled.

"You're putting me on? Come on, Simon, it had to be more than that."

"He was insane....suffering in pain. Now he suffers no more....after all....what are friends for?"

"Well, I never thought …"

Simon interrupted. "Do you really know what a hard blow is, Sweet Talk?"

"I think I do. I've had a few."

Simon shrugged his shoulders. In his opinion, she had no concept of what a hard blow was.

"I know you're cold about some things. Another man's life is one of them, but I also know that when we're alone you're awfully hot blooded. I like to think I have something to do with that. I think I'm good for you Simon. I think it's time for you to settle down with one woman. You could help me and Kate. We'd deal you a share."

Simon privately mused to himself, did she mean for him to settle down with her or Kate? Or maybe Jenny Sue was in the picture. "Caroline, there's some things you should know, things I've never told anyone else but it's the way I am. There's something inside me that likes the solitude....likes being alone....I'd never be happy settled down....I can't call a place home. I own nothing and nothing owns me....it's nothing against you....but I have to stay free."

"I know you got to have your room, Simon, but I can live with that. You can be by yourself anytime you wish. I won't crowd you."

Simon thought it but didn't say it, 'you mean like you're not crowding me now'. "I can't stay here, Sweet Talk. I'd never be happy and later it would just cause problems."

"Then take me with you. I won't be a burden. I'll earn my way. If I don't, then you can dump me, and I won't say a word." Caroline desperately wanted to be with Simon for the rest of her life. "Holiday carried his woman with him," she added, but then when she saw his reaction, she wished she had not.

For a brief moment, his eyes went cold. He set his jaw and his scar twitched. The Demon came because it made him mad to be compared to Doc Holiday. He quickly got the Demon under control. His expression softened. It was not his intention to make her miserable.

"I'm not Holiday. Please don't compare me to him again. He's dead now. Maybe carrying her around....put him in the ground. Who knows? With the way I am....drawing trouble like I do....it would only be a burden to you. If something were to happen to you, because of me....then I'd have your blood on my hands....for all eternity."

"Why ARE you so goddamn coldhearted, Simon?" Kate said, having overheard the conversation, as she came to the table and sat down.

"I don't know, maybe you can tell me.?"

"We don't know either. It seems the only thing you love is trouble. What made you that way? Are you capable of loving anything other than the violence?"

Simon almost got up and walked away. Instead he took a drink of his whiskey. Maybe talking about it would help, maybe. Writing about it in his journal had not got it out of his head yet.

"Whether it is coldhearted or callous....I don't know which....there's a tear in my soul....that I just can't stitch. The war saw to that, made me this way."

"Simon," said Kate, "there were a lot of men of men in the war. They all came back and settled back into a normal life. There's a lot of them right here in town. What makes you any different?"

Simon looked at the two women for a long moment. He decided to tell them about the incident when his taste for killing was born. Perhaps if he told them, they would leave him alone. He could only hope anyway. He leaned forward and placed both elbows on the table and cradled his whiskey glass in both hands. He spoke softly. "I kissed the blood....off my daddy's cheek....I held him in my arms....as he became limp and weak. The days counted five....I sat with him till he died. I never found my brother.... couldn't bury him all....I watched him blown away....by a Yankee cannon ball. I picked the body parts....out of the bushes and trees....dug both of their graves with my bare hands....down on my knees."

Kate and Caroline remained silent, now entranced by Simon.

"I wasn't afforded the courtesy to say any last words, didn't get time to grieve proper. During the ceremony the Yanks attacked again....this intense rage overcame me....I went crazy and killed many, many, blue–coated men. Some said at the time, too many." Simon took a small sip of his whiskey.

"But Simon, I'm sure others did the same, and they are okay now," said Caroline.

"Yes, I'm sure that is true, but not for me." Simon raised his glass to his lips using both hands, took a small sip and continued. "As I sat in the aftermath, in the bloody mess, something happened to me, I must confess. At that moment something was born inside me....this darkness people feel but cannot see. I sat there, sweat soaked, bloody from head to toe. I was looking around at the fallen men and came to realize....I had no remorse, no sadness in my eyes. The killing bothered me not, not a bit....and I knew right then that I liked it....really, really liked it. The men around me at the time told me I was coldhearted, for the manners regarding my kin….and for the ruthless hatred, directed towards those fallen men." Simon sipped on his glass of whiskey. "My superiors took note and began to....utilize me....all because they said I had this unique....ability. I, and a few others, did things in the name of war that in peaceful time we'd be in prison for.... and this darkness....unbelievably, yearned for more. Each foray took its toll....made even darker....my darkened soul. I began losing my emotion.... when I buried my daddy and my brother. All feeling was lost forever....it all died....when I lost my mother. The last time I cried....was when I got home....and found my mama had died. It was like all hope and happiness was viciously ripped from my soul....I have never found anything, or anyone to fill that deep black hole."

Caroline saw that Simon was serious.

Kate said "Good God–O–Mighty Simon. What did they do to you, you poor man? Is that when the rhyming started?"

Simon started to become agitated. He pushed away from the table and leaned back in his chair. He pulled his forty–five from its holster and began twirling the bullet cylinder with his left thumb. He now switched from speaking softly to talking in the same harsh whisper as he did when he was going to kill someone. His Demon voice, he called it. He took another long drink. "Perhaps you are right Kate. I think before I was a bit more genteel. Maybe what jumped inside me was a sadistic poet looking for a soul to steal." He spun the gun cylinder hard. "You know ladies.... people have wounds that can't be seen....some make us cold....some make us mean. Some of those wounds never scar....that's how we are made.... into what we are." Simon took the last of his drink.

"So you don't love anything, Simon, is that what you are saying? Do you have any love for me at all, just a little bit....maybe?"

"I know about commitment and duty and responsibility that's all. Love is not something I understand anymore."

Caroline spoke, her voice became excited. "Love, Simon, true love, is when you give up your heart and soul to someone. When you'll walk barefooted over rocks and stickers 'till your feet bleed to follow your man. It's when you're willing to give up everything you have or ever will have to follow him, that's true love."

"I've followed some men like that....then sent them to hell's gate....but I never did it for love....always did it for hate."

"I'm not talking about bounty hunting, goddamn it, Simon. I'm talking about a man and a woman for Christ's sake!"

"True love is beyond me....it's something I don't have in here." Simon pointed to his chest. "The thought of it scares me....it's my only fear. I don't ever want to feel like that again. What you're wanting is what I don't have any more. It was taken from me....the ability was drowned....all that I had is buried in the ground."

"But, Simon …" Caroline said.

Simon raised his hand signaling that he was tired of the conversation.

He is warped and twisted, but I love him anyway, thought Caroline. "You think I'm just a toy, don't you? You think I'm here to play with until you tire of the game and then can you put me away until you want to play again."

"Sweet Talk, you should know better....than to get love started....with a son of a bitch that's hot blooded....but coldhearted!" Simon drank down another whiskey, got up from the table and headed up the stairs, with his gun still in his hand.

Caroline picked up his empty glass and threw it at him.

The glass shattered on the railing close to Simon's face. A splinter of the glass lightly cut his face on his scar and caused it to bleed. He could not feel it, but he knew it because he could smell the blood. He never looked around. He stopped on the next to last stair and spun the gun around on his finger, caught it by the handle and deftly returned it to its holster. He continued up the stairs and went to bed.

Kate put her arms around Caroline's shoulders and gave her a small hug. "Don't judge him too harshly, Caroline. Simon is bad all right, but he's bad in a good way. He's got more guts than you could hang on a fence. He loves us, but in his own manner. He'd take a bullet for either one of us, but if you're looking for a husband you're shopping at the wrong store. Some say he eats glass and craps straight razors. Well, he might eat glass, but each time he does it just forms around his heart and makes him colder. You can't tie down the wind. You can only feel it, and that's what Simon is like. Enjoy when it comes, like you do on a hot summer day, and the wind comes and cools you."

"I'd take my chances, right now. I'd take anything I could get."

The next morning Simon came down from his room on the second floor of the saloon. He walked into the street and saw Kate and Caroline on the front porch of their house. He walked the short distance up the street to the house. He spoke before he got to the front steps. "Kate, Sweet Talk, I'm leaving this afternoon. Some business came up in Fort Worth. I talked to Jenny Sue. She's willing on the boarding house deal. I think it is okay to let her roam around and do what she wants to do. You're both right. She's got to learn to take care of herself from now on."

As soon as Simon had said the words of his departure, Caroline went into the house and slammed the door. Jenny sue joined Kate.

"Kate, I can explain it to her, but I can't make her understand it. I'm not suited to love anybody that someday I'll lose....it may not be right, but it's what I choose. I'd rather take the pain....of being cut or being shot.... than to have a love lost....whether I chose or not."

"But, Simon …"

"I'm sorry....that's how it is, I'm afraid....I can't help it Kate....that's how I'm made. I have to be on my way....it'll just get worse for her, if I stay."

"Will we ever see you again?" asked Jenny Sue.

"I'll be back....just like a bad cold....one morning you'll look up....and lo and behold."

"You take care of yourself, Simon," said Rebecca Ravenwood.

"Always, Jenny, keep a sharp eye."

"Bye, Uncle Si."

As Simon rode away a tear came to Rebecca's eye.

I told Kate and Caroline of how the Demon was born, I told them all,
but I'm not sure they can understand, how he comes when I don't call.
If I could spit him out I would ~ but then could I survive?
Do I have enough inside without him to stay alive?
Caroline is hurt, but she's better off than she can believe right now.
I made an excuse to go so maybe she could come to her senses somehow.
I'll go to Fort Worth for a while, hang around Hell's Half Acre.
Maybe I'll look for me a proper woman. Maybe I'll find me a taker.

Texas Rangers

Simon left Texas Sweet Talk, Big Legged Kate and Rebecca in Henrietta and went to Hell's Half Acre in Fort Worth, Texas. He wanted to see if there was anything in the Acre to hold his attention. He wanted to see if it had a different look to it than it did when he had stayed there with Caroline. He wanted to talk to the Texas Rangers about Nellie Jacks' killer. He needed to go to the Fort Worth National Bank and make a deposit.

In Fort Worth I met two I'd heard of, but to date had never met,
the Texas Rangers ~ Bennett Slaughter and "The Sandman" Everette.
They'd tamed a few it was told, between them the numbers were steep.
Slaughter is ornery like me and "The Sandman" got his name
from putting many a man to sleep.

The two Texas Rangers saw Simon enter the Waco Tap.

The Waco Tap was a loud saloon, maybe the rowdiest of all in the Acre. The Acre, itself, was rough and rowdy. One Fort Worth newspaper stated if there wasn't a cutting, or scrape, or gunplay, or if some prostitute didn't die from experimenting with morphine, then the Acre had had a good evening.

Before the Rangers could approach Simon, he abruptly left the Waco Tap. He journeyed to the outer edge of the Acre to Queen's Hall. This was a respectable gaming hall with some of Fort Worth's finest citizens in attendance. The patrons were not apprehensive that someone like the Rhymer would be in such their place. Others from the seedier side of the Acre, from time to time, ventured into this all male gaming establishment to try their luck. Most of those present knew of him by his reputation as a bounty hunter and a man killer. He was like the other gunmen that came, one not to be provoked. Some had seen a vague likeness in a posted picture but had never seen him in person. He was a larger man than they had imagined. They hoped he was here merely to gamble.

The two Ranges followed Simon to Queen's Hall and approached as Simon found a table. They wanted to make sure he was here for entertainment only, and at the same time they could tell him about the reward for Jedediah Drummond.

"Good evening, sir, we hate to interrupt, but are you not Simon Sublette?" asked the Ranger named Slaughter, tipping his hat.

Simon saw their badges. He knew this was not a social call. Simon stood up and nodded his head. "I'm Sublette. What a coincidence, I was coming to see the Rangers tomorrow. May I be of service?"

"My name is Bennett Slaughter. This here is Solomon Everette. We have been keeping an eye out for you. We received a wire from Sheriff J.T. Johnson in Marshall."

Simon motioned for the two Rangers to take a chair and waived for someone to bring some whiskey. Simon sat down.

The Rangers each took a chair, but they never got comfortable. They both sat on the front edge of their chairs, ready.

"I have heard of you, Mr. Slaughter, and of you, Mr. Everette. Your reputations precede you," said Simon. "I trust the wire was of a pleasant matter and this call is social in nature."

"We know about you also, Mr. Sublette." The words were polite and soft from Slaughter.

Simon received a hard stare from Sandman Everette as he spoke. "It seems your name comes up quite a bit these days."

Bennett Slaughter said, "People tell us you're a hell of a shootist, some say you have no equal one on one."

"Well, I wouldn't know about having no equal. My experience has taught me that even though you might be more skilled than most, there is always someone out there who is better. The trick is not to run into him."

"Well, that may be the case. The wire we received contained verification that you killed a man named Jedediah Drummond, it said you shot him to hell and stuck a knife in his ear. The sheriff, this J.T. Johnson, said he ruled it self defense. Regardless of how it happened, there was a federal bounty on Mr. Drummond. The proceeds are yours to claim."

"I ask him to let it be....but his ego was greater than his fear. Is that what you two came to see me about?"

"That's the main thing, but we also need to know your intentions while you're in Fort Worth. Are you here to apply your special talents or is this just for pleasure?"

"I can assure you, it is strictly pleasure, Rangers. I've had enough violence for a while. I don't chase it, but it does seem to find me, and too often for my taste, I might add."

"That's good to know," spoke up Everette. "Are you carring that derringer up your sleeve?"

"I see you have performed due diligence in regard to my habits. Is it illegal to have some small protection in the Acre?"

The Rangers were surprised at Simon's gentle nature and speech.

"No, not illegal, we know it can get rough here, but you react quicker than most."

"Then perhaps, to show my true intentions, I should surrender this little pea shooter." With a motion so fast the Rangers didn't have time to react, Simon's left arm moved and the derringer flew to his hand. Instantly he flipped it and laid it on the table in front of Everette. "I shall recover the weapon when we meet tomorrow. Is that satisfactory?"

The Rangers had heard of this move from others, when they recounted their stories of him in action. Seeing it in person was akin to a magician pulling a card from his sleeve.

"That's the best move I've ever seen, Mr. Sublette. Is that how you are so successful in your endeavors?"

"It has served me well in times of duress."

"I'm sure they were all legal, Mr. Sublette," remarked Bennet.

Simon tried not to speak in rhymes, but sometimes he had no choice.

"I never performed the act....on any man who was innocent....every man I ever planted....deserved to have his life spent."

A lovely young lady arrived with a bottle of whiskey and three glasses. Simon poured himself a drink, but the Rangers declined.

"Planted 'em huh," Slaughter replied, "Now that's one I haven't heard before. Have you ever heard that Sandman?"

Simon took a sip of whiskey and replied before Everette could answer. "Plant them....just like in an orchard....instead of trees you plant bones....it's the place where the lifeless go....to make their homes."

Damn, there it was again, the speaking in rhymes. They came mostly without him thinking about them.

Everette said, "I guess we'd better be careful, Bennett. He's talking in rhymes. You know what they say when that happens."

Simon smiled. It was a soft smile. "I do speak in rhyme, from time to time. It usually doesn't matter, simple mindless chatter. It's okay....simply a habit I've acquired over time....it comes natural....the words just pop into my mind."

"Well, it was good to meet you, Mr. Sublette. We have others we need to attend to. Come by tomorrow and we'll help with the documents for Drummond."

"I could sit still for that. By the way, don't worry about these city folks....I always give them a wide berth....you see, a man's reputation....is the only value he's really worth."

"Mr. Sublette, we know about your reputation during the war. We know you received several medals and served the Confederacy with great honor, and we'll give you generous latitude for that service. Do both of us a favor and keep your current reputation in check, and then we can keep this little meetings of ours strictly social."

The two Rangers left and wound their way through the crowd to the front door. "Bennett, I believe that boy is touched a bit."

"He can be touched all he wants with his rhyming and all, just as long as he doesn't touch nobody else. Then we might have to touch him, know what I mean?"

"Yeah, I reckon that would be a good fight, don't you? Can you believe that move he made with the derringer? Damn that was fast, wasn't it?"

"Uh huh, it'd be a damn good fight, but you know what. He scares me!"

"He's the only one that ever has then. I thought you were fearless."

I'll go to see the Rangers in the morning and collect my due.
It sure is nice getting paid to do something that I really like to do.
They tipped their hats and took their leave.
They knew all along that I had my derringer up my sleeve.
But I had another derringer in my boot, for just in case,
so I wasn't walking around naked, if trouble I had to face.
I guess we're opposites but the same. They hunt for trouble I don't.
They'll give a man a chance to surrender, I won't.
I had that feeling, the feeling that I sometimes get.
that I'd cross paths again with Bennett Slaughter and Sandman Everette.

Looking back it makes me wonder,
what the citizens would do if they knew what was in their midst,
and the carnage that could be reeked with my guns dancing in my fist.
What if the Demon that lies within was suddenly evoked,
because some citizen, for careless reason, caused me to be provoked?
Would they panic, run and scream and break into a sweat?
Would then come Bennett Slaughter and "The Sandman" Everette?
Bullets would fly, people would die, women would cry,
I might even die, and why it started no one would know why.

I have to control it better, my temper tends to run a little too hot
I'll try harder not to kill so quick ~ whether I like it or not.

Simon finally wrote about one of his reoccurring nightmares.

<u>*Ghost Gunfighter*</u>
It was a Sunday, a day like any other day.
I stepped outside and saw him at the end of the street.
It was blistering hot ~ and sweltering outside.
I guess it was about time we finally did meet.

The wind was howling ~ the dust clouds flew in the air.
The dirt stung like bees when it hit your face.
But it didn't matter ~ neither of us was giving any ground.
We both stood fast for the fight ~ both holding our place.

He moved carefully ~ he started unbuttoning his coat.
Cautiously he started with the button on the top.
I had dreamed this many times, and now I really knew.
That once this got started neither of us could stop.

He threw his coattails aside ~ moved them out of the way.
On his hips were strapped the cold harsh killing steel.
My hackles raised ~ my skin crawled up my spine.
The electricity and danger in the air ~ I could feel.

His eyes sparkled in the sun ~ they shone like diamonds.
They twinkled like they do when someone in pleased.
I knew from the sparkle ~ knew he faced the sun.
So the momentary advantage I had seized.

I don't think he ever saw me move ~ blinded by the sun.
He was staring straight into its brightest glare.
I thought my shotgun got him ~ split him like a rail.
But when the smoke cleared, he was no longer there.

Hell, I thought he was real ~ was it fact, or not so.
Perhaps it was an apparition or maybe a haint.

Something had been standing at the end in the street.
I guarantee you this ~ that whatever it was, it now ain't.

I walked back inside and there whatever it was sat.
Blood oozed from his wounds ~ bleeding all over the place.
I drew out my forty–five, quickly cocked the hammer.
And shot whatever it was square in its' ugly old face.

It fell from the table, and I took my carving knife.
And from its' body its' ugly old head I did sever.
But then the parts jumped back together and walked off.
And then I knew I'd be rid of him ~ NEVER!
~

Scream, Scream Banshee scream.
Come and awake me from my dream.
Shrieking, howling, come to my bed.
Drive the other demons from my head.

~

It's getting harder for us gunfighters to exist.
Wonder how much longer I can go on like this?
How do you right what's gone wrong?
How do you feel, when your heart is like stone?

Simon walked up the stairs and into the Texas Rangers headquarters. He immediately saw Bennett Slaughter.

"Morning, Mr. Slaughter, I trust you had an uneventful evening?"

"Sublette," Slaughter said, greeting Simon tersely. "I trust you did also?"

"I'm here for the Drummond reward you mentioned. What do I need to do?"

Bennett handed Simon the reward flyer for Drummond.

It surprised Simon the amount of money being paid for Drummond's death. He didn't show his surprise to Slaughter. He almost chuckled, this kind of money, and he only protected his own life. He silently wondered why J.T. didn't collect the money for himself. How would Simon have ever known?

"Drummond was a mean man, wasn't he, Sublette? What was he doing in Texas?"

"He came to kill me....but instead got his just due....isn't it wonderful getting paid....to do what you love to do? You and I are alike, I suspect.... except you don't get to collect."

"That's true, but it's a different motivation. A good thing your cousin J.T. ruled it self defense. Why did he want to kill you?"

"Why does any contract killer what to kill anyone, the money."

"Do you know who hired him?"

"He was contracted by a corrupt sheriff and federal marshal in Shreveport. They and one of their friends killed the owner of the Marshal mercantile was the report. I went to retrieve the body and to find out why.... they didn't want the truth known, so they wanted me to die."

"Is this your suspicion or do you have facts? Did Drummond verify your accusations?"

Simon reached into his vest pocket and removed a folded, yellow piece of paper. He handed the paper to Slaughter. It was the telegram sent from Shreveport to Drummond authorizing the kill. It didn't have a name signed, only the initials, FMS. "I have no substantial proof, just this. Drummond was tough, but he wasn't very smart to have kept this on his person."

"Any idea would who the initials FMS would be?"

"I think it stands for Federal Marshal Stevens. He's the one in Shreveport."

"Could be, if you are correct, it more than likely stands for Frank Miles Stone. He was the sheriff."

"It doesn't matter to me anymore. Do what you want with it. I do need to inquire into another circumstance, the killing of Nellie Jacks in Henrietta. I understand the Rangers tracked down the shooter and disposed of him."

"You mean the lady that owned Nellie Jacks' Saloon? Her real name was Mariselle Morzelle. She never did marry the man Denzel Jacques, just used his name, or a variation thereof. Did you ever hear of a man named Hock Alderson? He was a petty thief and rustler. He had a warrant issued for killing a deputy in Comanche. He was on the run and Miss Morzelle got in the way."

"Are you sure he was the one?"

"As sure as I need to be, our man, Rock Wardlaw, caught up with him at Burkburnet. He didn't want to give in to arrest and was shot and killed as the result. We have no reason to carry on."

Simon finalized the arrangements to have the reward money transferred to his account at the Fort Worth National Bank. He left the Ranger headquarters and began the walk to the corner of Main and First streets.

The reward for Drummond was substantial,
that plus the sale of the farm, and I don't ever have to work again.
I wonder how much money it'll take to get the killing out of my skin.
Maybe I could get one of them head doctors to come and cure me.
Turn me into a gentleman, instead of whiskey I'd have afternoon tea.
Hell, when he finished, I'd be a gentleman, but he'd have all my money,
then I'd have to kill again to earn a living ~ now isn't life funny?

Life is full of trials, each one a separate test,
some are simple tasks ~ some are drawn out quests.
With the passage of each one we are made to be more wise.
We live a little longer and we get more knowledge behind our eyes.

Simon had always been frugal with his money, only using enough to pay for room and board, his whiskey and his women. Even in these endeavors, he was not a spend thrift. He now had enough money he could actually buy any kind of place he wanted and settle down out of harm's way. It had crossed his mind on more than one occasion. He would send for the money when he got to Melina's place. Surely, they had a safe bank in Arizona.

Simon met at the bank with Major K. M. Van Zandt, one of the principals of the Fort Worth National Bank. Simon transferred all his holdings to the bank based on the reputation of Major Van Zandt. Simon knew him well and served with him for a brief time in the civil war.

"Simon, it's good to see you again. It looks like the world is wearing worse on you."

"Well, I'm okay. There's some proceeds coming from the Texas Rangers and I wanted to insure the transaction."

"There is a substantial sum of money in your accounts and I have some personal concerns. You haven't made any arrangements for disposal in case of your demise. Given your life style, it would make sense for you see our attorney and draw the proper papers, unless of course you want me to have it all." Van Zandt laughed. "Do you have any heirs?"

"I have no one. None anyway I want claim." Simon gave the bank attorney the name of Brock Deaton, Sweetwater, Texas to be his executor.

Fort Worth proper was too civilized for him, and he grew tired of the happenings in the Acre. His blood itched again. He still liked the rowdy unsophisticated saloons in the smaller towns. After concluding his business at the bank he went to the hotel to gather his things.

Sandman Everette and Rock Wardlaw came to the Ranger headquarters after Simon had left. "Mornin' Bennett, has our Rhymin' boy been by yet?"

"Yeah he was in early. He was waiting for me on the front steps."

"Did you discuss why Drummond was in Texas?"

"He said he came to kill him, but he killed Drummond instead. He thinks the sheriff and federal marshal in Shreveport hired Drummond to kill him. He believes the two were masking the murder of the Marshal mercantile owner, a friend of his. He didn't have any concrete proof, or so he stated."

"Guess all's fair in love and war, huh?" said Rock.

"Yeah, but they're both the same to a man like the Rhymer."

"Think so?"

"Yeah, a man like the Rhymer just loves his killing. He asked about the murder of Mariselle Morzelle, the lady from Henrietta. I told him about how Rock killed Hock Alderson. Do you know what the crazy son of a bitch said? He said, "If you don't mind, when I see him, I'm going to kill him again. Then it'll be complete, my treat.""

I'll be damned, Nellie Jacks, or Jacques, really was Mariselle Morzelle.
I'll send Kate and Caroline a note the next time I write a spell.

Rebecca Goes Home

As Simon was leaving Major Van Zandt and the bank, he thought he heard his name being called. At first it was faint, like it was far away. Each time he thought he heard his name being called, the voice became louder. He turned in the direction of the voice.

He saw Rebecca Ravenwood running toward him calling his name. She finally caught up with him and had to wait a minute to catch her breath before she could speak. Simon waited patiently.

"Simon," said Rebecca, still breathing hard, a bead of sweat running down her face. "I've been looking for you everywhere! I thought for a minute I was going to miss you. It occurred to me more than once that I might have to spend the best part of my life looking all over Texas to find you."

Simon took her by the shoulders and looked into her eyes. The hairs on the back of his neck came to attention. He sensed something wrong by the tone of her voice.

"What's the problem, Jennie Sue?" Simon said, "What is it you want me to do?"

Rebecca finally caught enough of her breath to speak in a normal tone. "First, Simon, I want you to start calling me by my real name. It is Rebecca, you know. And secondly, I need your help. It's something that is of no concern to you, and I know how you feel about things like that, but I'm asking anyway."

Simon didn't speak. He only continued to look deep into her eyes. His concentration almost unnerved Rebecca.

She steeled herself and looked back into his eyes. "I'm going back to reclaim what is rightfully mine. I'm going back to claim my inheritance of father's ranch and all of its holdings. I'm not a saloon girl. I'm not a boarding house, bawdyhouse, or any other kind of house worker. And I'm damn sure not a bucket maid to the ladies of the evening."

Simon started to say something, but Rebecca wouldn't let him.

"Caroline and Kate were both good to me, and I'll be forever grateful. They helped me when probably no one else would have. If it were not for them, I might not be sane today. I have repaid them for all they have done, but it's time for me to be where I belong."

"You want to go to the ranch, with your father?" asked Simon.

Rebecca nodded her head. "Yes, I want to go to the ranch and to him. I want to look him in the eye and see if I can find forgiveness."

"What brought all of this on, Rebecca? What has happened to make you want to go home?"

Rebecca took a deep breath. She led Simon out of the street and into a nearby hotel. They found a quiet table in the hotel's bar. She was nervous. She needed to sit down to tell all of this.

Simon saw that she was nervous and was struggling to speak. He ordered two beers thinking it might help her relax. It would certainly help him.

She waited until their drinks arrived and then answered Simon's question. "I overheard you talking to Caroline and Kate about how you came to find me. You told them about a man named E.J. Pilgrim and how he was hired to find me and was never heard from again."

"We don't have to go through this you know."

Rebecca stared hard at Simon, put her glass to her lips, took a sip of beer and continued. "Well, last week I was helping Kate cleanup, and this big burly man walked in. It was rather late into the evening, and only one or two other people were in the saloon. He was well into his alcohol. He started to brag to these other men about the easiest two thousand dollars he'd ever made."

Simon's eyebrows rose making his face into a scowl. The hairs on his neck moved again.

"He had some more to drink and then told them the story. He said he was paid to go find this girl the Comancheros had captured. He took the money, but in fact he never went. At the end of the story, I went over to him and asked him his name. He told me it was E.J. Pilgrim."

The hairs on Simon's neck bristled, she had his full attention. The blood rushed to his scar. Simon felt the Demon. He told him to be at ease.

Rebecca continued. "Then he grabbed me and forcibly pulled me into his lap. He asked me if I was ready to pleasure him. I told him I was. Kate damn near fainted, but she didn't say anything. We went upstairs and he tells me the story again, at my urging, he tells me everything. He told me the real reason he didn't try to find the girl, was that the brother, and that would be Daniel in this case, had paid him extra not to. So as it turns out, Daddy paid him to rescue me and Daniel paid him to leave the state. He sat there laughing at his good fortune. He was sitting on the bed naked, and when he continued to laugh about it, I lost my temper and hit him in his privates. Then I took one of his guns and stuck it in his mouth and said, 'Was the girl's name Rebecca Ravenwood?' When he nodded his head yes

I said, 'Well, I'm her!' His eyes got wide with terror. That's when, Simon, I pulled the trigger.'"

Simon gulped down the rest of his beer and signaled for another with a side of whisky.

"Kate came running upstairs scared to death. She thought he had shot me. When she saw what had happened, she collapsed against the wall. Then Caroline came rushing in, she must have learned it from you because she stayed calm; she kept her senses about her. She told me I'd have to leave. She said she would cover for me, but I'd have to leave. That's when I decided I was going back and get what's mine. You know, Simon, I've always blamed my father, but now I know the truth. I don't know why I am surprised. Daniel was always mean to me. It was a perfect way for Daniel to get me out of the way and inherit the ranch and all the Ravenwood fortune. Well, that's not going to happen now. And that's why I need your help."

"You're right," Simon said, "It's not my fight. There's nothing in it for me."

"I had this crazy thought about a man who killed thirteen Comancheros, all by himself, to rescue a young girl in distress. I had this crazy thought, he might, just might, not mind doing it one more time. The reward could be more than you ever dreamed."

Simon didn't answer. She was right though, he didn't mind. Something drew him to Rebecca, but he couldn't explain what it was.

"More than you ever dreamed Simon, Daddy's rich you know."

Simon sat back in his chair and drank down the second beer and the side of whiskey.

"I don't want, or need, your money. You know Daniel, given his desire to be rid of you, might have arranged the kidnapping to begin with. There's no telling what he will do when you show your face. He'll just kill you. I guess I could even the odds some. If you are going, I don't know how I could keep this off my conscience."

"There's something else that might interest you," said Rebecca with a twinkle in her eye, "something suited for you. Daniel, no doubt, has hired some real lowlifes, and you'll get the chance to kill all of them. Rid the world of a few more ne'er do wells, ease the suffering of mankind," Rebecca grinned.

Even before she had spoken Simon had made up his mind to help her. His reasoned he didn't have anything to do anyway, why not spend the next week or so in the company of one of the prettiest women he had ever seen—even if they didn't sleep together. Plus, she did need protection. Simon grinned, his scar twitched. "When do we leave?"

Now I'm off to the X–Bar–T, the Ravenwood lass, and me.
Take back what's hers is what we're out to do,
and in the process, rid the world of a lowlife or two!

Simon wanted to catch the train.

Rebecca wanted to go on horseback, to enjoy the countryside, to take in all the sights.

Simon warned her that since it was early spring the weather could turn bad at anytime—and he certainly didn't want to go through that again.

Rebecca won the argument. It was settled. She and Simon would ride from Fort Worth to the X–Bar–T, north of Tascosa in the Texas Panhandle.

During the ride, Rebecca told Simon of how Daniel had treated her as a child. He was always mean and hateful. When they were about to catch the train from Boston to Texas, Daniel tricked her into going for some cookies, and she had almost missed the train. She now realized it wasn't just brotherly mischief but brotherly malice. He pushed her out of a tree when they were young, and he claimed it was accidental. Now she was beginning to wonder. When she was pushed out of the tree she had landed on a sharp rock on the ground, and it pierced her hip and left an unusual scar. The scar was in the shape of a horse's head. Her father liked to tell everyone that if something ever happened to Rebecca, they could identify her by the horse's head scar on her hip. It always embarrassed her for him to tell people that.

She told Simon how the Comancheros had treated her. She told him of the pain she was made to suffer at their hands. She told him how they kept her hands tied together and kept her feet hobbled so she couldn't run. She told of the humiliation of having one of those foul men watch her every time she had to relieve herself. Some of the more brazen men would try to take her after following her when she went to relieve herself. The only time they removed the hobbles was at night when they would come and forcibly have sex with her. The sex wasn't in private either. It was always by the campfire so everyone could watch. They would even have sex with her when she was in her monthly cycle, they didn't care, and they were all foul. Sometimes she would have to accommodate more than one man each night. She told Simon that she finally steeled her mind as not to feel any pain, any emotion. She tried to do things to them to get them to kill her, but they never did. She even defecated on one when he was inside her, and he only laughed. That's how foul and despicable they were. She was trying desperately to get a knife or gun, so she could take her own life. She tried once to swallow an entire shirt so she would choke to death, but she had been caught. She once crawled over five hundred yards to the river to drown herself, but they caught her and their reward was to have sex with her in the water. She laughed, where in the hell was a good water moccasin when a girl needed one. She told Simon she had gotten pregnant but took care of the problem with a sharp stick late one evening.

Simon was amazed at what he was hearing. He was seeing another side of the remarkable young woman. She was as tough inside as he was.

She said another group of what she supposed was also Comancheros came and wanted to buy her. The name of the leader was a man named Moon.

Simon knew of the man named Moon. And said she was lucky that Moon didn't buy her, because he was meaner and fouler than Willie Patch Eye.

Rebecca told Simon she tried to get them into a fight, so they would start killing each other, and maybe she would get caught in the cross fire. She said she wanted Moon to win because there were only three of them. She could handle three better than thirteen.

She was looking for anything when Simon finally came. She told him that when she saw the dynamite strapped to rider she tried to crawl closer, but Willie Patch Eye threw her backwards far enough that he actually saved her life. It is ironic, she said, the one person I had come to hate the most in this world saved my life. She asked Simon why he didn't kill her as he had promised her father he would do.

His answer shocked her. He told her that the dynamite was supposed to have killed everyone in the camp, including her, but that when he got there and found her still alive, he didn't have the stomach to finish the job. He told her he always fancied himself cold and uncaring when it came to killing, but she was one he couldn't kill. Killing all the Comancheros was enough for one night. He said after he had killed all of them the idea came to him that he could take her to Texas Sweet Talk and Kate and that maybe they could heal her. Perhaps put her back together again, and somehow make a life for her. He told her he knew she was in shock, and he thought at the time she might not ever recover. After all, what had happened to her was one hell of a shock to the mind. He was surprised when she found him in Fort Worth—but it was a good surprise.

As they rode along they discussed many subjects.

Simon asked her about the money and the boarding house she left. Rebecca responded, "Simon James, I gave all the money and the boarding house to Kate and Caroline for helping me. It wasn't a life for me. I mean what young girl would want to spend their life being ridden five or six times a night by some horny old cowboys looking for meaningless sex, and most of them being randy as hell to boot?"

Simon didn't respond. He looked at her, grinned and nodded.

Rebecca asked Simon about the girl back in Oklahoma.

Simon rode on in silence for a moment then turned to Rebecca and replied.

"Well, it was never meant to be....I was in love with her but her father didn't like me. So one day he cornered me....and he pulled first....and then the Demon came....and satisfied his thirst. As he lay dying....I knew I had committed the ultimate sin....had killed her father....and she could never, ever love me again."

"Simon, I'm so sorry. I apologize for prying."

"And, Rebecca, I haven't loved anything since, easier that way."

"But Simon, don't you love killing, everyone says you do."

"It doesn't bother me, Rebecca, if it has to be done, but contrary to the belief of some, I don't love killing. I certainly don't do it for fun....there are just those who are destined to die by the gun. Guys like Ivory Joe....they get the chance....but then won't go."

"Have you ever thought, Simon, why you ended up like this?"

Simon turned almost side saddled so he could face Rebecca. "I think about all time....why was I picked to be a gunman who talks in rhyme? I won't know until I meet my maker. Why can't I be like other men....I know no matter how hard I try not to....I'll will to do it again."

"Aren't you ever afraid, scared of losing your own life?"

"Am I afraid? Yes, I am, although it may seem the opposite is true. My experiences have taught me the whole world is created on fear. When a snake strikes, it is out of fear. Believe it or not, he's afraid of you. That's the way I treat my enemies....with fear. I strike before they do. And I know that is what gives me my edge."

Rebecca gave him a look that said, 'You really do love it or you wouldn't do it.'

Simon turned on his horse so he now faced forward again. Then he turned his head toward Rebecca. When he spoke it was a gentle voice,

"Someday in honey....bees will drown....and someday....I too will go down."

Rebecca asked Simon how he had come to talk in rhyme. It was the most unusual trait she had ever seen in a person. He told her that when he was young he would write little poems to this mother. His father thought it to be a girlish trait, but his mother loved it. That's why his father had been so careful to teach him all the manly things, hunting, trapping and of course guns. He was taught to throw Bowie knives, hatchets and daggers of all sizes, and to be accurate in his aim. When he, his brother and father would go camping, his father would randomly throw a knife or hatchet at him. They might be eating or simply walking the trail. He had to be constantly on alert to avoid being hurt.

His father also taught him to how to fight. He never made him fight though. William and William's friends did that for him. They were older and, with Simon being the youngest, they always picked on him. He had to fight back, and at first he lost. When he was fourteen or fifteen, he had a fight, and to protect himself, he hit his assailant in the face with a shovel. The blow knocked the older boy down. He had to be pulled from the boy by the others before he would quit hurting him. After that, one on one, the older boys were no longer a match for him, and they showed him respect. He guessed, in looking back, that was the first time his demon came to him, but he did not recognize it. He told Rebecca that he didn't think in rhyme, but the sentences just came out that way. One day he stood to speak, and it came out in a rhyme, and he'd been speaking that way ever since. At first the rhymes seem to come mostly when he was agitated. And now they come whether he is agitated or not. The journal he kept was written mostly in verse and he didn't understand that either.

X–Bar–T

Simon and Rebecca arrived in Tascosa at sunset in the middle March. They had been lucky on their trip with the weather. The Texas Panhandle was enjoying an unusually warm spring—and Simon was glad for that.

They secured rooms at the Aladdin House hotel, and while Rebecca was getting a hot bath, Simon went to the saloon next door to have a drink. It was the same saloon where he originally had met Caroline Endryl, Texas Sweet Talk. The saloon was crowded. Simon found a place at the end of the bar; he could see the whole room from there. Rebecca came in and in trying to make room for her, Simon accidentally knocked over a man's glass, spilling his whiskey on the floor. Simon apologized and ordered the man another drink.

The man took offense, partly because he was half drunk, and mostly because he was one of those men who just liked to fight.

"Clumsy bastard, watch what you're doing!" the man spoke with venom in his voice.

"I'm sorry, mister, my mistake, barkeep, another drink for this gentleman here." Simon motioned for the bartender.

"You spilled the whiskey on my new boots, you think just sayin' you're sorry, makes it go away sod–buster?"

"I guess not. Jones, make it a whole bottle for this gentleman here."

"Look at what you did to my boots, look at 'em. Why don't you just get down on your knees and lick 'em clean? Maybe your sorry ass can do that!"

Rebecca got a towel from the bartender and started to bend down to clean the man's boots.

Simon stopped her. He lifted her up by the arm.

When she stood up, she saw that the Demon had come to Simon's face. The scar twitched and it was blood red. Shit she thought. I can't stop him now, but I can get out of the way. Rebecca moved against the wall away from the bar.

"Mister, you ever make a mistake before....do you want to make a fight for whiskey spilled on the floor?"

The man squared off toward Simon. His jaw was set.

Simon pulled back his coat to reveal his gun. As he was doing so, he silently flicked the derringer into his left hand. The man was already dead and didn't even realize it yet.

"A shoe shiner, a licker of boots, I'm not....I just send men to hell where it's hot."

Jones came from behind the bar and got between Simon and the man.

Simon moved Jones to the side so he could see the man's face. Then he spoke his killing line. "Tell me loud mouth....why have you picked tonight to die? Want to go to hell....and ask the devil why?"

Jones managed to get in between the Rhymer and the man.

"Dillon, this man is the one called The Rhymer. He has apologized and made amends. Take the bottle he bought, get one of the pretty girls, and have some fun. That's all we're all here for is fun, right, not fighting. A little whiskey ain't gonna hurt them boots. Hell, by noon tomorrow you'll be knee deep in cow shit anyway."

With the bartender standing between him and the loud mouth, the unsuspecting man did not see Simon pull his forty–five. Simon raised his hand, resting the forty–five on the bartender's shoulder, and pointed the gun at the man's face.

Simon spoke again. "So what do you think....want to die over a spilled drink?"

The man named Dillon had heard of The Rhymer before. He had heard it from Joshua Ravenwood, Rebecca's father. He had also heard it from Daniel. He looked at Simon and then at Rebecca. He remembered that Daniel said some day someone would come claiming to be Rebecca, but that she would be an imposter because the Comancheros had killed her. He would eventually take on The Rhymer, but he would wait for his friends to help him. He took the bottle and left.

Rebecca left early the next morning and rode out to the ranch to see her brother and father. She remembered Simon had cautioned her about Daniel's propensity for violence toward her, but she was not afraid. She stopped on the hill overlooking the ranch. It was the first time she had ever seen it. It was grand, more magnificent than she had imagined. Cattle roamed over the open plains and down near the river. She didn't know how many, but it was several hundred in her estimation. She knew there were more, but she had no idea of the vastness of the X–Bar–T. The main house was fenced in and sat in a dense stand of trees. The river was about one thousand yards from the gated entrance. It was a wonderful view from where she sat.

The only thing she had ever heard about the Texas Panhandle was that it was void of trees, windswept and barren, save for the prairie grass. That might be the case elsewhere but not here. This place was beautiful, more beautiful than she could ever have imagined. Boston could not compare to what she was beholding, and it was something she never thought she would see. She sat for a long time enjoying the view. Slowly, she moved her horse toward the main gate.

Daniel met her at the main gate. He refused to acknowledge her. He refused to let her see her father. Daniel told her his father was really sick, and he could see no one, especially an imposter. There he stood looking at his own sister, and he would not acknowledge that she was alive. A man joined Daniel. It was the same man Simon had spilled whiskey on the night before, Dillon. As they stood and argued with Rebecca, another man approached her from behind. He struck Rebecca in the head rendering her unconscious. They tied her to her horse and the three of them rode away from the ranch.

The only thing that saved her that day was Simon. He had been watching. He had followed her from a distance to protect her, to observe and to get his bearings. His suspicions about Daniel were true. He was violent—and deranged. He had to be deranged to viciously attack his own sister.

The men took Rebecca to a lime pit, about two miles east of the main ranch house. They removed Rebecca from her horse. One of the men started slapping her to make her wake up. The slapping raised red welts on her face. Finally, Rebecca awoke. The man who had been slapping her spoke.

"I'm glad to see you awake. I never could screw a woman while they were sleeping."

Rebecca, even though groggy, knew what was about to happen. They were going to rape her, kill her and throw her in the lime pit. She spit in the man's face and kicked the other one hard on the shin.

When one man pulled a gun, a shot rang out. The shot came from Simon's Sharps rifle. The bullet from the rifle hit the man in his right temple, splattering hair, bone and blood over both Rebecca and the other man. When a fifty–caliber bullet fired from a Sharp's rifle struck a man, it was devastating. With a head shot like this one, there wasn't much left where the bullet struck. Simon made a mental note to have the sights on his rifle checked. He was aiming for the man's chest.

When the shot hit the man, the one named Dillon froze in terror. Rebecca instinctively, instantly, grabbed his hand gun from his holster.

Simon quickly approached from his vantage point. As he dismounted, he saw it was the man from the saloon. He spoke directly to him while Rebecca kept the gun pointed at his chest.

"The noise of the gun fills the air....what once was, is no longer there....no bone, no skin, no hair."

Simon then hit the man across the face with the butt of his rifle. He bent down and grabbed the man by his hair pulling him up and bending him back over his knee.

"See the smoke, smell the powder?"

Dillon nodded in agreement. He feared for his life, and he had good cause.

"It's the devils' breath....when it comes it brings death....you go tell Daniel there is more where this came from....you tell him, you warn him, something evil his way comes!"

Simon then slammed the man's head on the ground. As Dillon lay there getting his senses, Simon tended to Rebecca. He took out his handkerchief and wiped the skull and skin fragments from her face and hands.

"Nice brother that Daniel, I saw the devil in his face....you'll have to kill him to take your place."

Rebecca looked deep into Simon's eyes. She knew what he was thinking, but she didn't want to think that way. Before she turned Simon and the Demon loose, she would seek a peaceful solution.

"I can't do that. There's got to be a better way. Somehow I'll get in to see Papa, and he can give me some advice."

As the sun was setting in the West the next evening, Simon left Rebecca at the hotel. She didn't want to go to the saloon with him. As he walked out of the hotel door, he saw Daniel and Dillon. They entered the saloon ahead of him. Simon went back into the hotel. He went to Rebecca's room and told her they were in town. He gave her one of his extra guns and told her if anyone came through her door to shoot first and ask questions later. She pleaded with Simon not to kill them. It went against all his senses not to end it now but agreed to try it her way. He would give it a chance, but on the next act of violence, he would kill Daniel and all of his supporters. Simon did not enter the saloon. Simon got his sawed–off shotgun and went to wait in the alley back of the hotel.

Just after ten o'clock Daniel and Dillon approached the hotel. They could not see Simon in the cover of darkness in the alleyway of the hotel. Something made them both stop instantly. They turned toward the alley. It was the noise that made them stop. It was the unmistakable noise of the hammers of a shotgun being cocked for firing.

"The hotel is off limits....you only got a minute. One shot can take the both of you....ever seen the damage a shotgun can do?" Simon said in a menacing voice.

"We're just going to see to the woman who's making the foolish talk that she's my sister," replied Daniel.

"There's no need to talk, it's time to embrace....it's time for your sister to take her place."

"That woman isn't my sister. She's an imposter just trying to rob my family and me. My sister is dead."

"You're wrong....I saved her from the Comancheros hell....I know she's for real....you know as well."

Daniel's face became mean, sinister; it was the look of evil. "You're just saying that for personal gain, you son of a bitch. How much is she paying you to lie for her?"

Simon stepped from the dark of the alley.

Daniel was taken aback by the look on Simon's face. The deep blue eyes were cold and fixed on Daniel's face. Simon's scar was blood red. The shotgun was only a few feet from their faces. They could see his trigger finger twitching.

The trigger finger was talking to Simon, *Come on my friend, let me squeeze, cut 'em in half, down to their knees.* "I don't know why I don't kill you and this other....you're one sorry excuse for a brother."

Simon watched Daniel and Dillon ride out of town. He had obeyed Rebecca and let them live—the Demon didn't know why. Another mistake perhaps, letting them live went against everything he had ever learned and against the feeling in his stomach. He got his rifle and went to the roof of the hotel. He watched and waited for the rest of the evening. The moon was bright and Simon could see the shadows of the men in the distance. Abruptly, the two riders split. One man continued to ride straight, the other turned and started back toward town. His senses were now at their peak. The Demon came. He couldn't tell which one was back tracking and returning to town, but he knew he would be in for a surprise when he got there.

Simon wondered just how dumb they thought he was. Did they really think he would go to bed and go to sleep? He could only surmise they had never dealt with someone like him before. He had dealt with plenty like them—wanting to die when a better solution could be had.

Simon watched the rider circle to the opposite end of town. Simon watched him dismount and rapidly walk to the dark shadows of the buildings. Simon left the roof and went to a position inside the back entrance to the hotel. From this position, he could also hear anyone coming in the front door.

The back door of the hotel creaked as it was slowly opened. The light from the doorway showed the face of the person opening the door. It was Dillon. Daniel sent him to do the dirty work.

Simon could see the terror in his eyes when he saw Simon and the shotgun. Simon hit him in the face knocking him backwards into the alley. Simon wanted to kill him, then and there, but he was respecting Rebecca's wishes to try and settle this peacefully.

"Are you deaf? Figure it out mister....why would Daniel want her dead....if she really isn't his sister?"

The man moaned and groggily got to his feet. The place where Simon had hit him with the sawed–off shotgun left a big red welt on his cheek. The man's hand moved instinctively to his gun. Simon put the sawed–off shotgun against his cheek.

"So you want to die do you....fighting someone else's feud....then be thrown out with the trash....be left for insect food?"

Dillon didn't want to die and he moved his hand away from his gun.

"I'm just taking orders," he said.

"Well, take this order....and listen good....go ask Mr. Ravenwood if she's real....he'll tell you so it can be understood."

I told Rebecca when you mix dirt and water you get mud.
Do you know what you get when you mix dirt and blood?
She couldn't answer. No words came from her breath.
I told when you mix dirt and blood ~ you get death!

The next night, just before midnight, Rebecca, with Simon along side, entered the main ranch complex from the back, through the dense cover of some tress. Quietly, as Simon stood guard, she found the room where her father was confined. She entered through the window. Silently, she went to his bed, and they spoke in whispered tones. Rebecca was glad to see her father again.

He was elated to see his daughter. It brought a light to his face. He was glad that for once the Rhymer didn't do as he said he would.

She saw he was sick and told him she was coming to help nurse him back to health. She left him happy.

Simon was on edge standing guard. The sawed–off shotgun was ready. Simon made sure that his finger was not on the trigger. Sometimes the sawed—off shotgun and his finger would talk to each other and all hell would start whether Simon wanted it too or not.

Rebecca came back outside through the window. They were silent on their way to the horses and left the ranch without incident.

Rebecca told Simon that Daniel was holding her father hostage. True, he was in ill health, but he still could walk without help, and his mind was a sharp as ever. Rebecca said her father told her he would intervene and would help, but until he had everything in place for her to be careful. Daniel was a sick man, crazed with the power of it all.

When they were out of hearing distance from the ranch, Simon began to sing. He liked to ride and sing even though he didn't' have the voice for it. It made him feel good.

> "Pistolero, Pistolero, where do you roam?
> Pistolero, Pistolero, where is your home?
> He's fought many battles, he's killed many a man,
> He stood beside Villa when he fought for the land,
> He fought in the mountains and in the valley below,
> He is a Pistolero from Old Mexico.
> He's killed for the money, he's killed for the gold,
> He's killed for a lady whose heart he must hold,
> He's killed all over where ever he's to go,
> He's a Pistolero from Old Mexico.
> Pistolero, Pistolero, where does it end?
> Pistolero, Pistolero, who is your friend?
> He rode through the west, he rode all alone,
> He'd do his killing and then be gone,
> He'd ride from the law, he'd lay real low,
> He's a Pistolero from Old Mexico.
> Pistolero, Pistolero, why do you run?
> Pistolero, Pistolero, is it 'cause of your gun?
> He's fought many battles, he's killed many a man,
> He stood beside Villa when he fought for the land,
> He fought in the mountains and in the valley below,
> He is a Pistolero from Old Mexico.
> Ooooo, Ooooo, Old Mexico....Pisto....ler....er....O!"

When Simon finished singing, Rebecca commented that the song sounded more like him than some gunfighter out of Old Mexico. Simon told her it was probably so but it was hard to get anything to rhyme with Texas.

As they rode back to Tascosa, he asked Rebecca why the human species couldn't be peaceful. Why a man can't go to a saloon, have a few drinks, tell stories and enjoy the company of a woman without some loud mouthed shit heel making trouble? Like the man, the other night in the saloon in Tascosa, wanting to make a fight over some spilled whiskey. It would have been just as easy for him to walk off as it would have for him to stand and make a fight. Simon wondered why there were men who were curious as to what their guts looked like on the inside. There they would lay, on the floor, with their belly opened up like a can of beans, blood spewing from the cavity, and then they knew. He had written about it before, and had spoken about it earlier. It came to him again, skin, and hair, and bone all gone—when the bullet hits the bone.

The next afternoon Rebecca and Simon sat in the saloon, eating lunch, and watched cautiously as three men approached. One of the men was the one Simon almost had to fight two nights before over the spilled whiskey, the one from the lime pit, and who had come to the hotel, the man named Dillon. The red welt from the sawed–off shotgun was still visible. One man Simon had not seen before. The third man was Carl Boyd, the farmer Simon had helped when he took the job to find Rebecca. Simon readied himself. He moved the derringer to his left hand and raised the sawed–off shotgun under the table to the level of the men's crotches.

They approached cautiously. The man Simon had not seen before introduced himself as Harpo Patton. The other man, the one with the red welt on his cheek, introduced himself as Dillon James, the ranch foreman. Carl said he was glad to see Simon again. They told Simon and Rebecca that Joshua Ravenwood had sent them. They had been summoned by Joshua at breakfast this morning. They were informed that Rebecca really was his daughter and that Daniel was poisoning their thinking. He told them this, but they were skeptical as to whether or not Rebecca was the true daughter and not some fake that had tricked a sick old man—fooled him enough to inherit a vast fortune.

"He told us it was true, but we came to see it for ourselves," spoke the man named Harpo. "Mr. Ravenwood gave us a picture of his daughter. You do kind of look like her, but it could only be a strong resemblance."

"Yeah," said Dillon, "lots of people look like other people. But Mr.

Ravenwood said there was one sure way we could know you. He said you, and only you would know what it is. He told us but we want to see if you know."

Carl said, "Mr. Sublette, we're not questioning your sincerity, please understand that."

Rebecca gave the men a harsh, stern, look. Then she smiled. Without caring who might see, she stood from her chair in the back of the saloon, and slowly unbuttoned her riding pants. She lowered her riding pants far enough to show her underpants. Then she slid one side of her underpants down far enough to reveal a scar on her right hip. It was the scar caused by the fall when Daniel pushed her out of the tree.

Simon's nose flared. He almost became aroused. He saw the milky, silky skin. He thought he could smell her womanhood. Only inches separated him and the three others from her sweetness. The Demon told him to pay attention. It still could be a ploy to divert his attention. The Demon didn't like sex, just killing. At this point, Simon didn't care what the Demon liked—and he was changing his mind about his feelings toward Rebecca Ravenwood.

After the men got over their initial shock of Rebecca pulling down her pants, they looked at the scar. It was just as Mr. Ravenwood had said; it was the shape of a horse's head.

Harpo spoke, "Excuse me, may I?" He pointed toward the scar.

Rebecca nodded her head in agreement. Simon held the shotgun at attention under the table.

Harpo reached over and touched the scar. He ran his fingers up and the down the scar to verify that it was real.

Simon wanted to do that, but he didn't plan to stop at just feeling the scar.

The Demon spoke to Simon. *Simon, don't let your attention divert, calm down, stay alert.* Goddamn Demon thought Simon.

"I don't see how a person could fake that," said Harpo. "That scar is real. Mr. Ravenwood said it was the only way we could know it was you." Harpo pushed back his hat and scratched his head. "All this time Daniel said that you were dead. He said someone might come. He said if she did she would be in disguise, but the scar proves it. Mr. Ravenwood was right. Meeting you, I can't believe all the bad things Daniel has told us. Why does he hate you so much?"

Rebecca replied, as she pulled up her underpants and buttoned her riding pants. "I don't know why. Ask him. My father always said the one slinging the mud is usually the one who's pouring the water on the dirt."

"Yeah, I've heard him say that," said Carl. "I'm sorry they treated you so bad. What can we do to help?"

Simon spoke to Rebecca, but his eyes never left the three men. "Rebecca, do you want me to kill them....for being on the wrong side of you....or do you want to forgive them....for they know not what they do?"

Rebecca gave Simon a gentle pat on his leg. "It's okay, tell the Demon to go away for now."

"I don't trust this Dillon James....he works for Daniel....not in your father's name."

"No, I was misled. Daniel lied to me all along. I apologize for my mistakes. I'll help make it right. Please, give me the chance."

Rebecca nodded in agreement.

Simon was wary.

The men told Simon and Rebecca that right after she had shown up at the ranch, Daniel sent for some additional help, some professional help. They said he had sent for a man named Harley Coale.

Simon had heard of Harley Coale. He was one of Johnny Ringo's early on Texas friends. Harley Coale's reputation was he was a psychopath, and he was like Simon. He shot first without conscience or worry of consequence. Harley had spent three different terms in prisons in Texas and Arizona. Simon knew he would have to kill Harley, as soon as he saw him. He knew he would have to kill Daniel too. If he cut off the head, the body would die.

They told them Harley was meeting some of the ranch hands the next night in the saloon on the south side of town, the one near the stock pens.

Simon took note of this and decided to give them a welcoming party. They wouldn't be expecting him—and surprise would be in his favor.

Rebecca rode out to the ranch later that evening without Simon. She was going to sneak back into her father's room and talk with him again. It was very dangerous for her to do this, but she had no choice. When she got to the window, she saw Daniel in her father's room. He was bending over the bed with a pillow in his hands. It took Rebecca a few moments to realize what was happening. Daniel was suffocating his own father! She went to open the window to stop him but someone grabbed her from behind. She used her boot and stomped as hard as she could on his toes. The man eased his grip on her and yelled in pain. Rebecca turned and saw she had the upper hand on her attacker. She grabbed the gun from his holster and shot him in the genitals until the gun was empty. Then, even though the gun barrel was almost too hot to hold, she took the gun by the barrel and beat the man until he was unrecognizable.

Quickly, she threw open the window and went inside. It was too late. Daniel was gone. She rushed to her father. What she found sent her into an uncontrollable rage. Her father was dead, and Daniel had killed him! The son of a bitch, thought Rebecca; the son of a bitch just killed their father.

Not caring for her welfare, Rebecca rushed into the living area, looked around and saw the rifle on the wall. She grabbed it and went looking for Daniel but couldn't find him. She was near where her horse was tied when she heard the commotion.

"There she is," a voice rang out. "She's the one that killed Mr. Ravenwood."

Rebecca quickly made for her horse and rode fast to find Simon.

"Why'd ya send for me for?" asked Harley Coale as he dismounted and walked toward Daniel, he was tired and grumpy after his long ride. "She's just a girl and god almighty damn, she's your sister. Why have you turned so hard on her?"

Daniel shot Harley a stern look.

"I hear she brought someone with her", said Harley, then he spit tobacco juice on the ground, "a body guard of some sort?"

"Yep, a gunman, some ruffian named Sublette."

Harley raised his eyebrows, "Wouldn't be Simon Sublette, would it?"

"Yeah, that's him. Ever heard of him before?"

"If it's the same one I've heard of, they say he talks in rhymes?"

"Yeah, we ran into him. He talks in rhymes all right."

"Do you think it strange, some sweet flowery son of a bitch to be a body guard?"

"I don't think there is anything sweet about him, Harley," said Daniel. "If it's who I think it is, he is a man called the Rhymer, war hero. Mean son of a bitch, killed his mother with a kitchen knife. Sat on her stomach and ate a piece of pie while he watched her die."

"I've heard the stories, but only in passing," said Harley as he spit more tobacco juice on the ground. "Actually, I didn't think he was for real. All the stuff I heard I figured was made up." Harley paused for a moment and then said, "But it don't mean shit to me."

"It might be the death of both of us if we aren't careful. I want him dead, the sooner the better."

"Piss on him, I'll kill the sweet talking son of a whore, as soon as I see him! Maybe he can recite us a verse as he lays there gasping his last."

"Harley."

"Yeah."

"Just hope he doesn't see you first."

Rebecca explained the whole thing to Simon the next morning. They waited all day for the sheriff to come. It didn't happen. This fact worried Simon. He could only guess the sheriff was being paid by Daniel. How many corrupt lawmen were there in Texas?

Harpo, Dillon and Carl were the ones that came. They came to help. They knew who killed Mr. Ravenwood and now their lives were also in danger. They had to leave the ranch or face Daniel's new henchman. By the fact that Daniel had not reported this, they knew Daniel was keeping this a private matter. The sheriff wasn't involved because Daniel did not report the incident. They knew if Daniel got the sheriff involved, then the truth might come out that Rebecca really was an heir to the ranch. They knew what Daniel had in mind. He was going to kill them, Simon, Rebecca, any supporters, and be rid of them forever.

Simon knew he must go on the attack. If he let them form a plan, he and Rebecca didn't stand a chance. He would have to divide and conquer.

Simon told Rebecca, Harpo, Dillon and Carl what needed to be done. Carl was finally going to get his chance to fight and help Rebecca. They went to the south side of town to the Equity Saloon where Harley Coale was to meet with the ranch hands loyal to Daniel. Simon told Rebecca to guard the back entry of the saloon. Harpo and Dillon waited across the street guarding the front of the saloon. If any of them came out, they were to kill them—even if it was Daniel. Though Harpo and Dillon were reluctant, Rebecca was eager; she hoped Daniel would be the one to run. Carl was placed beside the men's horses. If they got past Harpo and Dillon, Carl could do his job. Simon armed him with a long barrel shotgun.

Simon's mood shifted to one of a controlled rage. His mindset was the same he had used during the war. The enemy was in the saloon, and it was his sworn duty to eliminate each one. The Demon was in his eyes. Why else would one man enter a hostile saloon to have a gun fight with five men? The Demon thought it was a fair fight. Simon couldn't do it without him.

Simon entered the Equity Saloon by the rear door. He went to the bar and stood with his back to the wall. He didn't order a drink. At a table in the back corner of the saloon sat Daniel Ravenwood, Harley Coale and three other men. None of the men saw him enter through the back door. If it had been Simon, he would have posted guards. And when they saw Harley enter, Simon would have killed him on first sight. Simon would use this mistake to his advantage. He paused only to size the situation and where each man sat. No matter how many men were present, there was always one weak one, one back shooting coward. Simon knew he could take him last.

Then one of the five men turned his head in Simon's direction. Daniel spoke and pointed towards Simon. "There's the blood thirsty son of a bitch now."

None of the men moved toward Simon. The odds were five to one and Simon guessed it made them over confident. They didn't respect Simon. It was a mistake Harley Coale had not made before. It was a mistake he would never make again.

Simon replied. "It's been a long time....since I've satisfied my thirst.... any of you maggots want to be first?"

As Simon spoke, he studied Harley Coale. He would kill him first. Harley Coale's face was blistered. He had sores on his cheeks and along the side of his face to his eyebrows. It looked like he had stuck his head in a fire. Simon thought Harley's mind was the same way—opened sores and blistered.

The blistered Devil in plain view ~ gazing at me.
I was going to kill him first ~ then Daniel ~ then the other three.

The sores and blisters didn't make Simon feel sorry for him though, he was going to kill him anyway, and enjoy it. Humans shouldn't have to look upon a man like Harley Coale. And there was no telling how many innocents had died at his hand. If he were allowed to live, how many more would eventually suffer from this brain–blistered, opened sore, ugly, coldhearted, piece of shit, some called a man. Simon was glad he hadn't eaten—he would have thrown up.

Harley Coale grinned, revealing broken, discolored teeth. He glared at

Simon and spoke. "I'm surprised. I heard you couldn't look at a man in the face and deal with him. I heard you was a quick shootin' back shooter."

A grandfather clock started to chime. Simon saw it was ten o'clock. *Simon, when the clock chimes ten; let me loose again. The clock signals their end. Ten times it will chime, then I will kill them....me the Demon, he who talks in rhyme. When the gong hits the last bell....we will unleash HELL!*

Simon saw the one man move. Without hesitation, he raised the derringer and unleashed the Demon, and the Demon unleashed his fury.

"Guess I should act the part," he said as he shot the man dead. The man had only turned his head and Simon shot him in the eye. "How's that for a start?"

The shot caught them off guard. Before Harley Coale could react to Simon's attack, the sawed–off shotgun roared and removed his head. Some of the collateral buckshot sprayed the other men. Daniel and the two other men dove for the floor. Simon moved toward the front door for a better position. Daniel used this as an opportunity to try to escape. He crawled for the back door. One of the men crawled for the front door. It was the one Simon had picked as the coward. The other man attempted to roll under the table but was met with a forty–five bullet from Simon's gun. The bullet struck his arm. The next bullet Simon fired struck the man in the stomach. Shot in the belly is a slow way to die. Simon thought it would be good if he bled to death—it made the Demon happy. A shot came from the front door. Simon knew that either Harpo or Dillon had shot the coward. Actually, the man had slipped past Harpo and Dillion's bullets. It was Carl Boyd that fired the shot that killed the man.

Daniel rose to his feet and ran to the back door. Simon fired at him but missed. Rebecca was in the back alley of the saloon. He headed for the back of the saloon to help her.

Daniel raced out the back door. When he opened the door with a rush, he ran straight into Rebecca and the rifle she held. He knocked her into the wall of the adjacent building spilling the rifle from her hands and causing her to lose her balance and fall. His instincts told him to kill her, but if he stopped Simon would catch him. His only chance he thought was to run away down the alley and find his horse. He gave Rebecca a big smile and ran down the alley toward the street. If Rebecca or Simon were going to shoot him, it would have to be in the back.

Rebecca watched him run away. Rebecca was mad at herself for not being better prepared. She grabbed the rifle, aimed, and pulled the trigger.

The rifle missed fired, the chamber had become clogged with dirt. She slammed the rifle against the wall in frustration.

Simon came out of the back door of the saloon to see Daniel run out of the alley, quickly mount his horse and ride away. Where the hell was Carl?

Simon found his big gray horse and followed Daniel all the way to the lime pit. Simon caught up to him there, the place where Daniel had initially intended to bury Rebecca.

Into the Devil's den ~ him and disciples four.
Then hell broke open ~ death sprang as before.
In the ensuing madness ~ the blistered mind was slain.
Evil threat's now removed ~ ne'er to hurt again.
The Demon within me ~ slew the Devil's own.
Sent him home to hell ~ with his face all gone.
The disciples then three ~ killed one by one.
Lying gasping, bleeding ~ 'till the dying was done.
The Devil was followed ~ escaping into the night.
In dark of blackness ~ I extinguished his light.
Light returns to the land ~ no more festering diseased.
The Demon back to rest ~ happy now he's pleased.
As the madness lightens ~ sanity shows its face.
The land is rid of evil ~ peace settles in its place.

<u>*The Order of the Kill*</u>
It is crimson real ~ the order of the kill,
and it starts with a flick of the wrist.
First is the fast ~ the coward is last,
through the smoke and gunpowder mist.
You'll be stone ~ if you guess wrong,
and earn a permanent place on Boot Hill.
Take deadly aim ~ in the killing game,
and in choosing the Order of the Kill.
Rhymer

Simon found Rebecca back at the hotel with Carl, Harpo and Dillon. She was still shaken. He comforted her.

"What happened, Carl, I thought you were to guard the horses?"

"Sorry, Simon, I ain't ever killed a man before and I got distracted. Sorry."

The next morning Rebecca and Simon rode out to the ranch and met Harpo Patton, Dillon James and Carl Boyd. Rebecca gathered the remaining ranch workers and explained what had happened the night before. Rebecca told them that she was taking her rightful place. And just so there weren't any questions, she showed them the undeniable birth mark, the horse head scar.

One or two asked about Daniel. Simon told them he had run away and probably would be back, but to keep a sharp eye and for them to protect Rebecca.

Simon told them, "Things have a way of getting around....if something happens to Rebecca....hell comes back to town."

The ranch workers, each one, knew what he meant and knew it was not an idle threat.

That evening while they were dining in the main house, Simon told Rebecca he was leaving the next morning.

She wanted him to stay and told him so. She said she didn't think of him as an uncle anymore. Her feelings had grown much stronger. She told him she thought she was falling in love with him.

"Rebecca, my feelings toward you have changed, too....but I don't know if I can return that love to you."

Rebecca took Simon's hand and placed it on her thigh. "I know how we can fix that."

Simon strongly resisted the urge to grab her and ravish her. Getting involved with him was no good for a young woman like her. Eventually, it would only get her killed.

"No, Rebecca, I can't stay. You need to find yourself a handsome young man....someone who is good at working the land. It's the same everywhere I go....I can't stay....someone will get wind of it....and come to kill me someday."

"I don't care. We can handle it."

"No, we can't....it is always the same....blood mixes with dirt....and innocent people get hurt."

He told her he was flattered, but in his own way he was leaving to save her life, just like he had told Texas Sweet Talk. It was his excuse for not wanting to get tied down.

The next morning, as the sun peaked over the cottonwood trees, Simon mounted his horse to leave. Rebecca squinted into the sun, looking up at Simon, sitting there on his big gray horse. Rebecca hesitated, but she had to ask. She needed an answer to the question she had been postponing. She had to ask him before he left.

"Simon, what about my brother, where is Daniel, really?"

The big gray horse and Simon turned away from Rebecca. Simon gently turned the horse back, so he could face her. Just the mention of Daniel's name made Simon mad. How could a brother treat a sister with so much hate? He spoke as gently as he could but his scar betrayed him. It turned crimson—and it twitched once.

"When we came here....we tried the easy way....but then had no choice....Daniel resorted to gunplay."

Rebecca bit her lip; she was hoping Simon would tell her anything, anything but what she feared.

Simon continued, "So I had to turn loose the lightning....of the Demon's terrible gun."

Rebecca couldn't help it. She knew what was coming. A tear ran down her cheek.

"Your father no longer breathes....neither does his son."

Rebecca tried to speak but couldn't.

Simon wondered why Rebecca would cry over someone like Daniel, who had tried to kill her at every chance. He guessed women were just that way. Simon turned his horse to leave, and then looked back over his shoulder.

"Stay in good heath Ravenwood's daughter....if you need me....wire the Palomino Place....in Sweetwater."

Before she could speak Simon spurred the gray mare and rode away.

When she returned to the house, she found this note lying on the kitchen table.

FIRE
Fire is needed and does some things well.
Fail to respect its power and risk all hell.
Fire scorches the land, then all is born anew.
I am your fire, this is what I have done for you.
I can't stay, the land is now rid of the chafe and debris.

My job is done, and you no longer need someone like me.
You can see fire, smell it, but can never hold it in your arms.
You can feel its warmth, but get too close ~ it will cause harm.
Fire destroys what fuels its heat, it is natures must.
In doing so, it kills itself, turns itself to ashes, dust.
After all the bad men die ~ so will I.
Simon,
Take care Jenny Sue!

Simon rode south, towards Sweetwater.

The Chatter Man

A tear in my eye, wind on my face.
Am I the cleanser of the human race?
So it seems ~ I'm always in the right place.
Smell of a woman, feel of lace.
Many would gladly take my place.
But most would faint with what I face.
The Rhymer was asked to kill again.
I do it gladly, do it with a grin.
Those who are evil, they won't last.
The Demon will kill them with a shotgun blast.

Simon thought about the Pistolero song and what Rebecca had said about it being about him. As he rode for Sweetwater, he sang and tried to make up different words.

"Pistolero, Pistolero, where do you roam?
Pistolero, Pistolero, where is your home?
He's fought many battles, he's killed many a man
He stood beside Lee when he fought for the land
He'll kill again, but knows not, who next is
He is a Pistolero from out in East Texas.
He's killed for the money, he's killed for the gold
He's killed for a lady whose heart he must hold
He's killed all over, but knows not, who next is.
He's a Pistolero from out in East Texas.
Pistolero, Pistolero, where does it end?
Pistolero, Pistolero, who is your friend?"

Simon sang it, but he liked the Mexico version better.

Simon got to the Palomino Palace just after noon on a Saturday. He entered the back way as he normally did during the day. He was hungry, but he wasn't too tired after his trip. After his eyes adjusted to the dim light, he walked to the bar and took a stool at the end. He didn't see Cordell, Brock Deaton, or Lettie.

I was in Cordell's place, for a drink and to get something to eat.
My plan for dessert, was to take Lettie upstairs and have something sweet.
The fellow serving the food was new and talked in a constant stream.
Hell, most the time he talked just to him himself, or so it did seem.

The man behind the bar placed a shot glass in front of Simon. "Good afternoon stranger, what's your pleasure?"

Simon ordered a ham sandwich, a beer and a bottle of whiskey.

The man placed the beer and whiskey in front of Simon. "I don't recall having seen you in here before, mister, where you from?"

"Just get my food. Where I'm from is of no never mind."

"That your horse out back? Are you from Texas, or from some other place?"

"Just bring the food, please."

The man left and returned with the sandwich. He placed the sandwich in front of Simon and gave him a napkin. "I didn't catch your name, mister. You got a name?" the chatty bartender asked.

Simon didn't answer. He picked up the sandwich and took a large bite.

"What's that, a shotgun? Sure is a short barrel. It makes a wide pattern, I bet. Where'd you get that scar? Bet it hurt didn't it?"

Simon was trying to eat, but the man continued his incessant questioning. Simon chewed a bite of the ham sandwich, swallowed, took a drink of the beer and then spoke.

"Tell me something Chatter Man....are you part parrot....or uh....some other kind of bird? You haven't gone more than a second....without saying a word."

The man stopped and looked at Simon.

"You probably don't even realize what you do....did you learn that somewhere....or does it come natural to you?"

The man didn't know what to say. He just stood there staring at Simon.

"Don't get me wrong. I'm not saying it is bad, but please shut it off around me....I just want to eat in peace....and be left be."

Tandy Ledbetter saw Simon ride into Sweetwater by the back road and tie his horse behind Cordell's saloon. He went to the Mercantile and told Brock Deaton of Simon's arrival. Cordell Pitifore was there with Brock.

"Mr. Brock, Mr. Simon jest rode up. He went over to the Palace no more 'n' two minutes ago. Want me to tell him you all will be along directly?"

"No need to, Tandy, Cordell and I are through with our business here, so we can all go. I think he will be okay until we can get there. Not even Simon can get into trouble in a few minutes or so."

Simon heard a voice from across the bar. "Excuse me there, mister, he doesn't mean anything by it. It's not any reason to get your feathers all ruffled. He's only being friendly, no reason to be rude."

Simon looked across the bar from where the voice came. He knew the face, but he couldn't put a name with it. The man seemed to be agitated. Simon went back to eating his meal.

The man continued, "He's just a waiter. It doesn't seem to bother anyone here except you. And besides, he didn't mean any harm."

Simon's scar turned a pale red, and it twitched, ever so slightly.

"I wasn't rude....I asked him politely. I simply want to enjoy my meal....I would like to do it quietly."

"He can talk all he wants. Leave him alone."

Simon's blood quickened. Damn why was this man interfering? "Mister, whoever you are, this is between me and the Chatter Man....to you it should be no never mind....so just keep out of my business....while my mood is still kind."

Someone behind Simon gently touched his gun arm at the elbow. Simon allowed his eyes to move from the man of his focus and look to his side. He saw it was Brock Deaton. He looked back at the man interfering with his business. Simon had selected him to be the first to die, if it went that far.

"Brock, me and the Chatter Man here....were having a friendly little chat....then nosey here butted in....does he know a man could get hurt like that?"

The man across the bar studied Simon. He was weighing his options. Finally he spoke. "If I'd had a couple of more drinks, I'd just give you a go."

Simon grabbed his bottle of whiskey and slid it down the bar near the man's hand. "There, when you've drank enough courage let me know."

Another man stepped to the right of the first man. Simon didn't care. The derringer was pointed at his privates. The man was not aware of how close to death he was.

"I don't care what kind of mood you're in. Leave the man alone!"

Simon grinned, well now he could kill two of them. "So what will it be....make a fight....or leave me be. Want to flip a coin....see which one I shoot in the groin?"

The man looked at Simon's left hand and saw the derringer. One false move and he would be singing soprano in the choir, if he lived to tell about it.

The 'Quickening' was in full force. The Demon spoke to Simon. *One more twitch of the scar....let's kill everyone in the bar.* The Demon was afoot and dancing around the two men. Simon started to cock the hammers of the sawed–off shotgun. The sawed–off shotgun was talking to his finger. Hell was only seconds away.

A third man spoke, "No need for all this posturing. He only wanted to know your name. My name is Cyrus Wendell. I have the Twin Aces Ranch south of town. Do you care to introduce yourself?"

Brock Deaton knew what was about to happen. He stepped to the side of Simon and grabbed the barrel of the sawed–off shotgun. It was a brave act. Brock was well known to the men, and they respected him. Brock addressed his speech to Cyrus Wendell.

"Cyrus, let me handle the introduction," said Brock as he pointed to Simon with his right hand. His left hand was still holding the barrel of the shotgun. "His name is Simon, Simon Sublette. He is a very good friend of mine. He isn't the fastest gunman you ever saw, but he'll kill those two and you too, hell, maybe the whole bar before any of you can even draw. He is the man they call the Rhymer. I feel sure most of you know his reputation, and I promise you he'll live up to it and kill you without regret. Let's just back from this and close the matter. It doesn't make any sense, Cyrus, to get killed over some meaningless chatter."

Damn I was impressed. Brock Deaton spoke in a rhyme.
And the Chatter Man ~ well he hadn't said a word the whole damn time.

"We didn't know who this stranger was. With all that's going on who's to know," Cyrus said, "They didn't mean any harm, Brock. They were just trying to help out. We'll finish our drinks and be on our way."

Cyrus Wendell and his two hired hands finished their drinks and left the Palomino Palace. When they reached their horses Cyrus said, "He's a mean one, this Rhymer. Since he is Brock's friend we're going to have to do something about him, the sooner the better."

I can't be left alone long enough to even eat a bite.
The Chatter Man's talking almost caused a fight.
But others interrupted our personal conversation.
If Brock had not stopped me ~ they would have died without reservation.

Simon stayed on alert until the men left. A man could not even eat a sandwich any more without someone wanting to get killed. What was the world coming to?

Cordell said, "Simon, when did you come in?"

"I just kind of drifted in on the wind."

"I thought the wind had an evil smell to it today."

Simon struck a match and lit Cordell's cigar. He looked at him hard. The comment was like a little knife jabbed into Simon's heart.

"It's good to see you too, Cordell....when did you get so righteous, pray tell?"

"It's good to see you, Simon. And you are my dear friend, but you are an evil son of a bitch when you get a mind to be killing somebody. How you fixed for money, are you okay?"

"I'm okay. Why? You want a deposit, in case I shoot the place all to hell?"

"Yeah," he laughed, "give me four or five hundred for starters. Then we'll just put the rest on your tab."

Cordell laughed. Simon did too. The patrons went back to what they came to do. The music started to play, and The Chatter Man started to talk.

Simon called the Chatter Man over to his side. To everyone's surprise Simon apologized. You could have knocked Cordell over with a feather.

"Chatter Man, my name is Simon. I am sorry for all the ruckus and commotion....I'll make it up to you if you have the notion."

The Chatter Man spoke, "It is good to meet you. My name is Dan, Dan Sam. He offered his hand to Simon. Simon took his hand and they shook in agreement.

Brock Deaton looked at Simon and said, "Simon, I didn't realize you were so opposed to a little conversation?"

"Conversation is okay....being nosy rubs me the wrong way. I don't mind a little talk....but I'd never heard a man like the Chatter Man before.... hell, he's talked nonstop....and I've been here an hour or more."

"Might have seemed like an hour, Simon, but you have only been here 'bout ten minutes, maybe the Chatter Man just hit the wrong nerve."

"Maybe so, I was only asking the Chatter Man....how he got such a trait....I didn't say anything mean....and I meant no hate. I asked him nicely to shut it off....when he was around me....I just wanted to eat in peace.... and to be left be. Then Cyrus's men butted in....why, I don't know....but that's when the trouble began."

Cordell said, "I know it wasn't any of his business, but I do appreciate you backing down and letting it be."

"I didn't back down Cordell. I eased off. There's a difference."

"Yeah, yeah, I know. I know it's an ego thing. Either way it's over. Let's have a drink shall we?"

"Who the hell are they anyway?"

"The one was Cyrus Wendell. He's one of the richest men around. As he mentioned, he has large ranch, the Twin Aces, south of town toward Abilene. The other two were his right–hand men."

"Hell, I've heard of him, used to be just a cowboy, looks to me like he's getting above his raising. The other man, I know the face but can't place a name."

Brock Deaton said Cyrus was one of the richest men around.
He owns a big ranch, the bank and some other stores in town.
That's the trouble sometimes with the rich.
They think they can butt in whenever they get the itch.
But someone should tell Cyrus to be careful to who and what is said.
Sometime, someplace, it might just get him dead.
Guys like me don't care if he is powerful and rich.
If he butts in again, I might just kill the nosey son of a bich.

"One was Blackie Overton. The other man is Jack Whitechapel. He came here from the Lincoln County war. He once was a deputy in Tularosa. Before that he was in St. Louis."

"Yep", Simon said, "that's him. I knew I recognized him from somewhere. He was ineffective then, probably ineffective now."

Cordell handed Simon a piece of paper. It was a telegram telling of Rooster's death.

Simon expressed his appreciation and explained he had received the news earlier. He was forever in Cordell's and Fendley's debt for helping with Rooster.

Cordell said, "Hell, Simon, we were sure you were dead this time. These travelers said those two cowboys from Tularosa finally got the best of you. We told them we had heard that before, but they swore this time it was true. So when I saw you at the bar thought maybe your ghost had come to town."

"Cordell, I am a haint....some men can see me....and some men cain't.... some are glad to see me....some men ain't."

"Now, Simon, don't get all boiled over and twitchy. No more friends than you have. You shouldn't be running off the ones you already got."

I raised my glass to Cordell and took a drink. What he said caused me to think.
Cordell, B.D., Tandy and Moses, are the only men friends I have, the others I lost.
I would be served best to protect these relationships at all cost.
Then there's Sweet Talk, Kate and Lettie of the female persuasion,
but they're not true friends, just acquaintances I see on occasion.
Melina Madera, for her I hold a special place.
If I concentrate hard enough, I can taste her and see her face.
And then there is the young, delectable, Miss Rebecca Anne Ravenwood.
And yes I would, I would have her, if I could.
Abigail is the most special, but I fear I have lost her forever.
If so, can I forgive myself? I would think I could not ever!

"We just heard about Drummond," said Brock.

"I made a mistake with him, B.D....must be getting old....he was a hell of a lot meaner....than all the stories told."

"It must have been a hell of a fight?"

"I shot him three times....but he never flinched or showed the pain....we fought teeth and knives....I finally killed him with a blade to the brain."

"Some are saying that since you killed Drummond, you're the best there is."

Simon thought for a moment, swirling his whiskey around in his glass, weighing the impact of Brock's statement. After a few moments, he answered.

"What they say is of no matter. It won't cure the consumption."

Simon drank down a last glass of whiskey, and then left to relieve himself.

Cordell turned to Brock. "Foul mooded son of a bitch tonight, isn't he?"

"Yeah, but that's when he's at his best, when he's got a good burn working!"

"You ever wonder what goes on behind those dark glasses of his?"

"I try not to. It would probably scare the hell out of the both of us."

Simon returned and Brock took him by the arm and led him out of the saloon.

"Come on I want you to meet someone. I've been trying to get you to meet this person, but you keep running off."

Simon and Brock walked toward the Mercantile. "I want you to meet my ..."

Before Brock could finish the sentence, Simon interrupted him. Simon saw a woman coming out of the Mercantile and down the steps into the street. He rushed from Brocks side toward the woman. It was Abigail Sweeney.

Abigail saw Simon and hurriedly ran to him. Simon opened his arms wide and embraced her. They hugged in the middle of the street. "I thought I had lost you, thought I would never see or hear from you again!" said Simon excitedly.

"I sent you a letter telling you I was coming here. I guess you never got it."

"I sent you one too, telling you I was leaving Arizona. I guess they must have crossed paths. It is really good to see you, Abigail. What a wonderful surprise."

"What's going on here, you know each other?" asked a surprised Brock Deaton.

"Yeah," said Simon, "Abigail saved my life once, and I'm forever beholding."

"You mean when she was a nurse, in the army?"

"Yes, Brock, it was when I was in Fort Defiance. We found Simon half frozen from a winter storm, and I helped him heal."

"I'll be damned. Anyway, Simon, Abigail here, well, she's my wife now."

Simon stood back appraising the situation; he was holding Abigail now by her shoulders. Even though he was surprised and shocked, a large smile came to his face. "It couldn't happen to a better couple. My two favorite people, congratulations are at hand."

"So, Brock, just how do you know Simon, and why haven't you mentioned it before?" asked an equally surprised Abigail.

"Don't rightly know why I haven't mentioned it. I know I've been meaning to. Anyway, Simon and I met when we chased down some rustlers once, on the ranch when I worked for Mr. Harris. He saved my life."

"Really, now I think that would be worth mentioning to ones wife, wouldn't you, Simon!"

Abigail was now more pleased than ever she had saved Simon. He had gone on to save the man she fell in love with.

The three of them strolled down the street to find a good place to reminisce.

Abigail and Brock married, what a wonderful treat.
Isn't it strange how fate works, and two strangers meet.
It is curious how each one never mentioned me to the other.
Maybe knowing someone like me isn't what they druther.
Fate has thrown the three of us together for some odd reason.
Perhaps this is the place to settle, maybe, finally it is the season.

Lee T. Moon

Brock and Simon were in the Palomino Place just before lunch drinking coffee. Brock had a slow burn working on his temper because of the bickering and fighting going on about the new barbed wire fence. Chatter Man Dan Sam was sweeping the floor. Cordell came bursting through the door.

"God damned ill breds. These town councilmen make me so mad I could fight."

"Want to fight Cordell, who we gonna pick first?" piped Brock.

"Any of them. They're all stupid. Dumb as a new born chicken."

Brock and Simon started laughing.

Cordell left for the back room.

Brock noticed Simon's head suddenly snap around and his nostrils flared open. Brock thought he could see the hair on the back of Simon's neck stand up. "What is it, Simon?"

Something—or someone is coming—Simon could smell it. He rose from his chair and went to the door to look out onto the street.

It was one of those Texas days when the sky was colored with a hint of dust. A yellow, dusty haze draped the town. The Texas wind was blowing wisps of dirt, moving the dirt about in a swirling motion and slamming them against the weathered buildings. A small dust devil swirled in front of the saloon. At the end of the street, three dogs were fighting. Simon could hear their yelps over the howl of the wind. An omen he thought. He whispered, softly, to no one in particular. "Three dogs fight, devil winds in the dust....turn loose the Demon, I must. Evil comes to stalk the street.... men will die, blood and sand will meet."

Chatter Man Dan Sam heard Simon's whisper and froze in his motions of sweeping the floor. It scared him.

"What's up, Simon?" asked Brock again, when he heard Simon muttering to himself.

"Trouble is on the way Brock....coming with the noon sun....men will die....before it's said and done."

"How do you know, Simon, can you see them?"

"The Rhymer told me. There is badness on the way....coming in as three....they're coming to try....to try and kill me. But the Demon is ready for these evil three....it'll take a lot of dying today, trying to kill me."

Brock gave Simon a strange look. He had never considered that there were two people in Simon's body until Simon talked of the Rhymer in the third person. He was going to say something, but Cordell and Dan interrupted their conversation.

They had brought in some fresh cooked pork ribs, hot barbecue sauce and potato salad. The potato salad was made the way Simon liked it best—with lots of mustard.

Simon loved pork ribs and potato salad.

"Come and eat", said Cordell, "all this talk about fighting has made me hungry. Maybe this will take you two's mind off of hurting somebody for an hour or so."

"Well, I guess it's the next best thing. Are you in, B.D?"

"Just don't get your fingers in the way of my teeth."

I was eating lunch with Cordell and Brock in Pitifore's saloon.
Three scrounges came in, hired guns, one was the bastard, Lee T. Moon.
They ordered drinks and stood at the end of the bar.
If a man was looking for trouble, he wouldn't have to go very far.
I knew Lee T. Moon and one of the other two.
The Demon told me what they'd come here to do.

Three men rode into Sweetwater from the south as Simon had predicted. They rode through the dusty wind and the dirt devils. They rode to the Palomino Palace and tied their horses to the hitching post in front.

Simon could hear their spurs jingle as they walked across the wooden front sidewalk. When they walked in, Simon never looked up. He could see them, without moving his head, in the mirror behind the bar. It was these three that the Demon had told him were coming. In a voice barely above a whisper, Simon spoke. "Vultures have come to roost, I see....B.D., you and Cordell leave....they only came for me."

Brock and Cordell did not move. Cordell sent Chatter Man Dan Sam to the bar to get the men a bottle of whiskey. They already reeked of whiskey, so maybe more would dull their senses some and make them easier to kill. That was Cordell's thinking. He knew why they had come too. It was this damn barbed fence causing the trouble. He knew Simon was going to have to kill them, or at least die in the trying. There was no way around it.

Lee T. Moon was a Comanchero, the one that had wanted to buy Rebecca Ravenwood from Willie Patch Eye. He was hired by the cattlemen, mainly Cyrus Wendell, to help in the fighting over the coming of the fence.

He did not like Simon and Simon certainly did not like Lee T. Moon. The other two men with Lee T. were also Comancheros.

Every time Simon saw this breed of man, he thought about Rebecca. It made him instantly want to kill them. If it weren't for the promise he made to Moses, he would have risen from his chair and killed all three. Then he could finish his lunch in peace.

One of the men with Lee T. was a nervous, jumpy little man. Simon thought he looked like a weasel. He had a pointed straight nose, funny shaped ears and beady eyes. He was dirty. His hair was a greasy mess. It was hard for Simon to eat with him in the room. It looked to Simon like he had been wiped all over with a piece of greasy bacon. Simon wanted to kill him just for that, for disturbing his lunch. John Wesley Hardin would have killed him when he walked in the door. The Demon would have killed him too. *Let's kill the greasy sum—bitch....it'll only take one small twitch.*

The third one was a man Simon recognized, a man everyone called Vibora Chavez. He got his name from a fight he had with another man. Chavez bit the man in the side during the fight and a few days later the man died. Everyone said it was from the bite wound. After that everyone began calling him Vibora, Spanish for rattlesnake.

The Chatter Man applied his trade. "I haven't seen you here before, must be strangers. Are you passing through or are you looking for work? I hear they're hiring at the ranches around here. You look tired, here, have some whiskey and maybe it will perk you up. My name is Dan, what would yours be?"

"Bottle of whiskey, boy", said Chavez, "and two glasses."

"Only two glasses, but there are three of you, should I get one sarsaparilla? Now which one would be the sarsaparilla drinker? Let me guess."

Lee T. Moon rudely grabbed the whiskey bottle and the two glasses and shoved Dan backwards out of his face.

"I didn't mean any harm mister, just being friendly. I bet you work for Cyrus. Most of Cyrus's men are crusty like you. I bet you're the sarsaparilla drinker. What are you all doing here anyway?"

Lee T. took a drink from the bottle and spoke. "Put a cork in it sweetie, where we're from and what we are doing isn't a concern for you."

Lee T. Moon turned toward Simon and spoke. "Hey Sublette, we're working for the cattle ranchers, why don't you come and join us? We could use another gun."

Simon spoke, not looking up. "No interest here, it isn't my cause. I don't even know what you're fighting for."

"We fight for money, Rhymer, lots of money. The cause doesn't matter, just the money. You should join us, and then you won't be killed with your fence loving friend there." Lee T. pointed to Brock Deaton.

Simon's scar twitched violently. It caused him to bite his tongue as he was chewing his food—and that pissed him off. Simon finished the month full of ribs he was eating and moved his plate to the center of the table. He then said, "We're not looking for trouble Lee T....just go and leave us be."

Lee T. Moon said, "We ain't gonna give you no trouble, Rhymer. We just want you to come to our side. Now what's the problem, you afraid of a little skirmish?"

Simon turned his head and looked straight at Lee T. Moon. "I want no trouble with you, Lee T.....so please leave me alone....don't bother me about this....take your friends and be gone."

Moon looked at his companions and said, "See. I told you he talked funny. Told ya he said shit that rhymed."

Simon, never taking his eyes from Lee T. and his friends, whispered to Cordell and Brock. "Cordell, get Chatter Man Dan Sam out of the way, and then go get Moses, and tell him to get here soon. I'll talk to them as long as I can. B.D., get the hell out of here, no reason you to get shot because of me."

"I ain't leavin' Simon," said an agitated Brock Deaton. "If they want me, now's the time, you heard 'em. Anyways, I can handle sons of bitches like these."

Cordell rose from his chair and left out the back door to go and find Moses Fendley. Dan Sam remained behind the bar.

The three hired killers continued to harass Simon and Brock with their talk, and they continued to drink lots of whiskey.

Lee T. spoke up, "Heard what you did to Patch Eye."

"I don't know what you mean....how could little old me kill all thirteen?"

"I was thinking the same thing, but that's the word going around. I told 'em you were good but there ain't anyone that good. Told 'em it sounded like fluff to me."

These three they were starting to chafe me a bit.
I only knew of one sure way to get them to quit.

They won't go ~ I can't make them leave.
Guess I'll have to kill them ~ no one will grieve.

Simon got up from his chair and let his arms hang long and loose. "Okay, let's skirmish. You must speak a different language than me, Lee T.....you haven't heard a word I've said....why is it that during the middle of the day....you three want to end up dead?"

The three Comancheros started to laugh. The man who looked like a weasel had a high–pitched shrill for a laugh.

The Demon talked to Simon. *Maybe they think you're funning....or perhaps they think you're sissified, and that you should be running.*

Lee T. said, "Now, Rhymin' Simon, you can make this easy. Come on and join up with us. Just shoot your friend there as a good faith gesture and we all can be on our way."

When Simon heard the name Rhymin' Simon, his scar twitched violently. This was as good of a reason to kill them as any. "I've already fought a war, where too many innocents died....so just leave me alone....I'm not joining your side."

Lee T. laughed a nervous laugh, grinned and had another drink.

Brock Deaton slowly rose from his chair and moved over toward the piano to separate the line of fire. The three men did not react to his movement and seemed to have lost interest in Brock, for the moment. That was fine with him. It would be easier for him to help Simon kill them.

Where are Moses and Cordell? *It's coming....I can't slow it....and it's gonna be hell.*

Vibora slapped the bar, then picked up something and put it in his mouth and ate it. It was a bug, a cockroach, or something. He'd eat any creature.

Simon had heard that about him too.

Then he started to laugh, a laugh born of nervous malice. It went right to Simon's spine and gave him a chill. He knew it wouldn't be long now. They were close to having their nerve. His laugh served as a warning sign to Simon.

Come on Moses....get your ass across the street....come help me in this killing feat.

Cordell went out the back door, crossed over to the other side of the street and walked rapidly to Moses Fendley's office. Moses was not there. Cordell began the search for Moses. He hoped he would find him before the shooting started. He was more afraid for Brock's safety than he was for Simons.

Finally, Cordell located Moses at Tandy's livery stable. "Damn Moses, come quick. Lee T. Moon's in town and him and two others have Simon cornered over at my place. Deaton is with him too. We need to hurry."

Moses Fendley raised his eyebrows, "Yeah? Well, I don't know who has cornered who. Lee T. is a bad one, but I suspect he hasn't ever seen anything like Simon before. Come to think of it, not many men have."

Tandy said, "That's right, Mr. Simon's like a hot horse shoe, he ain't something you want to take holdt of. No sur,makes whelps and blisters come up on your ass. And it don't take peoples long to let go of him neither, no sur, jest causes pain, jest causes pain. Why Mr. Simon could raise a blood blister on a boot." Tandy reached for his shotgun.

"Where are you going with that scatter gun?" asked Moses.

"With you and Mr. Cordell, there's three of 'em. Gonna put the odds to our favor."

Moses answered harshly, "With only three against Simon, the odds are still in his favor. Kind of like throwing hens into a coyote pen, Simon will eat them, guts feathers and all. Now put up the scattergun and go find the Doc and the undertaker. Have them come to the saloon, and hurry up about it."

Tandy went for the doctor and to find the undertaker.

Cordell and Moses started toward the Palomino Place where Simon was dealing with the three Comancheros. Half way to the saloon they heard what they were trying to prevent, gunfire rang from the Palace. They ran the rest of the way.

Lee T. Moon and companions were leaving Simon no choice. He knew had to kill these men. They had come to do one of two things, either recruit him to their side, or kill him.

They left me no selection. I had to kill them, my instincts kicked into gear.
I'd take Moon first, the Weasel man last ~ he had the most fear.
The Demon came and I was calm. The derringer slipped into my left palm.

I'll give Chavez some bugs to eat, Simon, and I'll do it soon. I'll bury him in a grimy grave, beside the Weasel Man and Lee T. Moon.

The Weasel Man said, "Lee T., I think he's old, and I think he's slow. I think all that sweet rhymin' has softened his taste for killing."

Simon had an instant dislike to the Weasel Man. His voice even sounded like a weasel. It was like his laugh, a high–pitched whine.

"You know Lee T.....the Weasel Man may be right....but he might be wrong....which is it....are the angels singing me....or you a song?"

Moon was grinning, but suddenly his face got hard, and his eyes became a squint. "Harley Coale was my friend."

"You need better friends than Patch Eye and Coale. They are like the Weasel Man. None of them were born....just shit out on the side of the road. So have a go....if you think I've slowed!"

Brock was too scared right now to laugh at Simon's comment. Any other time it would be funny.

Better get here soon. I'm going to kill Lee T. Moon.

The Weasel Man stood away. "Let's kill him, Moon, and get it over with. It'll save us the trouble from havin' to do it later on."

Simon now realized their true intentions. Get him to join their side and kill him somewhere along the way. Simon turned his icy glare toward the Weasel Man. "You don't the balls I suspect....you going to do it....or stand there with shit in your neck?"

Sorry Moses, but I tried as hard as my senses would allow, but I have to kill this vermin, and I have to do it now. The Demon can't wait, it is fate.

Weasel Man's head and eyes darted rapidly back and forth to Lee T.
He was weighing the odds of me, against the three.
They were drinking lot, let them, the whiskey would soften their brains.
This old, slow snake would show how much venom I had left in my veins.

The Demon spoke to Simon again. *Well Moses will just miss his chance. It's time for me, and these three to dance.*

Suddenly, out of the corner of his eye, Simon saw a knife coming in the air. Vibora had moved to the side trying to catch Simon off guard. Dan Sam saw the move too, and in his own way of trying to help, raised his broom to deflect the knife.

The broom obstructed Simon's vision and caused him to change his target. Simon drew his forty–five and had to fire the derringer at the Weasel Man instead of Lee T. Moon. He fired another shot at Vibora, and as he moved to his side, he stumbled and fell over a chair. He got to his knees, saw Lee T and hastily fired at him. He then sought cover behind the bar. Bullets were flying everywhere. He didn't know where Brock Deaton was.

Dan Sam was crouched down behind the bar with Simon. He had been shot in the arm. The event had happened too fast. At this point, he didn't know if he had shot anyone or not. In the mirror above the bar, he could see Lee T. Moon's head, behind an upended table. He couldn't see anything else.

Brock said, "Come on out, Simon. The goddamn bug eater and the Weasel man are dead. This other chicken shit is hiding behind a table, but I got him cornered."

Just like a coon up a tree, o' Brock's got Lee T., said the Demon.

Simon stood up, cautiously, behind the bar. He saw where Moon was crouching behind the table. Deaton was behind the piano and had a direct line of fire on Moon. Moon was a dead man if Deaton were to have such a notion. It was Simon's intention to walk straight to where Moon was crouching and kill him.

Simon walked out from behind the bar. "Lee T., you're the kind of man....that's a disgrace to our state....is the money so good....that it's that easy to hate?"

Simon was catching his breath. He walked straight to Moon. He looked over and the lunch of pork ribs and potato salad was still on the table. He could see the heat still rising off the ribs.

"Now you know it, Lee T.....I'm not slow, and I'm not old....I'm going to kill you now....because my lunch is getting cold."

As Simon was about to pull the trigger and end Lee T. Moon's life, Moses and Cordell came running into the saloon through the back door. Moses was not happy. He had on his lawman's face, and his look was not friendly.

Moses spoke loudly, "Simon, put the gun down. It's my show now!"

Simon reluctantly lowered his gun, but did not put it away—it was ready just in case.

Deaton explained the whole scene and what had happened to Moses. "Boy, Moses, you should have seen it. It was the damndest shooting exhibition I've ever seen. He got one of them when he was falling backwards and the other one as he dove behind the bar. He shot both of them dead center in the heart."

Moses raised his eyebrows and gave a little whistle. "Pretty damn lucky, Simon, you probably couldn't do that again in a hundred years."

Simon looked at Moses. "Don't have to." Then Simon gave Moses a little grin.

Moses spoke to Lee T. Moon. "Lee T., get out from behind that table."

Lee T. rose to his full height, dusting off his clothes.

"Give me your gun, then get on your horse and get the hell out of here. And tell Cyrus not to send anymore of his cowardly assed gunmen to my town. Next time I'll do the killing'!"

When Lee T. reached for his gun to hand it to Moses, Moses shot him, dead center in the heart. Another gunshot rang out simultaneous with gunshot from Moses, striking Lee T. Moon in the left temple. Simon and Brock Deaton jerked their heads towards Moses in surprise. They saw the other shot had come from Chatter Man Dan Sam.

"I don't like to be touched like that. He shouldn't have been so rude," Dan said as he handed the gun over to Moses.

Simon said, "Hey diddle, diddle, the cat and the fiddle....call the coroner soon....the Snake and the Weasel are dead....Moses and Chatter Man killed Lee T. Moon."

"Goddamned vermin, I never did like him anyway. This was as good a reason as any. Come to town, bothering innocent citizens and shooting up a reputable establishment like this and messing up a fine plate of pork ribs. I find you guilty and sentence you to death." Moses took Simon's gun and then shot Lee T. Moon again. "Now you can have credit for all three. Who is to know the difference?"

Simon said, "Well, there're three more for the Bone Orchard....someone plant them quick....even full dead....the Weasel Man is making me sick. Hell....just set them on fire....it's what I'd do....souls are going to be in flames....bodies might as well be too."

Simon walked outside to get a breath of fresh air. The smell of the blood and the Weasel man almost made him vomit. He braced himself on the hitching post with both hands and took several long breaths. When he regained his composure, he noticed the wind had quit blowing. The sky had cleared and was now a deep rich blue. At the end of the street, one of the dogs was laying on a porch licking his privates. This was eerie, too eerie, even for Simon.

Moses came outside. "Simon, you know you're going to have to leave this part of the country, don't you? They won't let you be an innocent bystander, not in this wire thing. Both sides are fearful that you'll join the other. One of them, out of sheer fear, is going to kill you. You're just too damned dangerous to be left sitting around."

"I think I will pay Cyrus Wendell a call....on my way out of town....he came to kill me, I will end this for once and all."

"Cyrus is my problem. You let me handle it, as we agreed?"

Simon nodded. He agreed but was against his better judgment.

FATE came calling ~ it's sometimes strange what it has to give.
I have always lived to be on the go ~ but now I must go just to live.
They met their defeat,
in the sweltering heat,
three Comancheros with guns for hire.
They didn't care for which side,
that they finally died,
they sold themselves to the highest buyer.

Tandy Ledbetter and the undertaker came up the stairs as Simon and Brock were leaving the Palomino Palace.

"How many boxes we be needin', Mister Simon?" asked Tandy.

Simon spoke to Tandy, "Lee T, the Weasel and the Snake....now all dead for the barbed–wire sake."

Brock Deaton said, "Two planters and one manure bag."

"A manure bag?" asked the undertaker.

"Yeah," said Simon. "One of them was just a piece of shit posing as a man. Get my things ready, Tandy. I'll be leaving in a couple of days."

"Moses, who's paying for this?" asked the undertaker.

"Pack them up and send them to Cyrus, they're his," said Brock.

Tandy went into the saloon and saw the carnage of the gunfight.

If the truth was known, Simon had only killed the Weasel Man. In doing so he had saved Brock Deaton's life, again. Brock Deaton had been the one who shot and killed Chavez as Simon dove behind the bar. Brock did not want anyone to know what he had done. It was a lot easier to let everyone, including Cyrus, think that Simon had done the killing. By nightfall the citizens of the territory would be talking of how the Rhymer, single handedly, had killed three more Comancheros. No one would ever know the whole truth. I would add to his reputation—and his legend.

After the undertaker had the bodies loaded in a wagon, Simon gave him a note to give to Cyrus.

'Don't send no more weasels or Comancheros or bug eating Mexicans ~ with love, from a poet."

Tandy walked over to Moses. "Mr. Simon says he's leavin'. You makin' 'im go?"

"No, it's not me. He's got to go for his own good. They'll just send more. They're afraid of him, so they'll have to kill him before it's over."

"Maybe so, Mr. Moses, but they best not come a half steppin'."

"I hear that. These three did."

"And iffin' I'm here, they's gonna have black all over their ass!"

Brother Hood of the Gun
Be them a saint,
or be them a sinner,
in a duel there's only one winner.
The loser falls to the ground,
when the killing done.

Be them a criminal,
or be them the law,
it applies to them all.
They are now bonded by the
Brother Hood of the Gun.

Rhymer

The Bone Orchard
Three more for the Bone Orchard.
Three more their maker to meet.
Give me them boots.
They don't need nothing on their feet.

Pick the gold from their teeth.
I'll make that watch mine.
The gold will pay for the burying.
And they won't need to be keeping time.

Get those pistols and rifles
The Bone Orchard needs not a gun.
The damp and the underground critters.
Will, in time, get the job done.

The Bone Orchard is a place.
Where we plant those we kill.
Each town has one with a name.
Most just call it Boot Hill.

Rhymer

Thoughts Before Leaving

Simon wrote the two poems sitting in the hotel dining room before he went back to the Palomino Palace for his last evening with Lettie. He was getting soft, he felt. He was feeling some guilt for being with Lettie with Abigail so close. Maybe it was a good thing, this guilt.

The night of the killing of Lee T. Moon, Simon dined with Abigail and Brock, at their small house, on the ranch where Brock worked. It was the most peaceful setting he had been in since eating at home with his mother and the rest of his family. How long ago had that been? Simon was at ease.

In a discreet moment when Brock was out of the room, Abigail confessed. "Simon, I'm embarrassed to say this, but I must confess. When you were sick at the fort, I…," Abigail paused, "I, uh…I read your diary."

Simon grinned. "You're left handed, aren't you?"

Abigail nodded, "Yes, why do you ask?"

"I knew you read my diary. When I took it out to write some more I noticed it was tied wrong. So I figured you read it."

"It didn't make you mad, my reading your private notes?"

"What good would that have done? You saved me and I was beholding. Besides, it's only a diary. I have nothing to hide, especially from you."

Abigail gently touched Simon's hand, and she smiled. She was relieved.

Simon gave Abigail an envelope. He told her if something were to happen to him, she should open it and follow the instructions. It was his full intent to come back and retrieve the envelope someday. He made Abigail promise not to read it before hand. Abigail giggled and made the promise.

I'm not much for armies. I had my fill in the Great War that was fought.
Masses of men being told to kill and doing so without rational thought.
I watched thousands fall, fighting they said for the sovereignty of state.
They went in mass, following the swarm, killing without hate.
I didn't like being told who, where, and when I had to kill
I didn't like it then, I don't now, and I never will.
I watched my daddy and my brother and my friends fall in battle after battle.
I fought beside them, but we were sent to slaughter like herds of cattle.

It was my last evening with Lettie.
I watched as she slowly took off her garments.
I was lying in bed drinking, waiting for a glimpse of that feline varmint.
There it is, the Devils Triangle.
Just looking at it causes a man to go all a flush
I said some things to Lettie, she laughed ~ but she never did blush.

Brock Deaton met Simon to have breakfast before he left.

"B.D., it just doesn't make sense, being forced out like this. It doesn't seem right. A man forced from his a land because he wants to be neutral in a fight."

"Stay and fight then, it's going to happen. We want to avoid it at all cost, but Cyrus and the others don't."

"I got no stake in this, B.D. You're not even fighting for your own land. If you were, it might be different. I'd stay and help, you know that. To fence or not to fence, they could save a lot of blood if they would just stand back and look around. The fence isn't coming. It's here, and it's here to stay. I'm not a fence man. I still prefer the land like it was when the wind was wild and free."

"You're right, Simon. The fence is here, and it is the future. We haven't hurt anything or anyone. We left the water open. There's plenty for everyone, but no, hell no, they still come and cut our fences, and that cost us a lot of hard earned money. Then when we put it back up they come and try to kill us. This is something I believe in and whether it's my land or not, I am going to make a stand. Someday I'll have something here. So I'm going to make a stand. This is what I want."

"You got gumption, B.D. A man shouldn't itch for something he isn't willing to scratch for. I admire a man with principles. This just isn't mine. Thinking back, you should have let me kill Cyrus and his friends that afternoon in the bar."

"Probably, but he's just part of the problem. No, we got to battle the whole lot of them. Listen, I'm really sorry you got to go. I was kind of getting fond of having you around all the time. Abigail is too. Let me know where you are. I'll write when it's over. Go to Juarez, hang out and wait."

"I'll let you know. Maybe Juarez, maybe Arizona, maybe Tascosa, I don't know which."

"Not going back to Nellie Jacks?"

"Too wild for me, I'm ready for something tamer. I think some peace and quiet is what I need."

Simon thought about the X–Bar–T. Rebecca was one fine young woman. With her ranch and his money, he could enjoy the good life for a long time to come. He debated between the X–Bar–T and Melina. Which would it be? Melina, or the X–Bar–T?

<u>*When the Wind was Wild and Free*</u>

When the wind was wild and free,
prairie grass stood deep to knee,
and the buffalo blackened the western plain,
and the Indian knew no white ~ by a white man name.

The rivers ran deep and crystal clear,
the Great Spirit renewed Earth each year,
and game was plentiful for trap and hunters bow,
and seed was bountiful ~ for the wild wind to sow.

The tree of the forest was tall and plenty,
the Elk, the Deer, the Eagle were many,
and the air smelled sweet, forever you could see,
and the waters were pure ~ when the wind was wild and free.

No homes needed to lay a head,
animal hide blankets on ground for a bed,
and the spirits were in harmony with the creatures of the land,
and some were called wild ~ and some were called man.

Then the iron horse came, belching smoke and flame,
with him ~ the Others came,
and they brought disease and famine, pestilence and the barbed fence,
and civilizations were changed ~ the wind not blowing free since.

Sit we now in the ring of ceremonial fire,
chant the songs ~ spirits to conspire,
and the wild wind causes the herds to grow,
and if you watch ~ you can see it blow.

It comes in day or darkest night dream,
the vision of that ancestral scene,
and ages past float on smoke to me,
and I am there ~ when the wind ~ was wild and free.

Chapter Seven

The Beginning of the End

I've been watched over ~ wrapped in a four–leaf clover,
so far life's treated me pretty good.
But I'm not tempting Mother Fate, getting caught up in the fencing hate.
I'm leaving like McFinley said I should.
I just don't like this ~ it is a rather bad situation.
These local cattle people wanting me to be a part of their association.
If I don't side with them, they think I'm with those who want the fence.
I'm caught in the middle ~ when they're warring there is no common sense.
Now I don't have anything in particular against the fencers.
But I don't like fencing in the open range.
Lots of people say it's the new way coming,
and that eventually the west will change.
They should sit down and work out some kind of agreement.
But with the way it's going, the killing is coming and so is the bereavement.
I've packed up my gear. This isn't any of my concern.
I think at first light to Tascosa is where I'll return.
Ah, Rebecca Ravenwood, I can close my eyes and picture her plain as day
I'll send her a letter and tell her I'm on my way.

Simon weighed the pluses and minuses of each place he thought about going. Arizona with Melina was alluring. But her sexual pleasures were outweighed by the fact the saloon was public and there would always be trouble when tempers, alcohol and sex were involved.

Rebecca and the X–Bar–T Ranch offered the solitude Simon was seeking. The ranch was large and he could stay and help her and be sheltered from the public and hopefully away from situations where the Demon would take control.

As Simon rode out of Sweetwater in the early morning, he rode north to Tascosa. He sang this song as he rode.

"Lay me down in a field of lilies.
Lay me down in a field of wheat.
Lay me down in a den of lions.

Or with scorpions at my feet.
Lay me down in a field of flowers
Lay me down in a field of stone.
Just lay me down in Texas.
It's where I call my home."

He had seen this poem many, many years ago on an Indian grave near Fort Smith, Arkansas. He had remembered it to this day. For some odd reason, he had never chosen to sing it. Was it an omen? As usual, Simon changed the words to his own liking.

After he finished singing the song, suddenly, without provocation, the Demon came to Simon. It came in such a rush his scar twitched, violently and his right hand jumped so hard he jerked the big gray horses' head turning him to the right.

The Demon spoke to Simon. *Why you running Simon James....don't you know they'll be calling you names? Brock needs your help just like all the others....he's all you got left....he's like your brother.*

The big gray horse reared up and snorted. He began to prance like he too had a demon inside.

Simon leaned forward in the saddle and patted the big gray horse on the neck apologizing for the violence.

The Demon made him think about his decision not to help Brock, his good friend. Actually, he was the best fried Simon had. And then there was Abigail. He owed Abigail for saving his life. He wouldn't be able to live with himself if he let anything happen to Abigail.

The Demon spoke again. *You helped the little girl with Mountain Red.... you helped Wes when he needed to be dead. You revenged the storekeeper when it wasn't your fight....you helped Rebecca twice to set things right.*

Brock and Abigail were worth helping just as Rebecca and the others had been, maybe more so. Why not help them? Would he be killed—maybe? Was he afraid? No! His mind was racing. Hell, Sweetwater was as good a place to die as anywhere. At least they couldn't say he was running. That's what the song said he was singing; just lay me down in Texas.

The Demon hadn't left Simon, it spoke once more. *Let's sneak up on them Simon....let's kill the fence cutters....unleash me....I'll go through them like a hot knife through butter. We have to help Brock and Abigail....don't let Cyrus send them to hell.*

Simon knew the Demon was right. It came to him like a bolt of lightning. He finally realized this was what he had been searching for these many years. He was at ease here, even if trouble was on the horizon. This was now his family. Brock, Abigail, Moses, Tandy and Cordell—they looked after him and genuinely cared for him. He must stay. He knew it was his fate.

He halted the big gray horse and turned in the saddle and faced southeast. When the sun hit his eyes and the yellow–red daggers hit his brain, he knew then that he would kill Cyrus Wendell. The shotgun leaped into his hand and he laid it across his lap.

The Demon came again. *Simon, we can prevent this war, finally, my friend, we know what we are fighting for. Halleluiah!*

He gently turned the big gray to the direction of Cyrus Wendell's ranch. He decided that at nightfall, he and the Demon would sneak onto the ranch and kill everyone they could find. Maybe this was one war that would end before it got started. Nobody could blame him. He had left town this morning. Moses Fendley would just have to deal with it. Brock was his friend—and—as he had said before, what are friends for?

The Demon grinned, it was pleased, and Simon's scar twitched once more.

Simon circled around a small hill and was facing the sun when the shot came. He felt the impact before he heard the blast. The shot came from far away, probably from a Sharps Rifle. He heard a second shot, but it only kicked up dirt underneath his horse. The first shot tore open a huge hole in his left chest. The shot came from behind Simon. It came from two men who had been trailing Simon to make sure he left town, two of Cyrus Wendell's men. The man whose bullet struck Simon was one of the men from the bar incident with the Chatter Man. The one named Jack Whitechapel. The other man was Blackie Overton, also involved in the altercation with the Chatter Man incident.

Out of the clear blue sky on a brisk spring morning,
two shots were fired, they both came without warning.
The bullets came from behind, knocking me to the ground.
I was hit and bleeding before I heard the sound.
I needed protection and made it up into some rocks on a small hill.
I inspected my wound, it isn't good, the bleeding might cease if I lay still.
They ambushed me, probably thinking I was riding over to the other side.
Guess they figured I'd be one less hired gun if they shot me and I just died.
You know of all the things, I did I didn't think my end would come this way.
The blood and pain are so bad ~ I don't think I'll last to the end of the day.

I put some gunpowder in my wound, fired it, to keep it from getting infected.
I think my left arm is shot to hell ~ no movement can be detected.
I hear him in the rocks, he's hunting for me for where I lay.
If he finds me, then the son–of–a–bich will join me in death today.
I yelled at him "Hey mister, do you want to die?
Come with me and we'll both look the Devil in the eye."
The pain is easing up, I think maybe I'm beginning to heal.
Then I realize, when you are about to die, this is what you feel
I'm getting cold, but it is spring and this isn't right.
They say it is the coldest right before it becomes light.
I ask myself, why is it now, that I have to die.
Soon I'll see the Devil and ask him why!

Simon was knocked from his horse by the blast. The gray horse he rode was accustomed to gunfire and did not shy when the shot came. Simon was hurt real bad. He hooked his right arm into the stirrup of his saddle and urged the horse up to a small hill covered with rocks. He thought he could get some cover there from their next attack and could patch his wound. This wound was different than most other wounds Simon had received. This one was deadly serious. He managed to get some gunpowder into the wound and lit it with a match. The pain was almost unbearable. But it did slow the bleeding. Simon could hear the man looking for him. He wanted the man to find him, so he would have company when he went to hell. He was spitting up blood and the wounds to his arm and chest were deep. It had to have been a fifty caliber bullet. Nothing else he knew of caused this kind of damage. His breathing was labored. He knew part of his lung had been pierced.

He called to the man but no answer came. He was talking to the wind; the back shooting coward had ridden away. Simon knew he was dying; he did not have enough strength to mount his horse and ride for help. Using the sawed–off shotgun as a brace, he managed to stand and get his saddlebags. Then he sat down with his back against a large rock. The rock slanted in the ground to make a perfect chair back. With his face to the morning sun, he wrote his last words in his diary.

The sweet spring wind brushes my lips with a kiss.
Its wispy warm fingers, caresses my neck and face.
They embrace my heart and soul with comfort and bliss

The sounds and scents of God, emanate from this place.
I am at peace, finally, the turmoil, trouble, I will not miss.
Somewhere, in the distance, I hear, Amazing Grace.
The kiss the wind blew ~ was the kiss of death
I now breathe my last breath.
Simon

Simon leaned backwards against the slanted rock. He closed his eyes and felt the warm morning sun on his face and the gentle spring wind in his hair. He placed the diary in his lap. Thoughts of his family came to him. The Demon came for the last time. *I guess we were finally dealt a losing hand, so I am off to inhabit another man.*

Papa D

The old man sat in his rocking chair on the front porch, slowly moving back and forth. An easterly wind was gently caressing his leather–like weathered face.

"Rain's a coming, Zack. Better help your grandpa get the windows down. Granny would get mad at us if we let it rain in."

Little Zachary Deaton jumped up and ran inside. "Gonna rain, Granny. Papa D said to get all the windows shut."

"Go on back outside, Zack. I'll tend to the windows. Go on now and keep Papa D company."

A gentle rain began to fall. Softly, it caressed the big white house and the windowpanes. It sounded good when it hit the ground and made that soft splashing noise. Brock Deaton and his grandson sat on the porch, enjoying the smell of the fresh rain splashed against the dirt and the slow sound of the drops hitting the roof of the house. It was a good time for Brock. He was a lucky man. He had lived a good full life, surviving, even helping put to an end, the barbed wire fence war. He had married, had two children, and now he was blessed with five grandchildren. He tried not to show it, but Zack was his favorite.

On Brock's ranch, the Double S D, up on this rocky, craggy hill, was a grave marked with a small white cross. Brock refused to discuss that grave with anyone. Abigail Sweeney Deaton knew the story of the grave, but she was the only one Brock ever told. His two children were told it was a friend from the war of the fence. Brock did not tell Moses, Tandy, or Cordell it was Simon's grave. They assumed Simon had ridden away never to be heard of again.

"Papa D, I asked Daddy 'bout that grave marker. He told me he didn't know anything about it, and that it's not polite to ask. Why?"

Brock looked up to the hill, but he didn't answer.

"Who's up there, Papa D, whose grave is it? I saw you up there this morning when I got up early."

Brock looked at Zack. He had never discussed with anyone, other than Abigail, who was buried in that grave. He did not tell anyone, not even Abigail, about the subsequent events. Brock rose from his rocker, grabbed his cane for support, and went into the house.

Zack thought he had made his Papa D mad. His dad had told him not to ask his grandpa about the grave, not ever. Now he had made his favorite person in the whole world mad. His dad would be furious, too, when he learned that Zack had asked about the grave when he had been told not to. Zack thought he might get a whipping for this.

Brock went into the bedroom, opened the closet door, reached back into the closet's darkest recess and pulled out the old worn leather saddlebags. Carefully, he opened the saddlebags and reached inside. Gently, he removed a diary bound by a red ribbon. He cradled the bound pages like a man holding a baby and hobbled back to the porch to a waiting, scared Zack.

Abigail saw him walking out of the bedroom holding the diary. "What are you doing with that?"

"I'm going to let Zack read it."

"I guess thirteen is old enough. Is it all there?"

"Mostly."

"Mostly, is something missing?"

"Well, it's all here except what happened at the end."

"You know you never told me and I never asked. You only told me they killed Simon. I always guessed there was more. You want to tell me now?"

"You mean like confession is good for the soul?"

"Do you need to confess, Brock?"

"Well I remember what Simon said once. Heaven is only open for a few moments, and hell is open all night long. There were things that happened I kept from you for good reason but I can't think of that good reason now."

"Take the diary to Zack. I'll get some coffee and we'll talk a spell."

Brock returned to the porch and Zack. He sat down, covered his tired old legs with a blanket and looked up to the single white cross on the rocky hill. He motioned for Zack to come and sit by his side.

Zack was relieved and happy.

"Zack, I've never told anyone about that marker." Brock's voice was low, slow, controlled. "He was a friend of mine, a good friend, and he saved my life more than once." Brock tapped the loose bound pages with his finger. He read from a page he had written in Simon's diary. "This was the diary of the Rhymer, Simon James Sublette. He was a gunfighter, poet, philosopher, and may God rest his violent soul. He was killed upon that hill. He was back shot. He didn't deserve it, but he probably lived longer than a gunfighter should. The ranchers didn't want to face him, Zack. He was just too damn mean for his own damn good. Any man has the right to meet his enemy and meet him face to face. He didn't get the chance. Zack, I want you to take this and read it. Be careful it's old, and it is very dear to me. Take it somewhere safe, where you won't be found. There are things in here your mamma and papa might not think you're old enough to know. Read it good, Zack, study it well, read between the lines, read it twice. Let's keep this our secret, okay?"

Zack looked at his Papa D. He saw his grandpa was serious. He liked having a secret with his grandpa. He knew he was special, this proved it. Zack looked strangely at his Papa D. He had never seen him with a tear in his eye before. Carefully, Zack took the diary and sneaked around behind the barn, and then he made a mad dash toward the rocky hill. No one would look for him there. He untied the ribbon and began to read, just as his grandmother had some thirty odd years ago at Fort Defiance. Zack had read, some other place, about this man named Simon Sublette. He was legendary in some parts of Texas. He always knew that his Papa D had grown up in that era, but he had never associated his grandpa with gunslingers and killers. He read the first page of the diary. It was scribbled in Brock Deaton's hand writing.

It read: This is the journal of the life of Simon James Sublette, born July 6, 1846 and back shot on Friday, May 8, 1885. He is buried near Sweetwater, Texas on the Double S D Ranch, on a small rocky hill. He was my friend, and I am fortunate to have known such a man. May God have mercy on his soul. Brock Angus Deaton. July 6, 1885.

Zack couldn't read fast enough, he eyes and hands tore over the pages.

Abigail brought the coffee to the porch and joined Brock. "Have you read the dairy, Brock?"

"Yes, a few times actually. Have you read it?"

"No, not since Fort Defiance, I guess you know then that I had feelings for Simon early on. I think I might have loved him but I never loved his lifestyle."

"I loved him, too, like a brother. I didn't know about your feelings at the time, but sensed it I guess. I knew how you felt about me so it never caused me any concern."

"I guess that's my confession." Abigail sipped her coffee and waited for Brock to speak.

Brock said, "Here is what really happened. I heard the shot that fateful Friday morning. It echoed across the sky. For some reason I knew what it was and rode as fast as he could in the direction Simon was heading. I saw two men and when they saw me, one of them rode away toward the west. I chased that man and cursed his name. I yelled at him, 'Jack Whitechapel I'm going to kill you, you son of a bitch.' Whitechapel ran scared, he was a coward. He was never heard from again. The other man came out of the small hill where Simon is now buried and circled back toward town. I didn't know who he was until later. I found Simon, barely alive, in the rocks on that hill. He was unconscious when I arrived and I knew Simon could not survive such a terrible wound. I tried to stop the bleeding and plug the huge hole in Simon's chest. He was badly hurt and I knew a doctor couldn't help him. I tried to get him on his saddle but only ended up hurting him more. Simon briefly awoke, and he told me not to tell anyone he was dead. It would keep the fear in his enemies, and in my enemies. Simon said it might go bad for me and you if they really knew he was dead. He said a bizarre thing, said it right before he passed on." Brock took a sip of coffee. "Could you get me something a bit stronger?"

Abigail patted Brock's leg, rose from her chair, went into the house and returned with some whiskey.

"Abigail, what he said was, when I get to hell....I'm going to kill the devil and end hell for all time....they will say hell was frozen over....by he who talked in rhyme. That was the exactly what he said."

Abigail smiled, "That sounds exactly like something Simon would have said."

"You know Simon always wanted to be buried in Texas, and at least he got his wish. I laid Simon against the large, leaning rock and sat with him until he drew his last breath. I buried the man I had come to know and love. I cried, and that made me even madder." Brock poured some whiskey into his coffee cup and took a small drink. He smacked his lips, then continued. "I went to town, vowing to find Simon's killer and kill him. By happened stance, I heard this man in the Palomino Palace tell of killing Simon. I looked and saw it was Blackie Overton, Whitechapel's partner. I followed the man outside and confronted him. I told him if you blink, you die in the dark."

"And?" said Abigail.

"He blinked, Abigail. I killed him with my knife so not to make any noise. I killed him in revenge for Simon. I killed Blackie Overton. I would have killed him even if he had faced Simon straight on. Simon was my friend and I needed to expel the anger. I was never questioned about the killing. Moses might have suspected, but Moses did not like that kind of man either. It could have been the note I left implying that Simon had come back and killed the man.

"So you wrote that note they found on the killer, not Simon?"

"Yep, it was me. Here lies a sneak shooter, all dead in a heap. Cyrus Wendell, you have a date with death to keep."

Abigail poured herself some whiskey. She was speechless.

"I was riding back to the ranch, and I came upon Cyrus Wendell, alone on the road. Just seeing Cyrus and knowing he had ordered the death of Simon caused me to lose my temper again. I killed Cyrus with two gunshots to the head. Just like he did to Simon, I struck without warning. I did not give him a chance to defend himself. I then left another note on Cyrus's body that implicated the Rhymer. The note read, this man sent others to kill me but they didn't get the job done. Now I'm coming in the cold of the night, and I'm going to kill everyone. All should stay inside, lock your doors in fear, I am in the darkness, and death is near."

Brock took a sip of his coffee and whiskey and looked at Abigail.

She reached over and patted his hand.

"When they found Cyrus's body, the others became fearful of their life. They feared the Rhymer. He scared the living Jesus out of them. As you know, the killing of Cyrus was the incident that brought the fence war to its end. Moses never knew. That Ranger that came afterwards, that Rock Wardlaw, was convinced Simon did it so they never looked to me. And that's why I asked you not to tell who was buried on that hill. I sent letters to Melina and Rebecca."

"I saw a buckboard up there once, didn't know who it was. So he was killed on that Friday and not Sunday like you said."

"Yes, I know I lied but, I was protecting me, you and our future. Forgive me?"

"Always!" Rebecca leaned over and kissed Brock on the forehead. "You did good, Brock Deaton. Do you feel better now?"

"Yes, yes I do! Rebecca wrote back and asked me to put yellow and red wild flowers on his grave each spring and kiss his headstone for her."

"I guess it's time we mark his grave proper. Let's go to town next week and get him a proper stone for you to kiss. We were fortunate Simon smiled and blessed us with his generosity. We got to buy all this land a lot earlier than we planned."

"We were fortunate indeed. We got to know and love a man like Simon, and then were benefactors of his kindness, in life and death. I was overwhelmed when I went to Fort Worth to settle his affairs and found the small fortune he had amassed. And, Abigail, when he turned around that morning to come and help us he in effect probably saved our lives.

He stopped the fence war even though he was dead. We owe him a lot. I am certain he saved many lives in addition to ours."

Abigail held up her coffee cup in a toast, "To Simon."

Brock touched her cup with his.

Abigail was glad she now knew the truth.

They both smiled. They were overcome with joy and love.

Zack read all day. He carefully retied the diary, hid it under his shirt and made his way back to the ranch house. Abigail, from the window over the kitchen sink, saw him come from the direction of the rocky hill. He stole into the barn and hid the diary in a box where he thought it would be safe.

His mother was the first to see him. "Where have you been all day son, haven't seen hide nor hair of you?"

"Just been playing, Mamma. What's for supper, I'm starved?"

"Pork ribs and potato salad and maybe a piece of Granny's pecan pie if you'll give the thanks."

"Pork ribs, yippee, it's my favorite of all."

A big smile came to Papa D's face. He knew another man whose favorite food was pork ribs. He enjoyed the thought.

Zack slept hard that night, with visions of the Rhymer dancing in his head. He had a hundred questions for his Papa D.

The next day Zack took the diary and climbed to the hayloft in the barn. He read the entire book again that day. Again like the day before he slept hard and all night dreamed of his Papa D and the Rhymer.

The next morning Zack caught up to his Papa D at the chicken coop. He made sure they were alone. "Papa D, I finally finished the diary. Read it two times, I did. Did you actually do what this diary says? Did you really kill a man?"

Brock Deaton looked away. He looked at the cross on the hill for a moment, and then he found an old barrel, turned it sideways, and sat down, drawing Zack near. "Zack, I always thought someone would come along who might understand about the diary. Your mamma and daddy are too gentle for such things. You, however, you're like me when I was young. You have my mannerisms; you have a different attitude than them. I believe I can tell you things, now that you're old enough, and trust you to believe that the way we acted was necessary for the times. I can trust you, can't I, Zack?"

"Papa D, you could never do anything wrong in my eyes, not even killing a man. I can keep a secret. Mamma and Daddy always say to turn the other cheek, but I know that sometimes I got to fight. I just don't tell them about it."

"That's right, and don't ever forget it. If you can avoid the fight, do so, but if you can't then be mean and vicious, win anyway you can. Now this is our secret. If your mamma or daddy ever found out about the diary, why they'd come un–sprung for sure."

"Papa D, they do sometimes for no reason anyway. Mamma's already sissified Aaron. I listen to them and mind them, but it doesn't change the way I think."

"That's good, Zack. You got good instincts. Just trust yourself, that inner feeling about what's right and wrong, and don't ever change directions. It'll lead you good."

Brock stood up and spread some chicken feed on the ground. It was funny; watching those chickens peck reminded him of what Simon had written about his friend Boyce, the Chicken Man. It brought a smile to Brock's face. He thought a lot about Simon lately.

"Papa D?"

"Yeah, Zack."

"What's it feel like to kill a man?"

Brock led Zack back to the old barrel and sat down again. Zack sat facing him, cross–legged, Indian style. "Zack, killing a man isn't any good. But you'll learn as you get older that there are evil men in this world, and in order for decent folks to survive and be civil, those men must be killed. Some are suited well to do the killing, some are not. But killing, nonetheless, still isn't any good. I hope you never have to see it. The Rhymer was like that Zack. He just wanted to be left alone, to live some kind of life. He didn't like wars or bad cruel people, but he was suited well to killing. Like a glove on a hand, it fit him well. He was suited better than anyone I ever saw or heard tell of. A lot of innocent people lived longer because of him."

"It's a great story, Papa D. He's who's buried on the hill, isn't he?"

"Yes, Zack, he's the one lying under that marker. The Rhymer is buried up on that rocky o' hill. That's where I found him when he was back shot, so I buried him there. It's the only thing that stony o' hill is good for, holding the Rhymer and a bunch of stones.

"Just the Rhymer's bones and lot's of stones, Papa D, and a patch of wildflowers shinning blue. Ought to name it Rhyme Stone Hill, that's what we ought to do."

When Brock heard Zack speak in that rhyme a cold chill traveled up his spine. He thought, for a second, that he had heard Simon's voice again, coming from his grandson. Brock looked at Zack, and Zack realized it then too. They both started laughing. Brock rubbed the top of Zack's blond head. Brock knew Zack was smart for a boy of thirteen.

"Papa D., do you think the Rhymer went to heaven?"

"I don't know, Zack. I hope he did, but it's hard to tell. Whichever way he went, I'm sure he went shouting. He was bad at times Zack, but in a good way. I don't know how God judges men like him. If I had anything to do with it, he would have gone to heaven. Guess we'll just wait and see."

Brock Deaton grabbed his cane. He and Zack started the slow assent to Rhyme Stone Hill. On the way, Brock Deaton told Zack all the stories that weren't written into the diary.

"You know who killed him don't you, Papa D?"

"Yes, yes I do."

"Will you tell me?"

Brock and Zack found a rock across from the leaning stone on Simon's grave.

"It was two men who worked for a man named Cyrus Wendell. At the time Cyrus owned the Twin Aces ranch. If you look south of here you can see part of that ranch. I own that part now. It was two men named Whitechapel and Overton that killed Simon. I chased Whitechapel away that day. Overton was found dead later on."

"Papa D, what's this other poem here in the diary?"

"Let me see it."

Zack handed his grandpa the poem from the diary.

To some he was a hero,
To others he was a nightmare you know,
—when he talked in verse
—hitch up the hearse
He killed some fast and killed some slow.

He was from Texas most guessed,
But I'm sure, one time he confessed,
—his name was Sublette
—he was the Rhymer yet
And in his gunplay he was surely blessed.

For his friends he was always there,
To the bad he was never fair,
—with derringer and shotgun
—he got his killin' done
don't call him Rhymin' Simon unless you dare.

Kate

"Do you remember, in the diary? The woman named Big Legged Kate?'

"I remember. She was one of those nasty ladies, wasn't she?"

Brock nodded his head in agreement. "She wrote me after she found out and sent me the poem and I put it with the diary. That other poem, the one written by the one he called Texas Sweet Talk was given to him by her, I suspect somewhere along the way."

"Papa D?"

"Yes, Zack."

"Did you kill that man named Overton?"

Brock showed surprise when Zack asked the question. "The newspaper said Simon killed him. Then he went to the Twin Aces ranch and killed Cyrus Wendell. There were notes left on the bodies written in rhyme and signed by the Rhymer."

Zack scratched his head, "Papa D, how could the Rhymer kill them when he was already dead?"

Brock stared off, looking south. "He was the Rhymer, Zack. He had a powerful Demon in him. Perhaps it was the Demon."

Zack looked at his grandpa skeptically.

"Run on down and help your granny with supper. We'll talk more tomorrow.

Rhyme Stone Hill

"Zack, take this diary. It's yours now for safe keeping. Someday, someone will come along you can share it with. It's our secret until then."

"Yes, Papa D, it's safe with me. I know a very good place for hiding stuff."

Zack would keep his Papa D's wishes, at least as long as he and his Granny Abigail was alive. He could not wait to tell someone. He was proud of his Papa D. He was the Rhymer's best friend, and he had killed a man. Now who would not, or could not, be proud of that.

Zack awoke early the next morning. He knew his Papa D would be going up to Rhyme Stone Hill just like he did most every morning. However, this day Zack was too late. He looked out the window and saw his grandpa, with his trusty cane, shuffling along, almost already to the top of the hill. He quickly splashed water on his face, pulled on his clothes, and stole another look out of the window. He could not see his Papa D.

Brock Deaton reached the top of the hill. Damn, he thought, this hill gets steeper and steeper every day. He laughed. His legs must be getting shorter, too. It now took him twice as many steps to reach the top as it did before.

Brock sat down, his back against the large, leaning rock where he had sat with Simon when Simon died. Brock and Zack had named it the Rhyme Stone. He loved it up here. He was closer to God somehow. He could talk to Simon, and he could see his entire holdings from atop this hill. He took off his hat. The morning sun felt good on his face. He looked at Simon's grave, then closed his eyes and leaned back.

It was there, just as Simon had done, leaning against the Rhyme Stone, that Brock Deaton breathed his last.

Abigail buried Brock Deaton on Rhyme Stone Hill beside the grave of Simon James Sublette. She put a small white picket fence around the area. She removed the crude stone that had served as Simon's marker all these years. She had matching headstones made for each of the most special men in her life. Their headstones read:

Simon James Sublette

July 6, 1846—May 8, 1885

Protector, Friend, Poet

Gunfighter

Brock Angus Deaton

May 1, 1850—April 15, 1916

Husband, Father, Lover

Abigail went to the barn and made her way to the tack area. She paused at the saddle hanging on the wall, the saddle with the knife mark where Simon's leg had been cut away. She slowly ran her finger across the knife mark. It brought an image of Simon, an image of him smiling. The image warmed her. She opened the storage bin beneath the saddle and the reins Simon used to control the big gray mare. She moved aside an empty gunny sack and retrieved the worn, collection of papers, tied with a red ribbon.

Abigail went back to the main house, got her favorite blanket from her bed and made her way to the large front porch. She sat in her rocking chair and wrapped herself in the blanket. It was early May and there was still some winter in the spring air. She untied the loose bound papers, found the right page and began to finish reading The Dairy of a Gunfighter. A tear came to her eye, and she was smiling.

Epilogue

The Brotherhood of the Gun (enhanced version)

Suffering and pain ~ from shotgun came,
blood and flesh blown into the air.
With the flesh all gone ~ you can see to the bone,
what once was, is no longer there.
Go on the attack ~ shoot some in the back,
there aren't rules when the lead is slinging.
No rules of any kind ~ for those shooting from behind,
for the victim the funeral bell is ringing.
Cheap whiskey for drinking ~ causes bad thinking,
causes some men to be cruel and mean.
They will stand and fight ~ be it wrong or right,
and some will kill to earn the green.
Rifles, pistols and more ~ scatterguns, derringers galore,
the implement of death was of no concern.
Stand out in the street ~ your fate to meet,
once you cross the line you can never return.
Shoot at will ~ a crooked gambler to kill,
for dealing himself an extra card.
If they steal your horse or cow ~ or insult you somehow,
you get your gun and deal with them fast and hard.
Be ye saint or sinner ~ there's only one winner,
when you stand and do the gunman's duel.
Blood spills to the floor ~ a life is no more,
death comes and the dying is cruel.
The gun has no heart ~ it just not part,
of its' make–up or construction.
It responds to the finger ~ smoke and power linger,
in the aftermath of its' deadly destruction.
Some kill for the treasure ~ some for the pleasure,
but it doesn't make any difference why it is done.
For criminal and the law ~ it applies to all
they're now bond by the Brotherhood of the Gun.

About the Author

Eddie L. Barnes grew up in the Texas panhandle town of Pampa. He traveled extensively throughout the southwestern states during his career as a computer salesman. He now lives in Horseshoe Bay, Texas with his wife Carole, and enjoys golf as much as he can.